A Dangerous Desire

"WHAT ARE YOU DOING?" Macky tried to slide away, setting off a jingle of coins in her pocket. "Are you going to steal my money?" she asked.

His hand stopped in midair.

"No. I'm going to build a second fire. Then I'm going to find us something to eat. Then what I want to do is—"

But he didn't move. In her attempt to step back, the greatcoat had parted, exposing two bare legs that went on forever.

Macky gasped.

Bran's pulse quickened as he imagined sliding his hands along those legs, imagined capturing those lips, exposing those breasts. For a long moment they stared at each other, only a shaky breath away from touching.

"What I want is . . . to kiss you," he said in a voice so hoarse that she could barely understand him.

The air was tense. Macky could hardly breathe. She felt such a trembling in her limbs that she couldn't move.

Gathering her senses she said, "But a preacher wouldn't—"

"No? Maybe I'm not a preacher. Suppose I'm something else?"

"Should I be afraid of you?"

"Yes," he said, staring down at her. "Maybe you should."

The Redhead

and

The Preacher

—◆—

SANDRA
CHASTAIN

BANTAM BOOKS

New York   Toronto   London   Sydney   Auckland

THE REDHEAD AND THE PREACHER

A Bantam Book / November 1995

ISBN 0-553-56863-9

Published simultaneously in the United States and Canada

Bantam Books are published by Bantam Books, a division of Bantam
Doubleday Dell Publishing Group, Inc. Its trademark, consisting of the
words "Bantam Books" and the portrayal of a rooster, is Registered in U.S.
Patent and Trademark Office and in other countries. Marca Registrada.
Bantam Books, 1540 Broadway, New York, New York 10036.

The Redhead

and

The Preacher

Prologue

ALONG THE MISSISSIPPI—1836

He woke to the smell of smoke and the sound of his sister's terrified screams.

With his teeth chattering in fear, he pulled on his ragged trousers and crept down the stairs, his small body hugging the shadows.

Three threatening, mean men—river pirates, he judged from their clothes—were circling his mother and his sister. His father lay crumpled and still on the floor by the door, his head split open by an Indian tomahawk. A fourth man waited in the shadows.

"Papa," the boy whispered. "Get up, Papa."

"We gave you our money," his mother was saying. "Why'd you have to kill him?"

His sister's screams turned into painful whimpers, her arms crossed across her chest as she tried to cover her bare breasts. One of the men reached out and touched her, laughing as she cringed. "Leave her alone," his mother pleaded. "Take me instead."

Helplessness, anger, and some kind of animal instinct reached inside John Brandon Lee and told him that these men were the spawn of the devil his mother had warned him about. Bile rose bitter from his stomach, almost choking him as he searched for something that could be used as a weapon by an eight-year-old boy.

The woodpile by the fireplace.

The man in the shadows laughed. "Come here, girl."

Brandon forced himself to look away. Slowly he began to inch his way around the room.

"I said get your butt over here, or by God, I'll kill this old woman."

"You touch my daughter and God will smite you where you stand, you devil!"

"Get away from me, you old crow!" the leader said.

There was a cry and a thud. Then silence.

Hot, wet tears rolled down Brandon's cheek. He didn't know what to do. They'd killed his father and hurt his mother. Then his sister screamed again.

And the man laughed.

Instead of a limb from the woodpile, Brandon spied his mother's fire poker, the end of it still resting in the hot coals. He jerked it out and lunged toward the man who was fumbling at his britches.

"Stop it! Stop hurting my sister!" Brandon cried, striking out with as much force as he could manage. Someone grabbed him from behind and pulled him back, but not before he drew a cry of pain from the man holding his sister.

"God's blood, the whelp scorched me!" the man swore and slapped Brandon's face, slinging him across the room.

The next few minutes were burned forever into his mind. His sister continued to scream while the men used her. Then she hushed and Brandon knew she was dead. Sheer hate filled him as he committed to memory what he saw.

"Let's make it look like an Indian attack, mates," the young leader said as he lifted a bow and a quill of arrows from where he'd dropped them by the door. "I'll spray a few arrows around. You take their scalps and—kill that boy. No point in leaving any witnesses."

Brandon stood, stiff and unmoving, determined not to show fear. One of the thieves drew his knife and turned to Brandon's mother. A second man leaned over his sister. It didn't matter, they were both dead.

Then, knowing that he too was doomed, Brandon made one last attempt to charge the devil who laughed and raised his bow. The arrow caught Brandon in his eye, the force of it and the searing pain knocking him backward. The last conscious thing he knew was sheer agony, the man's cynical laugh, and his own vow of revenge.

Chapter One

ᴹCKENZIE KATHRYN CALHOUN consoled herself afterward by saying that she hadn't intended to commit a crime the day she took part in robbing the Bank of Promise in Promise, Kansas.

But the morning it happened, it wouldn't have done her any good to claim innocence. It was far too late. The people in Promise had long ago given up on the rangy, red-haired girl who wore men's clothes, quoted from the classics, and called herself Macky. She was considered as peculiar as her father and as wild and out of control as her shiftless brother had been.

Had Macky been anybody else, the town might have shown some consideration over her having buried her peace-loving father one day and learning the next that her brother, Todd, hadn't shown up for the funeral because he'd dealt himself four aces in a crooked poker game. There was nothing unusual about that, except this time he'd been shot to death by another gambler who caught him cheating.

Macky could have told them that she had to sell her father's horse to pay for his funeral and her own horse to pay for her brother's, but nobody asked. All she had left the day of the holdup was a mule named Solomon, her mother's cameo, and a worthless farm with the mortgage due. All she wanted to do was buy a stone for Papa's grave and find a place where she could belong. Her plan to get even with the banker who'd cheated her father might fail, but that morning it was the only hope she had.

It was late April, the time of year when spring crops should be planted, but not on Calhoun land in Promise, Kansas. It was fitting, Macky thought, that a light snow had fallen the night before, scalloping the prairie with white ruffles like the fading memory of frothy waves back home in Boston's harbor. Like everything else in her life, even the earth seemed to be moving away from her.

She closed her eyes for a moment to stop the spinning in her mind while she considered what to take with her. Deciding that it would be warmer to wear her clothes than carry them, she donned two of her brother Todd's shirts, his trousers and his work boots, stuffed with rags so that she could keep them on.

Instead of the braid she normally wore to restrain her unruly mass of red hair, she tucked it beneath her papa's felt hat. Finally, she rolled her only dress in her bedroll, along with the last of the cheese and bread.

Macky never had cared much about looking like a woman, but today even Papa wouldn't have recognized the washed-out shell of a person she'd become. With her mother's brooch tucked into the pocket of Papa's coat, she mounted the mule and started into town.

As she rode away, she looked back. There was nothing else of value left; there were no more livestock, no food supplies, only a rundown house ready to collapse in the wake of the next windstorm. If her father hadn't died of heart problems, he'd have died of starvation for there was no money left for seed that wouldn't grow.

The only thing that gave her pause was leaving her father's books. Carrying them would have been only a sentimental gesture for she'd memorized them long ago. Of all the things she'd lost, her conversations with her father would be the things she'd miss most.

Pulling her gaze away from the dismal scene, she gave the mule a slap on the rear. Today was Friday and payday for the banker's cowhands. She had better hurry if she was going to catch the man before he left for his ranch. As she rode, she rehearsed her plea to the smart-talking money-man who'd sold her gentle, scholarly father a worthless piece of land where nothing would grow but rattlesnakes and sagebrush.

If the banker-turned-land-dealer refused to buy back the land, Macky would sell her mother's cameo for enough money to buy a ticket on the noon stage heading for Denver. The brooch was the last thing she owned of any value, that and Solomon, a mule so ornery no one would buy him.

Macky gave little thought about where she would go now. Her family had been outcasts every place they'd ever been; Papa with his fine education and inability to earn a living and Mama and Todd who always refused to try.

She didn't expect to find a place where she fit in. God only knew where she'd ever find something she was good at. No man would want her as a wife; she was too outspoken, too plain, and she couldn't cook. She might have been a schoolmarm, if she'd had the temperament and had been submissive enough to satisfy those who paid her salary. She might have been a governess if she'd paid more attention to her mother's lessons of deportment.

But Macky was taught to think, to express herself and to do it openly as an equal. Macky sighed. The only thing she had to offer was something nobody would want—a quick mind.

About a mile outside of town, a hawk swooped down, clasped a frightened jackrabbit in his talons, and flew away. The sound of his wings spooked the mule, who stepped into a gopher hole and bolted. He deposited Macky in the middle of the trail and, braying at the top of his lungs, took off with her bedroll.

Macky let out an oath as she watched him race away. She was still fuming when four hard-riding men crested the hill and came to a stop where she'd fallen. One man was leading a horse with an empty saddle.

"Looks like you got trouble, boy!" The stranger who seemed to be the leader glanced at the disappearing mule, then moved closer. He had a scruffy gray beard and a bloody bandana tied around his forehead. He was riding a black horse with a fancy silver-trimmed saddle.

Boy? One look at the cold expression in his eyes made Macky decide that being a boy at this point was much safer than being a girl. She nodded and came to her feet.

"What's your name, son?"

"McKenzie," she answered in the deepest voice she could manage.

"Heading to Promise?" another asked.

"Yep."

"Folks there know you?" the leader asked.

Again, she nodded. They knew her, but that wasn't likely to do these men any good if they were looking for someone to put in a word for them.

"How'd you like a ride the rest of the way to town, pick up a dollar or two? We got an extra horse." The leader nodded at the black horse trailing behind them. "One of my men had a little accident a ways back and—stayed behind."

Macky would have said no, but if she walked, she'd miss the noon stage. Once she made her decision to leave, catching that stage had become the most important thing she'd ever do.

She studied the man making the offer. She had nothing for them to steal and, as long as he didn't know she was a girl, accepting his offer was less likely to give her away than refusing. Besides, Promise was only a short way down the trail, and once she reached town, she'd separate herself from these rough-looking men.

"Much obliged."

Macky grabbed the saddle horn and vaulted onto the horse, kicking him into a steady gallop to keep up with her new companions. She wondered where they'd come from and what had happened to the man who stayed behind. All the horses had been ridden hard; their coats were icy with frozen perspiration. Why were they heading for a town that had little claim to fame other than the attempts by a few homesteaders to raise crops in an area where the only year-round water belonged to one man?

The leader slowed his horse, allowing Macky to come abreast of him. "What kind of place is Promise, kid?"

"Small," she answered.

"We're heading there to do a little banking. You can watch our horses while we're inside."

That hadn't been part of Macky's plan. At the moment, however, she couldn't see a way out. Maybe it wouldn't matter. The bank, standing between the blacksmith's forge and the dressmaker's shop, was the first thing they'd come to.

The men reined in their horses in front of the rustic building and slid to the street mushy with melting snow. Macky, anxious to separate herself from the strangers, stopped her horse in front of the smithy's shop. She was already in enough trouble with the town; riding in with a group of strangers would only make matters worse. She'd just tie the horse to the hitching rail and disappear.

She soon found *that* wasn't going to work. "Watch the horses, boy," the man with the beard said as he climbed down and dropped the reins to his horse.

Two of the riders stationed themselves beside the front

door of the bank while the leader and the other man went inside. Before Macky could figure out how to get away, gunshots rang out. Seconds later the two men ran out of the bank.

"That's far enough, Pratt," the sheriff's deputy called out from the roof of the general store across the street.

"Drop the money and throw down your guns," Sheriff Dover ordered. Macky couldn't see him where he was standing in the alley between the bank and the blacksmith's shop. "We got word from the federal prison that you were heading this way. Just let me have the money."

Pratt? The sheriff had called the man Pratt. Everybody in the West knew about the infamous Pratt gang. One outlaw suddenly dropped to the ground, rolled away from the door and got off a shot. The deputy fell, but not before he'd wounded one of the robbers.

The man by the door found cover and opened fire. The sheriff responded with a barrage of bullets, grazing the horse's haunches as Pratt mounted. The frightened animal reared up. In his attempt to stay on his horse, Pratt lost control of the flour sack he was carrying, flinging it behind him toward the startled Macky who caught it instinctively.

Macky, who'd been paralyzed by what was happening, suddenly realized that Pratt and his men had robbed the bank. At any moment the sheriff would step out from the alley and see her. With the money in her hand, he'd believe that she was a part of the gang. She'd come to town to ask the banker for money and she'd been caught in a holdup.

Desperately, Macky kicked her horse into action and rode into the blacksmith's barn. She slid to the ground and slapped her horse on the rear and watched him gallop out the back.

Macky followed the horse. When she'd hoped to find something she was good at, she hadn't expected it to be a crime. She could only pray that all the attention had been on the shooters and that nobody had recognized her in Papa's coat and hat. No matter, her chance of selling her brooch had been ruined and it was almost time for the stage. The stone for Papa's grave would have to wait.

Desperately, she looked around. Perhaps the dressmaker would buy the cameo. Macky knocked on the shopkeeper's back door, found it open and slipped inside. "Hello?"

Moments later a woman peered furtively from a small room opening off the shop. Seeing that Macky was alone she came forward, facing Macky with distaste and disbelief. "Yes?"

Macky had never visited her shop and nobody knew that better than the proprietor. "Yes, I wonder if you can help me?" Macky started to reach in her pocket and realized she was still holding the flour sack filled with money.

"What are you looking for?" the seamstress asked icily.

"I'd like—" Macky reached for her cameo, heard the sound of coins jingle in the sack and stilled her movements.

Considering how she was dressed, she could understand the dressmaker's attitude, and after what her brother had done, the sheriff would never believe that Macky was an innocent pawn. Now she could be in even bigger trouble with the outlaw Pratt. He was sure to come after his money. Becoming a criminal was the final insult in her life.

Then it came to her. She didn't have to sell the cameo now. She had money for her ticket if she wanted to use it. Granted, it wasn't hers, but she'd been handed a means to administer justice to the man who'd cheated her father and so many others. She'd take the money her father had been swindled out of, plus interest. It would buy her a ticket out of Promise and stones for both Todd's and Papa's graves—at the banker's expense. Later, she'd return the money that wasn't truly hers.

Macky calmly considered her next move. The sheriff hadn't seen her, only the outlaws and the deputy, and from what she'd seen the deputy's wound looked fatal. The dressmaker didn't know what had happened for she'd obviously been in her workroom with no view of the street. If Macky was lucky she still might get out of Promise.

Macky made up her mind. Providence had provided.

"I'd like to buy a dress and a bonnet and cape. Quickly, please. I—I have a pressing engagement."

The seamstress studied her as if she thought Macky's pressing engagement might be with a ragman, then turned to her rack. "I do keep a few skirts made up but they might be a little small for you and the only blouses I have are probably too big. I could alter a dress by tomorrow."

"No, get the skirt and shirtwaist. I'll wear them."

The woman pulled the clothing from the rack and handed it to Macky. "You can try them on behind the changing screen."

Keeping an eye on the door, Macky quickly shed her brother's clothes and pulled on the unfamiliar women's garments, wondering how on earth anybody could wear such things. By the time the commotion outside died down, Macky was wearing a pale blue shirtwaist and darker skirt over her brother's drawers and had covered it all with a dark blue serge cape.

She reached inside the sack and withdrew enough money to pay for her goods and buy her ticket on the stage. Then she looked around for a means to conceal the rest. Getting on the stage holding a flour sack would only call attention to herself.

Hurrying now, she selected a tan-colored portmanteau in which she placed her old clothes and the flour sack. She added a second shirtwaist, a flannel nightgown, and a petticoat.

"Might I suggest this?" the seamstress said, holding out a blue velvet drawstring purse. "For your traveling money."

Macky took the purse, paid for her purchases, and placed the remaining money inside. When the coins clanked together she looked around and picked up a lacy handkerchief to cushion the sound.

At the last minute she selected a blue bonnet with a pink rose on its crown and poked her red hair beneath it.

After registering the seamstress's haughty disapproval,

Macky glanced at herself in the mirror and bit back a very unladylike oath. The dressmaker was right. The blouse needed altering, but with the cape to cover it, nobody but Macky would know that it gaped open between the buttons. There was nothing she could do to hide a skirt that fell two inches short of covering her heavy work boots.

So be it. The people in Promise didn't matter anymore and the citizens of Denver wouldn't care what she looked like. She'd just keep traveling until she found a place where she could belong.

When the driver, Jenks Malone, crawled up on the stage, he cast a dubious eye on the odd-looking young woman who ran from the dress shop to the stage office, then boarded the coach at the last minute.

"Females," he muttered, "always late."

She was looking around as if she were searching for someone. Another minute and he'd leave her behind.

The only other traveler was polite and well mannered enough. According to the stationmaster, he was a preacher, "Brother Brandon Adams, headed for Heaven."

But most preachers didn't wear fancy clothes or a black patch over one eye.

And most preachers didn't carry a Bible in one hand and a gun in the other.

Still, everybody along the line knew that the folks in Heaven were expecting their new minister. And if this man looked like the devil instead of a messenger of the Lord they wouldn't care. But he made Jenks uneasy.

Jenks wasn't sure that even a man of God could do much about the trouble in Heaven. If the federal marshal couldn't find out who was running the miners off their claims, Jenks doubted the Lord would care.

Trouble was no stranger in the West. Lately the stage line had suffered a mess of it on the weekly run from Leavenworth to Denver to Salt Lake. Five days ago, Jenks had lost his own coach to an Indian attack. He'd managed to make his way to the next way station to wait for a new assignment. When the driver on the incoming stage came in roaring drunk, the stationmaster sent for Jenks to finish the western run.

Giving the horses a flick of his whip, Jenks moved the coach out. They were due in Denver by the next day, and there was Indian country to get through first. Indians and the Pratt gang who'd broken out of the territory prison and robbed the bank in Promise only minutes earlier. The deputy and one of the outlaws had been killed. But the sheriff had caught one and wounded another. Only Pratt and a young boy who'd been riding with them had escaped and they were likely heading west.

Jenks had a bad feeling about the trip, even if the Lord was on their side.

Chapter

Two

John Brandon didn't move as the new passenger boarded the stage. He'd been alone in the coach since he and the previous driver had buried the real preacher just inside the Kansas line.

That driver had found a bottle of whiskey in the preacher's things, and by the time they reached the next station, he was roaring drunk. Fortunately, a substitute had been available to take the coach into Promise.

For Bran, the change in drivers was a stroke of luck.

His luck improved even more when the stationmaster in Promise took one look at Bran carrying the preacher's Bible and assumed that he was the Reverend Adams. For Bran, that cover seemed ideal and he didn't correct him.

Now there was another passenger, a lone woman, and it had been Bran's experience that nothing appealed to a woman more than a man of God. If he allowed it to happen, he'd be forced to make conversation all the way to Denver.

Leaning his head against the back of the seat, his face covered by his hat, he hoped that she'd think he was asleep. He'd learned long ago that his senses could discover much without the aid of his eyes and that good luck was as valuable as good planning.

Good. He winced over that word. He'd lost any goodness in his life the same time he'd lost the sight in his eye.

Bran wished he hadn't been able to see or hear the night the thieves pretending to be Indians had swooped down on his family's small homestead along the Mississippi.

What he'd lived through that night had forever robbed Bran of love, a family, and any hope of a normal life. The outlaws had come for the money from a year's crop of indigo and skins. They'd murdered everyone but the eight-year-old boy, who was saved by an arrow that lodged in his eye, causing a paralyzing pain that convinced the outlaws that he was dead. Then they'd burned the house. The last memory Bran had was of the gang leader, a silhouette of black against the orange flames of the cabin. That vision had been forever burned into his mind.

The commanding general at the nearby fort found the cabin burned to the ground and the boy half unconscious. He put the blame on the Indians he'd been sent to restrain instead of the river pirates.

Later, John had tried to explain that the gang of men who murdered his family were white but nobody would dispute the officer's claim. The general offered John to a local farmer. Alone and filled with anger, he'd run away from the fort authorities, who were no better than the thieves. But the memory of his sister's screams and the killer's laugh had driven him ever since.

Later, the Choctaw Indian tribe who'd taken him in and saved his life called him Eyes That See in Darkness. They thought he had special powers; he could see in the dark. And he'd stayed with them, determined to learn to kill.

Later, he'd accompanied the tribe west to the lands they were assigned in Oklahoma. Along with his Indian brothers, he'd attended the missionary's school where he studied the white man's Bible, the same one his mother had read to him as a boy.

The wound in his eye healed, but nothing healed the scar in his heart, and as he grew into a man he made a vow that if it took the rest of his life, he'd find the outlaw who'd been responsible.

For the last fifteen years he'd wandered across the country, looking, searching, hiring himself out as a private avenger of evil. As a gunfighter he found and punished thieves and murderers of every kind. But the man he sought was still out there.

Always, he watched for a rangy man of authority with an odd laugh, to no avail. Now Bran was on his way to a little mining town called Heaven, just outside Denver in the Kansas Territory. He'd been hired to find out who was causing accidents and holding up the gold shipments from a mine called the Sylvia.

Assuming the identity of the minister had seemed a ready-made cover for his mission. Now, in the coach, he amused himself by listening, feeling, allowing his mind's eye to discover the identity of his traveling companion.

Female, he confirmed. The driver had called her ma'am.

A good build and firm step because the carriage had tilted as she stepped inside, and she'd settled herself without a lot of swishing around.

Probably no-nonsense, for he could see the tips of her boots beneath the brim of his hat. The boots were worn, though the clothing looked new. The only scent in the air was that of the dye in the cloth.

Practical, for she'd planted both feet firmly on the floor of the coach and hadn't moved them; no fidgeting or fussing with herself.

Deciding that she seemed safe enough, he flicked the brim of his hat back and took a look at her.

Wrong, on all four counts. Dead wrong. She was sitting quietly, yes, but that stillness was born of sheer determination—no, more like desperation. She was looking down at rough red hands and holding on to her portmanteau as if she dared anybody to touch it. Her eyes weren't closed, but they might as well have been.

The stage moved away in a lumbering motion as it picked up speed.

The woman didn't move.

Finally, after an hour of steady galloping by the horses pulling the stagecoach, she let out a deep breath and appeared to relax.

"Looks like you got away," he said.

"What?" She raised a veil of sooty lashes to reveal huge eyes as green as the moss along the banks of the Mississippi River where he'd played as a child. Something about her was all wrong. The set of her lips was meant to challenge. But beneath that bravado he sensed an appealing uncertainty that softened the lines in her forehead.

"Back there you looked as if you were running away from home and were afraid you wouldn't escape," he said.

"I was," she said.

"Pretty risky, a woman alone. No traveling companion, no family?"

"Don't have any, buried my—the last companion back in Promise."

Macky risked taking a look at the man across from her. He was big, six feet of black, beginning with his boots and ending with the patch over his eye and a hat that cast a shadow over a face etched by a two-day growth of beard. There was an impression of quiet danger in the casual way he seemed to look straight through her as if he knew that she was an impostor and was waiting for her to confess. "What's wrong with your eye?"

She hadn't meant to ask. Asking questions would be considered bad manners. In the past, manners were something in which she'd never taken much stock. Now everything had changed. The memory of the dressmaker's frosty glare made her acutely aware of her ill-fitting lady's garments and bonnet.

Skirts and petticoats didn't make a lady and she'd already reverted back to her old way of saying what she thought without regard for the consequences.

"I'm sorry. 'A fool utterth all his mind.' "

Bran couldn't help responding in kind. " 'Answer a fool according to his folly.' "

She looked at him in surprise. "Plato?"

"No, Proverbs." He let a few seconds pass before he went on. "I lost the eye a lot of years ago."

"Forgive me. Your eye is none of my concern."

The man wearing the eye patch wouldn't normally have continued the conversation, but he'd never come across a woman who not only read books, but quoted from them. His interest sharpened. He couldn't resist the impulse to learn more about her. "You have a name?"

"Yes. Do you?"

"Indians call me Eyes That See in Darkness."

Macky studied him carefully, giving the impression that she was measuring him as a man, not an enemy. "Why?" she asked with no attempt to conceal her curiosity.

"Thought I could see in the dark."

"What do other people call you?" she asked.

He studied her in return. Though she was young, she neither played the coy young maiden nor the piously proper woman he was accustomed to. In short she met him head-on. He frowned. "Depends."

"Fine, it's your business," she said and pressed her lips firmly together. She didn't have to talk to him.

She gave the man in black a furtive look. His face was hard, chiseled with sharp edges, smeared in dark shadows. She knew better than to think he was interested in her. There was something about the Calhouns that turned people away.

Even the widows back in Promise who once made overtures to her father had cooled when her father spurned their attention. Later, when her brother, Todd, started hanging out at the saloon in town, those same widows quickly let Macky know that they had done their Christian duty in welcoming the Calhouns, but that welcome had come to an end. Thereafter, Macky had avoided the town.

Macky had missed Todd's boyhood teasing but she didn't miss the sullen, resentful man he'd become. She'd still had her father then, and that, she'd told herself, was enough. Todd would sow his wild oats and then come home. But he hadn't.

Across the carriage, Bran was aware of the girl's scrutiny. He felt himself giving her a reluctant grin. She was a feisty one, his peculiar-looking companion with wisps of hot red hair trying to escape her odd little hat. She had a strong face and a wide mouth. But what held him were green eyes that, no matter how frosty she tried to make them, still shimmered with sparks of silver lightning.

The Indians who'd named him would have called her Frozen Fire. She might be dressed like some dowdy school-marm, but there was more to her than her appearance indicated. In fact, he doubted that she cared much about clothing. And she damned sure didn't know how to choose a hat.

"I'm called Bran," he said slowly.

Bran decided she was definitely running away from something, but he couldn't figure what. He should back off. Planning the job waiting for him in Heaven was what he ought to be doing. He would be working for a woman. He'd never worked for a woman before and she hadn't liked his stipulation that his identity be kept secret.

John Brandon Lee had stopped using his real name fifteen years before when he'd killed a man who'd been beating an Indian boy. A warrant had been issued for John Lee's arrest. The only thing that had saved him in the years since was the fact that the only witnesses had been Indians. They'd identified the killer by name but their descriptions had been deliberately vague and confusing. Nobody ever knew that in later years John had dropped that name and taken a new identity, that of a half-breed gunfighter called Night Eyes.

Now he'd surprised himself again by giving her his real name. There was a growing sense of intimacy inside the coach. She seemed to be genuinely interested in him as a person, but wary at the same time. He considered getting out, saddling the horse tied to the back of the stage, and riding into Denver alone.

Bran had always found women ready to make a casual relationship with him more personal. They seemed attracted to danger. But this one didn't. And that cool independence had become a challenge.

Maybe a little conversation would shake the uneasy feeling that he was experiencing.

"What are you called?" he asked.

"Trouble, mostly," she said with a sigh that told him more than she'd intended.

"That's an odd name for a woman."

"That's as good as you're going to get," she added, lifting a corner of the shade covering the open window.

Good? There it was again. "Good is a rare quality in my life." He took a long look at her. "But I'm willing to reserve judgment."

He was doing it again—extending the conversation. Something about this young woman was intriguing. "Truth is, I'm a lot more likely to appreciate a woman who's bad. Wake me when we get to the way station."

Macky's eyes flew open. She was ready to tell him where he could go, but the brooding one-eyed stranger had covered his eyes with his hat and within seconds he was snoring. Macky hadn't had much experience with men, but she had the feeling that he might be laughing at her. She ought to be used to that but somehow this time it was disturbing.

Well, two could play that game. With his face covered, he couldn't be watching her. And no matter what the Indians thought about his sight, Macky didn't believe he could see through his hat.

Through the crack between the shade and the window opening she watched for some time as the stage moved across the open prairie. But her eyes kept moving back to the man. It was just because she'd never seen a man with an eye patch, she told herself as she studied him more carefully.

His fine leather boots were splattered with mud as if he'd come a long way. She'd noticed a saddle strapped on top of the coach and a horse tied to the back of the coach. His black greatcoat showed signs of hard use but his trousers were of fine cloth. His shirt was white, tied at the neck with a thin black ribbon tie, and the striped fabric of the waist-coat looked like the one Papa always wore when he went into town.

Papa. A pang of regret pierced her. She'd left town so quickly that she hadn't even stopped by his grave to say goodbye. But he wouldn't have wanted her to grieve. Eternally optimistic, if he were the one sitting in the seat across from Macky he'd say, "Don't look back, girl. Find a new star in the heavens."

But the only star she was likely to find was the one pinned on a lawman's vest.

Her father was a schoolteacher when Todd was born, barely making enough money to support his family. Todd was thirteen and Macky was eight when Papa had made the desperate decision to go West and make a new start running a trading post along the Missouri. But he'd been a better teacher than merchant. The move and poor health aggravated by the climate had hastened her mother's death.

The only fond memory Macky had of that time was the daily exchanges she had with her father. They'd had little else to do except try to outwit each other with puns, hypotheses, and verbal exchanges.

During her mother's long illness, all attempts to turn Macky into a real lady were forgotten. Instead, she had learned to use her mind and speak her thoughts. When

Mama died, Papa had sold his store and, sight unseen, bought a ranch in Kansas. It was only when they got there that they found out the land was worthless.

Macky had tried to talk her father into returning to Boston, but the banker who'd surveyed off the plot and sold the land had filled Papa's head with dreams of fortunes to be made in raising cattle and wheat. Papa had used the last of their money to buy cows and settled down to become a rancher.

But Todd, by then a gangly sixteen-year-old, had no use for or skill with a horse or a plow. Planting a garden for food and riding the range to keep up with their cattle had fallen to Macky. When the drought killed the crops and the cows had to be sold for food, Todd moved into the town that had sprung up, turning to drink and cards. Macky held the banker responsible for that.

Now, when she didn't need it any more, Macky had more money than she'd ever seen. She might have felt guilty over it, but the man whom she'd stolen it from had stolen much more. He'd taken her papa's dream. The gold and silver coins that lay heavy against her thigh seemed cold payment for his theft.

Todd and Papa were gone. Now, Macky was leaving. She shifted her weight and tried not to look at the long muscular legs filling up the space between the seats, but she couldn't help it. She focused on his hat, an expensive black Stetson. A jaunty silver feather had been pinned to the leather band. The feather seemed as out of place for a man so devoid of warmth as the Scriptures he quoted.

That's what was bothering her, she decided, the aura of danger he carried with him. It seemed impenetrable, and was the only explanation for the uneasy feeling in the pit of her stomach. She tried to keep her breathing light, in order to conceal her agitation.

But she soon decided that it wasn't only the lack of air that was bothering her. Her stomach was reacting just as oddly. Resolutely she pulled her attention away from her companion's hat, allowing her gaze to fasten on the seat across from her.

Beside him, on the hard leather bench, was a black object, an object that, after a moment, she recognized. A Bible. The man was carrying a Bible. What did that mean? Was he some kind of missionary? He'd said something about Indians. Maybe he'd been sent to convert the heathens.

Heathens.

Outlaws.

Bank robbers.

Sinners.

Macky, on her way straight to hell, was traveling across the prairie with a man of God. The Lord had sent an escort to make sure she got what she deserved.

She took a deep breath. Maybe, but if so, she was going to put up a struggle. She'd tied the drawstring purse containing the money left from purchasing her ticket around her wrist. She placed both hands on her travel case, shifting her sitting position in hopes of relieving the tingling sensation that continued to needle her.

The man called Bran might have eyes that could see in the dark, but unless he'd been watching during the bank robbery, he couldn't know what she was carrying in her case.

Once they got to the way station she'd buy a horse and make her own way to Denver. She'd always looked after herself. Now, thanks to Pratt, she was wealthy enough to buy her future, as soon as she decided what she wanted.

Letting out a quick little sigh of relief, Macky tipped her bonnet to cover her eyes. She had to make decisions and she had to make them before she got to Denver. With any luck the sheriff wouldn't know that the boy holding the horses had been Macky Calhoun.

But there was an even greater danger. Pratt may have been captured; she hadn't waited to see, but he knew that her name was McKenzie and that she had his money.

And, he'd already escaped once. The little jail in Promise

was nothing compared to the prison where he'd been held before his escape.

Macky had changed her appearance. Surely nobody would connect the woman on the stage with the robbery. Once she got to Denver she'd use her other name, Kathryn—no, Kate. And she'd make certain that nobody learned anything about her past. After she figured a way to return the bank's money she could move on, maybe even travel to California.

McKenzie Kathryn Calhoun, the person she'd been for the first nineteen years of her life, had to disappear so that nobody could link her to the robbery.

Before the world learned that Macky Calhoun was an outlaw.

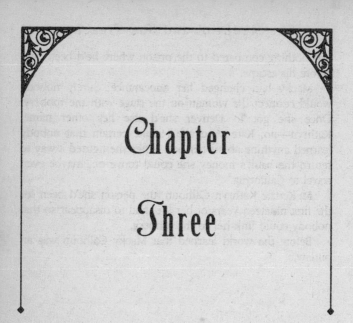

Chapter

Three

By late afternoon, Macky was chilled to the bone and wishing she had the cheese and hard bread that had been tied up in her bedroll. Heaven only knew where Solomon had ended up or who was eating her food.

It was good that the mule had run off, though. If and when he was discovered, the good citizens of Promise would likely think that something had happened to Macky and not even look for her. With any luck the townspeople would have been too busy watching the shootout to pay any attention to the boy holding the horses.

Even if the dressmaker mentioned selling a woman a skirt, nobody would believe it was Macky Calhoun, who didn't even wear a dress to her own father's funeral. The banker would foreclose on the land and sell it to another hapless family and the Calhouns would be mercifully forgotten.

Muscle-weary from holding herself erect and trying to

keep the money still as the coach bounced, Macky finally gave up and lifted the window curtain. All she could see was open prairie.

She allowed herself to slump slightly, leaning her neck back against the hard seat. The way her stomach was gnawing on her backbone she was glad the stranger was still sleeping, else he'd think he was about to be eaten by termites.

No matter how hard she tried to focus on her problems, her thoughts were drawn back to the man who called himself Bran. His boots scraped against the foot of the coach when it hit a bump in the trail. Occasionally his knee touched hers, setting off a fresh tightening of the nerves in her legs.

She decided that her feeling of anticipation was much like that of a moth being drawn to a candle flame. Even though the flame burned, the creature couldn't control its attraction.

As they rocked back and forth, a certain tension started to build. In spite of herself she began to wait for the point at which they would touch. If her brother had been there he'd be taking bets on the next encounter. And, as likely as not, losing.

An unusually deep hole bounced Macky into the air, unfastening her cape and jingling the money inside her velvet purse. Damn banker! Why hadn't all his payroll been in paper money? Why hadn't she left the coins in the portmanteau instead of carrying them on her person?

Don't be silly, Macky, even honest people have coins occasionally. It was just that the sound of those coins seemed to call attention to her, announcing to the world that she was a bank robber.

"Better find a way to stop that jiggling around," the stranger said, in a low, rough voice that gave the impression he didn't talk a lot. "You'll be accosted before you go ten feet outside this coach."

"I have no intention of being robbed," she said and untied the drawstrings from her waist. No point in trying to conceal what she was carrying. If her traveling companion had been interested in robbing her, he'd already have done so.

Macky tied the coins in the four corners of her handkerchief the way she'd seen her mother do long ago. "But I thank you for your advice," she added in a rare show of proper training that would support her new identity in Denver.

"Wasn't talking about the money," he said, tipping his hat away from his face with one black-gloved finger. His piercing dark eye came into view, focusing first on her chin, then traveling insolently lower. " 'Let your loins be girded above.' "

Macky followed the line of his vision to her chest. The open cape revealed where her blouse gaped between the buttons, exposing bare skin beneath.

"You wall-eyed peeping Tom!" she swore, promptly forgetting her plan to adopt a new identity, then tugged the front of her shirtwaist together. "How dare you quote Bible verse while looking at my—my private person?"

"Wouldn't, normally. Personally, never did have much patience with women who bound themselves up in layers of clothes, but in your case that's a mite safer than opening yourself up to be ogled."

He didn't even try to conceal his amusement. Not many women were so blunt in their speech or so foolish as to threaten a man like him. Any other time he might have reminded her that she was alone and at his mercy.

Instead he reached inside his greatcoat and drew out a small black cigar, then leaned forward to strike a match against the bottom of his boot, taking a long open look at her bodice.

Macky couldn't remember ever having blushed before; she'd never had a reason to do so. But, so far as she knew, a man had never seen her breasts before either, certainly never looked at them with such open appreciation. She pulled one side of her cape over the other and retied it.

"I can see how you got the name Eyes That See in Darkness," she snapped. "You're like a hawk, studying the field for his supper."

A moment of fear flashed in her eyes, then was quickly replaced by determination. She refused to be intimidated by anybody—ever again.

Bran recognized that second of panic and regretted that he'd caused it. Whatever she was running away from must have been pretty bad. In a rare moment of kindness he reached back and tried to soften the effect of his words.

"I told you to call me Bran."

" 'Brand' as in 'cattle brand'? Isn't that an odd name for a preacher?"

"Bran, without a *d,* as in 'devil.' " A suggestion of a smile wrinkled the corners of his mouth. "You think I'm a preacher?"

"Never knew but two men to carry a Bible around. One was a peddler and one was a preacher. How do you make your living?"

He should never have dropped his guard, but he found himself responding again. "Only answer to the law, a future wife, or Saint Peter. We can eliminate the first two and we aren't in heaven yet."

He drew in the smoke and let it out slowly. Macky felt as if he could see straight through her clothing, but she had no intention of letting him know how uncomfortable she was. It came to her that this was a test. If she couldn't stave off one man, how could she hope to find a place for herself in Denver where she'd heard that women were rare?

"Only thing I'm sure of is that I'm nobody's future wife, certainly not yours."

"Not interested in a man?"

She would have spit if she could. "Nope!"

"Expect to go West alone?"

"I do."

"Full of grit, aren't you?"

"I can take care of myself."

"None of my business," he said wryly, "but next time you put on that garment, turn it around. My guess is that there's more room for your 'private person' with the front of the shirtwaist in the front."

She thought back to the woman in the dress shop and the smug smile she'd given Macky when she studied her in the new clothes. Damn woman. She could have told Macky. But she'd let her go out of the shop looking like the ignorant know-nothing girl she was.

Macky suddenly swung her purse, catching the man's cheek with a heavy whack. Wasn't his fault that she'd reached the end of her control, but he was the one who had caught the brunt of it.

He didn't move when she hit him. Then, like one of those lizards that flicked out his tongue and caught his prey in the blink of an eye, Bran flipped his cigar out the window and jerked her across the seat. He turned her around, folded his arms across her chest, and spread his legs, pulling her bottom close to him.

When he spoke, his voice was tight with fury, not from her attack, but from the unexpected rush of heat that came when he put his arms around her.

"Had a few black eyes in my day, woman, but they were honest in the getting. Being slapped for telling the truth is something I don't take kindly to."

At that moment the sound of gunfire broke out and a barrage of bullets pelted the carriage door. The driver yelled and the horses began to gallop. The stranger pushed Macky down across the seat where she'd been sitting only moments before, shielding her body with his own.

"The devil's pitchfork! What are you trying to do," she cried, trying to twist out from under him, "smash the breath out of me?"

He curled his arm around her waist and shoved her even

farther down until she was in the foot of the carriage with his knee planted against her chest.

"Now shut up," he said, "and stay put unless you want to expose your private person to one of those outlaws shooting at us.

"Outlaws?"

Fear swept over her. Could Pratt have learned where she was? She bit back the curses she'd been about to let fly. The stage lurched drunkenly, throwing her assailant off balance. Righting himself, he drove his leg between Macky and the seat so that he could stand and jerked the curtain down.

More gunshots followed.

Looking up from where she was wedged between the seats, Macky could see bullet holes in the door. She wished she'd never seen those bank robbers, never taken the money. She could have left it behind in the dress shop. Instead, she'd drawn a gang of outlaws who were trying to kill them.

Instead of returning fire, the driver had to concentrate on keeping the stagecoach under control. The preacher was the only other man around. Macky had the absurd thought that the preacher might do better with a gun than a Bible.

Bran swore and Macky watched in surprise as he drew a gun from beneath his greatcoat. Bouncing around in the foot of the carriage, she was uncomfortably close to her protector. Expensive dusty boots disappeared beneath the fine black trousers covering muscular legs that now straddled her body. He was all man and the most masculine part of him was within touching distance. And given the rutted trail and the horses' speed there was little she could do to avoid touching.

He'd lost his hat, exposing a mass of jet-black hair that curled across his shoulders. Frowning, he slowly raised his head to peer out the window. Quickly he got off one shot, ducked, then lifted himself to fire a second one.

The sound of pounding horse hooves seemed temporarily diminished.

"Got one," he said, as if he were talking to himself. "Still two of them."

"If you'll let me get up and give me a gun, I'll help."

"I don't have another gun, ma'am, and if I did, I wouldn't let you waste the bullets."

"I'm as good a shot as the next man."

"Don't doubt it." And he didn't. Bran took quick aim and squeezed the trigger. "Now there's one left. Must be the leader—horse has a saddle trimmed with silver."

Macky felt her heart lurch. Silver-trimmed saddle? It was Pratt. She thought he'd been shot. As she listened, the sound of the third horse was growing fainter, as if the rider were turning back.

The trouble would have ended there, if the wheel hadn't hit a rut and cracked, careening the coach around and slamming it on its side. Already in a panic, the horses dragged their heavy burden for a short distance, then broke their traces and raced away, leaving the travelers stranded halfway between Promise and Denver.

Inside the carriage the two passengers had no time to brace themselves. When the coach tipped over it flung Bran backward, slinging Macky against him, her chin slamming his forehead against the door with a star-gathering thud.

When the commotion finally ended, Bran lay still, trying to sort out the situation. Pain shot through his head and he was having trouble focusing his thoughts. He blinked and tried to move only to discover that he was trapped beneath a heavy weight.

Groggily, he opened his eyes. He was half covered by a very feminine body which, even in his addled state of mind, had a pulse-raising softness. The loss of her bonnet had freed a mass of wild red hair that tickled his face and clouded his vision. The steady ache of his head didn't stop his awareness of a pair of firm breasts pressed against him. Her chin was resting on his forehead and his left arm was holding her bottom against the part of his body that responded faster than his muddled mind.

Her cape had pulled apart at the neckline and now covered them both like a blanket. As he attempted to lift her he was treated to a view of her blouse, which had fought a gallant, but losing battle. The buttons, now ripped from the shirtwaist, were caught in the folds of his waistcoat, leaving her breasts fully exposed. She was wearing nothing beneath.

Macky tried to scramble up, succeeding only in planting her knee into the body under her.

"Good God, woman, are you trying to emasculate me, too?"

He slid his hand between them and used what strength he had left to help her stand.

"Get your hands off my— What in the name of all that's holy are you doing?"

He let his hand drop. "Trying to survive purgatory!"

"For a preacher, you have a strange inability to distinguish the difference," she said, then bit back her anger as she realized that the man she'd been dressing down was bleeding.

Or rather he had been bleeding, both from his forehead and, from the looks of the panel he was leaning against, the back of his head as well.

"You're hurt," she said. "Were you shot?"

"I think not, but I don't seem to have any feeling in my lower body."

"Oh, my. Let me see." She slid one knee between his legs and wedged the other one beside him. She pulled back the greatcoat and looked for blood.

"I don't see any bullet wounds. But you may have broken something," she said curtly and slid her hand inside his shirt.

Bran could have argued but the intimacy of her touch shocked him into silence.

"What are you doing?" he finally croaked.

"This may hurt, but we have to know if you broke anything."

The numbness in his body was brought back to life by

her touch. When she pulled her hands out of his shirt and began to run them down his legs he couldn't hold back an oath.

"Here?" she questioned as she moved her hands back up his leg.

"No! I'm all right, I told you."

She moved her fingertips across his groin, prodding and kneading his flesh.

He groaned. Any fear he had that his condition was permanent disappeared as a rush of blood pooled and swelled that part of him that responded to a woman's touch. Unless he stopped her, she'd discover his rapid recovery.

"Stop it, woman! I told you I'm fine. Unless you want me to return the examination, you'll stop fondling my body."

"How dare you, you conceited jackass! I don't know why I was worried that you were hurt. I ought to be concerned with my own . . . condition."

"Let me," he said, sliding out from under her and sitting up, with his back against the floor of the overturned carriage. "I insist."

Amidst a flurry of skirts and tangle of limbs, she managed to stand and back away, ready to protect herself if he attempted to lay a hand on her. "Don't you dare."

"But I do, until I know you're not wounded."

"I hit my head and my stomach feels like it's full of prairie dust," she said quickly, "but I'm not hurt."

"Can you get the door open?"

It was then that Macky realized there were no sounds of life, other than their own breathing inside the coach.

The coach was on its side. She managed to turn around, twisted the handle of the door and pushed against it. It flew open, letting the fading sunlight inside.

Cautiously, she poked her head out of the open door and looked around. Nothing but prairie, and a purple shadow of mountains in the distance.

"I think we're alone," she whispered, the enormity of the

truth washing over her like a rush of cold air. "I don't see the driver."

"I think I'll worry about me—us first, beginning with getting up."

But it wasn't as easy as he'd expected. He was still dizzy and his legs were as wobbly as a newborn calf. "Damn! When you said you were trouble, you meant it."

"What does that mean?"

"It means that you have the hardest head in the Kansas Territory."

She felt a twinge in her chin and took in the blood on his face with sudden understanding. "Did I do that to you?"

"You had a hand in it," he said, grabbing the bottom of the window as he tried to lift himself. He thought back to their earlier position and grinned. "Guess that makes us even."

She reached down to assist him, her movement pushing her cape open to reveal her exposed breasts. "Sir!" she gasped. "How could you take advantage of me when I was, when we were—"

"I didn't, though if I hadn't been nearly knocked out by the force of your lovely chin, I might have."

"Get your own self up," she blustered, jerking her hand back and grabbing her cloak to cover herself.

It took her a moment to realize that there was no jingle of coins. She reached beneath her cape. Gone. Not only her purse but her carrying case as well.

"You stole my money," she accused as she watched the stranger grit his teeth and force himself to a standing position.

"You forget, ma'am. I was underneath you." He glanced around the coach. "Your purse is probably somewhere along the trail with my gun, flung out the window when the coach was being dragged by the horses. Horses!" He caught hold of the carriage and looked around. Without horses they could be in big trouble.

His worst fears were realized. There was no sign of any

living thing. They were alone. Night was coming and with it
the intense cold of the prairie. At least the woman had a
warm cape. Still, they couldn't survive long out there.
They'd have to face the elements and possibly Indians as
well. With the Arapaho and the Pawnee at war there were
too many hostile Indians in the area.

He'd spent the best part of his life staying away from
innocent, headstrong women. Now here he was, stuck with
one who didn't have sense enough to know the difference
between the back and the front of a dress, who was worried
about her missing purse when they didn't even have a gun.

Bran lifted himself through the open door and slid over
the side to the ground, wincing as the jolt set off a fresh
round of pain in his head. He touched his head, feeling the
sticky evidence of his wound. Apparently his hat had gone
the way of his companion's purse.

Macky saw him flinch and felt a twinge of guilt that
she'd been responsible for the accident. She scrambled out
of the fallen carriage, strode to the back of the coach where
Bran was studying the surroundings.

"Everything is lost," she whispered. "Even my travel
case—" *The wages of sin.*

"No," Bran corrected her. "It's behind us. I can see something back down the trail where the coach turned over. If
I'm lucky, my gun and my hat will be there."

But Macky had already started back toward the patch of
color. She could see the wheel, lying where it had rolled to a
stop. And something else, a bundle that took shape as she
came closer.

"The driver." Macky ran toward the man and dropped to
her knees beside him. He was still alive, a bullet through his
shoulder. "Are you all right?"

"As all right as a man who's been shot can be," he
rasped. "Sorry about what happened, ma'am."

"Can you walk?"

"You're durn right I can," he blustered. "I was just lying
here gettin' my strength."

She helped him to his feet and watched as the preacher picked up something, then walked slowly toward her, taking in the driver and studying the landscape around.

"What about your head wound?" she asked as he neared.

"I'll live."

"Unless whoever tried to hold us up comes back. We have a stage, but no horses."

"So we walk."

"A preacher with a Bible, but no gun."

"So, we'll pray."

"I don't have a lot of confidence in that," she said.

"Neither do I," he snapped.

She didn't answer. She didn't really want to believe that the men chasing them were after the stolen money in her travel case. Instead she looked around for the blue velvet drawstring bag and the preacher's hat. They were nowhere to be seen.

"Good shooting back there," the driver said. "Do you see any of the outlaws?"

Bran shaded his eyes and searched again. "No. I guess the one who got away must have picked them up."

"Who were they?" Macky asked guardedly.

"Probably that gang that held up the bank back in Promise," the driver answered. "The ticket agent told me that one of them was riding a horse with a silver-trimmed saddle."

"Surely it wasn't the same man," Macky said. "There could be more than one saddle like that around." She tried to convince herself that Pratt couldn't have known she was on the stage. Still she couldn't be sure and the thought of being stalked out here in the desert was daunting. "I mean . . ."

She looked up at the two men who were waiting for her to finish her statement. "The sheriff probably caught them," she finished uneasily. She couldn't figure out how they got away.

Bran studied her gravely. She knew more than she was admitting about what had happened back in Promise. Her quick departure was becoming more suspect. Sooner or later he'd do a bit of discreet questioning. For now he'd just watch her.

Watching her was becoming an interesting task since she'd lost that awful-looking bonnet, allowing a riot of rich red hair free across her shoulders. Any thought that she was odd-looking had vanished when he'd seen her hike up her skirt, throw shapely bare legs over the window of the coach and slide to the ground.

Trouble, as he'd begun to think of her, was an intriguing young woman. She had the kind of mouth that made a man lust to taste it at the same time she dared him to try.

He could tell that he was making her uneasy, studying her so seriously. She quickly averted her eyes, turning to the driver, spying the gunbelt strapped to his hips. "You have a pistol. If the thieves return, you can protect us, can't you?"

The driver worked his shoulder and winced. "Not likely, ma'am. They got me in my shooting side." He unsheathed his pistol and handed it to Bran. "You take it, preacher. You're a better shot anyway."

Bran took the weapon, examined it, then inserted it in his own holster. "Ammunition?"

The driver pulled back his jacket to reveal the bullets in the loops of his gunbelt. "Some, enough maybe."

"Good man. At least we're not helpless. I think we'd better get out of here, before the bandit who got away decides to come back. Any idea what he was after?"

"Not unless it was the mail. Ain't carrying nothing else on this part of the run, 'cept you two. Going the other way, sometimes I carry gold from the mines. But they usually send a couple of guards then."

"Look, isn't that the mail sack?" Macky asked, pointing to a bag lying against a rock.

The driver struggled to the bag and tried to lift it, groaned and let it fall back to the ground. "Don't think I can carry it. What about it, Reverend? I'll take your Bible if you'll tote the mail. Can't afford to lose it. That new Pony Express is already getting the mail across country faster than we can."

"How far to the way station?"

"Too far to walk before dark," the driver said. "Maybe we'd better find a place to make camp."

"Make camp?" Macky could sleep on the ground as well as the next one, but she was famished.

Bran studied the driver, then looked down the trail. "Let's get to that outcropping of rocks just ahead," Bran said as he picked up the mail bag. "At least it will give us some protection from the wind." He turned his head, speaking under his breath to Macky. "I don't suppose you have any beans and bacon in that carrying case, do you, Trouble?"

"Afraid not." He didn't have to tell her that she'd have been a lot smarter filling it with food instead of nightgowns and petticoats. "I'd appreciate it if you wouldn't call me that. I had nothing to do with our attack."

"Maybe not," Bran said. "But the name still fits."

"Let me help you, Mr.— What is your name?" Macky asked the driver.

"Jenks Malone," the driver said, pressing his hand against the circle of blood spreading beneath his fingers.

Macky took a step toward the grizzly old man. "You need medical attention before we go anywhere, Mr. Malone."

"Call me Jenks and I can wait," he insisted, through clenched teeth that said how painful the injury really was. "Right now, we gotta find shelter away from the wagon. Cover our trail."

As if on command the wind sprang up, whipping Macky's cape like a sail as she tried to collect it around her. Leaning against the strong current of air, she headed off down the rutted trail, the wind erasing evidence of her footsteps as she walked. Her case was heavy. She was cold and the growls of her stomach sounded more like tigers than termites.

To add to her woes, she faced the worrisome possibility that Pratt might be behind them. At least he was looking for a boy named McKenzie, not an odd-looking woman and a dangerous one-eyed man carrying a mail bag in one hand and a Bible in the other.

Chapter

Four

$\mathcal{B}$RAN PRODUCED a small bottle of whiskey from inside his coat and told Macky to use it to clean and dress the driver's wound.

"Where are you going?" she asked.

"We need food," he said, and walked away.

Macky watched him for a moment, then turned to the injured man. Jenks Malone was lucky. The bullet had passed through his shoulder, leaving a clean wound. The ruffle from Macky's newly purchased flannel nightgown served as a bandage, but as the sun fell behind the mountains and carried the heat with it, Jenks became far too cold.

Macky's compassion overruled her personal comfort and she unfastened her cape and used it to cover him. Ruefully she studied the front of her shirtwaist and blushed. Moments later she'd removed the offensive article of clothing and replaced it with her brother's shirt and Papa's coat. At least she was warm, even if she was wearing the clothing that would identify her to the bank robbers.

Bran returned, carrying a small rabbit. He glanced at the woman's change of clothing but didn't comment. If anything, he decided, she looked more at home in men's clothing than she had in the ill-fitting garments she'd worn before.

He wondered how old she was. About twenty, he'd guess. But women in the West were usually married by then. And she'd been quick to defend her status as single. Maybe too quick.

Bran put aside his reservations about calling attention to their location and built a small fire. The driver needed heat and they all needed food. If they were being followed, the bushwhackers already knew where they were, and he knew enough to know that the Indians didn't need fires to find their targets.

Soon the rabbit was roasting. The smell of the fat hitting the burning brush made Macky's mouth water, yet she stayed away, reluctant to get too close to Bran until finally the cold forced her to the heat.

"What about—the outlaws?" she asked. "Will they come back?"

He could have told her he was more worried about Indians, but he didn't. "Depends on what they were after. You wouldn't know anything about that, would you?"

She forced herself not to show a physical reaction to his question. He might be too close to the truth. "No. I don't know anything about those men. Maybe they planned to rob us."

"Could be." He motioned for her to sit and tore a chunk of meat from the roasting animal and handed it to her.

"How's Jenks?" he asked.

She blew on the meat, passing it back and forth between her fingers until it cooled. "The bullet passed through. He lost a lot of blood, but I think he's all right. There's no fever yet."

"There could be by tomorrow, if not from the wound, from exposure. Never know out here. The sun could fry us or the weather could change and bring more snow."

Macky glanced up at the clear black sky and shivered. One star was brighter than the rest. It blinked at her like a faraway candle. A wishing star, she thought, remembering the times she and Papa had looked up into the heavens and made a wish on the first star of the evening. "Do you think we'll make it?"

"We'll make it," he said, putting a strip of meat in his mouth and chewing slowly. "Don't suppose you have a blanket in that case?"

"No, just a nightgown and some other clothes." *And the money from a bank robbery.* She wished she'd never started out for town this morning, wished that Papa hadn't died and that Todd hadn't been driven to desperation. But her wishes had never came true before; there was less reason to believe they would now. "What about feeding Jenks?"

"He needs his rest more, and come morning, he'll need water." The one-eyed man stood and looked around. "I think there is enough brush. Try and keep the fire burning. It will protect you from wild animals and take the chill off."

"Where are you going?" The only thing worse than having him stare at her was having him leave her alone.

"For water. There was a canteen and other supplies in my pack. We spilled them somewhere along the trail. I'm going back for them."

She scrambled to her feet, reaching out to take his arm before she thought. "But it's dark. How will you find them?"

"I'm Eyes That See in Darkness, remember?"

The scream of a coyote cut through the night like a sharp knife. Macky didn't realize that she'd moved closer to the stranger until she felt his hand press against the small of her back.

"He isn't close. Sound carries a long way across the plains."

"I know. It's just that I . . ." To her horror, water began

to gather in her eyes. She hadn't even cried when she'd buried Papa. Now, she began to sniffle. Tears rolled down her cheeks and she leaned her face against the man's chest to hide her weakness.

"You're tired and afraid," he said, continuing to hold her. She hadn't seemed the sort to cringe at the sound of a wild animal, but he liked the idea that she was vulnerable. "That's understandable. Anyone would be emotional under the circumstances."

"I'm not emotional," she protested, but instead of pulling away, she clutched the silky material of his vest.

"Of course you are," he said gently. He didn't like the feeling that she needed protecting. He'd never allowed anyone to get past his guard before. Never getting involved had been his shield—up to now.

Now, he found himself saying, "Don't worry, Trouble, I'll keep you safe from whoever's after you."

"Nobody's after me!" she snapped. "You don't understand. If I am emotional, it's because I—I buried my father and my brother in the last two days. Then we were shot at. A man is wounded and we're out here in the middle of nowhere. I think that gives me the right to be emotional."

Anger made her even more appealing. She was very beautiful and she didn't even know it. Trouble was big trouble for she had the kind of innocent appeal that made men do foolish things. "I'm sorry about your family." His voice tightened. "What happened?"

"It doesn't matter," she said, taking a deep raspy breath. "Not any more. I'm sorry you lost your hat. I liked the feather."

"It doesn't matter."

She continued to rest her cheek against his chest. As they stood, Bran remembered a night long ago when a small boy had buried his family. He understood her pain and, for just a moment, he shared it. Then the driver groaned and the moment between the two of them was gone. Macky pushed herself away and hurried to the injured man.

By the time she'd checked his wound and turned back to the fire, the man the Indians had called Eyes That See in Darkness was gone. For the next two hours she dozed, rousing frequently to check on Jenks and to pile more brush on the fire. The stars faded and the fire burned down.

Bran returned to the campsite as the sky was turning light. The woman was curled in a ball beside the bed of orange coals, sleeping with her face resting on her arm, her back against her portmanteau. Bran felt his heart lighten unexpectedly, then scowled. He still wasn't convinced that the bandits hadn't been connected to her, though he could tell she hadn't been lying about her father and brother. Nobody could fake that, not even a woman.

He studied her face in the firelight. She was an odd contradiction in her skirt that was too short, heavy work boots, and a man's shirt and coat. Her hands were rough from physical labor; he'd learned that when she'd attempted to help him in the carriage. Now, resting in sleep, her mouth had softened and her hair reflected the fire of the coals, making a kind of copper frame for a face that was strong yet innocent.

The driver was awake, watching as Bran dropped his pack and drew out a canteen. "You see anything out there?" he asked, his voice weak and thready.

"Just a couple of lizards and a coyote. The coyote made off with the hardtack and biscuit I had in my pack."

"The horses?"

"Gone, for now. Maybe I'll see the black that was tied to the coach when it gets light."

The driver nodded. "There was coffee beans, a jug of water, and some jerky in a poke under the seat."

"I found it. Don't know what kept it from spilling out. How far to the way station?"

"About half a day's ride, but somebody will come looking for us when we don't get there. We're already overdue."

"Maybe, but when?"

Jenks licked his dry lips and tried not to stare at the canteen Bran pulled from inside the greatcoat.

Two sips was all Bran allowed the wounded man before he recapped the container. Building up the fire once more, Bran was very tired. His head still hurt. He wished for an hour's sleep before they began their trek to the way station.

Half a day's ride. That probably meant a day's walk, if they were lucky. Bran didn't want to think about somebody looking for them. He was afraid that somebody might finish what they'd started earlier.

Bran had heard about Pratt's gang, but their paths hadn't crossed. From what he knew, holding up a mail coach seemed a little tame for cutthroat bank robbers.

At least they had some water, jerky, and coffee. He carried the driver's pistol with enough ammunition to keep them in food, but they wouldn't last more than a few minutes if they had to fight off more outlaws. He glanced at the carrying case against which his redheaded companion was lying.

Idly he wondered what she was concealing inside. He'd been surprised to find her wearing a man's shirt and coat. Still, he had to admit that the rough work clothes fit her. She might have been a boy, except for the long red hair and her breasts.

The brief tantalizing look he'd had at her bare breasts had stayed with him as he walked back to the coach. Just thinking about her body brought an unwelcome tightening in his loins. "Damn!" The last thing he needed was a woman who spoke to his needs and didn't even know she was talking.

He told himself that a woman who donned her blouse backwards wasn't exactly the kind of feminine company he'd choose. He had the feeling that Trouble was better acquainted with masculine attire than what she'd been wearing when she climbed on the stage. She was awake.

•   •   •

"Let me have your nightgown."

Bran had gathered a large stack of underbrush. Then he moved the driver closer to the fire.

Macky watched what he was doing. She couldn't figure his actions out. "You're going to burn my nightgown?"

"No. I'm going to make a shelter."

"Why?"

"Once the sun gets up, it could get very hot in here, sheltered from the wind. Or it could rain. Jenks will need a cover."

"We aren't going to leave him, are we?"

"I'm not going with you, lass," the driver said. "I'll just slow you down."

"Of course you are. We'll help you, won't we, Mr.— Bran?"

"No," Jenks Malone said. "You go on to the station and send someone back for me and the coach. I'll keep the mail sack here with me."

"But you don't have food or water."

"He'll keep the rest of the whiskey and part of the jerky," the preacher said.

"Absolutely not! I won't leave him behind. Where does a preacher get whiskey anyway?"

Macky didn't know why she was arguing. The plan made sense. But they'd nearly lost the driver and, as irrational as it seemed, she couldn't face leaving anyone behind.

Bran put his hand on her shoulder. "Why does a woman carry a man's shirt and coat as a change of clothes?"

She knew he could feel her muscles contract beneath his touch and feared that he'd misunderstand. She was sure of it when he said, "Perhaps it would be better if you stayed with Jenks. I can travel faster without you."

"Stay here?" She was torn. She couldn't be sure about the bank robbers and Jenks needed her. But her feelings about allowing the stranger to walk off across the prairie alone was even more worrisome.

"No, lass," Jenks said. "You go with him. He might need

help. If somebody doesn't get to the station, we're all lost. I'll wait for you."

Rationally, Macky knew that he would make better time alone, but irrationally something stopped her from allowing him to go.

"Make up your mind, Trouble. Do you stay or go?"

Jenks was right. She'd done what she could for him. Making certain that someone got to the way station was what he needed now. "I'll go. Are you ready to leave?"

Bran looked at her. "You have any long pants in that case of yours?"

"Why?"

"You'd make better time if you weren't wearing a skirt."

Macky knew he was right. But if it was Pratt who attacked the stagecoach he'd be more likely to recognize her if she were dressed in the clothes she'd worn back in Promise. She couldn't risk discarding her skirt and she couldn't be too curious about the outlaws.

"Don't worry. I won't slow you down."

They gathered as much brush as they could, leaving Jenks surrounded by brambles. Finally, satisfied that he had enough to stay warm, Bran took a long look at his traveling companion. He hoped he wasn't making a big mistake. "All right, let's move out."

Macky lifted her portmanteau and started to follow.

"You're not planning to drag that along," he said, taking the carrying case from her hand, surprised at the weight.

"Of course I am. I'll carry it."

"Don't be foolish. You'll never be able to keep up. Besides, who do you plan to dress for? There's only me and, I assure you, I don't care what you wear."

Macky blushed. She knew he was right. But she couldn't abandon the money. How would she return the part of the money she didn't have a claim to?

Bran's expression dared her to argue. "If you can't wear it, you'll have to leave it behind."

Macky grabbed on to that idea. "Just a minute." She

dragged the case to the outside of the biggest rock and opened it. She stuffed paper money in her pockets and inside her shirt, managing to carry part of it. The rest she'd have to leave until someone could return for Jenks.

She tucked a few of the gold coins into the sleeves of her torn blouse and shoved them inside her coat pocket. Then she refastened the case and tugged it back inside the stand of rocks, leaving it beside Jenks.

"Don't worry, lass, I'll keep it for you."

"Thanks, Jenks. We'll get back for you soon."

Moments later she was charging along behind the preacher. Adding the money to her clothing did keep her warmer, but walking through the clumps of prairie grass was hard. It caught in her skirt and slowed her down, making her stumble. Not so, her companion. Even with the head injury he'd refused to let her treat, he set a steady pace that would have daunted most people.

But Macky kept up.

The ruts in the trail made a thin brown line across the plains. She set her eyes on the horizon, willing her feet to keep moving. A brisk cold wind swept across the plains, tugging at her hair. She was grateful for the heat of the sun as it climbed higher in the sky.

In spite of their dire circumstances there was something stimulating in the air, something that made Macky feel at home. The Kansas Territory had become a melting pot of people and ideas. Farmers, bent on escaping the close confines of the East, were pouring down the Overland Trail looking for a new life, fleeing the growing discord between the Northern and Southern states.

The finding of gold and silver in the mountains drew a different breed, some greedy, some merely independent, risk takers and mountain men.

But with the arrival of the Pony Express, news moved west as fast as the settlers. The politicians back in Washington were determined that Kansas be admitted to the Union as a free state, although some of its settlers owned slaves.

Papa had never owned slaves but he tried to be fair to both sides. He'd watched the growing discord between the North and the South and considered their western journey as a way to avoid being forced to defend either side. Still, he always spoke his mind, something a Boston schoolteacher was unwise to do.

And that made him just as unpopular in the West.

Politics didn't interest Macky. Always responsible for her father and her brother, she'd never given much thought to what she wanted. She'd certainly never fit in as a society woman back in Boston. Now, walking across the prairie, she realized that under different circumstances, she could easily have joined the pioneer women who walked alongside their wagons, following their men to a new land.

Idly she allowed her mind to build on that picture. What kind of man might she have married if she hadn't had Papa to care for?

Certainly not a man like her present companion. Bran didn't look like the rough-dressed men she'd seen pass through Promise driving wagons pulled by oxen. She wasn't exactly certain what a circuit preacher in the West looked like, but she was reasonably sure that they didn't carry guns and wear fancy black boots.

And there was the eye patch and his story of being named by the Indians. Was he an Indian fighter? According to Papa, those men wore buckskin clothing and coonskin caps. They were hard-drinking men with bad teeth and they didn't bathe.

Nothing about Bran fit any of those descriptions. But Macky knew as she struggled to keep up with him that this was a man she could depend on.

"Enough daydreaming, Macky," she whispered. "You're no more likely to be a pioneer woman than wear a satin skirt to a ball."

"Daydreaming?" The preacher's question startled Macky. She hadn't realized that she'd spoken aloud. More, she hadn't realized that she was dreaming. Fantasizing was as foreign to her as the skirt she was damning. Certainly she'd never done it before.

But neither had she robbed a bank nor followed a man wearing a black eye patch across the prairie before.

They stopped at midday, took a few sips of water and set out again. By this time the wind was gone and Macky's paper insulation was beginning to make her very warm. But she couldn't remove her coat without revealing the lumpy presence of the money inside her shirt. Worse, she needed to find a place to stop, a private place.

It was mid-afternoon when she caught sight of an indenture in the landscape. A line of trees, with leaves just beginning to bud out, snaked across their path, bringing the horizon closer.

"Ah, Mr.— Bran," she began, stopping to wipe her forehead on her sleeve. "I need to—I mean, do you intend to stop anytime soon?"

"When we get to those trees up ahead, we'll stop. Why? Are you getting tired?"

"No. I have to—"

He looked over his shoulder, took in the embarrassment on her face and understood. "Can you wait until we get there? If not, I'll turn my back."

"I'll wait," she said, tightening her muscles and picking up her steps.

Just as she'd decided she wasn't going to make it, they reached the copse of trees and the small stream running through them.

"Excuse me," she said, and headed for a section of brush that hid the stream from view.

Bran moved upstream in the other direction, allowing privacy for both of them and using the time to study their crossing place. The melting snow from the mountain ranges in the distance had caused what was normally a shallow stream to become much deeper, the current stronger.

There was nothing to do but wade across. Maybe camping here would be best. Then they'd go on to the way station in the morning rather than chancing an unknown trail in the dark.

As he walked back to where the trail crossed the creek he began to whistle, warning the girl of his approach. Grudgingly, he admitted that she'd been a better walker than he'd expected. He'd set a fast pace and she'd kept up with no complaints and no whining.

She was smoothing her skirt as she came to meet him. Her body was hidden by the loose-fitting jacket but there was something odd about her shape. She had to be wearing several shirts to look so lumpy.

"We have to cross the creek here," he said.

She glanced at the swiftly moving water and winced. "Isn't there a shallower place?"

"Not that I can see. Upstream it's wider but just as deep, and you can see that downstream the water takes a narrow path. The trail wouldn't cross here unless this was the best place."

Macky swallowed hard. The water wasn't that deep. She could see the bottom clearly. And she was wearing sturdy boots. But what in hell was she going to do about this skirt?

"Can't you just hike your skirt up over your knees?" he asked as if in answer to her thought.

Sure. You've already seen the top half of my body. Now you're asking to see the bottom. Why hadn't she worn the trousers? She glared at the amusement she was certain lurked in his stern expression.

"I'll get across. Just lead the way."

Macky watched as the preacher took off his greatcoat, tied it around a rock and threw it across, and stepped into the stream. Following his suggestion, she pulled her skirt through her legs and tucked it into the waistband, then stepped into the icy water. Taking a few steps, she felt the swift-moving water. So far, so good. She could do this.

She would have made it, if she hadn't slipped on a rock and dropped the heavy blue fabric of her skirt into the water. The current caught it and dragged her downstream before she could right herself. Even then she might have managed, except for the awkwardness of her movements caused by the restriction of her money-stuffed garments.

The clatter of coins, the string of oaths, and the splash of water caused the preacher to turn back toward her from the far bank. This time he made no attempt to hold back the laughter.

"Let me help you," he finally said, holding out his hand.

"No, thanks. I fell and I'll get up!"

In the end, however, she was forced to allow him to pull her up. When he caught the hem of her skirt and lifted it from the stream she followed the line of his vision. The clear water magnified the whiteness of the skin and the trail of blood that seeped from the scratch on her knee, just below the hem of her drawers.

"You're hurt," he said as he reached down and lifted her in his arms and started toward the other side. "And you're heavy. You feel like a supply sack. What are you wearing under that coat, everything you own?"

"Yes! Let go of me—this minute!"

"This minute?"

"Yes!"

"Certainly!" He stepped to the bank and let her go, allowing her to fall on the marshy earth like an armful of stovewood.

"Ohhhh! I have never met anyone so infuriating. Couldn't you have put me down like—like a gentleman?"

"You said let go. I did." She was trying to squeeze the water from her skirt. Though the bottom of her coat was wet, the top of her body had stayed reasonably dry. But Bran knew that the frigid water would turn her into a chunk of ice in minutes. From the look of her blue lips she was already beginning to feel the cold.

He'd have to chance building another fire so that they could dry their clothing before night set in. "Let's move upstream, away from the crossing, and I'll make a fire." Bran began gathering sticks and limbs. "We can't go on until you're dry, and by that time it will be getting dark. We'll camp here for the night."

Teeth already chattering, Macky followed him. "What about Jenks?"

"He's better off at the moment than you are," he replied. In a short time a fire was blazing. But even the fire didn't stop the chill.

"Take off your jacket and skirt and drape them over these rocks," Bran finally said, "and I'll see to your knee."

She glared at him. Take off her skirt? Her clothes might have to be dried, but she'd turn into an icicle before she'd stand there nude.

"You need to see my knee? What's the matter? Haven't you seen enough of my—me? First you rip the buttons off my shirtwaist. Now you're asking me to expose myself? What kind of crazy man are you?"

"I'm the man who is going to show you crazy if you don't do as I say. Here, you can wear my greatcoat while your clothes are drying."

He flung the dusty garment at her and stalked off downstream. "When I get back I want your clothes draped by the fire and you sitting quietly beside them."

Macky would have said something but she sensed that her rescuer was very near doing what he'd threatened. Considering what he'd find if he undressed her, she decided that she'd be better off doing it herself. Moments later she'd draped her skirt and jacket over two large rocks near the fire and donned the preacher's heavy coat. She removed her boots and pushed them toward the heat, leaving her wool-sock-encased feet turning into ice.

If she removed her shirt she could cover her feet, but the money would have to be hidden. Did she have time to do that before he returned?

The sound of footsteps told her no. Quickly she emptied the gold from the torn shirtsleeves into her pocket and tied the fabric around her feet.

The water-soaked skirt began to steam and the socks

gave off an odor of wet wool. Bran dropped a second pile of limbs behind her, knelt down and reached for the front of his coat.

"What are you doing?" Macky attempted to slide away, setting off a jingle of the coins in her pocket.

His hand froze in midair. "I was going to examine your knee."

"My knee is fine."

His face showed obvious displeasure. "I thought you lost your purse."

"I did."

"You apparently have an unending supply of coins. Is that why you wanted to bring your travel case along?"

There was no arguing with the truth. Macky decided that admission to his charge was the only way she'd stave off being forced to tell him about the bank robbery.

"Yes. Are you going to steal my money?"

"No. I'm going to build a second fire. Then I'm going to find us something to eat. Then what I want to do is—"

But he didn't move. In her attempt to step back, the greatcoat had parted, exposing two bare legs that went on forever.

Macky's lips parted, making a small circle as she gasped.

Bran's pulse quickened as he imagined capturing those lips, sliding his hands along those legs, exposing those breasts. For a long moment they stared at each other, only a shaky breath away from touching.

This time it was the shrill cry of a bird ruffling the tree limbs that broke the silence.

"What I want is . . . be rid of you," he said in a voice so hoarse that she could barely hear him. "Before . . ."

The air was tense. Macky could hardly breathe. She felt a trembling in her limbs that had nothing to do with the cold. Half of her was burning, half shivered. She'd never felt such odd sensations before.

Gathering her senses, she said, "But a preacher wouldn't—"

"No? Maybe I'm not a preacher. Suppose I'm something else? A gunfighter, maybe."

"Should I be afraid of you?"

"Yes," he said as he stood and moved away. "Maybe you should."

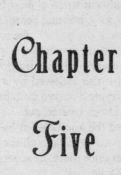

Chapter Five

*B*RAN STOPPED from time to time and inclined his head as though he were listening. Macky could tell that he was worried about the fire drawing attention to their campsite, but, like him, she didn't see that they had a choice. Dry clothing was necessary and the sooner the better.

He started a second brush pile several feet behind the first one. "Two fires will heat the air faster," he explained as he lit it. "Keep them going. I'll get food."

"What about the jerky?"

"We need something more nourishing. Save the jerky for tomorrow when we're walking."

When Bran returned he was carrying a tin bucket, rescued from the water's edge where some earlier travelers had dropped it, and another rabbit that he set to roasting on a spit over the fire. The bucket, placed in the second fire, soon sent the aroma of coffee into the night air. Macky's stomach started a fresh round of protesting. She wasn't sure she'd ever satisfy her hunger again.

When Bran finally cut strips of meat from the rabbit she reached for them eagerly, burning her tongue in her haste to eat. "How do we drink the coffee?" she asked. "We have no cups, unless you have another bottle in your pockets."

"There are other ways." He headed downstream and she heard the rustle of brush followed by a splash. When he returned he was carrying a curved limb from which a newly grown offshoot had been twisted out.

Then he enlarged the knothole left by the branch with a knife, using a rough stone to smooth the inside. After rinsing the crude dipper once more, he scooped up some coffee and handed it to Macky.

"Where'd you learn how to do that?"

"The Indians. I lived with them after my family died. They taught me many things."

"What happened to your family?"

Bran took the dipper back and refilled it. He looked down at the murky liquid, swirling it around as if he might be seeing things, things that made his expression turn hard and cold.

She didn't think he was going to answer when he finally said, "River pirates. They raided our farm one night, stole the money from a year's work, then killed my father, my mother, and my sister. Then they burned the cabin. There was nothing left."

As if it were responding to Bran's sad story, a coyote let out a low moan in the distance, only to be answered by a second animal far away.

"Is that how you lost your eye?"

He swallowed the coffee in one long gulp, then refilled it and handed it back to Macky. "Yes. The leader of the gang thought he killed me, too. He laughed. I've never forgotten the sound of that laugh."

She blew on the steaming liquid. There was more, but Macky could tell he wasn't ready to share everything. She had the feeling that not many people knew as much as she. Pushing back her natural need to sympathize, she asked a less painful question. "Which tribe did you live with?"

"Choctaw. In Mississippi, until they were driven west."

"Driven?"

"Herded like cattle," he said, his stark face not showing any signs of emotion. But his eyes couldn't hide the pain.

"But you went with them, didn't you? Why? You were a white boy."

"Army offered to send me to a white family. I liked the Indians better."

Though Macky knew little about the man, she had the firm conviction that if he started something, he saw it through. "I don't know much about the various tribes," she admitted, hoping to draw him out. "We lived in Boston where there were only immigrants. What were the Choctaw like?"

"They became my family. They were good to me."

That was it. They were family and they were good to him. That was all that mattered in a child's world. Not the suffering of the tribe, nor what her father had described as inhuman cruelties inflicted on the Indians. "What happened to them?"

This time he didn't answer. After a long silent moment he stood and turned her skirt over so that the other side would face the heat. "Still wet. It'll be dry by morning."

When he knelt beside her, Macky tried to sidle away.

"No, being close will keep us warm."

"But . . ." She tried to protest, then realized that he wasn't listening. He smoothed the ground, then lay down on his side, pulling her tight against him.

"Mr. . . . Bran . . . Preacher—whatever you are, I don't feel right about this. I'd prefer to sleep apart."

"Then you're going to be cold."

He started to pull his greatcoat away, exposing her legs and lower body to the cool air. He was going to leave her without cover. What kind of man would do that?

The answer was simple. He'd given her a choice and he'd abide by her decision.

"Fine," she snapped. "I'll just cover myself with my skirt."

She sat up, reached out for the garment, touched thé still-damp fabric and let it go. For a moment she felt tears well up in her eyes. Everything had gone wrong since Papa died. Everything. Now she was going to freeze to death out in the middle of nowhere, that or sleep with a man who had her stomach playing leapfrog with her lungs.

She let out a deep, ragged sigh, folded her arms across her knees and leaned her forehead against them. All the money from the Promise Bank couldn't help her now. As if to remind her of how helpless she was, the eerie scream of a wild animal rent the night silence.

Unconsciously, she shifted closer to Bran who, by now, seemed to have gone to sleep without showing any further concern for Macky. As the fires began to burn down, the air between them cooled.

Macky added more brush, then took an unemotional look at her plight. She couldn't help herself or poor Jenks if she froze to death. If lying close to the preacher would provide additional warmth, then that was the sensible thing to do.

Except for the money. A man wouldn't have to have much sense to feel the padding beneath her shirts and Bran was a smart man.

Making up her mind, she stood up, draped her wet skirt around her, and dashed into the bushes along the creek. Quickly she hid the money behind a log, then returned to the fire where she dropped to the ground and scooted beneath the greatcoat, planting her back against her tormentor's.

Without a comment, he turned, gathered her into his arms and pulled her close, covering the lower part of their bodies with his coat and their upper bodies with her father's.

"What in hell?" He sat up. The woman's bottom was covered with a soggy mass of wet cloth.

"What? What's wrong now?"

"Take those wet things off."

Macky shook her head. "I will not. And they're my—my undergarment."

"And they're wet. Off. Take them off and then we'll try again." He lay back down and closed his eyes.

Macky squirmed. This wasn't working out. The wages of sin were upon her and she didn't need a preacher to tell her. Finally, with the threat of freezing to death at hand, she shimmied out of her drawers and flung them alongside the skirt, then crept back under the coats.

If Bran had said a word she would have hit him with his Bible. He only opened his arms and resettled her inside them. The fire warmed her feet and his body offered a cozy little burrow for the rest of her. He even provided his arm as a pillow.

She could feel his strong thighs pressed against the back of hers, his body buffering her from the cold, his arms folded across her providing warmth and a sense of protection.

Giving a last reluctant sigh, she closed her eyes. She could do this, she decided. By morning her clothes would be dry. The sun would warm the earth and they'd get to the way station.

Bran knew the exact moment the girl relaxed and started drifting into sleep. And he knew that he wouldn't be so lucky. Her hair tickled his nose. With her bare bottom pressed intimately against him, and her legs—dear God what legs—rubbing against his own, he was going to have a long night.

Suddenly she wiggled again, arranging her body so that they were completely touching. He trembled with the need to plunge himself inside her.

"Are you cold?" she asked, rousing herself sleepily.

"No—yes."

"Can I do something to help?"

"Yes! Stop wiggling your bottom and go to sleep!"

She grew very still, fighting the urge to move against him.

It was very hard not to, especially when she could feel his heart beating against her. But she didn't know what else to do and she knew that she was keeping him from resting.

Finally, a long time later, she fell asleep. Once, Bran thought he heard a horse gallop by, but it kept going. When the sky began to lighten, Bran rose to build the fire back up again. He'd only fallen asleep once. And when he woke to find his hand beneath her shirt, holding her breast, he'd stilled his movement, but he'd found it difficult to let her go. For the rest of the night he simply held her, like a father might hold a child, comforting, nurturing.

Damn it, he didn't want to feel like that. He didn't want to feel responsible for her safety. He'd never been able to protect the people he cared about. He hadn't been able to stop the deaths of his own family, nor that of his Choctaw brother. Caring sealed their death warrant. He had no intention of caring about this woman.

In the state of half-sleep he allowed himself, he argued that keeping the girl warm was only a matter of survival. But by morning he couldn't ignore that he was as hard as a stallion in the middle of a herd of fillies. He hurt and he knew if she awoke and found him throbbing against her, she'd be frightened.

He pulled away, covered her with his coat, and left the camp.

Macky had been having a wonderful dream. Everything about her had been alive and warm. She'd felt strange new feelings, feelings that made her want to tighten her muscles and release them. She pressed herself against the pleasurable warmth that was touching her.

That hot feeling took over her. Her body felt as if it

needed relief, but this time it was different. Her very skin seemed to burn and twitch and her private parts were trembling with fire.

Then, suddenly the pressure disappeared and she knew that she was alone. "No," she whispered, wishing the dream would return. She didn't want it to go. She didn't want to wake. She moaned, then burrowed beneath the duster, seeking the return of warmth. Moments later she came suddenly awake.

"Bran?"

But there was no answer.

Macky heard the sound of fire crackling dry brush. Her skirt was lying across her feet, dry and still warm from the fire. And she was alone.

Quickly she climbed out from beneath Bran's coat and shimmied into her drawers. Before he returned she reclaimed the money she'd hidden and packed it beneath her shirt. She lay back down and pulled the coat back over her.

Sometime later, Macky heard the spit of water dripping into the flames. She opened her eyes to see the tin bucket back in the midst of glowing coals.

Bran was squatting beside the fire, adding fresh water to their coffee beans from the night before.

The night before. Her heart skipped a beat as she remembered how they'd slept, how he'd put his arms around her. She'd shamelessly pressed herself against him, seeking his warmth. And he'd held her, keeping her safe, while making no demands. Whoever this man was, she trusted him.

"Good morning, Bran," she said, brushing sand from the back of her arms and running her fingers through her tousled hair.

"Maybe. Need to get to the station. Without trouble."

She glanced around, grateful to see that he was focused on the fire, then stepped into her skirt and stood up, fastening the button at the waist. "Is something wrong?"

"Out here without a horse? Guess not."

The beard on his face was even heavier, making his

already dangerous-looking face even more forbidding. "I never knew a preacher to talk so little. Are you always so pessimistic?"

He cut a sharp glance at her. "Yes."

"No joyful noise from you, huh?"

" 'A fool's mouth is his destruction.' "

"Or, 'Fools rush in where angels fear to tread.' "

"Proverbs?" he questioned, with reluctant admiration in his mind, if not his voice.

"Nope, Alexander Pope. Which translates roughly to 'you may talk like a preacher, but you could be a "wolf in sheep's clothing." ' Aesop's Fables."

Bran couldn't think of a proper response. If she'd been lovely in the dark, she was even more appealing with the flush of their exchange on her face. She ought to be frowning. Instead she was smiling, her mouth challenging like some temptress. Her green eyes were a soft emerald color in the sunlight; they'd match the leaves of the willow trees in summer. And they were teasing him.

In spite of her dowdy clothing and the fact that she was alone, his independent traveling companion had a quick mind that had been used for more than just womanly chores. She was becoming more and more intriguing.

"Drink your coffee," he said, dropping the dipper in her lap. "We have a rough walk ahead of us."

Remembering that one brief lapse the night before, Macky understood that the light of day had turned them back into strangers. She took the dipper and filled it with the strong coffee. She wished for some honey to sweeten it. She wished for a smile from her stern companion or at least a word to suggest that they were friends.

But it wasn't to be. The coffee was bitter as sin. She didn't know yet what the man was.

Morning burst across the prairie like Macky's childhood memory of a saffron veil over one of her mother's sky-blue hats. The thought made her smile. Her steps came a little lighter and for just a moment she found herself humming.

Bran, leading the way, fell back a step, allowing her to come alongside him. "Always this cheerful in the morning?"

"Yes."

"They called you Trouble. Why?"

"It was my father's name for me. I always seemed to get into something. I was never content until I did everything my brother did. Then later . . . well, it was good that I had learned."

"Undaunted" was the word for his companion. She'd taken everything that had happened in stride and made the best of the situation. Her attire might be outlandish, but it couldn't hide her beauty and her strength. He had the feeling that nothing stopped her.

Even spending the night in the wilds with a stranger.

"What did your brother do?"

Bran watched the light go out in her eyes.

"He cheated at cards. Another gambler shot him."

"And your father?"

"My father had a bad heart. The land and the town finally killed him. He was all I had left."

Thinking about her brother and her father seemed to take away her brief flare of optimism. Macky shaded her eyes and peered across the flat brush-strewn landscape. When she squinted he knew she'd seen the thin, snaky trail of smoke visible in the distance.

"Look, smoke! Is it the way station?"

"Could be the way station. Could also be Indians, or even the outlaw that got away. Best we take care."

Macky slowed her steps. Now that they were nearly there she wasn't sure that she was ready for what might be ahead. In spite of the risk, the danger, there was something invigorating about having survived.

From the time she rode into Promise, her life had changed. She'd become a bank robber, climbed on a stage, and been shot at. Now she and a devilishly handsome man were heading across a windblown prairie toward an uncertain end with an outlaw on her trail.

"Are you worried, preacher man?"

"I'm always worried, especially when I'm with a pretty woman who doesn't know the meaning of fear."

Pretty woman? Macky didn't know whether it was the unexpected compliment or that the man had uttered a full sentence of conversation that stunned her into silence. She had known few men in her life and none of them had ever referred to her as a woman, not even Papa. To Papa she was Trouble. To Todd she was just Sister, and to the town she was that wild girl. But never woman and never pretty.

She pulled her jacket tighter, covering her confusion.

Bran considered their approach, worried about what they'd find ahead. Often robbers hit the way stations. For all he knew the outlaws had circled around and were waiting for them.

He was down to a handful of bullets and flat out of ideas. Waiting until morning had given them time to dry off and rest, but now they were in full sight. And he had a woman to protect.

He glanced at her. She was impatient to be on the way, stamping her feet and flexing her shoulders. Her hair was tangled from their trek and the desert breeze. She might be wearing a man's jacket and shirt, but that glorious head of auburn hair would identify her as a woman from ten feet. Most women would be timid and afraid. She was like some renegade chief, spear raised, ready to charge.

"All right," he said, "let's see if Daniel is in his den." He started toward the smoke spiral, toward rescue, toward God only knew what.

"Wait a minute," Macky called out. "Why not let me go first? If there are outlaws there, I'll tell them you're hurt. That way you'll have a chance to size up the situation before you're into it."

"Let a woman go first?"

"What do you have against being cautious?"

"I don't call that cautious. I call that foolish!"

"My father didn't. He always let the most unlikely person scout out the situation. Said it caught the opposition off guard."

"Your father sounds like a smart man. How come he let a town get the best of him?"

Macky turned to face her companion, her eyes dangerously full of moisture. "Because of me and my brother. He wanted to give us a good life and didn't know how."

"Sometimes we can't save the ones we love, no matter how bad we want to," Bran said softly. "That's why I travel alone."

"Alone?" She swallowed the lump in her throat, concentrating instead on refuting his claim. "What do you call me, or don't I count as a person?"

"You're temporary trouble. And I never let trouble get the best of me, not for long."

Chapter

Six

They CONTINUED to follow the wagon trail across the plains until the way station came into view. Macky charged ahead, determined that the preacher wouldn't tell her what to do. He stayed with her for a while, then slowed.

The hot Kansas sun brought beads of perspiration to Macky's forehead. She'd never understood the sudden change of temperature in the West. When the sun set, the flat open plains became bitterly cold. But in the springtime, it could snow one day and still be warm, sometimes even dry the next.

From a distance, the station seemed quiet. By now she could see horses in the dusty corral. A dog wandered down the trail, then sat and watched as if he were too lazy to come any farther. Nothing about the scene caused alarm.

The door opened and a tall rawboned woman with thinning brown hair caught up in a bun stepped out, carrying a dishpan which she emptied over a patch of new grass sprouting beside the door.

"Hello!" Macky called and began to run toward the crude structure.

The woman looked up, frowned and stepped quickly back inside. Moments later a bearded man wearing a red shirt that fit too tight across his middle came to meet them.

"Morning," he said, studying them with surprise. "Name's Smith, stationmaster here for the stagecoach line. You folks run into some trouble?"

"We were on *your* stagecoach," Macky answered. "Bandits wounded the driver and tried to hold us up."

"Your driver's still alive," Bran added. "We left him back a ways, in an outcropping of rocks just off the trail."

"Know where that is. What about the robbers?"

"Winged two. One got away."

"Could be Pratt's gang. One of those new Pony Express riders came through here last night with the news. Pratt broke out of the federal prison and robbed the bank in Promise. He and the kid riding with them escaped with the loot."

Kid riding with him. Macky groaned inwardly. He was talking about her. And Pratt had escaped. She didn't want anybody to die, but she didn't want to think a hardened criminal was trailing her, either.

The woman came back outside, drying her hands on her apron. "Harvil, what are you thinking? Bring them folks inside. They're hungry and thirsty."

"Sorry," her husband said, walking toward the corral. "Go on inside and eat. I'll go back for the driver. What about the stagecoach and the horses?"

"Horses ran off. A wheel broke, but we can fix it," Bran said, reluctantly turning to follow Smith. He didn't feel comfortable leaving Trouble behind, but the stationmaster would need help. "I'll give you a hand."

"I'll go, too," Macky said, remembering the contents of

her travel case. "Jenks will need someone to see to his wound," she added.

"You'll wait here!" Bran's voice allowed no room for arguing.

Macky started to protest, then changed her mind. She was tired and she was hot. A cool drink of water would suit her fine. "Don't forget my case," she said casually.

By the time Mr. Smith had saddled the horses and rounded up a new wheel and replacement animals to pull the coach, Mrs. Smith had prepared canteens of water and food for the ride back.

"There's some bandages and sulfur powder for the wound," she said, turning to Macky. "Us women are going to do some gossiping and maybe have a cup of tea."

"Tea?" Macky couldn't keep the dismay from her voice.

Mrs. Smith gave Macky a wink and waved to the departing men. Once they were out of sight she turned back inside. "Now, about that tea. I like mine hot and spicy. What about you?"

She reached inside a wooden barrel and withdrew a bottle. "Sherry," she said, holding it up so that Macky could see the rich light color. "A stage driver brings me a bottle now and again, for when I have company."

Macky looked at the bottle. It was nearly full.

"I don't get many guests," Mrs. Smith said in a low voice. Then she smoothed her hair from her forehead. "I'll loan you a wrapper. You go out behind the building. My Harvil built me a showerbath out there. Get good and clean and then we'll have tea and cake."

The showerbath sounded good anyway. Macky took the wrapper and the wiping cloth Mrs. Smith handed her and went out the back door. The shower was easy to find. The grass around its wood frame was green. On top of the frame was a large tank. A pull of the rope released the water inside.

Macky looked anxiously around. There was no cover to shelter a person's body from prying eyes. Though, except for someone in the house, who would get close enough to see?

She thought about undressing outside for anyone to see. Then she thought about the dirt and dust she'd endured for the last two days.

She'd do it.

Moments later, Macky's coat, shirt, her skirt, and the ragged strip of fabric she'd tied her hair back with, all hit the ground. She stepped beneath the water, pulled the cord, and felt the sun-warmed water sluice over her tired body. Quickly she let go the cord, stopping the flow. Using up the full tub would be selfish.

She soaped her body with the grainy homemade soap she found on one of the braces, then released just enough water to rinse. Drying herself, she slipped the wrapper on and gathered her clothing. She'd have tea with Mrs. Smith, then she'd brush the dust from her clothes.

"My, my, you're a pretty thing," Mrs. Smith said. "I'm Harriet. What's your name?"

"It's—" Macky caught herself just as she was about to answer. She couldn't say McKenzie. That's the name the bank robbers were looking for. She couldn't say Macky. If anybody recognized her in Promise, Macky would be the name the sheriff was looking for.

"Kathryn—no, Kate," she said softly. "That was my mother's name."

Harriet Smith looked at her shrewdly. "It's a beautiful name. I'm proud to be visiting with you, Kate. How long have you been married?"

Macky hoped her shock didn't show on her face. For a moment she didn't know how to respond. "We—we haven't been together long," she answered vaguely in case anyone asked Mrs. Smith about her guests.

"Well, don't you worry. I was shy myself. There's a pot of stew for supper but we'll just have our tea before our menfolk get back."

The tea turned out to be weak—more sherry than water—but the cake was moist and sweet. The reference to "our menfolk" was harder to swallow. Macky's conscience nudged her. She'd never lied so willingly before, but she'd never been a bank robber, either.

As soon as her travel case arrived, Macky intended to find a way to buy a horse and head for Denver. She'd leave the preacher to explain their relationship if he hadn't already.

Mrs. Smith frequently refilled their cups. The afternoon gave way to early evening and the prairie turned cold once more. Macky glanced anxiously out the one window, wondering if something had happened, if the outlaws had come back.

"Fixing a broken wheel takes a spell," Mrs. Smith volunteered. "Don't worry, we'd know if something had happened. Harvil's horse would have hightailed it home."

"I—I was only worried about Jenks," Macky lied. It wasn't just the driver, it was also the money—and Bran.

"Why don't you take a nice nap while I fix us some food," Harriet suggested. "They'll be along soon."

Macky, suddenly very sleepy, agreed, allowing Mrs. Smith to lead her past the rope bed in the corner of the station into a back room where one large bed and several small hard-looking cots lined the walls.

"We have facilities for the stage passengers to lay over when there's trouble," she explained, "but more'n likely there won't be nobody else along for a day or two. I made you and the mister a bed by the fire."

Though unsteady on her feet, Macky managed to fold her shirts stuffed with bank money and placed them beneath the straw-stuffed mattress on the floor. At least it looked clean.

Macky lay down, pulled a ragged blanket over her, and before Mrs. Smith had left the room she was asleep.

An hour later when Harvil Smith, Jenks Malone, and Bran returned, she was sleeping so soundly that they decided not to wake her. Leaving her traveling case beside her bed, Bran made use of the same outdoor shower, ate heartily of the stew Mrs. Smith provided, and helped Jenks bed down by the big fire in the main room before announcing that he'd turn in so that he could get an early start the next morning when Harvil left with the stage.

Inside the room where passengers slept, Bran built up the fire, and lay down on the floor, covering himself with his greatcoat.

He still hadn't decided on a permanent cover. Announcing that Mrs. Sylvia Mainwearing had hired a gunfighter to protect her claim from whoever was stealing her shipments was what his employer had wanted. But Bran never went into a situation with guns drawn. A challenge often resulted in the death of the wrong target before Bran learned enough about the man he was after. More than once the culprit had gotten away. Now a condition of his employment was that no advance word of his arrival would be announced.

Only when Mrs. Mainwearing's solicitor back in St. Louis agreed, did he accept the assignment. He'd play it quiet for a day or two, check out the lay of the land, then call on his employer.

But what was he to do about the girl? No matter how tough she thought she was, she was still as innocent as a child, and she didn't have a tribe of Choctaw to protect her. She didn't even have a name. He couldn't help but wonder what she was hiding. And why?

Bran needed sleep; he'd had little of it in the last two days. Now when he had to rest his body, he was restless, the mere sound of his breathing distracting.

"Ah, darling," he whispered, "the wages of sin are death, and you're surely the devil's own temptation."

John Brandon finally slept, but only because he couldn't stay awake any longer.

Only because he knew he had to be alert if he wanted to find the man he was after.

Only because he couldn't allow himself to respond to the desire his body was suddenly feeling after months of being suppressed.

It didn't take a man of God to know that her papa had named her right when he'd called the girl Trouble.

The next morning Harvil hitched the team to the coach, and loaded the mail sack on board. Macky heard the movement of the carriage and the nickering of the horses. She opened her eyes with a start and quickly climbed from the bed, reeling from the headache that practically blinded her.

Though she'd fallen asleep as soon as her head hit the pillow, she'd dreamed, wonderful fantasies that seemed too real. Even as they disappeared into lost memories she knew that one of the participants had been a man with a patch on his eye.

Now she had to hurry, replacing her bank money in her portmanteau, and pulling on the badly wrinkled skirt and remaining shirtwaist, this time making sure it was closed properly.

By the time she was dressed and had managed to tie her hair back with a piece of cord she found hanging on the end of the bed, the stage was almost ready to leave.

"Good, I was about to call you," Harriet said as Macky entered the great room.

Jenks was sitting at the table eating flapjacks and drinking black coffee. Harriet filled a cup for Macky. "Sorry it isn't tea," she said with a wink.

Tea! Of course. The tea laced with sherry had to account for Macky's deep sleep and the headache. And possibly for the strange dream she'd had about Bran, about being in his arms again, about feeling his hands on her body.

"Thank you," Macky said, trying to conceal a blush which had nothing to do with Harriet's reference to the spirits they'd drunk.

"How are you feeling, Jenks?" Macky asked as she hurriedly polished off two cups of coffee and forced herself to swallow one of the flapjacks.

"I'll live, lass," he said, "thanks to the preacher's shooting and your fine doctoring back there."

"I had little to do with it," she protested, finishing the last of her food just as Bran entered the room. "And I'm not convinced that he's a preacher," she said under her breath.

"You coming?" Bran asked Macky.

"Did you think I'd let you leave without me?"

"You'd be smart to do just that."

"Nobody ever said I was smart."

Harriet Smith came around the table and gave Macky a hug as she stood. "Bring your man and come back for a visit again, Kate."

"Kate?" Bran's voice didn't bother to conceal his amusement. "Thank you, Mrs. Smith," he said as he steadied Macky's faltering step and whispered in her ear. "Kate? I don't think so. Trouble seems more appropriate for a woman wearing a blue wrapper."

Macky whirled around and started out the door, stopping only to pick up her traveling case. "And Eyes That See in Darkness is a better name than Bran for a man who goes snooping around in the dark." She didn't know how he knew what she'd been wearing, but she was beginning to have the odd sensation that he had done more than see in the dark last night. The shimmering sensation just beneath her skin had intensified the moment Bran had spoken.

Even in her innocence she knew that his knowing grin and the physical reaction that flared between the two of them couldn't be right. Macky might not know much about men, but she knew there were two kinds of women; the kind of women her brother visited in town when he'd come home drunk and reeking with cheap perfume, and the kind men married.

Macky Calhoun was neither. She was being chased by a killer and the one-eyed man she was traveling with was a devil. He was only trying to frighten her.

And damn him, he was succeeding.

•   •   •

As the day went on, Macky's headache only got worse. At
least she hadn't had to tolerate Bran's presence inside the
coach. Instead, he'd ridden on top, next to Harvil, who had
his rifle in his lap.

"Just in case we run into Indians," Harvil explained.
"The Arapaho, the Ute, and the Pawnee have been at it for
the last six months, ever since that new Indian agent was
killed. Don't guess they'll ever learn to live like civilized
men."

"Probably not, when supposedly civilized men have run
them off their land and killed their buffalo," Bran offered
bitterly.

They drove off, leaving Jenks at the way station to wait
for the next stage coming in. That stage would lay over to
rest the horses since there were no fresh replacements.

Macky tried to rest, but the rocking of the coach only
added to the pain in her head. If this was what came of
drinking spirits, she couldn't imagine why her brother ever
indulged.

The stage crossed the shallow, fast-moving creek at the
base of the mountains and Heaven came into sight by mid-
afternoon.

Through the curtainless window she saw the snow-
capped mountains gradually creep closer, and finally, a
crudely constructed mass of buildings came into view,
linked together like children playing Red Rover. The stage
came to a temporary stop and Bran climbed inside the
coach.

"No point in announcing my arrival," he said.

"You think they won't see you?" Macky said. "I know
you believe you can walk on water, but you haven't turned
into a spirit yet."

The stage took off again, jostling Macky, who wasn't
prepared for the sudden movement.

"No jingling this time," Bran observed with a smothered smile.

Macky ignored him, concentrating instead on the settlement she could see through the window. She was surprised at the number of buildings. She was even more surprised at the crowd waiting on the wooden sidewalk outside the stagecoach office.

Harvil drew the team to a stop. A mass of people moved forward, led by two men, one wearing a top hat and a black suit and a United States Marshal wearing a badge.

As Macky searched the crowd her heart sank. Slouching against the building at the rear of the delegation, freshly shaven, and wearing new clothes, was a man she recognized without question.

Pratt. He'd managed to follow her, or the boy named McKenzie. She glanced around, looking for a place to hide, a way out. There was none.

Pratt was waiting for her, but what would he do? He couldn't turn her in without implicating himself. He'd killed the deputy and that's what he'd do to her, if she were caught. *Slow down, Macky. How can he know that the woman on the stage is the boy who made off with the money?*

Maybe he didn't. Maybe he was taking the stage and leaving town.

Desperately Macky considered her choices. If she ran away she'd call attention to herself. If she stayed she just might get away with her deception. Particularly if the waiting crowd made the same mistake that the Smiths had back at the way station; that the preacher was her man.

The expression on Bran's face said that he wasn't any happier over their reception than she. He looked as if he would like nothing better than to leave the stage and disappear.

"Brother Adams, greetings! We got your letter saying you were on the way," the man wearing the top hat said as he opened the door and extended his hand to Bran. He caught sight of Bran's eye patch and for a moment his hand hung limply in the air before he caught himself and held it straight again.

"And Mrs. Adams," one of the women said, rushing forward to greet Macky. "The minister wasn't sure you'd be up to making the trip. The journey from St. Louis must have been dreadful."

"After we heard about the bank robbery in Promise we were worried about you, Reverend," another called out. "You didn't run into that Pratt gang, did you?"

"There was a little problem," Harvil said, climbing down. "Bandits tried to hold up the stage. The driver got shot, but they managed to get away. The driver was saved, thanks to these folks."

The man in the top hat tried to help Macky down from the stage first, but she quickly moved behind Bran so that Pratt couldn't see her. The man finally turned his attention back to Bran, who climbed out.

"We don't have much of a church yet, Brother Adams, but we Methodists know how to make our new preacher welcome. I'm Preston Cribbs, the new Pony Express station manager and the mayor of Heaven."

"You knew we were coming?" Bran asked in surprise as he reached back to pull Macky out.

The clipped way he had of speaking was back and Macky knew that Bran was not pleased with what was happening. She expected him to speak out any minute and tell them that he'd never seen her before the stop in Promise. But he didn't.

"My rider told us you were on the way. He stops at the way station, then comes cross-country," Mr. Cribbs explained, and held out his hand once more to Macky, who could no longer avoid climbing down.

"So, when we found that you'd be arriving this afternoon, we all came down to welcome you."

"Thank you," Macky said, her voice trembling in fear. She held her breath, waiting for his reaction when he got a good look at the new parson's wife.

At that moment the man wearing the badge stepped forward. "Aaron Larkin, here, U.S. Marshal. Did you get a good look at the outlaws?"

Harvil answered. "No, had their faces covered. But the preacher got two of them. The only one to escape was riding a black horse. Could have been the Pratt gang, but the regular driver couldn't say for sure."

Macky gulped. She was staring at a federal marshal and the sheriff in Promise was probably on his way. If she wasn't killed by Pratt, she'd be hung from the nearest scaffold by the law.

Macky glanced casually over the heads of the townsfolk at the bank robber, who studied her briefly for a moment, then turned his attention back to the stagecoach. She leaned down, smoothing her skirt, reckoning that the shorter she appeared, the less likely he'd recognize her. But all she did was draw the ladies' attention to the sad state of her travel-worn short skirt.

She heard a murmur ripple through the crowd. Then came dead silence. Macky raised her gaze to find all the attention was on her. She was caught in the most humiliating moment of her life. She had to act quickly before Pratt figured out who she was or Bran gave her away.

"Please," she began in a soft, strained voice, "call me Kate. I'm—we're very pleased to be here." That much was certainly true. Under other circumstances she'd be in jail, or dead. Anything was preferable to that, anything except the look of fury in the preacher's eye.

While it had suited Bran to use the minister as his cover until he got a handle on the situation, he never expected to have a wife. To save his life, he couldn't figure out what her angle was until he saw the fear in her eyes. She reached out and clasped his arm, holding on for dear life.

We're glad to be here? What in hell was she doing, formally linking them before this crowd? The last thing he needed was some half-wild female to be responsible for. But somehow that was what was happening.

The flame of her cheeks said that she realized how inappropriately she was dressed. He'd seen the lifted chins on the women. Yet she was standing up to them, proud and undaunted.

"Preacher Adams," the mayor went on, "would you and the missus like to adjourn to the saloon?"

"Saloon?" Macky repeated in a shocked voice.

"Don't look so surprised, Reverend," Marshal Larkin commented dryly. "They don't have a church yet. Until funds are raised for a building, the good Methodists of Heaven have been using the saloon as their meeting place. They've planned a meal and a social occasion in your honor."

"How nice," Bran said, feeling Macky's fingertips dig even deeper into his arm.

The marshal tilted his hat back and studied Bran. "Interesting eye patch, Reverend Adams. Not many men wear them. Have I ever met you before?"

Macky's eyes strayed back to the bank robber. Pratt pushed himself away from his spot against the building and walked around the stagecoach, casually studying the travelers. Macky followed his movements, catching his gaze head-on. The outlaw looked at her, puzzled for a minute, then smiled and nodded his head.

Damn! Had he recognized her? Macky didn't know. Maybe he hadn't figured it out yet. The headache she'd nursed since she awoke this morning came pounding back.

It was only a matter of time before Pratt would remember seeing those same green eyes on his young associate who'd vanished with his money. She had to do something to stop him.

"I don't believe we've met." Bran was answering the marshal's question. "In fact, I'm afraid—"

"We've—I mean I've never been out West before," Macky interrupted. "I'm originally from Boston and the Reverend Adams is from—" She looked at him helplessly, imploring him to go along. She'd long since stopped trying to decide whether she was putting alibis in an outlaw's mouth, or lies in a preacher's.

"Mississippi," Bran finished, questions flashing in his eyes.

They were in it now. With the marshal's gaze fixed on him and Trouble looking as if she were about to be burned at the stake, he had little choice.

Years had passed since he'd feared that old wanted poster from back in Texas. The Rangers had looked briefly for John Lee, who'd saved his Indian brother from a beating by a thieving army sergeant delivering cattle to the reservation. But with only a pen-and-ink sketch of a young man with an injured eye to identify the boy, and with many feeling sympathy for his act, Bran had never been seriously hunted.

Because his scarred eye could identify him, he'd covered it with the black patch which he'd worn ever since. The case was still open, but Bran hadn't worried about it for years. Until now. Maybe having a wife was good.

"Mrs. Adams and I would be pleased to attend the social," he said, gallantly folding Macky's arm over his. "Shall we, Kate, *dear*?"

For a moment Macky seemed nonplussed. She glanced around, then turned to Bran and smiled bravely. "Certainly, but I—" She looked down at her skirt and winced.

"Don't worry about the skirt," Bran said, "the good people of Heaven will understand that your clothing was destroyed in the wreck of the stagecoach."

"Of course," the woman closest to Macky said, with relief in her voice. "We certainly understand."

Bran felt the vibrations coming from his new bride and knew he'd better head off the approaching explosion. In spite of his profession, Bran had a strong moral code and he believed that God's servants shouldn't be ridiculed.

"The Lord will provide, Mrs. Adams," he said piously. "In the meantime, let us be truly grateful for what we have been given—a place of safe refuge from our enemies."

Macky tried to jerk away.

Bran held her tighter. At her startled look he inclined his head so that his mouth was close to her ear as they walked. "Now, what in hell are you doing, *Kate*?"

"What the hell are you doing?" she asked under her breath, then turned to the woman beside her. "We know that God works in mysterious ways, and our arriving in Heaven is truly a miracle."

Preston Cribbs nodded vigorously, turned and started across the street. "Yes, indeed. Let's ring the Heaven bell to let the sinners know that our minister has come."

The welcoming committee closed around Bran and Macky, pushing them even closer together. A shiny new bell mounted on the top of the saloon began to ring.

"I was a bit worried that your members might not recognize me," Bran said pleasantly, to the beaming members of his congregation keeping pace with his steps. In his own way he was testing his hope that nobody in Heaven had ever seen the preacher.

"Harvil's wife said you wore an eye patch," someone said, as if that identified him.

"Of course. Why would anyone doubt you?" Macky asked in exaggerated innocence, all the while keeping her eye on Pratt, who was still dogging their steps. "I never would."

She was very clever, this woman who'd proclaimed herself to be his wife just moments earlier. "And you've known a lot of ministers, haven't you, dear?"

"Only you." She blinked her eyes in what she hoped was a flirtatious gesture and smiled.

At that moment the church members broke into a lively chorus of "Bringing in the Sheaves" to accompany their march to the saloon, offering Bran the opportunity to ask his new wife a whispered question. "And why do you care what happens to me?" he asked, his voice barely more than a growl.

"Because," she snapped, "I'd rather be a rich wife than a poor widow."

Bran gave a dry laugh. "What in hell makes you think I'll ever be rich?"

"Why, this is Heaven, isn't it? I've heard that the streets are paved with gold."

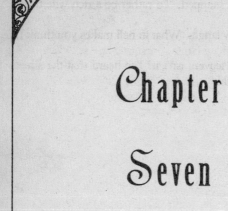

Chapter

Seven

𝕸ACKY KEPT REMINDING HERSELF that, for whatever reason, Bran hadn't corrected the welcoming committee's impression that she was the minister's wife.

For now, she couldn't ask questions. Later, when she'd gotten away from this crowd, would be soon enough to find out what kind of game the preacher was playing.

In the meantime, she was Mrs. Adams, Mrs. Kate Adams, wife of the new Methodist minister in the part of the Kansas Territory called Heaven. But she didn't believe for one minute that Bran was helping her out of the goodness of his heart, and though she'd started this charade, she wasn't sure she wanted to be used.

" 'Oh what a tangled web we weave, when first we practice to deceive,' " she said softly, trying to pry herself away from the pressure of Bran's arm against her rib cage.

"Or 'come into my parlor, said the spider to the fly,' " he

whispered as they moved through the swinging doors to the saloon.

Macky caught sight of the women standing around the edges of the room, circling a painting on the floor. "My goodness. It's a picture of a lady."

There was a laugh as one of the onlookers separated herself from the others and moved toward them. Her presence stopped the chatter abruptly.

"It's your face on the floor," Macky exclaimed.

"Yes, it's me. Good afternoon, Mrs. Adams, is it?" the woman said, her voice laced with amusement. "A good likeness, don't you think?"

"It's beautiful," Macky admitted, feeling all the more shabby in comparison to the saloonkeeper. She was even taller than Macky, but that was where the resemblance ended. Her hair looked like spun gold and her body was magnificent. There was so much of it, so nicely shaped, so openly displayed.

The marshal stepped forward. "Reverend, Mrs. Adams, this is Miss Lorraine Lake, the proprietor of Heaven's Bell, recently renamed in honor of the new church."

"Ah, yes," Preston Cribbs chimed in. "Miss Lake has been gracious enough to allow us to hold Sunday-morning services in her establishment, seeing as how she doesn't use it then, of course."

"Of course, your congregation believes you'll manage to convert me," Miss Lake said, turning her attention to Bran. "Who knows, maybe you will."

There was an instant connection between the woman and Bran, obvious to Macky if not to the others. Bran's lips quirked at the corners and he held out his hand. "Miss Lake, is it? I'm Brandon Adams, your new messenger from God. It's very kind of you to welcome my little flock of sheep to your—establishment, but it isn't Sunday, is it?"

"No, but your sheep are always welcome to join my other guests," Lorraine practically purred, pushing a long strand of golden hair behind her ear.

There was a collective gasp from the ladies of the church and Macky wondered how often they'd crossed paths with Miss Lake before. Based on the sheepish expressions of discomfort on the men's faces, she'd bet they'd all put a foot on the bar rail at one time or another.

Macky had been in the saloon back in Promise more than once, bringing Todd home—until he'd finally moved out and dared her to torment him again. But never had she seen a woman like Lorraine.

It was the devil that made her do it. Macky had no other explanation for her planting herself firmly against Bran's side and smiling up at him as she thought an adoring wife might do. "Do call me Kate," she said. "Mrs. Adams is just too formal. Thank you for making us welcome."

It wasn't Trouble's saucy remarks but the sharp heel of her heavy boot that caught Bran's attention and reminded him that his cover as a minister had to be complete or it could be ruined. He didn't know which, if any, of the men watching might be the one he was after. But for now, he'd better play it out—all the way.

"Yes. Thank you, Miss Lake," Bran said.

Macky's words hadn't erased the twinkle from Lorraine's eyes. The citizens of Heaven might be taken in by Macky's claims, but she was afraid that fooling Lorraine Lake was going to be a bigger task. She was certain of it when Lorraine said, "Maybe you'd like to begin our redemption by leading us in a word of prayer, Reverend, before we enjoy the refreshments the ladies of your church have prepared."

"I—I . . ." Bran was at a loss for words. If Macky hadn't been sure that he was masquerading as a preacher before, she was now.

The saloonkeeper went on. "I might even contribute something spirituous to the occasion—to welcome you."

I'll bet you will, Macky wanted to say. In spite of their story, Lorraine had taken one look at Bran and set her sights on him. To stay out of jail Macky needed Bran. She'd just have to find a way to keep him from Lorraine's clutches until she could get away. The method hadn't come clear yet, but Macky would find it.

"Yes," Marshal Larkin agreed, "a word of prayer might be in order."

It was the marshal's agreement, or his challenge, that forced Bran to gather his wits and bow his head.

The crowd grew quiet.

There was a cough and someone shushed someone else.

The silence continued.

Macky nudged Bran with her elbow and risked cracking one eye to study his face.

"Father of all," he finally began, "He who was there first, before any man or woman, or rain or wind or beast, hear our lament. We ask you this day to make our steps firm and our hearts good."

He stopped.

Macky took a chance and added, "Amen!"

The members of the congregation looked at Bran and back at each other, unable to hide their bewilderment before Mr. Cribbs let out an echoing "Amen!" The others followed and surged forward to shake Bran's hand and introduce themselves.

Reluctantly, Macky allowed herself to be separated from Bran by the ladies. They insisted that she taste every dish laid out on the bar, each giving her a description of its ingredients, each tactfully ignoring the nearly nude figure painted on the floor.

She followed their lead, dutifully eating meat pies, cakes, apple dumplings, and a few dishes she couldn't name. One very heavy woman with several chins held out a dish of what looked for all the world like animal feet.

"We don't have many hogs to kill, Mrs. Adams. But I always put the feet back to brine. You're going to love my pickled pig's feet."

It could have been the rich food after she had eaten nothing more than a bit of meat for days. It could have been overindulgence in Harriet's special tea or it could have been the sight of the pig's feet. In any case, Macky took a deep desperate breath and held her stomach as she began to heave.

"Oh, dear, I think I'm going to—"

"Don't you worry, child," Mrs. Cribbs said, nodding her head in understanding. "Come with me."

Before Macky knew what was happening she was out the door, throwing up beside the building.

"I know how it is when you're that way," Mrs. Cribbs said. "When is your time?"

Macky gagged again. "Any minute now, I'm afraid."

"But you don't look a bit like you're hiding something."

"Hiding something?" Macky remembered the money hidden inside her shirt.

"Boys always carry low," Mrs. Cribbs went on. "I guess the preacher is pleased."

Macky leaned her arm against the building and wiped her mouth with the scrap of cloth from her hair. "Boys?"

"Take deep breaths," her helpful companion advised. "I'll just wet my handkerchief in the water barrel."

Macky nodded. Seconds later there was a rippling sound in the water, followed by a damp cloth being pressed to her forehead.

"Let's get you up to your room, Mrs. Adams, so you can rest for a while. I'm sure the folks will understand once they learn about your condition."

"Thank you, and please call me"—Macky hesitated, almost forgetting her name change—"call me Kate," she finished. "All my friends call me Kate."

"Fine, Kate." Mrs. Cribbs opened the door and preceded Macky back inside. "We'll just slip up the stairs."

"The preacher's wife is spending the night in a—saloon?" Macky couldn't keep the disbelief from her voice. Even in a mining town that seemed a bit absurd.

"Only temporarily," said Mr. Cribbs, who was waiting by the door. "We are preparing a small house, just outside of town. It needs a bit of fixing up, but it will be fine."

Bran, lounging at the base of the stairs, lifted an eyebrow. "Are you all right, my dear?"

"She's fine," Mrs. Cribbs assured him. "A perfectly understandable occurrence. You all just go on with the party and I'll get Kate settled for a nice rest. Did you take her things up, Mr. Cribbs?"

"Things?" Macky straightened, felt her stomach complain, and swallowed hard again. "I'll be fine. Just tell me where the room is."

The last thing she wanted was someone opening her case. Judgment day would arrive before either she or the reverend was ready.

"I'll show you," Lorraine Lake said. "Follow me." She started up the steps and looked back over her shoulder. "Would you care to join us, Reverend?"

"Ah, no," Macky spoke quickly, feeling her face flame. "Do go on with the party. The congregation has been so generous. I'll go with Miss Lake."

"Lorraine," the blond-haired Viking corrected. "I'm real interested in learning about the Scriptures. Maybe you could help me?"

Bran frowned. "Maybe it would be better coming from me."

" 'Tis an ill cook that cannot lick his own fingers.' " Macky snapped. "That's from Shakespeare, not the Bible."

Bran smiled. "On the other hand, 'Blessed is the man that endureth temptation; for when he is tried, he shall receive the crown of life.' " He turned to the silent onlookers. "That's from the New Testament, and that will be the topic of my first sermon, 'The Temptation of Man.' "

"And women, too, dear." The sound of Macky's voice came floating angelically down the stairs.

Lorraine opened the door at the end of the hall and entered, indicating to Macky that she should follow. Once she was inside, the saloonkeeper closed the door and leaned against it.

"Now, what's going on here? Your husband is dressed like some fancy gambler and you look like a sheepherder's wife."

"And you look like a fancy lady, not a saloonkeeper."

Lorraine smiled. "Thank you, Kate. But that only proves that you aren't acquainted with either one. Are you really his wife?"

The devil's pitchfork. Macky didn't want the preacher, but damned if she was going to let this woman steal him, if that was what she had in mind. Macky didn't want Lorraine to cause trouble for him, either. He'd been good to her, protecting her, making sure she didn't catch cold or go hungry. She owed him a certain amount of loyalty, even if she didn't know who he was.

Macky stood straighter. "I don't know what you expected Bran's wife to be, Miss Lake, so I won't try to answer."

Lorraine let out a genuine laugh. "Good for you. You're going to need spunk to stave off those pious women downstairs. You may not look like the kind of woman the preacher would choose, but I like you."

Lorraine's smile was genuine. It was as if she'd relaxed and decided to befriend the preacher's wife for some reason that was beyond Macky.

"You mean you aren't going after him?"

"No. I saw the way he was watching you. But, just for the record, if he showed any interest in me I might trade my saloon for a tambourine. How'd you do it?"

Her question left Macky with her mouth open. "I really don't know—I mean I didn't—I'm a mess."

"Nothing wrong that the right dress and a little fixing up wouldn't cure." Lorraine cocked her head toward the portmanteau. "What do you have in that bag? Not more of the same, I hope."

Macky glanced down at her skirt. "Pretty bad, I know.

These are—borrowed. The rest of my clothes got spilled out along the trail when the stage turned over."

"I'll lend you something to sleep in," Lorraine said and left the room, returning moments later with a soft pink nightgown with lace along the collar and sleeves, a garment entirely different from what Macky had expected.

"Thank you," Macky said, ashamed at her wrong first impression of the woman who seemed ready to be a friend. "The accident left me ill-suited for Heaven. I wonder, Miss Lake . . ."

"Call me Lorraine."

"Lorraine. Would you help me choose some more suitable clothes?"

"Me? I hardly think the members of your husband's congregation would approve of that, Mrs. Adams. I'm the town's scarlet woman."

"Please call me Kate. I may not have any choice in who joins the—my husband's church, but I'll pick my own friends. I know what it means to be left out."

"Thank you, Kate," Lorraine said. "And don't worry. You just get a good night's sleep, and in the morning, I'll see that you're suitably dressed as the wife of the new minister. I only hope you know what you're doing."

Macky hoped she did, too. Right now all she wanted to do was find a way to avoid the citizens of Heaven for the evening. "And, will you tell all of them that I regret spoiling their party."

"Spoiling their party? Don't worry about that. They haven't had so much fun since I brought my girls to town. I'm going to be interested to see what happens when they find out that they haven't found a crusader to help them fight all this sin in Heaven."

"Crusader?" Macky's last question was lost in Lorraine's closing of the door.

Of course. She guessed that's what preacher's wives were supposed to do. Be good examples. That was a joke, having a bank robber setting the standards in Heaven. She'd gotten herself into big trouble this time. Sooner or later she was going to have to face Bran with an explanation. What on earth was she going to tell him?

That odd feeling in the pit of her stomach came back again. This time she couldn't blame it on the pig's feet.

Macky was tired, and a bit scared, for in spite of her bragging that she was as strong as most men, all this bravado filled her with doubt. Suppose she was discovered? She was no crusader. All she wanted to do was hide.

Moments later she'd burned the flour sack in the fire, hidden the money beneath the mattress, washed her face and hands with rose-smelling water from the pitcher, and swapped her dusty clothes for the pink nightdress. She'd never been so exhausted.

Forcing herself to forget about her situation, she stretched out on the soft, sweet-smelling bed. As she slid her arms beneath the crisp muslin sheets, she decided that, just for that night, she'd take her chances with fate. The die was already cast. Either she'd be branded as an angel or a sinner. She couldn't change what was to come.

There was, she decided as she breathed in the scent of roses, definitely something to be said for sin in Heaven.

Bran waited for Lorraine Lake to return. He knew she'd have questions for Kate. How would his newly acquired wife answer them? From the way she'd bristled at Lorraine's familiarity, he suspected that they'd collide head-on.

If the circumstances were different he'd have taken the woman aside and found a way to use her knowledge and position. But playing out his charade before half the town of churchgoers prohibited that.

For all he knew, she was involved with the man he'd come to confront. What was bothering him the most was her being alone with Trouble. She was much too innocent for Lorraine Lake.

He glanced at the painting on the floor and held back a

smile of admiration. He'd seen such artwork before. Some down-on-his-luck drifter with a talent for drawing would cover his drinking bill by painting a portrait on the barroom floor. This artist was better than usual and Lorraine Lake was a woman worthy of having her likeness captured.

For another half hour, Bran socialized with the members of the church, discreetly asking questions about the town residents under the guise of learning about his community.

Then he decided to meet the enemy head-on. "Marshal Larkin, isn't it a bit unusual for a mining settlement to have a federal lawman stationed there?"

"I don't have an office here. I actually answer to Judge Hardcastle in Denver, but Heaven is in my territory. I'm just in town at the request of Mrs. Sylvia Mainwearing. Since her husband, Moose, was murdered, she and many of the other prospectors have been besieged by outlaws."

"Her husband?" Bran had been hired by Mrs. Sylvia Mainwearing's solicitor in St. Louis. This information made him reconsider his position.

"Moose was a pretty rough character. They say Sylvia didn't much care for him when he was alive, but he was murdered and she's been distraught ever since. I've been trying without much success to find his killers. Maybe having a minister in Heaven will calm things down a bit."

"That's what we're counting on," the woman with the three chins said. "I'm Clara Gooden and I hope you know, Reverend Adams, I don't approve of you and Mrs. Adams staying in this place. I'm sure the Lord would be shocked."

Bran cast a wounded look at the woman whose intrusion was hampering his fact-finding. "Why, Mrs. Gooden, don't you believe that the Lord provides?"

"Why—why, yes, of course. But not a saloon like this. A man of the cloth ought to stay in a more appropriate place."

Bran gave her what he thought was a clerical look of disapproval. "Mrs. Adams and I are very grateful to be provided with a place like this."

"Well!" Mrs. Gooden whirled around and began to claim

her bowls. "Come, Mrs. Cribbs, Ethel. I think we've occupied Miss Lake's . . . establishment long enough."

"Yes," Mrs. Cribbs agreed. "We're so glad to have you here, Reverend. Oh, and Mrs. Mainwearing has asked us to tell you that you're invited to supper tomorrow night, if your wife's well enough. Sylvia sets a fine table, and when you're eating for two, good food is very important."

The eating for two didn't make much sense but Bran nodded. It was the perfect way to see his employer without arousing undue interest. He was glad to see that the uncomfortable gathering was coming to an end.

Dinner with Mrs. Mainwearing would give him the chance he needed to size her up without her knowing he was the gunfighter she'd hired. Bran had always made it a point to keep a low profile to protect his identity. Now he was being studied by a United States Marshal, a table of gamblers who probably knew most of the criminals this side of the Mississippi, and a town full of good citizens, any one of whom might give him away.

He shook hands with the men and followed the mayor outside the saloon. "Thank you for the meal. I'm sorry my . . . wife became ill. Must have been something she ate."

The men grinned at each other and slapped him on the back. "We understand. We've all been through it a time or two ourselves."

"About Mrs. Mainwearing," Bran persisted, "is she a member of the congregation?"

"No," said the round-faced man who had been identified as Mr. Gooden, the local general store owner. "But if she likes you, maybe she'll contribute some of her gold to build a church. Then we wouldn't have to hold services in the saloon and we'd be able to provide a better parsonage for you than Kelley's shack."

"Parsonage?" Bran hadn't considered that far ahead.

"It's too small and pretty rough for a young wife," Mayor Cribbs explained, "but it's the best we can do for now. I hope that Mrs. Adams will be tolerant until we can do better."

Bran's opinion was that Mrs. Adams would do better in the wilderness than in any kind of cabin. He was beginning to wish he'd never gone along with her ready acceptance of the misunderstanding. No matter how he looked at it, her pretense made no sense. And now he'd committed himself to being responsible for her safety. The whole thing had gotten out of hand.

Not only that, but she was already beginning to interfere with his reason for being in Heaven. Even now he was torn between pursuing his investigation and checking on her sudden illness. When he realized that the men were waiting for some response from him he asked, "Who is Kelley?"

"Kelley was a prospector," Mr. Gooden explained. "Never found any gold that we know of, but when his wife was killed, he signed over his claim to the church and moved on. And it was the best of the vacant houses around Heaven."

"So," Preston Cribbs went on, "we accepted his generous contribution and fixed it up for our parsonage. It'll be ready in another two or three days, if the weather holds."

"And where is this claim—shack?" Bran asked.

Lorraine stepped out onto the sidewalk. "Out by Pigeon Creek," she answered. "I hope you have a horse or you're going to have a hard time ministering to your flock from out there."

"No, I don't, not yet," Bran admitted. "But I'll look into that."

"We'll be leaving you then, Reverend," Mr. Cribbs said. "If it suits you, we'll take you out to the parsonage in the morning. Maybe you'd like to give us a hand."

Bran grimaced. Doing repair work on a miner's shack wasn't his first choice of duties. In fact, what he'd planned to do was use the time in the saloon to do some quiet asking around.

"Are you sure we don't know each other?" Marshal Larkin asked once more as they turned back into the saloon.

"Don't think so," Bran answered casually. "Where'd you come from originally?"

"The Carolinas. Been up north of here mostly, trying to settle the disturbance with the Mormons and trying to keep the Indians on the reservation."

"I'm from the South myself," Bran admitted. "Maybe we crossed paths somewhere along the line."

"Maybe," the marshal agreed, rubbing his chin in thought as they walked back inside the saloon.

Lorraine met them. "How about something stronger than punch, boys?"

"Sounds good to me," the marshal said.

Bran would have accepted a whiskey if they'd been alone, but carrying out his charade made him refuse. "Thanks, ma'am, but I guess I'd better go check on—Kate. Was she all right when you left her?"

"Your wife seemed fine. She was worrying about her wardrobe. She asked me to help her shop for something a little more stylish tomorrow."

Bran knew his face reflected his surprise.

"Don't worry, Reverend, I promise to make sure your wife looks as dowdy as the rest of the pious women around here. Unless you think our association will damage your cause."

"Of course not, Miss Lake. I'll be most appreciative," Bran responded warily. He wasn't at all sure that his new wife's reputation would survive the gossip. But knowing Trouble, he'd be willing to bet that she wouldn't care.

"What about you, Marshal?" Lorraine said with a smile and a fluttering of her lashes. "Are you going to let your job interfere with sharing an evening with me?"

"Of course not. I'm not on duty all the time and my superior isn't looking over my shoulder, like yours, Reverend Adams."

"A man doesn't always know who's judging him," Bran

said. It wasn't his superior who was worrying him. The citizens of Heaven might be a trifle too judgmental and Bran had already learned that the woman upstairs waiting for him was no angel.

He just hoped that she wasn't the devil in disguise.

Chapter

Eight

Macky slept soundly. When she finally opened her eyes purple shadows cloaked the room. Like a cat, she stretched and closed her eyes once more, breathing in the sweet-smelling bed, experiencing the feel of cotton sheets against her skin, the slinky satin of the spread caressing her cheek. She felt deliciously wanton.

Then she remembered where she was and the precariousness of her position. She should have remained on the stage and kept going to Denver. Now Bran was at risk. Bran! In alarm she raised up and peered at the empty space in the bed beside her. She was alone. She hadn't known what to expect, but she was relieved.

Or was she? For three days they'd traveled together, spending one night in each other's arms. Granted, it was for survival, but she couldn't deny that he made her feel safe. Time and circumstance, she reasoned, forced men and women to do what they must.

Even if her stomach felt like a field of clover drawing clouds of dancing butterflies, she'd managed to conceal her reaction from her protector. And he'd kept her warm, no, warm was much too mild for what she'd felt. There was a roiling heat, a kind of yearning with the promise of more.

But that was then, she admitted with an unwelcome sense of loss, and this was now.

From below she heard the tinny sound of a piano and the low murmur of conversation. She wondered how people slept in a place like this, then mentally chided herself as she realized that probably wasn't a concern.

She wondered where Bran was. She wondered what a preacher might do in a saloon and how he explained his absence from his wife's side. Obviously he wasn't holding a prayer meeting, and from the sound of the laughter downstairs, the customers were enjoying themselves.

It was ironic, even to her, that the last person she wondered about was Pratt. Was he still in town? Was he traveling alone?

Pratt and the marshal, not Bran, should be her chief concern. He held her immediate future in his grasp and the marshal would, sooner or later, begin searching for the bank robbers.

Macky slipped from the bed, walked to the window, and unfastened the shutters. The moon overhead was full and bright. It was still early, maybe not even midnight, and there were horses tied to the rail in front of Heaven's Bell. One of them, a small black horse, looked familiar.

Too familiar.

A closer look was what she needed. If she could see the saddle, she'd know if it belonged to Pratt. There'd be no mistaking the silver trim on the horn.

But what if Bran came and she was gone?

So what if he did? He had no claim on her. She could do what she wanted. Besides, the hour was long past the time a preacher should be at home with his wife. If he really was a preacher.

A shiver ran up her backbone. She had no claim on him, either. She wasn't really his wife.

The window opened out onto the roof that covered the wood-plank sidewalk. If she could climb out, she could find a way down without being seen. Her mind made up, she quickly changed into her brother's trousers and shirt. She had lost Papa's hat, but if she covered her hair with something, she could conceal its color and the fact that she was a woman.

A sock would make a fine cap.

"Phoo!" The sock was too light in color. It would stand out in the moonlight like a beacon. No man would wear a white stocking on his head. Desperately she glanced around.

The fireplace. Without a thought she ripped the sock from her head and put her hand inside. Then, avoiding the dying coals of the fire, she wiped the inside of the fireplace, turning the sock black with soot. Pulling it back over her head, she was satisfied that, in the darkness, nobody would see her.

The window opened easily and the roof seemed steady as she climbed out on it and made her way across the front of the saloon to the side. The streets appeared empty. Now all she had to do was find a way down.

Bran, leaning against the wall of the general store next door to the saloon, watched the street and considered his next move.

He was uncharacteristically restless and out of sorts. Not just because he couldn't get a handle on the situation in Heaven, but because, for the first time, he wasn't working alone. Any decisions he made involved another person.

If Trouble hadn't stepped forward and allowed the welcoming committee to think she was the minister's wife, he could have corrected their impression. But she had, and Lucifer's horns if he hadn't gone along with her.

An unmistakable tightening in his gut reminded him

that traveling under the guise of being a minister was one thing, but keeping up the charade was going to be something else. He wasn't normally a man who worried much about hoodwinking people if he stood a chance of finding the man he was after, but being a preacher could be difficult.

Having a wife could be even more.

Normally, he'd go to Sylvia Mainwearing as a half-breed drifter, looking for a job. But as the minister, he could call on anybody he wanted to under the pretense of soliciting funds and saving souls. And if he collected any pledges it would be a fair exchange for anonymity.

Each time he started a new job he hoped the man he was after could lead him to the cutthroats who'd killed his family. During the last fifteen years he'd located many men who started as Mississippi River bandits, but the man with the disturbing laugh remained free. And Bran couldn't give up. The search kept him going, gave his life purpose.

This time he had a feeling that he was on the right track. His Choctaw father would have said it was his second sight, the kind of unique instinct that had given him the name Eyes That See in Darkness.

The end justified the means, he told himself, and if Trouble was part of the charade, so be it. She'd made her own choices. Now she'd have to put up with him and whatever happened.

But hell, it was going to be hard. He let out a laugh. No, he was hard already and the night was still to come. Sooner or later he'd have to retire to the room the townsfolk had arranged for the new minister and his wife. He'd put off confronting that temptation as long as he could by taking a walk down one side of the street and back up the other. Now he delayed once again to have a last smoke.

He'd spent one night holding the girl in his arms to keep her warm and another night wishing he could. Until they were able to move into the cabin, he could see no way out of sharing the same bedroom. What had started out as a necessity was turning into a real problem.

As he'd watched her discomfort at the social earlier, he'd seen how uncertain she was under her show of bravado. Obviously, she was completely out of her element. But she'd forced herself to go through the motions, never once asking for help. He was more than a little curious about her past; it was imperative now that he know. Ignorance of his accomplice could be fatal.

Then, in a lull in the merriment filtering out of the saloon, came a voice. "Ding dong bells! No stairs."

The voice was little more than a whisper, but he instantly recognized the swear words of the woman he'd spent the last hour fretting over.

What in hell was she up to?

The sound of scuffling answered his question as two trousered legs suddenly dangled from the roof.

Bran stepped into the shadowed doorway of the store and waited. Whatever she was doing, she didn't want to come through the saloon to do it.

Suddenly she let go, landed on her feet, and fell forward to her knees. "Ouch!"

Bran almost reached out for her, then caught himself and waited. He'd been standing there long enough for his eyes to become adjusted to the darkness.

After a moment, she stood and scurried to the edge of the building and waited. Apparently she was satisfied that nobody had seen her for, hugging the shadows, she made her way into the street toward the horses tied at the rail.

Was she about to steal a horse? That activity seemed more natural for her than attending socials. But the marshal was already too interested in Bran. Having the preacher's wife guilty of horse theft was certainly not the kind of attention he could afford.

He almost called out to her when she moved around to the other side of one of the horses, examining the saddle. The sudden droop of her shoulders was obvious. What had she seen that bothered her so much? And what was she going to do?

Macky was wondering that same thing. She'd confirmed her worst fears. The horse was the same one she'd ridden into Promise in the company of the Pratt gang. Pratt must have claimed it and was still in town, looking for McKenzie.

Why?

He couldn't know that the preacher's wife was the Mc-Kenzie he was searching for, could he? She opened the saddlebag, running her hand inside. She didn't know what she expected to find, but when her fingers touched the velvet and she heard the sound of coins clinking together a knot formed in her stomach.

Pratt had found her purse along the trail, the purse containing some of the coins from the bank robbery. Surely that didn't prove anything. Would Pratt connect that to the robbery, to Heaven?

Her heart sank. She was about to be discovered. She'd lose everything and now she didn't even have the brooch to sell. Jail was a distinct possibility, or even worse.

The cameo. It had been in the purse. It was hers, the last thing she had that belonged to her mother. Digging deeper, she found it, closed her fingers around it and something else. She drew the objects out.

At that moment the doors of the saloon swung open, throwing light across the startled Macky, catching her in the act. Instinctively she ducked and started running around the corner of the building, tucking the cameo inside her pocket.

"Hold it, you little thief!" Pratt said, drawing his gun. "I'll kill anybody who steals from me."

Bran let her run by, then left his hiding place and stepped between the fleeing Macky and her pursuer. His voice was intentionally low. No point in calling attention to what was happening. "Careful, pilgrim. The Scriptures say that 'He who is without sin may cast the first stone.' Are you free from sin?"

The startled fugitive hesitated, then pointed his gun at Bran. "Get out of my way, preacher. The thief is getting away."

"What did he steal?"

That stopped the clean-shaven man for a moment. "Nothing," he finally answered, replaced his gun in his holster, turned back to his horse and climbed on. Patting his saddlebags and eliciting a jingle of coins, he seemed satisfied. "Sorry, preacher, I thought I'd seen him somewhere before. Guess I was wrong."

Bran wasn't so sure about that. He didn't understand what he'd just witnessed, but he knew there was more to it than a case of mistaken identity. An ordinary drifter wouldn't leave anything valuable unguarded in his saddlebags. Maybe the patrons of Heaven's Bell knew the man better than they wanted to admit. All the more reason for him to have a little talk with Lorraine.

Bran stood on the sidewalk and watched as the man rode away, then turned and went around the building in search of his errant bride.

Macky didn't know what had stopped Pratt from coming after her. But she seemed to have escaped. With her heart thudding in her throat, Macky pushed open the back door and peered into what seemed to be a dining room. It was empty.

She slipped inside. There were two doors, one leading into a pantry, the other into a hall where she found a set of narrow servant's steps leading to the second floor.

Letting out a deep sigh of relief she crept up, feeling her way in the darkness. The stairs led to the end of the hall across from the room she and Bran had been assigned. As she crouched in the shadows, she heard the soft laughter of Miss Lake, the proprietor of the Heaven's Bell.

"How long will you be staying this time, Marshal?" she asked.

The answering voice was deep but too muffled to be understood.

"No," Lorraine said. "Perhaps Reverend Adams isn't exactly what the town expected, but what makes you think that I would know him?"

There was a silence.

Macky was curious about that herself. Why would the marshal question Lorraine? Obviously, he was suspicious of Bran. If Marshal Larkin was asking questions about Bran, it only followed that he'd question Macky.

"Are you saying you don't like him, Lorraine? Don't lie to me. I saw the way you looked at him."

There was a low, amused laugh. "Them," she corrected. "He has a wife, remember? And if you think I looked at him with desire, you weren't looking at his wife."

"Wife? I still don't know what I think about her."

"Neither do the women of the congregation. I hope she's as tough as I think she is. Otherwise, those sanctimonious souls will have her tarred and feathered before she even knows why."

"I think she can take care of herself," the marshal observed. "With a little help she could be . . . appealing in a primitive sort of way."

"Leave her alone, Larkin. You're already flirting with Sylvia. She's more your cup of tea—respectable and wealthy."

Primitive? Why, that toad-sucking jackass!

"Kate is an innocent. I won't have you corrupting her!"

Crawfish and tadpoles! Lorraine was sticking up for her. Macky didn't know what to think about that for she too had seen the way Lorraine looked at Bran. And Lorraine had been honest in admitting that if things were different she'd be interested in him.

As innocent as she might be, Macky couldn't forget the feel of the soft mat of hair on his chest, the strength of the muscles in his legs when she'd examined him for wounds. How could she blame Lorraine?

But by damn, Bran was hers. Well, not really, but he belonged to her as far as the world was concerned. Besides, for now, she told herself, she needed him and she had no intention of sharing him with another woman. As for the marshal's suspicions, Macky had to let Bran know so that he could . . .

What? What did she expect him to do?

The sound of footsteps interrupted her thoughts. Someone was coming up from the kitchen. Macky scurried into her room and closed the door. Suppose it was Pratt, looking for her? Quickly she tucked the purloined jewelry behind the bed, shed her clothing, donned the sleeping garment, and dived under the cover.

Just in time. The door opened and closed softly.

Macky didn't dare open her eyes to see who was standing there. She was certain that it was someone she didn't want to have a conversation with.

Then she knew, without words or sight.

Eyes That See in Darkness was watching her. She could feel him. Not the preacher, nor Bran, but the dangerous man to whom she'd formed an unnatural spiritual connection. That same fluttery feeling filled her stomach and threatened to stop her lungs from drawing in air. Willing her breath to rise and fall evenly, she feigned sleep.

She was pretending to sleep when Bran entered the room to which Lorraine had directed him earlier. Deep shadows fell across the bed where she was lying, shrouding her face in darkness. She was covered by a satin spread that had slipped down to reveal a soft pink sleeping garment.

His plan to confront her about her past got lost in the sudden tightness he felt in his loins. Damn it all to hell, it was self-defense, he told himself, concern over her nefarious activities. What connection could she possibly have with the man from the saloon? Whatever it was, she was inviting trouble and it was up to him to protect her—in self-defense.

Bran massaged a dull ache gathering at his temples. Trouble. She'd warned him. But Bran wasn't prepared for this unexpected need to keep her safe. He was no gladiator, but he had the growing feeling that this woman was not as independent as she wanted him to think. And he already knew she was much too impulsive.

He'd had demons chasing him a time or two and he recognized that something powerful was driving her. Whatever had sent her running was important enough to force her to pretend to be his wife.

Bran was still having trouble with that word. He'd never had a wife and never expected to. But he'd had a mother and a sister once. He hadn't been able to take care of them. Now this girl had been thrust into his life and instead of walking away he was making himself a part of her.

Bran knew he'd committed too many cruelties, accepted too many assignments that ended in bloodshed, to let himself see this relationship as anything more than a means to conceal his identity while he searched for the man who was behind the mining thefts in Heaven.

Why, then, was he still standing there, staring at her?

Because without the ill-fitting clothing she looked totally different. Soft in sleep, there was a vulnerability about her that she wouldn't have appreciated him seeing. And it caught at whatever small bit of tenderness still lay hidden inside his heart.

That worried him. He'd always prided himself on his ability to remain focused on his objective. Using a woman to achieve his goal was one thing, but breaking his concentration was dangerous.

She moved, drawing her knees up and snuggling her chin beneath the covers like a child. Desire swept over him and he took an involuntary step toward her.

Suddenly her eyes opened and he heard her take a soft breath.

Then silence.

She knew he was there and she was waiting.

From the bed, Macky could see only the outline of the man, the fire beside him forming an orange backdrop for the black silhouette beside her bed.

She could hear his breathing and her own. What would

she do if he touched her? What had she done by letting the world think she was his wife? Why had he allowed it?

She moistened her lips and waited.

She heard a match strike and groaned. Any hope of escaping a confrontation died as the light flared on the table beside her.

"I think we need to talk. Christ! What in hell do you have on your head?"

"Oh!" The sock. She'd forgotten to take it off. Glancing back at the pillow, she saw the sooty evidence of the outline of her head on the linen case. "It's—it's a beauty treatment."

"I see. And what is it supposed to accomplish?" He struggled to hold back a smile as he moved closer.

"To make my hair more tame." She began to edge away from him. "I mean, a preacher's wife should look . . . proper."

"Somehow I doubt that the congregation would see it quite that way. How long does that stay on your head?"

"Ah, it's only temporary. I'll take it off now." She jerked the sock from her head and poked it under the soiled pillow. Anything to get it out of sight and stop his questions.

"I think it's time you told me why you let them believe that you were my wife."

She'd known the question was coming but she had no answer. "Why are you pretending to be a minister?"

"What makes you think I'm not?"

"I don't know," she admitted. "You know the Scriptures, but there is something about you that frightens me."

"You should be frightened. I'm a man and you're still a girl."

"I'm almost twenty."

"Why are you running away, Trouble?"

Dare she tell him? No. Telling him would only put him in danger. From what she'd seen of Pratt he wouldn't think twice about threatening Bran, or worse. And there was the marshal. Even if Bran truly wanted to keep her shameful secret, what would keep him from protecting himself by turning her in to the marshal?

No, for now, she'd keep her past to herself.

Until she could be certain that Pratt had gone and that the law wasn't looking for her.

"I was running away from—from a town that had turned its back on me, from a life that was over."

"Running away? Yes, I believe that. Is someone likely to come after you?"

She took too long to answer. "Yes, but he won't be looking for a minister's wife."

"Knowing you, I can believe that."

"As you pointed out," she went on, "a mining town isn't safe for a woman like me, alone. It was either become a preacher's wife or one of Miss Lake's girls and I'm not experienced enough for that."

"But you're experienced enough to be my wife?" He couldn't hold back a laugh. "I don't think you have any idea what that would mean."

She hadn't seen him laugh before. His entire face changed and suddenly it was hard for Macky to talk. After a long moment she put on her bravest front and answered. "I don't know what you're really up to, but it seems that pretending to be Reverend and Mrs. Adams will serve us both well—for now."

Bran stopped smiling at her statement. Obviously he was having more trouble carrying out their charade than he wanted to admit. She could tell from the set of his shoulders that he was going to say something to frighten her.

"Macky, we're here, in this room alone. I'm a lot bigger and stronger. Suppose I don't choose to pretend?"

She simply shook her head. "We've already committed a sin by lying, Bran, surely even you wouldn't make it worse by expecting me to—to . . ."

"Would that be so bad?"

"I don't know," she admitted. "I've never been with a man before."

He believed her. God help him, he did. And that thought made their situation even more precarious. "If you don't leave you could be asking for a different kind of trouble. I'm a man, not a monk, Trouble."

Her voice turned into a whisper. "Please, Bran. I can't leave here just yet. I'm sorry I intruded in whatever it is you're doing. But you can't—I mean we can't . . . Besides, if I leave, he—the town will only become suspicious."

"I want you to go, Macky. You aren't safe here."

"You mean because of the marshal?"

"What do you know about the marshal?"

"I heard him talking to Lorraine. He seemed curious about you. He was asking Lorraine if she knew you."

"Damn! All the more reason to send you to Denver on the next stage."

"No. I won't go." She sat up folding her arms across her chest. "Why is he asking about you?"

"Just his job, I guess. According to Mayor Cribbs there has been a lot of trouble in Heaven. I guess he has to be suspicious of everybody."

"Exactly. I think we both need someone to look after us. And Bran, I don't believe for one minute that you'll force yourself on me. I don't know what you are, but I trust you."

Bran groaned and turned away. She was impossible. She was stubborn. She was the most appealing woman he'd ever crossed paths with. And she was right; she was too trusting. "Don't believe that, Trouble. I'm a wicked man. And you'd do well to keep going wherever it is you were heading when you climbed on that stagecoach."

"I will, as soon as it's safe. But for now, unless you tell the world otherwise, I'm Kate Adams, the new preacher's wife. And since I am"—her voice gathered authority—"I insist that in public, you act like a proper husband."

"Oh? And where is this proper husband supposed to sleep tonight?"

"We're not in public. You can sleep on the floor by the fire. There's an extra blanket on the chest."

"I'm thirty-three years old, Macky, and I've spent a lot of nights on the ground, but I've never slept in the same room with a woman unless I slept in her bed."

He couldn't resist teasing her and he wasn't sure why. She was the last woman he ought to want to bed. As her face flamed in the lamplight, he knew that the teasing was torture and it was himself being tormented.

"Fine. You want the bed? Climb in." She came to her feet, her lips curled into an impish smile, pulled back the covers and held out her arms, inviting his entry.

Bran wasn't sure what she was saying. Trust was one thing, but this was pure foolishness on her part. She needed to know that. He'd show her what could happen if she didn't take him seriously. He began to remove his clothing.

She stood, stoically waiting, the firelight behind her silhouetting her shape beneath the gown, all soft and curvy. When he'd shed his trousers and shirt, he hesitated, waiting for her to make a move. His threat turned empty as he climbed into the bed, still wearing his underdrawers.

Macky leaned forward, planted a light kiss on his cheek as she pulled up the covers and turned back to the fire, where she unfurled the blanket and curled up on the floor.

"Nighty-night, Reverend, dear. I have to get to sleep. Lorraine and I have a big day planned for tomorrow."

"I heard." His statement was more of a growl and he knew that he was the one who'd been put in his place.

"Is there something wrong with that? I doubt your congregation will accept a preacher's wife in men's trousers. But if you'd rather—"

"Frankly, I don't care what you wear, but I doubt a preacher's wife would befriend the local saloonkeeper. You may damage your reputation."

"If I'm going to be a Christian woman who sets an example in the community, I'm going to do the Christian thing. If that bothers you, go suck a lemon."

"It doesn't bother me one bit, darling. I rather like the idea of showing those old biddies a thing or two. I'm just

afraid that any dress Lorraine picks out might do just that—
amply."

"Then I'm sure you'll preach a proper sermon on lecher-
ous and sinful thoughts, won't you, Reverend Adams?"

Long after Trouble pretended to be asleep, Bran lay in
the darkness listening to her breathe. "Are you awake?" he
finally asked.

She didn't answer.

"The one thing you do know about me is my name," he
said. "I'd like to know yours."

Just when he had decided that she really was asleep, she
whispered softly, "I'm McKenzie Kathryn Calhoun. But everybody calls me—used to call me Macky."

"Used to?"

"Macky got on the stage in Promise. But it was Kate who
got off."

"I hope not," Bran said in a voice so low that she barely
heard it. "I think Macky is still very much here. Kate's a
stubborn woman who insists on sleeping on the floor.
Macky is much more sensible. She'd get up here under the
covers where she'd be warm."

"Maybe, but Macky slept with Eyes That See in Darkness. The man in the bed is Reverend Brandon Adams and
he'd never soil an innocent girl."

Bran let out a deep breath.

"I think," he said, "that I liked Eyes That See in Darkness
and Macky better."

Macky didn't reply, but in her heart she knew that she
did, too.

"It took you long enough to get back here," the man on the
horse said, throwing his right leg carelessly across the saddle. "What happened?"

The reply was sullen. "We ran into a little trouble. The
sheriff was waiting for us."

"I heard. Where's the holdup money, Pratt?"

"I—I don't have it."

"What do you mean you don't have it? The word I got is that you and a kid escaped with the gold. Where's the kid?"

"I don't know. He got away in the shootout and I haven't seen him since."

"I trust you had a meeting place arranged."

There was a hesitation that Pratt hurried to cover. He intended to find that kid. He couldn't just disappear with the money. Sooner or later, he'd start to spend it and Pratt would know. "Sure, he just ain't showed up yet."

"So, you lost the money and now the sheriff is on your tail. Understand me, Pratt, I didn't break you out of that prison to have you mess up what I have going here."

"Robbing that bank was your idea." Pratt fingered the healing scar across his forehead. "If the sheriff comes here, I'll take care of him."

"What about the stagecoach? Was the kid involved in that, too?"

"No. The others were men I picked up. Don't worry, they're dead. That one-eyed preacher picked both of 'em off."

"About that preacher, I don't think I like having a stranger riding into town right now. Too much of a coincidence. Besides, I've seen him before. I just can't remember where."

"There's a lot of men wearing eye patches, but it don't look like it would be too hard to place a man like him."

"That's what bothers me. I can't."

The horse flicked his tail and moved about nervously. When Pratt took hold of his bridle he danced away.

"If he worries you, say the word and I'll take him out. I got a score to settle with him anyway."

"No, not yet. You'll get plenty of time for that. Just keep an eye on him for now."

"I don't know why we're hiding out up here. You've already claimed all the other land along the creek except the piece them church people are turning into a parsonage. I don't see why you don't just let me run them off like the others."

The big man swore. "It's too late for that. They've already filed the claim. I didn't expect that fool miner to sign everything over to the church. Then you get caught holding up that nothing little bank in Promise."

"How was I to know the sheriff would be waiting?"

"You use a lookout."

"That's why I picked up that kid."

"That kid who ended up with the money. Just don't make any more decisions on your own. I'll get rid of the preacher when the time comes."

He'd gotten rid of Moose. And, in spite of what Sylvia had said, nobody could prove that his accident was anything but. Even the law hadn't been able to stop the trouble at her mine. Now all he had to do was put the next part of his plan into action.

The mine would soon be his.

Bran left Macky reluctantly the next morning. He wasn't certain what she would do next.

As he stood, watching her curled into a knot beneath the blanket, he wished, just for a moment, that all this was behind him and that they were meeting for the first time. But that was a foolish wish and he knew that wishes were for children.

As he started toward the door he picked up his pistol and slid it beneath his jacket. Preachers didn't carry weapons, but he didn't intend to take a chance.

"Who do you plan to shoot this morning?"

Macky's voice was soft with sleep, and appealing.

Macky. Odd how easy it was to think of her that way. Kate might fit the minister's wife, but it was Macky who was rubbing her eyes and pushing herself up on one elbow.

"The first man who makes up to the preacher's wife," he said with an easy smile.

She gave a disbelieving laugh. "Then you might as well leave the pistol behind."

"I still wish you'd reconsider taking Lorraine with you."

Macky smiled. "You're really worried about my reputation? That's nice."

"Didn't I tell you I see into the future as well as the dark?"

She sat up, worry etching a frown on her forehead. "You do?"

"No, I don't, not really. I wish I could. It would make things much easier, for both of us." Suddenly the light-hearted exchange was over. Bran took the doorknob in his hand, unlatching the hook above it. "You'd better get in the bed, in case someone comes. I wouldn't want them to think I made you sleep on the floor."

"You didn't," she said, pulling the blanket around her as she stood. "It was my choice."

"If you were imposing some kind of feminine revenge, Macky, it worked. I could have taken the floor and slept better."

"Good, that's my revenge. A philosopher once said that 'no one rejoices more in revenge than a woman.'"

"It has also been said that the woman who seeks revenge often finds it when she least expects it."

"The Bible?"

"No, the man who gave me my Indian name. By the way," he added as he opened the door, "the first place a thief would look is under the mattress. You'd better find another place to hide your money."

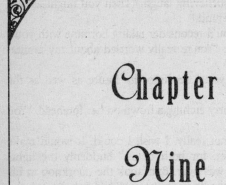

Chapter

Nine

𝒫ʀᴇꜱᴛᴏɴ Cʀɪʙʙꜱ was waiting for Bran when he finished his breakfast at Willa's Boardinghouse. The mayor had traded his top hat for something more serviceable to drive a farm wagon loaded with roofing shingles.

"Morning, Preacher. Are you ready to see the parsonage?"

"Of course." Bran climbed into the wagon. "I thought as we ride, you could tell me about the citizens of Heaven."

"Sure thing. You met my wife, Ethel, at the social. The general store here belongs to Otis Gooden and his wife, Clara. Across the street is our blacksmith, Hank Clay. He also runs the livery stable. Hank's not married, pretty close-mouthed about his past."

One by one, the mayor identified the people who owned businesses along the street that made up the town. As they left the businesses behind, the street became a rutted trail leading toward the mountains.

"What about the marshal? I noticed that you have a jail back there. Does Larkin always spend this much time in Heaven?"

"No, he's been assigned to our territory for a while. Seems like a nice fellow, but he's not making much progress on finding out who's behind the trouble."

"Seems like you'd have your own law officer," Bran commented.

"Had several. Either got killed or wouldn't work for what we can pay."

They'd left the town behind when the mayor began his apology. "Sorry about moving you out here, Brother Adams, but it was the only vacant house already finished. It may still be a mite bare, but the ladies of the church intend to have a housewarming and donate the items Mrs. Adams will need. And of course the Goodens will open an account for you."

"I'm sure Mrs. Adams will be pleased to have their help," Bran said, hoping that she at least knew enough about housekeeping to appreciate their efforts.

"Then later, as she gets closer to her time, they'll be here to help her out. We don't have no doctor, but Ethel's a pretty good midwife."

"Her time?"

"Her time to deliver. Mrs. Cribbs confided to me that your missus was expecting. They talked about it last night when Mrs. Adams got a bit sick."

Bran almost swallowed his tongue. Expecting? Why in God's heaven had Macky told them such a thing? He'd believed her when she said that she'd never been with a man. Then it came to him in a flash that left him stunned. She'd told him herself that her stomach was out of sorts. That explained why she was running away. Some man had done her wrong and she'd had to leave Promise to keep her sordid secret.

No wonder she was closemouthed and so protective of her money. She'd probably stolen it to safeguard the child's future, particularly if someone was coming after her. Bran had offered her a perfect hiding place. A pregnant minister's wife wasn't likely to draw attention like a lone woman with a child.

Bran didn't know why he was so disappointed. He should be relieved to learn the truth. Instead the answer only brought more questions. Macky might be impulsive and too independent, still, she hadn't seemed the foolish sort. If a man did her wrong, she'd get a shotgun and make him do the right thing.

Unless he was already married. Unless the man who'd wronged her had done so against her will. Unless she was afraid of him.

Like the man who'd pulled the gun, threatening her in the street.

"There was a man in the saloon last night, Mr. Cribbs, not one of your congregation. He was clean-shaven, with some kind of scar across his forehead. Rode a black horse with a silver-trimmed saddle. Do you know who he is?"

Cribbs turned a puzzled gaze on Bran. "I'm afraid I can't say. Of course, since word of the mine spread, there are a lot of strangers who ride in and out of town."

"Tell me more about the mine."

"Old Moose Mainwearing hit a mother lode on the other side of Pigeon Mountain. After that, prospectors covered these hills like ants at a Sunday school picnic. A few found some good color, but nobody ever hit it big. And one by one, their luck all went bad. Accidents, fires, landslides. Most of them just gave up.".

"What happened to Moose?"

"Moose liked to drink. He's the one who brought Miss Lake here, built the saloon for her. Talked the Goodens into opening the store. He financed most of the businesses in town. Then he married a woman from San Francisco. She tried to put a stop to his wild living, Miss Sylvia did, but one night soon after his wedding he had too much to drink, tumbled down a ravine, and broke his neck."

"Miss Sylvia?" Bran questioned innocently. "Why wasn't she at the social last night?"

"She's not a member of our congregation—yet. She don't hold much with churchgoing, but she's a powerful woman. Since Moose died every single man in the territory has courted her. But she turned 'em all down and took over the operation of the mine herself. These shingles came from her sawmill. She's managed better than anybody expected, but she's had her hands full lately with all the new trouble."

Bran's ears perked up. "New trouble?"

"Accidents inside her mine. Gold shipments being stolen between here and Denver. That's why the marshal moved in."

"Has he made any arrests?"

"No, but he thinks whoever killed Moose could be the same one who scared off Kelley so fast. When his wife died, he signed his claim over to the church and pulled out."

"So who do you think is behind the trouble?"

"I ain't got any idea. My guess is that it's somebody from Denver. If Moose's vein runs through Pigeon Mountain and comes out on this side, a man could make a claim if he already had staked out the land."

"Is that likely?"

"Hard to say. The last case I heard about, old Judge Hardcastle ruled that whoever opened the vein had the rights to the gold, even if it ran across somebody else's land. But the law in a mining town is pretty much made by the miners themselves."

"Judge Hardcastle lives here, too?"

"No, he lives in Denver, but this is his territory and lately I hear that he's bought some claims up the valley. Even made an offer on Kelley's place."

As they approached the mountain, the trail became steeper. In places there was no trail and the wagon bounced about like a rock in a landslide. To the left a wide creek ran merrily along, cutting a path through a chasm of rock.

"We take the right fork," Cribbs said as they came to a

split in the road. "The left one takes you straight to Mrs. Mainwearing's house."

"Where's her mine?"

"In the hills beyond. That's Pigeon Creek," Mr. Cribbs explained. "It crosses the road and runs behind your house. You'll have good water. Except when they muddy it upstream."

"Who muddies it?"

"There are still a few prospectors left up in the mountains. None of them have much in the way of equipment so they dig out the stream banks and pan in the water."

Bran could hear the sound of hammering. As they rounded an outcropping of rock, he could see the small shack nestled in the side of the mountain. It was built of logs but its roof had been covered with sod. Now the workers were pulling off the squares of earth and replacing them with shingles.

Bran tried to see the house from a female's point of view. He'd lived in much worse, but he thought that a woman would probably be disappointed in its crudeness. Then he remembered Macky's wardrobe and changed his mind.

The cabin contained a single room. The cooking was limited to the fireplace. There was a cupboard and two new shelves built over a freshly cut plank counter, which covered the woodpile. A double bed and a chest occupied the front corner of the room, a crude table and two benches stood in the other.

As far as he could tell there wasn't even an extra blanket if his new bride wanted to sleep on the floor. He looked at the fireplace and grinned. If she was inclined to continue whatever she was supposed to be doing with the sock on her head, she'd have an ample supply of soot to do so.

"I'm sorry it isn't more," Mr. Cribbs said. "But we'll improve it as we can."

Bran took off his coat and rolled up his sleeves. "Don't worry, Mayor, this will do just fine." The sooner they moved into the house, the sooner he could escape prying eyes and start his search.

Beginning with supper that night with his real employer, Mrs. Sylvia Mainwearing, and ending with a talk with Macky. If he was going to be a father he wanted to know what to expect.

When the bedroom door closed behind Bran earlier that morning, Macky was left with the feeling that she'd been bested in their conversation. She'd even told him her real name. What was she doing giving away her secrets to a man who wasn't revealing any of his own?

What had she proved by sleeping on a cold, hard floor?

Not only had she been uncomfortable, she'd left the bed so that Bran could search and find the money she'd hidden.

Money!

She hurried to the bed, sliding her hands beneath the mattress. The money was still there, along with the cameo she'd taken from Pratt's saddlebags, and something else she hadn't had time to examine last night—the silver feather from Bran's hat.

Macky had spent a good portion of the night trying to find some reason why Pratt might suspect that she was McKenzie. But Bran's presence so close by had kept her mind going in circles. If Pratt had spoken to the dressmaker and found out that a woman dressed like a boy had bought clothing and gotten on the stage, why hadn't he approached her?

And if the sheriff had arrested Pratt, how had he gotten to the dressmaker? It made no sense. And she wasn't going to find any answers hiding in her room. What she ought to do was follow Bran's advice; buy a horse and ride away.

Macky groaned. After representing herself as the preacher's wife, she couldn't even leave. Half the town and the marshal would start an immediate search for her. She'd have a bank robber, a sheriff, a marshal, and God only knew how many others on her trail.

No. Best that she stay put until she knew what was happening. Somehow, though she didn't want to admit it, as long as she was with Bran, she felt safe.

After searching the room for a new hiding place for her money, Macky decided that the only other spot was beneath the kindling in the woodbox. She'd only just finished replacing the wood when there was a knock on the door.

"Come in."

A serving girl entered carrying a tray containing a pewter pot, a cup, and a roll. "Miss Lorraine sent you some chocolate and a sweet roll, ma'am. May I prepare your bath?"

Macky didn't know how to answer. She'd never been waited on before. "My bath?"

"In the hip tub. I'll bring hot water."

"Oh, no! I'll just bathe in the basin, thank you."

The girl nodded and backed out the door, returning moments later with a fresh pitcher of warm water and a bathing cloth.

"Miss Lake will be waiting for you downstairs whenever you're ready," she said and left the room.

Macky quickly washed the soot from her hands and face, then gulped down the chocolate and ate the roll. Her stomach had never been so empty. Food had never tasted so good. She still cringed at the spectacle she'd made of herself by throwing up her food in the alley.

Pickled pig's feet. She couldn't even think about it without feeling her stomach lurch in protest. What must the women of the church have thought about her?

Not that it mattered. Macky Calhoun had quit worrying about what other women thought about her long ago and nothing she could do would make her into something she wasn't, even a preacher's wife.

With a sense of dread she donned the worn skirt and badly wrinkled shirtwaist. Her hair was another problem.

Without Papa's hat to cover it, she was faced with a mass of curls that refused to be restrained.

At last, in utter desperation she resorted to braiding it and fastening it with a bow made from a strip of fabric ripped from her petticoat. Finally she tucked a supply of gold coins and paper money into her pocket, opened the door, and stepped into the hall.

With her heart thudding in her chest, she offered a silent prayer that she wouldn't see anybody until after she'd gotten a decent wardrobe.

In the saloon, a boy was sweeping.

Macky paused and looked around. "Hello. I'm—I'm Mrs. Adams."

"Miss Lake be here in a minute." The boy studied Macky curiously.

Macky strode through the swinging doors onto the walkway. The sidewalk was filled with women carrying baskets doing their morning shopping. Laughing children darted around their mother's skirts and ran across the street. Heaven looked so normal.

"Morning, Miz Adams," one of the shoppers called out.

Macky managed to nod at the woman she recognized from the church social last night.

"Good, you're ready," Lorraine Lake said as she moved out the door and lifted her skirt. "Let's cross the street. Thank goodness we haven't had any bad weather in the last few days. The street is a mudhole when it rains."

Macky didn't miss the frowns of censure as she followed the beautifully groomed woman, dodging a carriage and two men on horseback who leered at her. "Where are we going?" she asked.

"There is a dressmaker just down the way. Her gowns aren't as stylish as those from back East, but she's good. Gooden's General Store carries shoes and hats made by the pious Mrs. Gooden. She won't carry merchandise she considers frivolous, but the dear soul actually has some nice things."

Remembering her experience with the dressmaker in Promise, Macky voiced her reservations. "The seamstress probably won't have anything that will fit me."

"Don't worry. If Letty doesn't have anything made up, I'll lend you something of mine."

Macky laughed. "Miss Lake, I don't think I have quite the shape to wear your clothes. Besides . . ."

"Please, call me Lorraine. And don't worry. I wouldn't dress you in anything that wasn't suitable for the members of your congregation. How long have you and Bran been married anyway?"

"Ah—not long. I'm surprised that there are so many women in town," Macky said quickly, changing the subject. "Why aren't the children in school?"

"There's no teacher. The mothers who know how to read and write try to school them at home. I offered to help out, but they couldn't trust their little darlings to a fallen woman."

"I can't imagine not knowing how to read. I've been reading all my life. How did you—I mean—"

"How'd a saloon girl learn? I knew a woman who was kind to me. She had a bad life too and helping me made it easier."

Macky could hear the pain in Lorraine's voice and was sorry she asked. "Have you been here long?" she asked.

"I came here two years ago, right after Moose Mainwearing struck it rich. Heaven wasn't much back then, mostly miners and drifters. Now with the army buying cattle, the stagecoach line, and the Pony Express, new people come in all the time."

"I think I may have seen one of them last night, from my window. He was riding a small black stallion with a silver-trimmed saddle horn."

"In here," Lorraine said, and stopped before a door with a real glass window displaying the dressmaker's wares. "I'm afraid I don't know. I could ask around if . . ."

"Oh, no. I just thought I recognized him. But I'm probably mistaken."

The proprietor came forward. "Lorraine, I'm so glad you dropped in. What can I show you today?"

She glanced past Lorraine, caught sight of Macky and stopped short, her gaze one of utter disbelief.

"Kate, this is Letty Marsh. Letty, meet the new minister's wife, Kate Adams. She lost her clothing in the stagecoach mishap. She needs something to wear."

"Well, I do have several dresses complete, except for the hem, but they were to go to Sylvia Mainwearing. I suppose I could let you have one of them."

"Oh, no! I wouldn't want to take someone else's dress."

"Don't worry," Lorraine said, "Sylvia has so many she won't miss one. Show us what you have, Letty."

Macky had been uncomfortable before, but never so much as she was while sitting on the love seat beside Lorraine Lake. Letty brought out three dresses, two of which were much too low-cut and elegant. Only the third dress, a checked gingham of green and white, with green ribbons at the sleeves and along the bottom seemed suitable.

"I don't know," Macky began, "they look much too sophisticated for me."

"Perhaps the green one," Lorraine said, "with a nice bonnet and a pair of leather shoes and a shawl, of course. Try it on, Kate. The color matches your eyes."

"Oh, I couldn't." She hadn't thought that far ahead. She didn't have proper underclothing, and her petticoat had been ripped. She looked like a plowhand.

"Why not?" Lorraine asked, selecting a soft pair of ladies' drawers, a crinoline petticoat, lace-trimmed chemise, and some stockings. "Slip behind the changing screen, Kate."

"I'll help you," Letty added. "If you aren't used to wearing crinolines, they're sometimes hard to get into. And,"—she studied Kate carefully—"you'll need a corset."

Wearing crinolines made from steel wire? And a corset? Macky couldn't imagine why anyone in their right mind would even want to. But the last thing she wanted to do was show her ignorance by admitting that she'd never even seen such garments. She owed it to Bran not to embarrass him.

Several mortifying moments later she was trussed up like a prisoner, dressed in the undergarments and the gingham gown. Stepping out from behind the curtain, she waited for Lorraine to burst out laughing.

Lorraine didn't.

Instead she nodded her head, circling Macky as if she were a prime steer about to be auctioned off. "This will do fine, Letty. If you'll add another strip of ribbon to the bottom, it'll be just the right length. Can you stitch up a couple more? Maybe one nice silk and another day dress?"

"Of course. I can have this one hemmed by suppertime and the rest ready next week. Will that do, Mrs. Adams?"

She couldn't speak and it wasn't entirely from the lack of oxygen in her lungs. She'd caught sight of herself in the mirror. Hallelujah! She was saved. Nobody, not even Pratt, would ever believe that woman was McKenzie Calhoun.

After arranging to have the dress delivered to the saloon, Lorraine led Macky across the street to the general store. She headed for the corner where the women's goods were displayed. Moments later, Mrs. Gooden came from the back, spotted Macky and greeted her warmly.

"Good morning, Mrs. Adams. I trust you're feeling better this morning."

"Yes, thank you." Macky recalled the incident in the alley and felt her face turn a miserable shade of red.

Then Clara caught sight of Lorraine and her lips drew into a wrinkled knot of disapproval. "What can I show you?" she said to Macky, deliberately ignoring Lorraine.

Macky couldn't offend Clara Gooden but she couldn't allow her to be unkind to Lorraine.

"Miss Lake told me that you carry a nice selection of women's shoes and hats. She says that you have excellent taste in hats. Can you help me choose?"

Lorraine ducked behind a counter of yard goods and waited for Clara's explosion.

"Why I—I—yes, I suppose I do."

"What do you think, Lorraine?" Macky held up a pair of serviceable brown lace-up boots.

Lorraine straightened up. "No. If you're going to buy those, you might as well keep what you're wearing." She came around the counter and reached for a pair of soft white kid slippers. "This is what you need."

Clara Gooden stiffened and let out a sniff. "Really, Miss Lake, I think those would be much more suitable for someone like you than the minister's wife. Perhaps a nice black, Mrs. Adams."

Macky couldn't help but show Mrs. Gooden what she thought about her attitude. "You're both right. I'll take the white ones for special occasions and a plain pair for everyday."

Along with the impractical white shoes and simple black boots, Macky purchased a silly-looking straw bonnet adorned with ruffles and changeable ribbons made by Mrs. Gooden. Lorraine added a soft cream-colored wool shawl to the stack, and Macky selected a drawstring purse made of green velvet and a white flannel nightgown with a high neckline. When they left the store the supply of coins in Macky's pocket had been a bit depleted and a beaming Clara had promised to create a new hat for Lorraine to wear to church.

Macky passed up Lorraine's invitation to have a midday meal at Willa's Boardinghouse, and elected to have her meals sent to her room instead.

She didn't know where Bran was and she didn't want to take a chance on encountering Pratt before she had her new wardrobe. The way she looked now, it wouldn't be hard for him to recognize his youthful accomplice from the bank.

She was sorry she hadn't gone on to Denver. But facing the sheriff in Promise was different from facing Pratt. She didn't think he'd go along with her plan to return the money. Now she'd let her vanity influence her into spending too much of it on frivolities when she should have been saving it for the future.

Yep, the devil was definitely dogging her footsteps. Her tangled web of deceit was slowly but surely imprisoning her. Macky Calhoun, bank robber, runaway, wife.

Oh, Papa, what in heaven's name am I going to do to get through this?

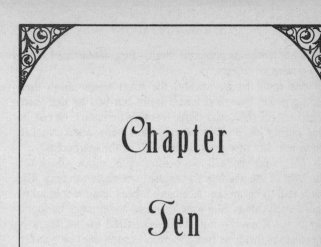

Chapter

Ten

Back in her room, Macky felt as if she were in jail. She'd never been closed in before, and she couldn't imagine what a prisoner felt like. Though, if she weren't careful, she stood a good chance of finding out.

With half the territory looking for the bank robbers, Macky couldn't understand why she was the only one who recognized Pratt. Of course he'd shaved the bushy gray beard he'd worn when he and his gang rode into Promise, and now he had a wound on his forehead which gave a curious tuck to his left eyebrow. But surely Marshal Larkin was accustomed to seeing criminals try to change their appearance. She smiled. If Pratt's appearance had changed as much as the kid who'd escaped with the money, she could understand.

Macky was out of sorts and fidgety. Where was Bran? He had no right to desert her like this. She didn't like not knowing what was going on. Bran—Pratt—Marshal Larkin. They were all threats.

She took the cameo and the silver feather from their hiding place. Pratt had found both, but had he tied them together? All she could think was that he hadn't, or else he was biding his time to expose them both. Macky tucked them into her new purse and took out the gold coins.

They were crude circles bearing an *S* on one side. From the light of the window she studied one more carefully. The coins had to be special. As a bank robber, Pratt would know about such things. She wasn't sure how, but once he found her purse along the trail, he'd recognized the markings of those coins inside as being identical to the ones he'd stolen from the bank. Then he'd stumbled on the hat with the feather.

Still, unless he'd talked with the dressmaker and the ticket agent, he couldn't know for certain that the purse belonged to her, or that the hat belonged to Bran.

With more questions than answers, Macky put the money away. There was a knock on her door. She hurried to open it, hoping Bran had returned. It was the boy from downstairs.

"I'm Tobe. Miss Lake had me fetch you some food from Willa's," he said, holding a tray covered with a white cotton cloth.

"Put it on the table, Tobe." She fetched him a coin from the change Clara Gooden had given her.

"Tobe, can you read and write?"

"Yes, ma'am. Miss Lake taught me. She taught me real good."

He took the coin and scurried out the door as if he thought she was about to test him. Macky thought about the saloonkeeper who taught a boy to read as she ate dumplings of beef and potatoes, dried apple pie with cream, and coffee. Too bad the town didn't appreciate Lorraine's big heart. Macky finished the food, covered the tray, and flung herself across the freshly made bed, considering the possibility of a real school. That was something the preacher's wife could do.

Minutes later she came to her feet and began to pace again. Where in west side of hell was the Reverend Adams? How dare he put her in this position and then just disappear. The truth was, there was nothing to hold her here. She didn't owe Bran anything.

Suppose he'd left Heaven without telling her? What made him think that she'd stick around while he waltzed about the countryside? He knew she had money. She'd just buy herself a horse. She ought to be prepared.

Moments later, Pratt and the marshal be damned, Macky marched across the street to the livery stable. "Hello?"

"Out back!"

She followed the sound of the man's voice to the rear of the stable where a blacksmith's fire was glowing hot. A large man, dressed in a leather apron, was pounding a piece of iron into a plow shank.

"How do you do," Macky began. "I'm Macky—Mrs. Adams and I'd like to speak to you."

The man went on pounding. Was everybody in this town rude? "I said, I'd like to speak to you. I want to buy a horse. Do you operate the stable?"

"I do."

"Good, I was beginning to think you couldn't talk. Do you have a name?"

He nodded at the sign on the side of the barn: H. Clay, Proprietor.

"Mr. Clay—"

"Good, you can read. I was beginning to think you couldn't." Hank picked up the bellows and blew on the fire, forcing the coals to flame.

Macky blushed. "I'm sorry. I'm just a bit out of sorts. I mean, I'm not used to being inactive. Could I do that for you? Seems to me it would be a lot easier."

Hank laid the bellows back on the table and took a good look at Macky. "Thank you no, Mrs. Adams. I'd be glad to sell you a horse. If you'll tell the preacher to stop by, I'll show him what I have."

"You'll do no such thing. It's my money—I mean I know horses. I'd like to inquire about prices, if you have the time."

Hank nodded, laid the piece of iron down in the coals at the edge of the fire, and turned into the stable. "Follow me." He led her to the corner of a small room he'd made into an office. "Have a seat."

"Why?"

"I have to look at my records. The only horses I keep at the stable are those I rent. My others come from a rancher south of Heaven." He reached for a ledger on the shelf. As he slid it out, a second book tumbled into Macky's lap.

Macky started to hand it back when she saw the cover. "Poetry? You read poetry?"

"Does that shock you?"

"Crawfish and tadpoles! I can't talk to you without riling you, can I? Seems like everybody in this town knows how to read and write except the children. I don't understand why you all wouldn't let Lorraine open a school to teach them."

"Lorraine?"

"Miss Lake. She offered to help teach the children and she was turned down. What's the matter, are you afraid she'd contaminate them?"

Hank gave a long, serious look out the window toward the saloon. Macky wondered if she'd made a mistake in mentioning Lorraine's offer. Certainly everything else she'd done since arriving in Heaven had been improper.

"No, I don't judge people," he said.

"But you don't do much about making them welcome either, do you? Look, I'm sorry. I'll just wait until Bran—Reverend Adams gets back to see about a horse. I may even decide to buy a mule instead. At least a mule can pull a wagon and a plow."

This time the burly blacksmith didn't try to conceal his shock. "You intend to farm?"

"I intend to—I don't know what I intend to do. Good day, Mr. Clay."

Back in her room, Macky threw herself across her bed as she continued to fume. What kind of place was Heaven where Lorraine's knowledge was rejected because she was socially unacceptable? Where the blacksmith read poetry and kept to himself? Where the preacher was expected to hold services in a saloon and the preacher's wife was a criminal? But all the time she was railing out at injustice she knew that the real fly in her ointment was that the man she'd taken on as her pretend husband had disappeared.

Across the street, Hank Clay caressed the spine of the book and studied the upper window of Heaven's Bell. Miss Lake's room. The preacher's wife was right. There ought to be a school. And Mrs. Adams might be the one to pull it off.

Macky didn't realize that she'd fallen asleep until a knock on the door awakened her.

"Yes?"

The same serving girl entered the room timidly, carrying a basket and the gingham dress draped carefully across her arm. She stepped aside for Tobe to bring in the tin tub. "Miss Lorraine sent me up with your new clothes and the tub. I'm supposed to remind you that you and the preacher are having supper tonight with Mrs. Mainwearing."

Macky watched Tobe place the tub by the fire and add more wood. Then he left the room and returned with two iron kettles of hot water. The girl draped the gown across the end of the bed and waited for the boy to bring two more kettles of water.

"There's soap on the washstand. I'll return shortly and help you dress, ma'am," she said, dropping a curtsy as she backed out of the room.

Macky stared at the tub. Surely they didn't expect her to strip off her clothes and sit in that little tin tub. It wasn't as if she'd never taken a tub bath. She had. But it had been a washtub with full sides and she'd been in her own kitchen. Suppose somebody came in?

Still she couldn't resist picking up the dress. She'd never had anything so lovely in her life. It even smelled new. She held it against herself and imagined, just for a minute, draping her market basket over her arm and going out to shop. Or better still, having Bran slip his arm through hers and fold her elbow across his.

With her eyes closed she took three steps across the room, nodding to invisible acquaintances and smiling up at her pretend husband. Pretend husband?

A bank robber having supper with Mrs. Mainwearing? Staring at herself once more in the mirror, she made up her mind. She might never do it again but this one time she wanted to dress up in her new gown and show that skeptical one-eyed man that she *could* look like a woman.

She took off her clothes and pinned up her hair, making use of the women's beauty articles that had mysteriously appeared on the washstand. With the soap in her hand she slid into the hot water and leaned back as far as she could to cover herself. For a few minutes she merely lay there enjoying the sheer luxury of having someone wait on her for the first time she could remember.

Finally, as the water began to cool she soaped herself, scrubbing her skin vigorously, then slid back down in the water to rinse.

Macky didn't hear the door open. But she was instantly aware of Bran's presence. In a futile attempt to cover herself she drew up her knees and clasped them to her chest with her arms, then turned to face Bran, bravely covering her panic with a frown of stern disapproval.

"Thank you for knocking, Reverend."

Bran, at a momentary loss for words, could only stare at the naked woman in the tub. He'd already come to the conclusion that she was prettier than she acknowledged. After seeing her in a nightgown, he'd spent the day convincing himself that his physical reaction was because he'd been without a woman for too long.

"Stop staring at me!" she snapped.

A tightening in his gut told him his body wasn't listening this time, either. He groaned. " 'Lust not after her beauty in your heart; Neither let her take you with her eyelids,' " he said. "Proverbs."

" 'Lying lips are an abomination to the Lord.' That's from Proverbs, too." Macky's voice turned into a whisper.

Bran rubbed his chin, feeling the bristles of a three-day growth of hair rasp against his fingertips. "I don't lie, Macky."

"Oh? What do you call letting the people of Heaven think you're Reverend Adams?"

"As I recall, that was your doing, not mine. I was about to tell them otherwise when you came forward. Suddenly, I had a wife."

"But you didn't correct their impression. You aren't a preacher, are you, Bran?"

"No, I'm not."

"And your name isn't Adams, is it?"

"No."

"I'm not Mrs. Brandon Adams," she said defiantly. "That makes you a liar, Bran."

"No, that makes me a fool. But I thought you needed to be protected. Now I know why."

She came to her feet without thinking. "You know?"

She looked like a pagan deity painted in the great museums, all lithe and rosy in the firelight. The sight of her stole his breath away, making him dizzy.

"I know."

His voice was rough, angry as he considered that another man had touched her, perhaps abandoned her. "And though I don't understand how you let it happen, I'll keep your secret for now."

"It wasn't something I planned," she said. "And I'm going to make amends as soon as I figure out how. I just got caught up in it before I could stop. What's your excuse for your lie?"

"I can't tell you, Macky. Not yet. It wouldn't be safe for you to know. Just believe me when I tell you it's important."

"I see. It's all right that you know about my sordid past, but you can't trust me to know the truth about yours?"

"It's the best way to keep you out of it. I've done some things I'm not proud of, but I'll protect you."

"Why?"

"Hell if I know. My Indian father said that all things happen for a reason. Why'd you agree to be my wife?"

"I always hankered to have a man who could see in the dark. Besides," she added, "I like your face. It makes my heart sing."

He couldn't stop his next question. "Does it sing often?"

"Never has before. All this is new to me, Bran. Other women have mothers to prepare them for these feelings. I've had to learn for myself. I'm just now beginning to under-stand what I missed."

At least she was honest. He wanted to give in to the need to pull her into his arms and tell her that everything would be all right. Instead, he picked up the towel and wrapped it around her. "I'm sorry I walked in on you."

"You should be. You shouldn't have left me here by myself all day. Where were you?" She stepped out of the tub, deliberately sloshing water on his boots.

"My, my! Is the preacher's wife turning into a nagging shrew?"

"I don't nag," she said, her voice painfully tight, "and I'm not anybody's wife."

She'd already told him that there was no husband. Now she'd said it again. Bran took a step toward her. "What about this man who may be coming after you?"

"Oh, Bran." She leaned her head against the fireplace and closed her eyes. "I just wish I could go back, that I'd never come into town that day, that—"

"You were the young innocent girl you once were?" he finished for her, fighting the urge to comfort her.

She sighed and began to dry her face and neck, shrinking down inside the cloth as if she were trying to hide. "Yes. I guess I do wish that. But we can't go back, can we? We have to live the life we've created for ourselves."

"Would this life be so bad?" Bran asked, knowing that such an idea was not only unwise, but impossible. "Would you hate being a preacher's wife?"

"Would you hate being a preacher?"

"Never thought about it. I suppose there are many ways to cure the ills of man. This may be the most ill-paid one. Hardly seems fair to ask any woman to share a life that depends on the charity of others."

Macky chose her response carefully. "I—I think that it is rare for a woman to have a choice about the kind of life her husband makes for them. If any man ever asked to marry me, it would be the man, not his profession that would matter. Not that such a situation is ever likely to happen."

"Who told you that?"

"My mother said that my papa filled my head with nonsense, that no man would ever want me. She was right."

That made him angry. It was one thing for her to disguise her beauty if she were hiding. But for her own mother to convince her that she was incapable of attracting a man . . . He lifted her chin with his fingertips and forced her to look at him.

"Macky, don't you have any idea how appealing you are? How much you stir a man's needs?"

"Me?" She shook her head and looked away.

"Damn it, woman, look at me. You do know what happens to a man when he wants to make love to a woman?"

He could tell that she didn't or couldn't believe him.

Bran didn't know who he wanted to strangle first, her mother, who'd made her feel so inferior, the men in her family who'd apparently reinforced that kind of thinking, or the man who'd used her and left her with a child.

He watched as she allowed a faint hope to shine in her eyes. His hands left her shoulders and slid down her back, drawing her close.

"Macky," he whispered, his breath catching in her hair. "Macky." He liked saying her name. "If you never believe anyone else in your life, believe me when I tell you that you are very special. I don't know who hurt you, but being with a man can be very good. Being with the right man can be a beautiful, loving experience."

"I don't—I mean . . ." She tried to step backward and found herself being held even tighter.

Bran felt her confusion. He ought to let her go. But he couldn't. He felt her unspoken pain that reached out and joined his own. "Under other circumstances, Macky, I'd show you. But it wouldn't be right. Just relax. Let me hold you."

Macky resisted at first, then gave in to the need to be held and hid her face against Bran's shoulder. The touch of his whiskers against her forehead felt like sand rubbing against her skin. Her heart was pounding. Their thighs touched, breasts and chest pressed together. Heat flared, leaving her trembling and weak. "You would?"

"I would," he murmured as he nuzzled her hair, feathering her cheek with soft kisses, claiming her lips at last.

Bran's mouth was soft, like velvet. She hadn't expected that. New sensations bombarded her, heating her skin to fire.

Bran groaned, and deepened the kiss. She'd never allowed herself to think about being kissed by a man, not consciously, but suddenly she was leaning against him, inviting him to show her the way.

He closed his eyes so that he wouldn't reveal the incredible yearning that sent his heart slamming against his rib cage. He tightened his muscles, growing rigid against her. Finally, he broke the kiss and stepped back.

"That shouldn't have happened," he said, his voice hoarse as he backed toward the door. Damn her eyes, why had she been so cooperative? What was it about this woman that made him want to take care of her? He didn't want to think how close he'd been to stripping away that sheet of cotton and taking her, then wondered why he'd stopped when she was willing. She seemed incredibly innocent and that pretense angered him unreasonably.

"You're right, Bran. Tomorrow morning, I intend to buy a pistol. To protect myself from men like you."

Macky knew that was a feeble threat. There was no other man like Reverend Brandon Adams. He was a man who knew how to make a woman forget her own mind. "I hope you don't plan to touch me again."

"I don't. In fact, maybe I'd better leave. I'll speak to Lorraine. I expect she'll find another room for me."

"No!" Macky shouted. "I mean, you can't. Someone would know and—well, it wouldn't look right."

Bran couldn't ignore the stricken look on her face. She was afraid, not of him, but of being left alone.

He let out a deep breath. He'd done a lot of bad things in his life, but this time he had to draw the line. Macky was right; he couldn't walk out on her now. He had sworn by whatever good was left in him to protect her. But protecting her didn't mean sleeping with her. Whatever the truth was, he wouldn't take a chance on bringing harm to a woman who was carrying a child. He'd have to continue the charade. "You're right," he said. "We have to go on as planned, no matter how difficult it is."

She gave him a skeptical look. "What does that mean?"

"Put on your new dress, Mrs. Adams. I'll be back for you in an hour. The preacher and the redhead are going to supper with the queen of Heaven."

As Macky pulled on the pristine white undergarments, she alternated between fuming over Bran's actions and fury at herself for giving in to him. She didn't know any more about handling a man than she knew about the women's drawers Lorraine had selected for her.

She managed to get the chemise and the drawers tied properly, but there were stockings, a petticoat, and her corset. Letty had strapped her into the harness at her shop, but now with its laces and cords it seemed to lie there and mock her.

A knock on the door brought her to a state of panic. Surely Bran hadn't returned so quickly. "Yes?"

"It's Polly, ma'am. The preacher said you was ready to get dressed."

"Come in, Polly, and—" Macky jerked the door open. "Show me how in tarnation you wear this—this thing."

Polly couldn't hide her smile. "Let me just put this curling iron on the fire to stay warm and I'll lace up."

Moments later Macky felt like a chicken, gutted and tied up to be roasted. All she needed was a larger fireplace and a spit on which to be skewered. "How's a person supposed to breathe?"

Polly giggled. "You take quick little breaths."

"Like when I've been running?"

"Or like you feel when a man . . ." Her voice trailed off and she turned to fetch the stockings and ties to hold them up. "Sit down, ma'am, and I'll put 'em on."

"That's all right, I think I can do that myself."

Macky sank down on the stool. She knew what Polly meant when she said a woman couldn't breathe around a man. She still felt like her lungs were suddenly too small. And that was before Polly had laced the corset.

Polly untied the ribbons at the bottom of the drawers and threaded the stockings up each leg and tied them above her knees with the matching ribbons.

Next, Polly placed the impractical leather boots with the tiny spool heels on her feet and began to fasten the laces. "We'll move the stool over here to the table and I'll do your hair before you put on your dress. I thought we could use the green ribbon in your hair."

"I don't know . . ." Macky said uneasily.

Polly began to brush out Macky's braid. Parting her hair in the middle, Polly pulled a heavy swatch of hair up on top of her head and anchored it there. Then she reached for the curling iron and fashioned a cascade of sausage curls that rippled down her neck.

Macky began to fidget. She was fooling herself with her expectations. Nothing Polly could do would tame the mass of hair she normally stuffed under a hat.

"Now, let me add the ribbons."

Moments later Polly gave Macky a hand mirror.

"It's—I look—I mean I never expected," Macky said in amazement.

"Now, stand up."

Then came the white ruffled petticoat, followed by the crinoline with the steel frame.

"You mean I wear all this under my skirt? No wonder you have to draw a body up to fit into it."

Feeling more uncertain, Macky raised her arms and allowed Polly to slip the dress over her head, and it fell softly over her shoulders.

Polly fastened the buttons up the front and stood back to look.

"The preacher is going to be very pleased. He ought to be back anytime now. I'll wait until after you leave to have the tub taken away."

"Thank you, Polly," Macky said, and turned back toward the mirror, still thunderstruck at what she saw.

After Polly left, Bran knocked on the door and identified himself. Macky hesitated, nervous about his reaction, then berated herself for caring what he thought. "Come in, Bran."

Bran opened the door and stopped dead still, unable to cover his shock.

The uncertain girl he'd spent the last hour trying to erase from his memory had been replaced by a woman who was absolutely breathtaking, as fresh as a copper coin and as vibrant as a desert sunset. He couldn't speak, and stood there like a man who'd never seen a woman before.

"Well?" she said, her voice trembling with barely hidden uncertainty. "Am I Macky or am I Kate?"

"Your papa was right. You're Trouble and I'm in the thick of it."

Chapter Eleven

"Am I properly attired?"

"You're very properly attired, Macky."

Macky's simple green checked dress with the high neckline and long sleeves was the exact color of her eyes. There was nothing provocative about it, except the way it hugged her breasts and nipped a waist much tinier than he remembered. The short cream-colored shawl draped across her shoulders formed an outer shell much like an opening rose revealing its loveliness.

But it was her hair that astounded him. It was caught up at the crown with matching green ribbons and fell down her back like ripples of fire. Her mouth quivered for a moment before she straightened and took on a look that dared him not to disapprove.

Macky felt as if Polly were lacing her corset again, her breath coming in little pants. But this time, it was definitely the man, not the corset, that caused her consternation.

While she'd been dressing, Bran had bathed, shaved, and changed into fresh clothes so new that she could smell the dye. He'd exchanged the dusty black clothes for a frock coat and trousers in a soft gray color. A pale green tie at his neck matched the green in her new dress, giving the impression that they were joined. Where he'd been dangerous before, now he was . . . delicious.

" 'Truly, to tell lies is not honorable,' Bran."

"Believe me, Macky, 'as a man thinketh in his heart, so is he.' And my heart is saying that the lady I'll be escorting this evening is more lovely than Solomon in all his splendor."

"Don't use those pretty words on me, Bran Adams, and don't quote Scripture, either. Aren't you afraid that God will strike you down for blasphemy?"

He considered her words before he answered. "No, I'd like to think He and I are on the same mission."

"Just the same, I'd rather you not flatter me. Just act like the preacher you're supposed to be and don't try to play up to me."

He held out a single white wildflower, slightly drooped, but still alive. "Does that mean I ought to throw this away?"

"For me?" she whispered, completely unsettled by the look in his eyes. "Where did you get this?"

"I found it behind the bathhouse where they empty the dirty water. It was growing amongst a stand of weeds, holding its head so high and proud, I thought of you."

"Me? Oh, for goodness sake. I'm not. You don't think . . ." But she let her words die as she saw the look in his eyes. He'd done a lovely thing and she couldn't spoil it.

"Thank you, Bran. It's beautiful. Nobody ever gave me a flower before." She stuck the blossom through the ribbons in her hair, lifted her head and gave him a smile.

"Tonight, you're Mrs. Adams, whose husband is very proud." He took her hand and lifted it to his lips. "You are very beautiful."

Macky blushed. At the touch of his lips, a shiver rippled up her backbone.

She wished she could hold on to the moment, but the longer he held her hand, the more uncertain she felt. "Hadn't we better go?" she finally asked, trying to pull some sense of reality back to the moment.

"Yes. Though, if it were up to me . . ."

Quickly, she removed her hand and swept past him out the door. For a moment Bran's flower took the edge off her worry that people would laugh at her clumsy attempt to look like a minister's wife. For a moment she forgot the uncertainty of the coming evening, of facing total embarrassment. And for that moment she held her head high and smiled.

Bran followed her down the hall to the steps that led to the saloon, his hand resting possessively against the small of her back. As they reached the bottom, the cacophony of sounds hushed and every eye turned toward Macky.

"Well, now, don't you look nice." Lorraine stepped forward and studied the couple. "Polly did a good job with your hair. Sylvia will be impressed."

Across the saloon, Macky caught sight of Pratt leaning against the bar. He nodded at her and her confidence vanished in a heartbeat. What on earth had made her think she could be something she wasn't? Only a few days before she'd been a farm girl. Then with no intent to do so, she became a bank robber. Now she was pretending to be a preacher's wife and the man who could expose her was looking at her with a cunning leer on his face.

Bran, almost as if he understood her fears, slid his arm around her waist and nodded to the saloon owner. "Thank you, Miss Lake. And I appreciate very much your taking my—"he swallowed hard and forced himself to say the words—"my wife under your wing this morning."

"Yes, thank you, Lorraine," Macky said, then bolted toward the door, surprising Bran with her sudden departure.

Bran said a quick goodbye and hurried after Macky. He

had the feeling that she might climb on one of the horses tied outside the saloon and ride blindly off into the night.

"Macky, what's wrong?"

"Stop trying to make me into something I'm not. I just look *nice*, like a minister's wife ought to look, nothing more."

"You do look nice," Bran said. "Why is that so hard for you to believe?"

"Because you're too good at lying. You know what I really am. You don't have to pretend with me you—you two-faced, smooth-talking gambler."

Angry words just tumbled out and Macky didn't know why. He didn't owe her any explanations. She'd forced herself on him, and if he behaved as a normal man, what right did she have to complain? Men kissed their wives. It didn't mean anything to Bran. He'd just been trying to convince her that she was something she wasn't. And she wanted to believe him. Until she saw Pratt and it all came tumbling back. She was a Calhoun and they were always failures.

She couldn't blame Bran for her foolishness. But in that one moment she had really felt like a woman, and those thoughts were nothing more than silly dreams.

If there was one thing Macky had learned from her father, it was that dreams only brought pain. Now, for a reason that she still couldn't understand, Bran was pretending that they were husband and wife.

And unless she were willing to face Pratt, or the marshal, or both, she would have to go along with anything he said, or did.

Her face flamed as she thought about how she'd felt when he'd come into the room, when he'd wrapped the towel around her and . . .

Macky swallowed hard. She was Mrs. Brandon Adams and there was nothing she could do about it, short of confess to her wrongdoing. But that wasn't the real problem. Even now she was trembling, all from his touch. She wished she had a sip of Harriet's sherry to give her courage.

Macky decided it couldn't get any worse until they walked past the blacksmith's shop into the livery stable. There, as a reminder of her peril, was the black horse with the fancy silver-trimmed saddle on the ground nearby. And in the next stall was a mule, a mule that looked very familiar.

"Solomon!" she said, before she realized she'd spoken out loud.

"Solomon?" Bran questioned, looking around. "Who's Solomon?"

"The mule. I mean he looks exactly like a mule I once owned. His name was Solomon."

The mule snorted and took a step toward Macky. *Oh no, you can't make up to me now, you ornery old cuss.* She turned away, trying to gather her thoughts. How on earth had he gotten here?

"Evening, Mrs. Adams, Preacher," Hank Clay said, wiping his hand on his shirt before offering it to Bran. "Got the buggy harnessed and ready."

"Nice horse," Bran said. "Is he for sale?"

"Nope. Belongs to a stranger, a miner, I think. I'm just stabling him." He looked at Macky. "If you're planning on doing any farming, I can make you a good deal on the mule."

Bran looked at Macky and back at the mule. "Where'd you get him?"

"Bought him off a drifter who stumbled on him out on the plains. He's a good animal, but he's stubborn."

"We'll take him," Macky said. "I mean we'll need a good farm animal, won't we, Brother Adams?"

"Why, yes, I suppose we will," he agreed. "Consider him sold, Mr. Clay. Now, Mrs. Adams, we'd better be going."

Bran caught Macky's arm just as she was about to climb up in the buggy. "Allow me to assist you, my dear," he said. Macky shrugged off his offer, swung her leg into the buggy, and caught the folds of her skirt and petticoat on the edge. Bran smothered a smile as her crinoline swung up, giving him full view of her long legs. In an attempt to right herself she put one hand on the bench and the other behind her, pushing the starched undergarment against her bottom, which threw the hoop forward, exposing her front.

"Tadpoles and crawfish!" she swore.

This time Bran couldn't hold back a chuckle.

The blacksmith quickly turned his back and, with a whistle meant to cover his smile, busied himself at his fire.

"All right, Brother Adams," she said in a voice that was barely more than a growl. "I can walk, but I can't sit down. Get up here and tell me how to manage this thing, unless you want me to expose myself to the entire town."

Bran climbed into the buggy and, with as straight a face as he could manage, took both her hands and pulled her up. Then he arranged the petticoat behind her so that it draped itself over the seat in back and her knees in front.

This time Macky couldn't even manage to swear. If she'd said a word she would have burst out in tears. Not only was she incapable of being a preacher's wife, she couldn't even wear a skirt properly. As soon as she got back to their—no her—room, she was going to put her trousers back on, and if Bran's so-called congregation didn't like it, they could just go suck a lemon.

Wisely, Bran didn't try to talk to Macky. He simply drove out of town, lifting his hat in greeting as he passed the townspeople along the street. Once away from Heaven, he turned the buggy off the trail and stopped the horse beneath a stand of cottonwood trees.

"Why are we stopping?" she asked through clenched teeth.

"I thought it might make it easier on you if I gave you a few lessons on wearing petticoats." He stepped down from the buggy and walked to the other side.

"Oh? And how many petticoats have you worn? Is that another of your professions?"

"No, but I have watched women wearing those contraptions. And I don't envy you at all."

She continued to look straight ahead. The softness in his voice said that he understood her plight. He wasn't laughing at her and she knew it. But she couldn't allow herself to weaken as she almost had when he gave her the flower. She didn't want him to be kind. He was already too much in charge of her life.

"I expect you have," she snapped, "and I expect you know as much about taking them off as you know about wearing them."

Bran gave a wry laugh. "I've done that a few times," he admitted. "Would you like me to show you that, too?"

Before she thought about what she was doing, she whirled around, caught her skirt in the brake and released it. With the buggy wheels rolling, she toppled out, landing in Bran's arms with a thud.

"Oh!" she said, instinctively throwing her arms around his neck to anchor herself.

Bran caught his hands beneath her bottom and held her hard against him as her crinoline flew up in the back.

Macky gasped in astonishment as she felt him pressing through the rough fabric of her petticoats between her legs. She raised her eyes in mute appeal, her gaze locking with his.

She felt her clothes tighten, her body becoming so sensitive that her breasts reacted to the soft chemise. They swelled and ached as her blood roared through her veins in tandem with the beat of her heart.

Or was it his heart?

"Oh . . ." she said again, this time in a low, intimate whisper. "I don't think this is helping me."

Bran tried to answer, but his throat was so tight that he couldn't speak. She was so damned open with her feelings, with surprise at her own response, with wanting him. How could she have let some man take her—before him? How could some fool have used her and left her with a child?

Tightening his grip on her bottom, he pressed her

against him, trying to erase the other man's touch, trying to imprint her body with his own.

"Bran, I . . ." Macky's head lolled back, exposing her breasts to him, and he couldn't stop himself from pressing his lips hungrily against the trembling cords in her neck.

For a moment he let go with one hand so that he would be free to touch her. As his hand began to move around her waist, she tightened her arms around him in a move so erotic that he realized he was only moments away from climax.

Gaining enough control to stop himself was the most difficult thing Bran ever did. But he tried to slow his breathing and carefully let her down. They were due at Mrs. Mainwearing's and there was no time to pursue this now.

Macky let out a little sigh. "I don't understand."

"We have to go. I'll try to explain all this later."

"All what, Bran?"

"Just get in the buggy, Macky. We're going to be late."

This time Bran didn't offer to help. He marched around the carriage and got in. Macky lifted her petticoat and, after several attempts, climbed in.

"Lift your skirts so that you have as much in the back as the front and sit in the middle, like a hen setting on its nest."

"Why are you so angry?" Macky asked, trying to calm her stomach and her racing heart.

"Macky, I told you. I know about the child."

"What child?"

"You don't have to pretend with me. I won't hold it against you. It suits you to have a husband for your baby and it suits me to have a wife—for now."

Macky stared at him, appalled. "You think I'm going to have a baby? Jumping Jehosaphat! Me?"

"Well, aren't you? That's what Clara Gooden said."

Confusion filled Macky's eyes. "Clara Gooden?"

"According to Mayor Cribbs, you got sick the night of the social because you're carrying a child."

Carrying low. Boys? Now the peculiar conversation came

back to her. Macky took one look at Bran's face and started to laugh. "Oh, Bran. Surely you don't think I'm going to have a baby. Why, who'd have me?"

"But you admitted a man would be coming for you. And you were afraid. I could see your fear."

Macky's laughter died. Bran really believed that she was with child. He thought he was protecting her from the father. "Oh, Bran, you silly fool. There is no child. It was the pickled pig's feet on top of Harriet's sherry that made me sick."

"But Clara—"

His eyes narrowed and he forced his eyes to the road as he urged the horse to pick up its pace.

"Bran, I don't know how it happened, but there is no child. No husband. There never was." The silence was long and painful. "I wish you'd say something."

He wished he could. An odd kind of relief swept over him. She wasn't with child, but it didn't make sense. No matter what she said, he knew that her fear had been real. "Then what were you running away from?"

Her moment of truth had come. She still couldn't believe that this man had been willing to protect a woman he didn't even know just because she was carrying a child. But what would he do when he learned that it wasn't one man he was protecting her from, but three; Pratt, the marshal, and the sheriff from Promise. She had to be careful with what she said.

"Believe me, Bran, you don't want to be involved. If the truth about me comes out, I could be hung."

"Why?" His voice was skeptical and hard. He was going to find out, whether she wanted him to or not.

"I'm wanted for—a crime. That's why I couldn't be recognized the day we arrived. I never meant to involve you. It just happened."

"Christ! You mean the law is after you?" That was the last thing Bran expected. He was a gunfighter, acting as a minister trying to avoid a marshal who seemed inordinately interested in his past. And the woman pretending to be his wife was a criminal?

"I'm sorry, Bran. If you want me to go, I'll leave."

"Leave?" That thought cut through him like a sharp wind. He didn't know why but he couldn't let her go. And until he could understand why this feeling was so strong, he'd have to follow the road he was traveling.

"No, Macky, it's too late for that. All we can do now is get through the evening. We'll sort it out later. For tonight, nothing has changed. I'm still the minister and you're still my wife. If the town believes you're carrying a child, so be it. Revealing the truth could result in both of us being exposed as fakes."

Worse, Bran. The truth could get me hung. Being hung might not be so bad, but she refused to die without returning the money and clearing her name.

Bran left Macky to her own thoughts while he concentrated on the coming meeting with his employer. He'd been brought to Heaven to solve a problem. He couldn't change his situation, but he could do his job, and find the person responsible for the trouble at the mine. The only outsiders he'd encountered were Marshal Larkin, and the mysterious man on the black horse.

And of course Macky. From the moment she'd come on board in Promise, she'd thwarted every attempt he'd made to push her away; she'd thrown herself into his life and he was making a place for her. Stealing a quick glance at her, he couldn't hold back a smile. Trouble, yes, but much more. She was bright and charming and independent. Too damned independent.

Without his help, she'd end up as some farmer's workhorse or in some brothel earning her living on her back. He couldn't let that happen. Somehow he'd become responsible for her, and sham or not, he had no intention of letting her past stop this job or ruin her future.

Not if he had anything to say about it.

From somewhere in the outcropping of rock ahead an owl hooted. The late afternoon sky had changed from blue to a hazy purple as the sun slid lower, draping the mountain range in shadows.

Past the barrier of rock, the Mainwearing house loomed like a white crown in the distance. The house was a Spanish-style adobe with a veranda that wrapped around the second floor. It was lit with lamps that shone like jewels in a crown. The fence posts, whitewashed like the house, were also topped with lamps, welcoming the guests' arrival. As they drew closer they could see a scattering of small white buildings and barns clustered around the house.

"Oh, my," Macky murmured, as the buggy came to a stop and a servant took hold of the horse's bridle. "No wonder you were concerned about my appearance. Mrs. Mainwearing must be very wealthy."

"She is," he said in a low voice as he helped her down.

"I know that I've endangered your position here, Bran, and I don't understand why you want me to stay. But I owe you a debt of gratitude more than you'll ever know. So just tell me what to do and I'll try my best."

"Just be yourself, Macky," he answered. "And maybe we can pull this off. Perhaps we can even convince Mrs. Mainwearing to donate some money to help build a church."

Macky let out a soft breath. He wasn't going to turn her in. She leaned back so that she could see his face. "I don't know what you're up to, but I don't think it's building a church. You'd do better if you flatter Mrs. Mainwearing like you did me. You're very good at it. What do you think?"

He looked down at her and, even with everything that had happened, knew that she was still the most appealing woman he'd ever met. "I think," he said, folding her arm over his, "not. You see, I have no interest in sleeping with her."

Before Macky could respond, the door was opened by one of the most handsome women Macky had ever seen.

"Reverend Adams," the woman said, her eyebrows lifted as if she were measuring the man. "I am Sylvia Mainwearing. Welcome to my home."

Bran released Macky's arm and took the hand extended to him, kissing it lightly before he reached back and drew Macky forward. "And this is Kate, my wife."

Sylvia glanced briefly at Macky, then planted her gaze on Bran with such intensity that Macky could feel the intimidation from where she stood.

"You're not what I expected," she said. "Neither of you."

"Welcome, Mrs. Adams," Marshal Larkin called from the room opening off the entranceway. "It's very nice to see you again. Come and meet the judge."

Sylvia looked displeased for a moment, then noting the frown on Bran's face, she stepped back and motioned them inside. "Yes, do come and meet my guests, Reverend."

"We'd be delighted," Bran said easily.

Bran was wrong. From the look on Mrs. Mainwearing's face, Macky could see that it wouldn't take many compliments for Bran to gain her favor. Macky swallowed back the hot anger that blazed inside and instinctively moved closer to the man who was not only her husband, but her jailer as well.

Bran put his hand on her back, urging her forward. "Is *this* the lion's den?" she whispered under her breath.

"Oh, yes, this is definitely the lion's den."

"Well, I hope you brought your slingshot."

"Wrong story, Macky. That was David."

She could have argued that she wouldn't feel comfortable with both David and Daniel as her escorts. Only her fear of the marshal, who had stepped forward to greet them, stopped Macky's need to flee.

"Judge," he said, "meet our new minister, Brandon Adams, and his wife, Kate," the marshal said, turning to the stately man standing beside the fire.

A judge and a marshal. Macky was dead. Even a Methodist minister in the middle of Sodom and Gomorrah couldn't save her now.

"A true Southern beauty," the judge said, smiling at her. "No doubt about it. Where are you from, missy?"

Bran started slightly. At that moment Macky knew Bran still wasn't sure of her. She was as much his jailer as he was hers. She felt an enormous need to prove to him that she could be trusted.

"I'm originally from Boston, Your Honor. And you?"

"From New Orleans. Came out to Denver to make my fortune after the last fire. A splendid, though slightly wicked place, New Orleans. But the folks there don't take to Americans too well."

Macky wandered closer. "I've never been there myself, but my father ran a trading post along the Mississippi, before we came to Kansas. Mr. Adams is from Mississippi originally, too."

"Interesting, we're all ex-Southerners. I believe the marshal is from that area as well."

"How long have you been married, Mrs. Adams?" Sylvia asked, coming to stand by the judge.

"Not long enough," she said.

"Not very long," Bran said at the same time, looking for a way to change the subject. "What brings you to Heaven, Judge Hardcastle?"

"This angel in red," he answered, smiling possessively at Mrs. Mainwearing. "I'm trying to convince her to come to Denver, for safety's sake," he said.

"Don't believe a word he tells you, Reverend Adams. He's interested in my money, just like every other man I've ever met. Except for Mr. Mainwearing, of course. He already had the money. He just wanted me. What about you, Reverend?"

"Oh, I already have a wife, Mrs. Mainwearing, but if you're offering me money, the church will be pleased to accept it, in the name of your late husband, of course."

She looked at him oddly for a moment, then asked shrewdly, "What are your plans for our town?"

"I'm not quite sure yet. I have to get to know the people of Heaven, find out what their needs are. Then I'll decide what to do. You have a lovely place here, Mrs. Mainwearing. That is an interesting painting over the fireplace."

Bran's remark drew everyone's attention to the framed picture of a crown, adorned by an ornate gold letter *S*, surrounded by lacy filigree against a black background.

"It's the crest which represents my mine, the Sylvia. In an effort to stop the thefts we recently installed a press that engraves all my gold with my own mark. That way we can always identify the gold from the Sylvia."

Marshal Larkin took a sip from his whiskey glass. "The first marked shipment of Mrs. Mainwearing's gold coins was stolen by the Pratt gang in that bank holdup over in Promise. We don't believe any of them have been used yet, but once they are, we'll get the thief."

Macky's breath whooshed out of her lungs. The *S* was the same as the letter on her coins. Everybody would know that her gold had come from the Sylvia mine. Pratt had seen it. Bran had seen it. And she'd spent some of the coins in Mrs. Gooden's store. She'd run from discovery only to set herself up to be identified. As always, Macky was in trouble.

Mrs. Mainwearing, the judge, and the marshal were all studying the painting. But Bran's full attention was focused on her. He knew about the coins. Macky had to find some way to get out of there. As if she were collapsing inside her crinoline petticoat, McKenzie Kathryn Calhoun did the only sensible, womanly thing. She fainted dead away.

Chapter Twelve

Macky's pretend faint scared the wits out of Bran, but he was able to act like a concerned husband long enough to get Macky out of the room. He didn't know what had set her off, but he could tell that she was ready to bolt.

Sylvia Mainwearing insisted on taking Macky upstairs to rest, shooing Bran out the door until the servants had made her comfortable.

"Now," Sylvia was saying, "we'll just get you out of your gown and into a wrapper. You can take a nice rest while I see that the men are fed."

"Thank you," Macky said gratefully, hoping that her tone was reasonably faint. "But I'll be fine. You go back to your guests."

The older woman studied Macky carefully, then agreed, but had one of the maids sit by the bed to watch over Macky. Mrs. Mainwearing gave her one last concerned look, then slipped out of the room and closed the door behind her.

Bran was waiting in the hall. "Is she all right?"

"She's fine, Reverend Adams. The mayor explained that your wife is with child. These things are to be expected. Shall we rejoin the others?"

Bran knew he had to talk to his employer sometime and this was as good a time as any. "Mrs. Mainwearing, is there somewhere we could talk, privately?"

Sylvia quirked an eyebrow, then nodded. "Of course. My private sitting room is just down the hall."

"That will be fine."

Bran followed her, rehearsing his story, wishing he had the wisdom that his Indian father had always predicted. Sylvia left the door ajar, but didn't bother to light more than the one lamp.

"What did you want to talk about, Reverend Adams?"

"Let's begin with my name. I think you know me better by Night Eyes. I'm sorry to have misled you, but as you know, I always keep my identity secret when I start a job."

Sylvia's eyes widened. Then she started to laugh. "You're my half-breed gunfighter? With an eye patch? I don't believe it. I will have to say that you're the least likely looking preacher I've ever seen. What did you do with the real one?"

"He died on the way here. I buried him on the trail. I didn't plan to assume his identity, but it happened and then it seemed like it was meant to be."

"Heaven-sent," she quipped. "Yes, I can see how you would. But how'd you get his wife to go along?"

"Macky isn't his wife. She—well, she doesn't figure in our situation. Now, we don't have much time. Suppose you tell me what's been happening."

For the next few minutes, Sylvia Mainwearing described how after Moose's death, the original prospectors had been scared off, followed by the attacks on her mine and her gold shipments.

"It's as if that outlaw knows exactly what I'm doing and when I'm doing it."

"And you have no idea who is behind it?"

"Well, obviously it's somebody who wants my money. The truth is, it could be anybody. It could even be somebody in Denver whom I don't know."

"What about the marshal?"

"Judge Hardcastle brought him here. He's done all he can. He's sent guards along with my shipments, he's posted his own men at the mine. I'm at my wit's end. The townspeople are tired of their men getting shot up. They're beginning to resent me so much that I don't even go into town. What am I going to do?"

"We need their help, Mrs. Mainwearing. The first thing I want you to do is get to know those people in town."

"I wouldn't know how."

"Well, I can think of one way. They're holding a housewarming for us, to help furnish Kelley's shack, the new parsonage. Why don't you come?"

He expected an argument, but to his surprise, she thought about it for a moment, then nodded. "Do you think they'd mind?"

"I don't think so, but it's a perfect way to get things started. People are inclined to gossip at social occasions, let things slip because they're among friends."

"Wouldn't it be better just to announce that you're here? Every crook in the West knows about Night Eyes."

"Yes, but nobody actually knows me. They think I'm a half-breed who lives a mysterious life as a loner. One of the conditions of my employment is that nobody gives out my description. You were told that, weren't you?"

Sylvia looked as if she wanted to disagree. "Yes," she finally said, "but wouldn't your reputation as a gunfighter be enough to stop him?"

"It just might make him lay low until I'm gone. I need everyone to believe that I'm trustworthy, that I'll be able to help them. That's where you can help."

"How?"

"You say that the people in town resent you, maybe it's because they think you are only using them, taking without giving back."

Sylvia gave him a look of sheer disbelief. "What in hell does that mean?"

"It means that what man takes from the earth, he must share for the good of all. You may have all the money in Heaven, but you don't have respect, and I think that may make a difference. Make a contribution to the church and see what happens."

"I might go to a housewarming, but I don't believe in all that religious stuff. Why should I give my gold to build their church?"

"You don't have to believe in religion to know that the Lord giveth and the Lord taketh away, Mrs. Mainwearing. You've seen it personally. Oh, I don't think God is responsible for your trouble, but you never know. Now, I want to check on my wife."

"All right, Reverend Adams, I'll go along with your plan, but only for a time. If you don't find out who's behind this soon, I'm going to tell the town that Night Eyes is here."

Back in her room, Macky was quietly steaming. Her fainting spell hadn't worked. She'd expected Bran to take her back to the saloon so she could find a way to get rid of the coins before Clara Gooden identified the minister's wife as the person spending Sylvia Mainwearing's gold.

Once the marshal learned she was a thief, he'd start asking questions about Bran. Macky had put him in danger and he'd only tried to help her. She was surrounded by predators, waiting to pounce.

And more than that, Macky had to find a way to escape Bran before he kissed her silly again and she lost whatever common sense she still had. The first thing she had to do was get rid of the maid guarding her.

That idea was temporarily set aside when the door opened and Bran slipped in, his face laced with concern. At his request, the maid stepped outside the door, giving them more privacy than Macky wanted.

"What's the matter, Macky?" he asked, perching lightly on the side of her bed.

She gave what she hoped was a convincing sigh and closed her eyes. "I'll be fine. Just go back to the party and don't worry about me."

"Don't lie to me. You aren't expecting so don't try to blame your little faint on that. What are you really up to?" Bran's hand lightly cupped her jaw, forcing her to face him.

"Honestly, Bran, it just happened. I think it might be this corset. Polly trussed me up like a Christmas goose and I can hardly breathe."

"You do look a little flushed," he admitted, still not willing to accept her story at face value. Without knowing what he was doing, Bran's fingertips moved down her chin toward the open neckline of her dress.

Macky gasped. It was becoming harder and harder to appear faint when her pulse was racing like wildfire, and the color in her face wasn't from fever. With Bran looking at her as if he were ready to strangle her and the marshal downstairs ready to send her to jail, she couldn't think straight.

"I've already caused you enough trouble. I—I mean it came on me so suddenly. I feel really ill, Bran. I'd like to go home—I mean back to the saloon please, before . . ."

"Tell me the truth, Macky. You aren't sick, are you?"

"I'm very uncomfortable, Bran. I really don't feel well."

She was going to brazen it out unless he could find a way to force her to explain. He needed to know what upset her. He couldn't carry this off without knowing the facts.

"Maybe you are coming down with a fever," he said, filling the washbasin with water and dipping a cloth into it. He wrung it, then began to wipe her face and neck. "I believe you'll be more comfortable if you have a bit more breathing room." He loosened a button, then another, his cloth roaming farther beneath her chemise and across her nipples. Bran felt her tremble.

When he started his caresses, he'd only intended to rattle her enough to learn the truth. But now that her breasts were visible in the lamplight he couldn't stop. God, how smooth and soft she was, how yielding.

If only they were back in their room at the saloon. If only she weren't so damned appealing. He was fully hard and he wanted nothing more than to push up her skirt and take her, right here, with a room filled with people below.

"Tell me what happened, Macky, you'll feel better."

"No! You're just saying sweet things to me again, Bran. And I want you to stop, right this minute!" Despite her words, he could tell she was aroused, maybe as much as he was.

"You're a very tempting woman, Macky. Since you do seem set on pretending to be my wife, maybe we should do more than pretend."

"Damn you," she swore. If he'd just kept touching her, coaxing her body into such wild yearnings, she wouldn't have stopped him. But he had to exact a price for his silence.

She sat up, her face flushed, her dress open and her breasts exposed. "I understand what you're asking, Bran, and you and I both know that I can't stop you. I can't imagine why you'd want me, but if this is what it takes to keep your silence, I'll pay your price. So do what you have to and stop torturing me."

Pay his price? She couldn't imagine that he'd want her? That was such a lie that he almost laughed. What in hell could she have done that was so bad that she thought she had to buy her freedom?

He wanted her like hell, but if he made love to McKenzie Kathryn Calhoun, it had to be because she wanted it, not because she was paying a debt.

He covered her breasts and stood.

"No, Macky. Not like this. I've never done a thing like that before and I won't now."

"I wouldn't have stopped you."

"I know. But a woman deserves respect. She deserves to be honored. I don't know what kind of dark secret you carry but I won't hurt you to learn it. I'll wait."

"For what?"

Until I've found the man I'm after. Until the man who is after you is satisfied. But he couldn't say that without doing more explaining than he wanted to do. Macky was the kind of woman who'd go after the crooks herself. No, he'd have to mislead her.

"Until you're ready to be honest with me."

She wanted to laugh. Honest? He wanted her to be honest with him? Did he expect her to confess that he was driving her crazy with wanting?

Did he not know about her part in the robbery? He had seen the coins, but did he look close enough to see the S engraved on them? Maybe not after the attack on the stage, but back in the room he'd mentioned her hidden money under the mattress. She sighed. Trying to control a lie was like trying to stop the spread of a broken egg, it simply slid through all her attempts to contain it.

"Does honesty work both ways?" she finally asked.

Bran turned back from the door and looked down at her. She was considering his offer. Her honesty for his. And he couldn't do that, and be sure she was safe.

He had a job to do, and for the first time he was allowing something else to interfere with his duty. Sylvia Mainwearing had paid for his services, not Macky. Yet she'd become as important as his mission. When had instinct become need? He didn't know.

Bran made a rare adjustment of his eye patch. He'd been given the name Eyes That See in Darkness and told that someday he'd learn why. He'd always believed his gift would lead him to the man who'd murdered his family, to the man whose laugh haunted Bran's dreams. He'd never doubted his quest, until now.

Now, Macky had distracted him and he didn't have the

power to resist her. He had to stop what was happening between them.

"You know I'm not a man of God, Macky. But I won't give you away, not yet. I'll keep your secret for now, but someday you'll have to face what happened to you, why you left Promise. It might not matter to the world, but it will to the man you love."

The man you love. That was an earth-shattering thought.

"You're not really a preacher, Bran. You don't have to be so noble. Since you're not in love with me, it won't matter in the end anyway, will it?" She turned her face to the wall and wished he would go.

"I don't know," he whispered.

He opened the door, and slammed it behind him. Moments later, Macky heard it open again as the serving girl reentered.

She was confused. Was Bran telling her that he couldn't love her? Wouldn't love her?

Who was he? Was what he made her feel a sin? What if they truly were married, would that change his anger? And why was he hiding in Heaven?

More importantly, she knew if she were discovered as the only one to spend coins minted with an *S*, Bran would be held accountable. She'd put him in danger.

To protect this man, Macky had to run away.

With an expression of anxiety, Macky sat up and peered beneath the bed, but the servant didn't respond. "I have to relieve myself." Macky said finally. The girl brought a chamber pot from behind a screen and placed it by the bed.

"You can leave now," Macky told her. When she made no attempt to do so, Macky stood, took the chair by the door and placed it outside, motioning for the maid to go. Reluctantly, the girl complied, and Macky locked the door behind her, before quickly shucking her crinolines.

Moments later, Macky made her escape, stepping through one of the windows onto the veranda that wrapped around the house, and tripped down the outer stairwell to the ground.

She would have gotten away, had it not been for the violent explosion that turned the sky into a shower of fire. Footsteps pounded. Doors opened and the guests suddenly joined Macky outside the house, staring in horror at the blaze that roiled up in the night sky in the distance.

"The mine!" Mrs. Mainwearing cried out.

Then the men were rushing toward the flames that had turned the sky an angry orange, shooting sparks into the blackness like the explosion of a Chinese firecracker. This time it was Macky who comforted Mrs. Mainwearing.

Bran and the marshal outdistanced the judge. By the time they got to the mine, fire was spewing out the mouth of the tunnel. The screams of a man inside spurred Bran toward the entrance. But the flames were too hot. He glanced around calmly to assess the situation. One thing he'd learned was that rushing into the center of a problem wasn't smart.

At the end of the rail tires that exited the tunnel were rough wooden carts used to move the ore from inside. Nearby, a trough still piped water down a sluice and into a stream that joined Pigeon Creek.

"Help me, Larkin. Let's swing the trough around and fill the cart with water."

Larkin understood Bran's intention and began pushing his weight against the rickety conveyance. Together they ripped the lower extension away, allowing the water to pour into the cart. Bran discarded his coat, submerging it into the water, wetting it thoroughly. Once the cart was full, he climbed in, took hold of the tongue inside the cart and began pumping it up and down. With help from the marshal, the cart rolled back inside the mine.

As the cart reached the flames, Bran took a deep breath and ducked his head beneath the water. He had no idea where the man was, but he figured that he could follow the sound of the screams.

Finally, just as the cart came to a jolting stop, Bran realized the screams had hushed. He lifted his jacket and raised his head into the heat. The inside of the tunnel had apparently collapsed at the site of the explosion. The cart could go no farther. A crackling fire eating at the support beams gave off enough light so that he could see the man leaning against the debris.

"Help me . . ." The voice was barely more than a moan.

Quickly Bran climbed over the side and fought his way to the man. Behind him a second cart rolled down the rails and crashed against the first one. Marshal Larkin climbed out and started toward the downed man. As he and Bran lifted the burned victim they heard the second cart start to roll.

"What the hell?" Bran looked over his shoulder.

"There's someone else. He's running away," Larkin said.

"Go after him," Bran yelled out. "I've got this one."

The marshal covered his head with his arms, ran behind the moving cart, and pulled himself inside.

Bran fought the intense heat and struggled to lift the injured man over his shoulder and get him into the badly leaking ore cart. There was little water left now and the smoke was so bad that he could barely breathe.

For a moment, Bran was thrust back into the past. He still felt the pain of the arrow in his eye when he'd come to and found the cabin filled with smoke so thick that he couldn't find his sister and mother. Only because his father's body lay near the doorway did he stumble over it. But even then, he couldn't pull the heavy man outside.

He refused to let it happen again. Grimly he climbed into the cart and, wetting his jacket once more, covered his head and began to pump. Beams fell and the smoke choked him, but Bran refused to stop. Finally, just when he felt as if his lungs would burst, they were in the open.

As the onlookers pulled the injured man from the cart, it was obvious that Bran's efforts had been in vain.

"Did you catch the other one, Larkin?" Bran asked as he staggered toward the lawman.

"No, the fool hit me and knocked me down. Before I could get up, he'd dropped over the front of the cart and disappeared. I lost him in the dark."

"Are you hurt?" the judge asked, coming to Bran's side.

"Well, let's just say I don't look forward to the fires of hell," Bran said, studying the marshal, who'd obviously fared better than either Bran or the man he'd rescued.

The miners had set up a bucket brigade and begun dousing the flames. Back at the main house, both the marshal and the judge recounted the heroics of Brother Adams, who'd risked his own life trying to save the fatally injured men who'd been trapped there.

"Too bad the other one escaped," Bran said. "He might be able to tell us who hired him."

Bran declined Sylvia's offer of assistance and climbed into his wagon, directing Macky to take them back to town. He'd said he wasn't hurt, but Macky took one look at the singed clothing and soot on his face and knew that Bran was not a man who willingly revealed his weakness.

He'd saved the stage from bandits who would have stolen her gold and paper money. He'd gotten her to safety and then gone back for Jenks. He'd protected her from Pratt by allowing her to pretend she was his wife, and now he'd risked his life to rescue the criminal intent on destroying the Sylvia. Her plan to leave would have to wait until she knew that he was all right—whatever the risk.

Lorraine met them at the saloon door, took one look at Bran's smoke-smeared face and ruined clothes and went into action. Before Macky could argue, he'd been taken to their room and was about to be undressed and bathed.

"Get the burn salve," Lorraine directed her girls, "and tear some bandages from a bed sheet."

Macky leaned against the wall and felt a stab of jealousy.

as another woman took care of the man who was supposed to be her husband. When Lorraine began to remove Bran's clothing, Macky roused herself.

"Thank you, Lorraine," she said, pushing herself between the saloonkeeper and the bed. "But I'll do that."

Bran's eyelids flickered open. "You're still here?" he asked and Macky wasn't sure whether he was relieved or resigned.

"Of course," she replied, then stopped and waited until Lorraine backed away and left the room. Once they were alone, Macky unfastened and stepped out of the petticoats that interfered with her nursing. She began to unfasten the buttons of his shirt.

"This isn't very smart of you," he said.

"Maybe not."

"But then, you've always found trouble if it was to be had, haven't you?"

She pulled the shirt from his body and began to clean his face gently with a cloth.

"You did this for me earlier tonight when I was . . . sick."

"Yes, but that was different."

"How?"

He groaned. "I thought you were only pretending to be ill."

She rinsed her cloth and began washing lower. "I was." She watched his skin pucker, the way his nipples retracted into tight little balls beneath the hair that covered his chest. "I was running away when the explosion occurred."

"I would have come after you."

"I know, Bran. Be still."

He should stop her, but he couldn't move. Tired beyond belief, with the hair on his arms singed and his muscles aching so that he could hardly lift his head, he lay, letting himself feel the warmth of a woman's touch, listening to a confession that only bound them closer. He knew it was foolish, that it couldn't last. That it wasn't smart to lower his defenses enough to respond to an emotion that wasn't only physical.

But her eyes were filled with concern and for just this one night he wanted to take what she was giving. "You ought to have let Lorraine do this."

"Why, shame on you, Reverend Adams. The very idea. Lorraine is a single lady." She rinsed her cloth again and turned her attention to his arms. "I have to clean your skin so that I can treat your burns." Carefully she washed away the evidence of the fire and the soot, until she'd bathed his upper body completely. When she reached for his drawers, he grabbed her wrists and held them tightly.

She could see the war in his eyes. Gone was the amusement he used as the shield to hide his need. He wanted this, yet he was struggling to deny himself the pleasure of her touch.

"You don't understand, Macky. Don't give me lofty ideals. Forget everything I said tonight. No matter what I claim, underneath I'm only a man."

"I understand that," she said. "But I have to do this for you." She reached down and unfastened his trousers.

To her credit she didn't gasp when she saw the unadorned results of her touch.

To his credit, he didn't flinch or try to hide his state of arousal when she washed the spot on his thigh where his trousers had been burned away.

"I'm sorry. I'm going to have to hurt you."

"I've been hurt worse."

"Your eye?" she asked quietly, continuing her ministrations.

"That, and the pain that comes from watching people you love brutally murdered and not being able to stop it."

"Your family?" She tried to focus on something other than his desire. "Tell me about them."

"My mother died trying to save my sister. They'd already killed my father. I tried to stop them, but I couldn't. After the bastards were through, they shot them with arrows and scalped them to make it look like Indians had done it."

She ripped the trousers and his drawers off, exposing his red-streaked feet and ankles. His worst injury was on his thigh, where the trousers had been burned, leaving a slashing mark. Macky risked looking at him. He'd closed his eyes.

"But you knew different," she said softly. Her voice seemed to distract him, almost without knowing he was doing so, he described the carnage that had so affected his life as a young boy.

"Were they caught?"

"No. But they will be, at least one of them will. The one who told the others what to do."

Despite his iron-willed control, the grim set of his lips told her how painful that deeply buried memory was. She looked down at this stern, dangerous man and knew how much she was beginning to care.

"There," she finally said, as she began applying the salve. "You don't appear to be burned so much as bruised. I think you'll feel better by morning."

Bran let out a deep breath, trying desperately to prevent what was about to happen, then gave in and pulled her across his body.

"Nothing will take care of my problem, McKenzie Kathryn Calhoun, except this."

When he kissed her, Macky didn't even try to pull away. She accepted him, both the intrusion of his tongue in her mouth and the feel of his rough hands on her body. She couldn't mount a protest, couldn't even find a reason to do it. She'd known how he felt, almost waited for him to claim her. This time he wouldn't stop.

Macky held herself very still. Only a low moan gave voice to her own desire. His heart was racing and when he pulled his lips from hers and moved down toward her breasts she couldn't hold back a gasp.

Through the haze of his desire Bran heard her surprised

cry. What was he doing? He'd sworn to protect her, to keep her from being hurt, and he was the one about to do her the most harm.

So what if she was giving him her permission, giving herself to him freely and with trust? It was that very trust that had to stop him. Sweat beaded his forehead. His body was screaming. His desire had stretched him almost past the point of no return, but he reached deep inside and forced himself to find the strength he needed. Gradually he was able to move her to her back beside him.

"No, darling Macky. Forgive me for behaving badly. I won't do this to you."

"What's wrong with me, Bran?"

"It isn't you," he groaned, "it's me. I won't take you just to satisfy my lust."

"What—" Her voice choked in her throat. "What if I wanted you to satisfy mine?"

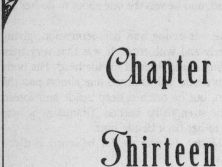

Chapter Thirteen

 Bran had never thought much about heaven or hell until Macky came into his life. At this moment he believed in both.

Earlier, she had found her own way of escape. She'd fainted. If it worked for her, it could work for him. For once he intentionally took the coward's route. Bran groaned, and pretended to pass out.

Macky swore in frustration.

If Bran thought that concern over the state of his health would stop Macky's inquisitive nature, he was wrong. It only gave her free license to examine his body.

She touched his lips, examining them intently with her fingertips before trailing them downward. As her caresses moved lower and lower, Bran felt the muscles in his stomach tighten, and the expansion of that part of him she examined next.

Bran bordered on total loss of control at Macky's touch

and whisper of awe. In another minute he'd have her beneath him and he'd—

"Ohhh!" he moaned, and turned over, shielding himself in self-defense. He couldn't believe what was happening. All he had to do was lie back and enjoy it, but he had to refuse what he wanted, what she needed as badly as he.

"I'm sorry, Bran," she said. "I didn't mean to hurt you. I really didn't."

He felt the bed move as she lay down beside him. From her restlessness he realized that she was as aroused as he. Only she didn't understand and he couldn't bring her to fulfillment.

"Oh, Lord, give me strength!" Macky's voice quivered as she spoke the words. "Make me strong. Make me— Ah, hell." She turned toward him, threw her leg across his thigh and her arm over his back. "There has to be more to being a wife than this. And you just look out, John Brandon. Sooner or later, I intend to find out what it is."

Once Macky finally fell asleep, Bran turned over, feasted his eyes reluctantly on her lush body and pouting lips, then reluctantly extricated himself from her embrace.

God had tempted David with Bathsheba and David had sinned. He'd tempted Sampson with Delilah and he'd lost his power. Now Bran was poised at the edge of the fiery furnace and the flames were coming closer and closer. He'd better find somewhere else to sleep.

The floor was not far enough away, but it would have to do. He didn't even need a blanket. He was burning with a heat that nothing could cool.

Not even sleep.

By the time Bran made it to the boardinghouse for an early breakfast the next morning, it was common knowledge that the man he'd rescued was a stranger. Preston Cribbs suggested Bran join the other members of the city government who were meeting down at the jail to discuss the implication of the explosion.

He'd managed to escape before Macky waked and now all he wanted to do was stay away.

"You don't look too bad," Larkin observed as Preston Cribbs and Bran entered the jail.

"Just singed a bit here and there," Bran said. "You?"

"About the same. We're both lucky, I guess."

"What about the explosion?" Preston asked.

"Accident, or deliberate, we'll never know," the marshal said as the men gathered in the vacant jail built by the citizens of Heaven.

"You don't believe the explosion was an accident, do you?" Bran asked. The other men, Otis Gooden, Preston Cribbs, and Hank Clay, each gave a reluctant shake of the head.

"Without witnesses, there's no way to prove anything," Marshal Larkin said, his wariness of Bran clear in his eyes.

"You didn't recognize him, Marshal?" Bran met the marshal's gaze, not hiding his doubt.

"Nope, and once I've seen a man's face, I don't usually forget him. It's a talent I have."

"Too bad he got away," Hank Clay observed in an unusual voicing of his opinion.

Otis Gooden agreed. "These things happen all the time around here. A man decides to do a little prospecting on his own and he blows himself and everything around him to blazes."

"Maybe," Bran allowed. What no one had said was that the man Bran had rescued had a stab wound in his chest. The marshal seemed ready to pass the wound off as being caused by the explosion, but Bran wasn't so certain.

"And maybe," Hank went on, "no reflection on you, Larkin, we ought to find us a local man to keep an eye on things. It's time we started making use of the talent we have right here in Heaven."

Preston cast a critical eye on the blacksmith. "What do you mean, Hank?"

"We need a full-time sheriff and I think that we ought to start a school."

Bran studied the blacksmith. He'd heard the man kept to himself, but he seemed more observant and wise than he was being given credit for. "I understand you've had several law officers," Bran commented.

"Yes," Cribbs confessed. "But as I told you, they don't last long in Heaven."

"Don't know why Moose ever called this place Heaven. He should have gone with its original name," Otis Gooden said in disgust.

Bran flexed his knee, still sore from the rescue. "Original name?"

"Early prospectors called the trail leading into the area Hell," Otis Gooden was saying.

Hank Clay tucked a pinch of tobacco between his lip and his gum with two soot-covered fingers. "It might have been cut out of the wilderness with good intentions, but folks used to say that once you got here, you either went to Heaven, or the other direction."

"Yep," Otis agreed. "Now they just say if you want to go to Heaven, you've got to go through Hell first."

Bran studied the men, trying to decide how best to phrase his questions. Being a preacher was a new experience for him. He was finding that people weren't always as open with a preacher as they were with a man carrying a gun.

"Mrs. Mainwearing seems to be the one hardest hit. But she seems determined to hold on," Bran said, abruptly changed the subject.

"If anyone can, she will," Preston Cribbs answered. "It's still hard to believe old Moose is gone. We miss him a lot."

"You miss him *now*," Otis corrected. "But there were times when us merchants could have done without his rowdy binges. And I know Lorraine could have. Sorry,

Preacher, but Moose did get a little out of hand before he married Miss Sylvia."

"Out of hand?" Bran inquired.

"Moose was good to us, all right. He brought all us to town and carried us till we could get set up," Otis explained.

Then Hank added wryly, "But there was times that we had to send up to Denver to restock after Moose tore the town apart."

"But about the accidents." Bran drew the conversation back to the issue. "Was Moose the only victim?"

This time it was the marshal who responded. "No, all of the prospectors have had a hard time of it. Of course, Heaven is no different from a hundred other mining settlements. Once Moose struck it rich, the hills were crawling with miners. There were tents every ten feet along Coyote Creek. They'd get enough dust to get drunk, then they'd gamble their claims away, or worse."

"Sometimes they started killing each other," Otis added.

"Anybody in Heaven seem to get more prosperous?" Bran asked.

"No, truth is, once the miners drifted off, things seemed to die down," Preston said thoughtfully.

"Yeah," Otis agreed, "even the bank closed. Moved all the money over to Promise."

That caught Bran's attention. "You mean the banker in Promise owned both banks?"

"Not any more. According to my Express rider, the banker got shot in the holdup."

The blacksmith spat a stream of tobacco out the open door. "Too many people connected to Heaven are dead, starting with Moose. Prospectors go missing or get murdered. Folks thought it was for their claims, but now I ain't sure. Kelley never found much color and he lost his wife."

"That's the man who built the shack—I mean cabin—you've refinished for us?"

"Yep, and speaking of that, we ought to get back to the hotel and collect your missus," Preston Cribbs said, getting to his feet. "We need to get you settled in the cabin before tomorrow."

Bran cast a cautious eye on the mayor. "Why?"

"Because we'll be having a little housewarming for you on Saturday night, before your first service on Sunday. You remember, I told you that the ladies would be bringing a few things to make you more comfortable."

First sermon. Housewarming? Christ! Bran suspected that Macky would be as happy to hear about that as he was.

The others fell in behind the mayor, marching up the sidewalk toward the hotel.

Bran moved more slowly than the rest, using his burns as an excuse to fall back to the marshal's side. "How long will you be here, Larkin?" he asked.

"Depends. I was about to head out when that explosion happened. Now, I don't know. Not that I'm convinced that it was deliberate," he added, "but Sylvia Mainwearing is an important woman in the territory. If this keeps happening, it might be safer for her to move into Denver."

"Is she likely to?" Bran asked curiously.

"Sylvia has had her pick of any man in the territory and she hasn't accepted any of them yet. She's determined to keep her money under her control. But she isn't safe any more. I tried to get her to let me recommend a good man to protect her, but she refused."

Bran knew that Mrs. Mainwearing had only refused the marshal's help, not the idea.

"You wouldn't be a candidate for her hand, would you?" Bran asked and was rewarded with a flinch which Larkin tried to cover by cutting his eyes to the hills and back at the street.

"Me? What makes you think I'd throw my hat in that ring?"

"I don't know. Even a marshal might like the idea of marrying a wealthy woman."

"Hell, no! A marshal makes a poor husband. And even if I was interested in a woman, it would likely be somebody like Lorraine who still recognizes that the man is in charge. With a woman like Sylvia I'd be afraid she'd hog-tie me and put her brand on my bottom."

Bran had heard enough lies in his time to recognize one when he heard it. The marshal was interested in Mrs. Mainwearing all right. But was it the woman, or the gold, that drew him? And did Lorraine know?

What was more to the point, did Macky know that the wagon piled high with goods parked outside the saloon was meant for her? He wondered if she'd really recognized the mule he'd bought, the one she'd called Solomon. He was already feeling a bit foolish for having made the arrangements with Hank, but they needed a mule, he told himself, if they intended to give the impression that they were settling in.

One look at Macky, as she came through the swinging doors dragging her portmanteau, told him that he was right about the mule. "Solomon," she said and broke into a smile.

For Bran, one look at Macky took him right back to the night before and he knew exactly how David and Samson felt.

Preston Cribbs and Hank Clay rode ahead, leaving Bran and Macky to follow along in the wagon. At the rear of the wagon they'd tied a roan-colored mare which Hank had offered to let Bran use until Bran could pick out one of his own.

The sun was high in the sky and not a cloud could be seen. In the distance the mountain peaks were still frosted white and Pigeon Creek was lapping at its banks from the melting snow.

Bran didn't mention the night before and neither did Macky. She hadn't expected to enjoy the morning. She didn't even know why she was still in Heaven. Until the explosion had occurred, she'd planned to be past Denver by now.

She hadn't seen Pratt that morning, but she knew he had to be around, waiting and watching. She had to be very careful. One false step could result in a prison term for her and put Bran in danger. She still didn't know why he was in Heaven, but her instincts told her that it had something to do with his family.

Knowing all that, she'd still packed her new clothes and the money in her traveling case and followed Lorraine down the steps to the wagon that was carrying her straight into a life of seduction and secrets.

Lorraine gave Macky a parting gift of a red feather quill and an absurdly small umbrella. "Are you sure you want me at the housewarming?"

"Of course I do, and bring Letty, too."

"Oh, Mrs. Adams, you're going to set this town on its ear. And I want to be there to see it. Thank you."

Macky had been a bit worried about leaving until she saw Solomon. Somehow when she saw her contrary old mule, it made her think everything would be fine.

Now, instead of taking flight as she'd planned, Macky was decked out in her gingham day dress, holding an umbrella and riding across the plains like a real preacher's wife out for a Sunday drive.

She ought to thank Bran for his kindness, but she didn't know what to say.

"Is he ours?" Macky finally whispered. "The mule?"

"You seemed to like him," he said.

"But that means . . . Surely you don't really expect us to move out here and set up housekeeping?" Macky asked under her breath as they rode along.

"Set up housekeeping? Never thought I'd hear that phrase in connection with me," Bran admitted wryly. "Never expected to be married, pretend or otherwise."

"But we aren't really married, Reverend Adams. It's more a matter of mutual need, I'd say. You need me and I need you."

He took in her perky umbrella and red hair. "A truer statement was never made, but I don't have to like it."

"Well—well—neither do I. I didn't ask to get gussied up last night and go to dinner with those men and I didn't ask to move out of the saloon."

"Moving out of the saloon into a cabin in the hills may test both our resolves, Mrs. Adams, but I don't see any way out of it."

"I suppose you'd rather stay at Lorraine's."

"Wouldn't folks talk?"

Macky gave Bran a grin of mock exasperation. "Somehow, I didn't suppose that you would worry about gossip."

Bran lifted his eyebrow at that charge. It wasn't the first time his wife-in-name had shown her sense of humor. He liked her willingness to accept hardship, but he wasn't certain how far her sense of propriety would go.

"Gossip doesn't bother me," Bran admitted, "but impropriety, now, that could be a problem." Bran gave a tsking sound and covered it nicely with a flick of the reins. "Impropriety could be considered a sin, or at least an undesirable trait in a minister's wife."

"I don't know how to be proper and I'm not your wife," she protested.

"You are for now." He grinned. "And I'm looking forward to some good homecooked meals."

Macky didn't swallow her tongue, but she came close. She could ride a horse, brand a cow, plant and harvest a garden. But cook? Not her.

Still, what choice did she have, short of confessing her crime? None. So long as Bran continued to go along with their ruse, so would she.

The wagon was unloaded and the supplies brought inside. Macky stood in the middle of the one-room cabin and looked around in dismay. Even the farmhouse where she'd lived with her father and brother hadn't been this bad.

Granted, there was a wood floor, a good fireplace, a table and a loft. But it was the rope bed in the corner that held her attention.

One bed.

Apparently unaware of her confusion, Bran directed the members of the congregation as to where the items should be placed.

"Take Mrs. Adams's carrying case up to the loft," he said. "For the time being I believe that she'd like to store her belongings up there. Wouldn't you, dear?"

Macky could only nod. Anything to remove the remainder of the gold coins from possible discovery.

Eventually the salt, flour, meal, and canned goods were arranged on the shelf over the worktable. The bacon and dried beef had been hung from the ceiling in the pantry outside the kitchen door. And she had enough pans to cook and enough bedclothes to cover the cornshuck mattress.

Macky allowed their helpers to think that she was simply overcome by the generosity of the congregation. In truth she was scared to death. So she had flour and meal and meat, what did she know about preparing it?

Papa had been the cook at home. Even after he became so ill that he could do little more than sit in a chair by the stove and stir a pot, he managed to feed himself and Macky. In the end all he could eat was broth, and Macky had learned to boil meat and stir in a bit of mush.

"We'll be getting back to town now," Preston Cribbs said as he looked around the cabin and smiled.

"Yep," Hank agreed. "All you'll have to do tomorrow night is make the coffee and have a cook fire."

"Thank you," Bran responded, standing beside Macky and sliding his arm around her waist. "We'll be ready."

"Good evening, then," the two men said, and turned to leave.

"Oh, by the way," Bran called out. "Mrs. Mainwearing will be coming."

Hank gave a disbelieving laugh. "She's going to mingle with the common folk?"

"Don't joke, Hank," Preston ventured. "You never know, she might. Long as Lorraine won't be here. She's never forgiven her for knowing Moose first."

"Knowing Moose first?" Macky's heart plunged to her shoes. *Please, God, don't do this to me.*

"I think you'll be pleased to know," Bran said as they watched the wagon pull away from the cabin, "that Sylvia agreed that she ought to mix with the townspeople more. It isn't much, but it's a first step."

"Yeah," Macky agreed, "to a war. I invited Lorraine."

Bran narrowed his eyes and stared at the wagon disappearing in the distance. "Macky, sometimes things have to get worse to get better. Lorraine and Sylvia might like each other if they gave it a chance."

"Bran, let's not get carried away with this Messenger of God business. You're not Adams and this isn't the Garden of Eden."

"I don't know," Bran observed, looking at the splotches of new growth dabbled across the plains like colors in a paintbox. "I wasn't there of course, but this could be a kind of Garden of Eden."

"I know that story," Macky said in a resigned tone. "This may look like the Garden of Eden to you, but there's one problem."

"What would that be, Macky?"

"The Garden of Eden came with a snake."

Chapter

Fourteen

AND THEN THEY WERE ALONE.

The silence was deafening. It shimmered like heat rising from the floor of the desert in the middle of the day. The only sound in the cabin came from a cricket, hiding somewhere in the stack of wood beside the fireplace.

"I'd better check on the animals," Bran said, moving toward the door as if he too was being affected by the feeling in the air.

"What should I do?" Macky asked, trying to shake her discomfort.

"It's late. Fix us something to eat and we'll forget about food later," he called over his shoulder.

"But—wait, just a minute!" Macky went after Bran. He was acting cold and distant like he had in the beginning. She might as well get this straight right away. "What do you mean, fix something to eat?"

"Cook, as in make biscuits. Make coffee. Fry some bacon. Surely you can do that."

She bit back a sharp retort. He did have a right to expect something from her. And God knew there was little enough that she had to offer. Preparing a meal shouldn't be too difficult, even without her father's directions.

"Fine, I'll see what I can do."

"You do know," he said seriously, "that we have to make this work, for a while anyway."

"When are you going to tell me what you're really doing here, Bran?"

"Like you, I can't tell you without putting you in danger. Just be careful, Macky."

She glanced behind him at Solomon. "Should I be afraid of you?"

"Maybe you should."

Macky had felt many things for this dangerous man who'd brought such new emotions into her life, but curiously, fear wasn't one of them.

"Well, I'm not. But you do give me cause for concern. I go around feeling like I'm holding my breath, knowing I'm about to be lambasted by the wind and not being able to do a dad-blamed thing to stop it. And none of it makes a lick of sense."

"I know," he answered, his voice hoarse and grainy. "You should catch the next stage and find another way to hide from whoever is chasing you. I ought to make you go."

"Why?"

"Because I'm not a good man, Macky. I can't promise that I'll be able to keep my hands off you if you stay. And, you're interfering with my job here."

She took a half step toward him. "What job?" she asked again. "Why can't you tell me? I don't care if you're not a minister. In fact, I'd be in a pickle if you were. And I trust you, John Brandon, no matter what you are."

He looked at her a long time before he answered.

"Don't trust me, Macky. There are dark things about me that you can't even imagine. I'll only hurt you."

"No you won't. And I may not know the truth about you, but I know that you're a good person. You're kind and caring. What's happened between us can't be bad, can it?"

Bran wanted to laugh. Oh, it was bad. How in hell was he going to be able to stay away from her when all he could think about was taking up where they'd stopped the night before?

"You're trouble, McKenzie Kathryn Calhoun."

"Because I know how to be honest about what I want?"

"And because you go after it."

"I do," she said. "I'd like you to kiss me, Bran. Just one kiss," she murmured, closing the space between them, justifying her need to be near him by telling herself that she'd probably end up in jail and never know what happened between a man and a woman. This was her only chance.

"Damn it to hell, Macky. You've got no business asking me to kiss you." Then every reservation disappeared as she lifted her face to meet his.

"Please, Bran."

Their lips touched, lightly at first, then more firmly. "Am I doing it right?" she asked as he nuzzled her neck.

"If you were doing it any better, I'd have you leaned against a tree with your legs around my waist—"

She opened her green eyes, wide with wonder. "Why on earth would you do that?"

"I wouldn't," he growled and thrust her away. "And I'm not. Macky, go back inside before I lose every ounce of control I have."

"Don't you like kissing me? I know that I'm inexperienced, but I thought I was learning. If there's something I'm doing wrong, just tell me. I'll fix it. We're going to have to spend a lot of time together. It seems to be a very pleasant way to spend some time, since we're married."

"We're not married, Macky. Not in the eyes of God."

"Oh, phoo! It seems to me that God wouldn't have made

something like this feel good unless it was all right for a body to feel it."

Bran let out an oath.

Macky was beginning to understand his frustration. She was feeling much the same thing herself. "So I make your body do crazy things. Good. I wouldn't want to think it was just me."

He would have taken her, right there, on the ground, except Solomon came meandering up and stopped next to them as if he were inspecting the proceedings.

"What the?"

Bran let go of her, blinking his eyes at the sight of the long-eared creature. "Thank God!"

"Solomon! You bad boy! I ought to turn you into fertilizer," Macky cried out. "Go away!"

The mule stamped his foot and let out an awful sound of complaint.

"Don't you argue with me. You ran off when I needed you and now . . . now . . ." She choked back her anger and frustration.

"He really is your mule?"

"Yes. I was riding him into Promise that day. He got spooked by a hawk and ran off. I would have had to walk. I should have walked, then I would have had plenty of time in town and none of this would have happened."

"What do you expect to do with him?"

"Plow our field, of course. Can you put him behind the fence with your horse?"

"Why not?" Bran caught the mule by the halter. "They're about as well suited as we are." By the time he secured the makeshift gate on the fence around the shed, Macky had left.

The source of his trouble was gone, but Bran was still as hard as a rock and even more frustrated.

Bran was as overwhelmed by Macky's innocence as her lack of guile. More and more he was convinced that whatever had happened to her was not of her choosing. Sooner or later he'd get the truth from her. But for now it was all a confusing mess. And he couldn't see it getting any easier.

Back in the cabin, Macky decided to change out of the dress and petticoat. Cooking biscuits would be enough of a challenge without having to worry about a skirt. Glancing out the window, she saw Bran filling the horse trough with water. She'd better hurry unless she wanted him to see how really inept she was.

She climbed the ladder to the loft, took a look around and felt her heart drop. Any idea she might have had of sleeping up there disappeared when she saw the dust on the floor and the spiderwebs strung to the low ceiling.

Quickly she removed her new clothes and donned her brother's trousers and shirt. The old work boots followed. As she shimmied down the ladder, she felt normal for the first time in days.

First she'd make a fire. Then she'd tackle the sack of flour. Making biscuits couldn't be that hard. She'd watched her father do it. All she needed was flour, grease, and milk. Well, maybe not milk. Water would have to do.

But first came the fire.

"That was a close call last night. The fire spread so fast, you almost got caught. Why'd you have to stab him?"

"Yeah, well, he figured it out and I had to move fast. I got the job done, didn't I?" Pratt, standing on the ground, looked up at the rider.

"At least he's dead. But I don't like bodies left lying around. People ask questions."

"Better than having somebody go looking for suspects."

"Next time, be more careful. What about the preacher? Did he get a look at you?"

"No, but it was close. Are you going to the housewarming?"

"Certainly. I want to know exactly what's happening.

Somebody in Heaven spent gold coins at the general store. I intend to know who."

I intend. Pratt bristled. That's the way he always talked. He made everybody who answered to him feel as if they were being looked down on, even when he wasn't on his horse. "Didn't that woman know who spent the money?"

"The forgetful Mrs. Clara Gooden couldn't recall. I think she was just afraid she'd have to give it back."

Pratt was getting tired of staring straight into the sun. "Some of the coins were probably used here in town anyway, weren't they?"

"Yes, Sylvia couldn't resist showing off the new engraving, but if she'd been the one who spent the gold, Clara would have said so."

"So, what happens now? I'm going stir-crazy with nothing to do out here. I'm ready to go back to town."

"Absolutely not. You're lucky somebody hasn't spotted you. We're too close to take any chances. Now this is what I want you to do."

Pratt took a step closer and smiled as the man on the horse gave his instructions.

Macky opened the sack of flour and took two hands full, dropping them in the chipped pottery bowl she found on the shelf. She needed grease. There was none. But grease came from frying bacon.

Macky sliced several chunks from a slab of bacon that Bran had brought from town. After almost singeing her eyelashes, she managed to set the skillet in the fire and plopped the bacon inside.

Moments later the sizzling bacon was spewing grease in the fire like gunpowder. Flames licked eagerly at the meat in the pan.

Macky's attempt to raise the skillet resulted in her pouring part of the grease directly into the fire and she had to jerk the pan away from the flames. Finally, with a burned finger and a splat of grease on her arm, Macky decided that if the bacon wasn't done, it was close enough.

She laid the meat on a plate, then poured some water from the kettle into the grease, sending a splattering cloud of smoke in the air. Finally, she stirred in the flour and shoved it back into the fire. Then she hung the kettle on a hook suspended from the other side of the fireplace.

By the time the water began to boil, her hair was hanging in wisps. Perspiration and soot ran down her face. And the smell from the skillet announced that at least the bottom of her bread was cooking, too much, too quickly.

"Horsefeathers!" she swore. "Even Solomon wouldn't eat this."

She squatted before the fire, wiping her forehead on her sleeve, wishing Papa had taught her to make bread, regretting her ignorance.

"What I deserve is 'just death, kind umpire of men's miseries,' eh, Mr. Shakespeare?"

A low familiar laugh answered. "Am I to assume 'there is death in the pot'?"

Macky came to her feet in a rush and whirled around. "Not yet, but I'm working on it. I think it was Aesop who said, 'don't count your chickens before they are hatched.' "

Bran walked past her and, wearing his gloves, lifted the skillet from the fire. "This looks—interesting. What is it?"

"Biscuits. That's what you ordered, isn't it?"

"I take it biscuits aren't your specialty?" He slid the edge of the knife under the clump of dough and, after several attempts, managed to turn the bread over. Shaking his head, he planted the skillet back over the fire and turned toward Macky.

Her eyes were shimmering with moisture, but Bran knew that the last thing he could expect from this woman was tears. She might very well swing the skillet at him, but she'd never apologize for her efforts.

"I don't think you have had any more experience cooking than I've had preaching," Bran said. "What exactly are you good at?"

"Plowing a field," she snapped. "Got one handy?"

He didn't mean to rile her further, but everything about her was deadly right now, especially her temper. Still, he couldn't contain a smile. Together they were like lightning in a storm, bouncing off the clouds and colliding with a streak of fire.

"Oh, Macky, what a treasure you are. How on earth are you going to manage what's ahead?" He took a handkerchief from his pocket, moistened it in a pool of water she'd sloshed from the kettle and began to wash her face.

"What are you doing?" she asked, her voice losing its fury as her stomach flipped at his touch.

"The question is, what have you been doing in here? You look like a scullery maid."

"That's probably a step up from being a farmer," she quipped. "And that's what I ought to be doing instead of this, if you don't want me to be a total embarrassment to you."

He found himself reassuring her. "Nothing you could do would embarrass me, Macky. If you can't cook, I'll teach you."

She groaned and closed her eyes. He couldn't mean that. If the truth came out, not only would she embarrass him, she'd be arrested. Instead of taking cooking lessons, she should take herself into town and confess her crime to the marshal.

But first, she had to make things right.

"There's something I need to tell you, Bran, about my past."

His fingers continued to hold her chin. "You don't need to explain anything to me."

"Yes I do. I never meant to get involved. By the time I was, it was too late. I shouldn't have kept going. I should have stayed to face my punishment."

"Macky, I know you. If you ran, you had reason."

She went on as if he hadn't spoken. "I saw him again, the man responsible. I was afraid he'd come after me."

Bran swore and pulled Macky into his arms. "Then there is a man involved."

"Not the way you think, Bran. I mean, we didn't even know each other. He just offered me a ride into town and it happened before I knew."

He didn't know what she was trying to say. She'd already told him that she wasn't going to have a baby, that her terrible secret could get her hung. Still, if there really was a man after her, Bran could protect her.

"I couldn't save my sister, but if I get my hands on the man who took advantage of you, Macky, I'll make him sorry he did."

"No," Macky said. "This man killed someone. He is very dangerous and he's after me because I—I have something he wants. I've made up my mind," she said. "I'll go into town and confess the truth to the marshal. I don't want to put you in danger."

The marshal, the same man who might recognize the preacher as a kid named John Lee who was still wanted for murder. He ought to let her go, if for no other reason than she wasn't safe with him. But if something happened and they took him away, who'd protect Macky?

"No, you can't do that," he said. "There are other things to consider."

His left hand was rubbing a circle on her back, spreading heat throughout her body. The intensity of his motion was even beginning to give off a scorched odor. "What other things, Bran?"

A burning smell.

"The biscuits! Bran, the biscuits are on fire."

This time when Bran attempted to rescue the skillet, he dropped it into the fire.

As if in an attempt to keep pace, the coffee boiled over,

falling into the pan, dousing the flames and spitting the scalding droplets across the floor.

"Well." Macky gulped in air through peals of laughter. "You wanted coffee and biscuits. Help yourself."

The moment of revelation passed while Bran and Macky laughed until they were out of breath.

Later they peeled the burned crusts from the bread and ate it with the chunks of bacon. The coffee, once Bran added more water and let it reheat, was just about right.

Then, without knowing why, Bran began to talk. He told her about the Choctaw tribe he'd gone to live with when his family was killed. He talked about his Indian parents, about the good times, and the bad ones. He told her of the terrible winters they'd faced in the West and how the white men constantly forced them off their land. Then later, he told her how the same government officials who were supposed to keep them supplied with food and goods cheated them instead. But he stopped short of telling her about his adoptive brother, Blue, and how he'd killed a soldier to save Blue's life.

Macky told him about their home back East, about her father's store on the Mississippi, and about her brother as a boy.

Neither talked about tomorrow or what would happen then. They grabbed on to the present and the sharing of their pasts. The evening passed in a rare mood of companionship that neither wanted to examine too closely.

As the fire began to die down, Bran banked it for the night and took the skillet to the creek to wash it. Macky put away the food supplies and swept the crumbs from the floor.

When Bran returned, he closed and bolted the door. "Macky, about what you were saying earlier. I respect your need for secrecy. Let's don't make a decision yet. Let's think about it until after the housewarming. There's plenty of time for you to talk to the marshal."

Macky wasn't so sure about that, but she agreed and placed her makeshift broom, made of a broken branch, in the corner. Her fears that she'd have to share Bran's bed were alleviated when he gave her a chaste kiss on the forehead and said he'd take the loft.

"But it's full of dirt and spiders," she protested.

"Just about right," he agreed, "for a snake."

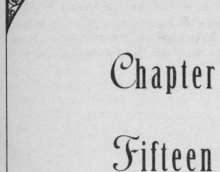

Chapter

Fifteen

LORRAINE ARRIVED at the cabin shortly after noon, driving a wagon filled with lumber. "Are you sure you want me here?" she asked Macky, not even trying to conceal the reservations in her voice.

"Absolutely sure. I need a friend."

"Hello, Reverend," Lorraine said as Bran came from the shed to greet her. "Help me unload these boards."

"What are you going to do with them?" Bran asked, pulling the planks out the back of the wagon.

"Hank Clay says he'll use these to make the tables." Lorraine glanced around, her gaze stopping at the stand of cottonwood trees near the creek. "Let's set them up there."

"Tables?" Macky echoed. "How many people do you expect?"

"Don't know. I've never been to a housewarming."

"Why not?" Macky asked. "I thought they were common."

"Never been invited."

Macky took the end of one of the boards and helped Lorraine carry it to the spot where Bran was piling them. "Heck, I was hoping you could tell me what to do."

" 'Fraid not. You've had more experience with church socials than me."

"I wish," was Macky's plaintive response.

"All I know is there will be children, ranch hands, and miners. They always seem to know when there is free food, and I heard Clara talking about musicians. I guess that means we'll—they'll dance."

Musicians? This time Macky didn't echo her words out loud. But dancing was something she'd never considered.

"And there's the marshal and the judge," she went on. "Clara even told me that she was frying chicken."

"Something unusual about that?" Bran asked, as he pulled the last of the lumber from the wagon.

"Frying chicken? No. It's her telling me that's unusual.

Macky followed Bran to the stack of lumber. She was as surprised at Clara's carrying on a conversation with Lorraine as Lorraine was. Maybe there was something to be said for a little meddling in the name of religion. "How are we going to make tables out of this?"

"Don't have to," Lorraine answered for him. "Hank Clay is right behind me with some legs he's put together at his shop. All we have to do is wait—look, there he is now."

Hank was driving his own wagon, stacked with odd-looking pieces of wood and iron, fastened into crosspieces which would support the wooden planks.

"Morning, Mrs. Adams," Hank said, crawling from the wagon. "We'll have these tables put together in no time."

Helplessly, Macky watched as Hank hitched his suspenders higher on his shoulders and rolled up his shirtsleeves. She'd seen more than one late snowstorm hit the territory, but this year, the surprisingly warm weather had continued, and in no time Bran and Hank had worked up a pleasant sweat.

As the tables were assembled, Macky and Lorraine worked together covering them with bed sheets sent by the women in town. By the time they were finished, Lorraine turned to Kate and studied her. "I think you have about enough time to clean up and dress while Hank and I start your cooking fire and put the coffee on."

"Oh!" Macky looked down at her pants and shirt and blushed. Though neither Lorraine nor Hank had commented, she certainly looked more like one of the miners than the preacher's wife.

"Clara says we'll have lemonade too, and maybe some punch, but the men will need coffee, particularly if somebody spikes the punch."

"Yes, of course," Macky managed to say, trying to hide her ignorance about social events. She'd attended one or two when she and Papa had first moved to Promise. But after Papa made it clear that he wasn't a farmer and had no intention of remarrying, the invitations had stopped coming. It looked as if she were about to learn.

Quickly Macky dashed into the house, assembled her green-checked dress, underclothes, and a drying cloth, and set out to find a private bathing spot along the stream.

"I'll take you to a good place, Macky." Bran's voice surprised her. She wasn't aware that he was behind her.

He walked along the bank, following the rip in the earth through which the water flowed. When Macky hesitated, he reached back and took her hand to assist her across the boulders and through the brush. "There's a pool up here where we can bathe, out of sight."

"We?" There was no hiding the quiver in her voice.

"That was a general statement, Macky. Relax, we have to get through the day. Don't get spooked before it even starts."

The thought of them bathing together sent a frisson of fear down Macky's spine and she stumbled, twisting her ankle as she fell.

Bran quickly lifted her up. "Are you hurt?"

"I don't think so. I just stepped wrong. Let me go."

Being so close to Bran was setting off more vibrations than the twisted ankle. Bran released her. She took a step forward, winced, and kept walking.

The pain in her ankle was sharp and searing, but she refused to give in. It wasn't going to stop her—but, wait a minute. With a sprained ankle she wouldn't have to reveal that she couldn't dance. Suddenly she let out a moan and reached back for Bran.

"Maybe I do need some help," she said.

Bran didn't have to be a scholar to see that Macky was exaggerating, but he couldn't figure out why. If she wanted to be hurt, he'd go along. "Of course," he said with a grin and swung her up in his arms.

"Bran! Put me down. I'm too heavy for you to carry."

"Macky, you're not too heavy. I'm a big man, or haven't you noticed? Besides, what kind of husband would allow his wife to walk on an injured ankle? Up ahead there is a deep pool where you can soak it in icy water. It'll keep down the swelling and you'll be able to dance a jig with the best of them."

Macky groaned again and this time it wasn't put on. This wasn't working out as she'd expected. Then Bran pushed through a growth of evergreen brush and they were beside a pool of water that came from a waterfall above.

"Oh, this is beautiful," Macky said, awed by the picture. "How did you know this was here?"

"I was looking for Kelley's mine this morning while you were sleeping."

"Did you find it?"

"I found where he'd been prospecting, yes. But I can't say that it looked promising." He put her down on a rock. "Let me help you."

He took the clothing she was clasping to her chest and laid it aside. Then he began to unfasten her boots.

She slapped his hand away. "I can do this," she insisted, unlacing and removing her brother's boot. "I mean, really I can. You can go now. I'll get back to the house by myself."

"Not until I'm sure you can get into the water. Take off your clothes."

"Not necessary," she protested, removing the second boot. If he laid a hand on her, she'd plunge into the water, clothes and all. Actually, that wasn't a bad idea. "I'd planned to wash these clothes anyway. If you'll help me, I'll just wear them into the water."

"That's an odd way to wash clothes, isn't it?"

"It's the way I always do it."

Biting back a grin, Bran assisted her to the bank and into the water. "When you're done, give a yell. I'll be listening for you." He turned his back, whistling as he walked away.

Macky waited until he was out of sight, then let out a sigh of relief. He was going to let her get away with it. She stepped into the pool.

"Brrrrr!" The water was cold enough to make chill bumps on an iceberg. It wouldn't take long to wash herself, if she didn't drown first.

The pool wasn't big but it was deep and suddenly her feet weren't touching the bottom. Her wet clothing had begun to pull her down.

"Horsefeathers!" She'd have to get undressed or she wouldn't live long enough to get to her own party. Quickly she slid out of the shirt and, kicking her feet madly, unbuttoned her trousers and shucked them in the water.

Bran heard her splash and the frantic sound of moving water. He let his whistle die. He'd give her a chance to enjoy the temperature of the melting snow before he returned. Then, just to punish her for the ruse, he'd sit and watch her freeze for a while before he helped her out. He counted slowly to ten.

"Macky," he called out as he retraced his steps. "It occurred to me that you might not be able to climb out." He reappeared at the pool and sat on Macky's rock. "Oh, I see you decided to soak your entire body. Not a bad idea. I'll just wait until you're done and help you up."

Now what was she going to do? Not only was she wearing nothing but her drawers and her chemise, but her clothing was hanging on a limb. If she climbed out, Bran would see her almost completely naked in broad daylight. If she stayed in the pool, she'd turn into an icicle. She'd stay.

Minutes went by, longer for Macky than for Bran, who was watching her with what he hoped was concern in his eyes. She began to shiver. Her lips turned blue. Then his amusement turned into concern. Punishing Macky was one thing, but he didn't want her to get sick.

"Don't you think you ought to get out now?" he asked.

She shook her head. If she opened her mouth her teeth would sound like woodpeckers tapping a hollow tree.

"Macky—don't be stubborn. I'll get your clothes."

She shook her head again.

"I know what you're doing, Macky. If you don't want to dance, you don't have to. I'll even turn my back. Just get out of that water, now!"

Macky was too cold to argue any more. She started toward the side of the pool and held out her hand for Bran. He turned his head as he pulled her up. This time she knew that his concern was genuine.

But Bran hadn't counted on Macky's playful nature, or her decision to take revenge. He hadn't counted on her strength, either. She gave a sudden jerk and he went sailing past her, landing in the freezing creek up to his neck in his clothes.

"Why, you scheming woman. You—"

She couldn't move fast enough to escape. Moments later they were both engulfed in laughter and rolling on the path with arms and legs entangled. Dried leaves and twigs stuck to their bodies like flour on frying chicken.

Then Macky made the mistake of looking up at the man lying on top of her. His patch had been shoved aside, revealing the wound where his eye had been.

"Oh," she whispered, as she touched his face. "The man who did this must have been a monster."

"Yes, I swore that night that I would never rest until he

was dead. Not because of what he did to me. But for what he did to my family. For a long time I wished he'd killed me."

"Why didn't he?"

"He thought he had. And in a way, he did. A part of me died along with my eye." A distant look crossed Bran's face for a moment, then he said quietly, "After that I knew what I had to do."

"What?"

"Find him."

"And did you?"

"Not yet."

"But that's what you're doing here?"

Lying there, in the silence, he finally decided to give her a part of his truth. "That's one reason," Bran agreed.

"Will you recognize him?"

"I don't know. He was in the shadows but I know he's a Southerner with an odd laugh. For fifteen years I've looked for this man. Thieves don't stop being thieves, they just change what they steal. Sooner or later, I'll find him."

"Maybe it's time to stop looking and put the past behind you," she said, wanting to comfort him. "Maybe we can look after each other." She raised her lips to his.

"I wish I could," he said, his voice hoarse. He'd felt nothing but emptiness for so long. He'd refused to let himself care about anything or anybody. She almost made him believe that together they could cast out the demons who'd been driving him.

Now this woman with the wild red hair was forcing him to open up and let her inside. He'd promised himself that he wouldn't kiss her again, even though every part of him wanted to claim her, brand her with his taste and touch. For this moment he forgot about where they were, about the people waiting back at the cabin, about those who were coming to a housewarming.

"Please don't worry," she said and pulled his head down so that their lips touched.

The kiss was inevitable. Every time it happened he was

astonished how she melted beneath his touch. Every time he explored her hot, sweet mouth he was stunned by the explosion inside him. He kissed her tenderly at first, then more fiercely. Her eyes were closed. Her fingertips kneaded his neck, then they slid down his back and moved beneath his shirt.

She was melting into him, her breath coming faster, her heart beating wildly. There was no mistaking her need, nor her invitation. She was asking, seeking, moving against him. He was as helpless to fight it as she. But he was a man who had learned control. He'd always been able to rein in his emotions and hold them tight.

Until Macky brought trouble into his life.

A rush of heat surged through his loins. He was so close to letting go. And she wouldn't refuse. Holding back was punishing her, making them both suffer.

His hand moved between them, seeking her breasts. He had to touch her, hold her. She was so soft, so yielding, so new. He felt as if he'd never been with a woman before.

Stop, Bran. You don't need this kind of want in your life.

Logically he knew he couldn't allow this to continue but his body refused to obey his mind's commands. Drawing on all his strength, he forced himself to pull back. Beneath him, Macky's eyes flew open. The shimmering green of her eyes reflected the storm of her uncertainty.

She gradually became still, relaxing her fingers that lay against his bare skin.

"Why did you stop?" she whispered.

"Because taking you would be a mistake."

"Why?"

Her question was honest and he didn't know how to answer it. "I don't know. Because it isn't right. Because I would be hurting you and you don't deserve that."

"I already hurt. Now we both hurt. Why?"

"Maybe I'm more of a preacher than I thought," he said and drew her to her feet. "We'd better get you dressed, Mrs.

Adams. Otherwise you're going to meet your guests looking like a catfish pulled through the bull rushes."

Macky should be upset, but she wasn't. There was a kind of quiet joy inside her. He was rejecting her, as he'd done from the beginning, but it was different. Sooner or later— What? She was very confused. She had thought he wouldn't want any part of her, but he did. She could tell.

He removed a leaf from her hair, tangling his fingers in the damp tendrils that fell across her shoulders. Then he kissed her. And she understood that his kiss said what he couldn't. It was a silent promise, a pledge of trust. She understood and she'd wait.

Macky stepped back. Her foolish action meant that she had to don her dress over her wet underdrawers and chemise. Bran waited, watching her. She smothered a smile. He may be pretending to be a preacher, but he was still a man and she saw no reason why he couldn't be both. She simply had to convince him of that. In the meantime, she couldn't help teasing him, making her movements slow and her body visible.

Hank accidentally brushed against Miss Lake as he reached below the table to steady the legs. He hadn't realized that she was there. She hadn't been so close when he'd leaned down. Now, as he raised up, they were standing thigh to thigh.

"I'm sorry," he mumbled and wished for the plug of tobacco in his shirt pocket. He felt uncomfortable being bare chested. He was clean, but being so close was too intimate.

"Don't be," Lorraine said with a smile. "Nobody saw. In fact, we're all alone out here, aren't we?"

"Yes, ma'am, but I guess the preacher and his wife will be back any minute." Hank wouldn't let himself look directly at the beautiful woman. She was moving her leg slowly back and forth against his, as if she knew what she was doing.

Except she couldn't. She couldn't know how many times he'd sat in the dark of the livery stable and watched her silhouette walk back and forth across the window shade. Since Mrs. Adams had mentioned that she might teach the children to read, he'd been even more aware of her.

"Hank?"

Her voice drew his attention back to her.

"Hank, do you have a girl?"

"No, ma'am," he stammered, trying to sound as if he were the ignorant blacksmith people believed him to be.

"In that case, I hope you'll ask me to dance tonight. Macky invited me, but let's face it, there won't be another man here who will dare ask me, and I know it's silly, but I don't want to be left out."

There was a longing in her voice. "Perhaps you'll be surprised, Miss Lake. Mrs. Adams has a way of seeing people in another light and making other folks see them that way, too."

Lorraine looked at Hank in surprise. She'd had the same thought but she didn't know anyone else had noticed.

Moments later, Lorraine looked up as Bran and Kathryn came down the path. There was no mistaking the flush in the girl's face, nor the proprietary way that Bran was assisting her. It was obvious to Lorraine that Bran was totally smitten, even if Bran didn't know it yet.

"Macky fell and turned her ankle," Bran explained. "That's why her hair is . . . mussed."

"Macky?" Lorraine's eyebrows raised at the affectionate name he'd given her. "Let's get you inside and I'll see what I can do to help. Can't have your congregation seeing you like this."

Bran helped Macky to a stool by the fire, gave Lorraine an odd look of appeal, then excused himself to go to the loft and replace his wet clothing with dry.

Macky ducked her head near the fire and concealed her face by rubbing the wet ends of her hair with a drying cloth. She could tell that Lorraine wasn't fooled. Macky didn't have a mirror, but she guessed that anybody, including Hank, would know that she'd been thoroughly kissed.

The kettle filled with coffee was boiling over the fire, sending its smell across the air. She could hear Bran's footsteps overhead as he changed clothes. Hank was outside hammering the table legs into the ground.

Once Bran left the cabin, Macky took her comb and began to rake it through her hair. She stopped and let out a deep breath, raised her head and looked miserably at Lorraine. "Have you ever been in love?" she asked.

"No," Lorraine admitted, laying her hand on Macky's shoulder. Then she rescued the comb and took over. "Have you?"

"I don't think so. Papa said it would happen one day. But he didn't tell me how I'd know."

"Ah, Kate, I can't tell you, either."

Macky was silent for a moment. "Please help me. I don't want to make Bran ashamed."

"You'd never do that, Kate."

"I'm really called Macky," she said. "I mean, Kathryn is my name too, but nobody ever used it before. I wish you'd call me Macky."

"I will. Does your ankle hurt?"

"It's all right. I didn't hurt it that badly. I just thought if Bran believed it was sprained, I wouldn't have to dance."

"Because you don't know how, is that it?"

Macky caught her lower lip between her teeth. "I never learned. No reason to. I never thought I'd go to a dance. In fact, I never thought I'd be in a place like this."

"From the look on your face," Lorraine observed, "seems like you're not too happy about it right now."

"I'm happy. Goodness yes, I'm happy. But I'm worried. Do you know Pratt?" Macky asked quietly. "That bank robber the marshal is after?"

"No, should I?" Lorraine asked, not hiding her confusion.

"He was in your saloon. I saw him, twice. I mean I saw

him leaving," Macky said in a rush. "He rides a horse with a silver-trimmed saddle."

"A lot of men come through the saloon, Macky, some I know, some I don't, some I don't want to know. Why, is there a problem?"

Macky wanted to tell Lorraine that Pratt was on her trail, wanted to ask Lorraine what she thought Macky should do. But she couldn't. She'd as much as promised Bran that she'd keep his secret, whatever it was, if he'd keep hers. If she confessed, she'd admit that claiming to be the Reverend Brandon Adams and his wife was a lie.

"No," she finally said. "I once knew someone who had a saddle like that. I'm just being silly. So much has happened that I don't know what to think about anything. Even Bran."

Lorraine laid the comb down. Taking Macky's chin in her fingertips, she tilted her face up. "Don't let it overwhelm you, Macky. No matter what he says, he cares. I can see it in his eyes, and I envy you for that."

"He cares about me?" Macky couldn't keep the wonder from her voice. "Sometimes I wonder."

"Believe me," Lorraine insisted, "and I've seen enough men without that look to know. Besides, you're not ignorant."

"I can recite most of the words of Shakespeare, the Greek poets, and even Benjamin Franklin, but what I don't know about being a woman could fill all those books and have some left over."

"Men can't always tell what they want, but when they find it, sooner or later, they know. Whatever you did to catch Bran's eye, I'd say, just keep it up."

"But I haven't done anything but let him kiss me."

Lorraine tied a ribbon around Macky's hair, drawing it up in the back so that she could pin it under. She considered Macky's comment. Everybody in town knew that she was carrying a child, even Bran confirmed it. So she couldn't be that innocent. Or could she?

"Macky, don't answer this if you don't want to, but have you ever been with a man?"

"Of course I have. Bran and I shared the same stage. We've shared the same room in your establishment. You've seen me with him."

"I mean, in the physical way, Macky. As a man lies with his wife, makes love to her, joins his body to hers?"

Macky ducked her head to conceal her blush. "I don't think I ought to talk about this with you," she said. "I mean, Bran would likely not approve."

But Lorraine didn't need to hear the answer. She could see the truth in Macky's face. She'd never made love to Bran, but she wanted him. And he wanted her. So, who was the father of Macky's child or, better still, was she really carrying one?

And how could she explain love to Macky when she'd never felt it herself? Lorraine lifted her head and caught sight of Hank through the window.

He'd been watching her.

As their eyes met, he dropped his head and found something on the ground which interested him greatly. He was buttoning his shirt and threading his fingers through his damp hair.

He looked like a man of the earth.

Lorraine felt a flutter of disappointment. She liked him without the shirt. She wondered how he looked without the trousers.

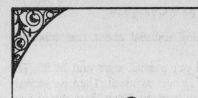

Chapter

Sixteen

Marshal Larkin studied his pocket watch and spoke to Bran, who was standing with the town fathers by the fence. "I'm beginning to wonder if Mrs. Mainwearing is coming."

"Maybe she heard that Lorraine would be here and decided not to come," Preston said, watching the women place the food on the table.

"Maybe, but I was out at the mine this morning. She said Judge Hardcastle was picking her up. I'm getting a little worried."

Bran pulled his attention from Macky, who'd been given a place of honor on a stool just outside the cabin door where she could watch the women trying to turn the cabin into a proper parsonage and the others preparing the food. "What were you doing at the mine?" he asked the marshal.

"I suppose it's all right to say now. Another gold shipment went out this morning. I sent an escort with it, but after the bank robbery in Promise, I'm worried."

"Was there something unusual about that robbery?" Bran asked.

The marshal pulled out a small cigar and lit it. "The regular wagons left for Denver as usual. Then we secretly shipped the new coins to Promise. From there they'd have gone on to California on the stage. It would have worked except that the Pratt gang decided to hold up the bank."

"Yeah, it was almost like Pratt's gang knew they were there," Hank Clay said as he joined the group.

"And then," Bran added, "there was the explosion in the mine."

The marshal shook his head. "We still don't know whether that was an accident or not. It turns out the man who was killed had been newly hired and the other men said he seemed awfully nervous."

Something was wrong but Bran couldn't put a finger on it and he hated that nagging feeling. He did know that whoever was behind the trouble was not an ordinary criminal. Sylvia had hired Bran to find the culprit, but he didn't have a lead on the guilty party.

Larkin drew on the cigar and tapped the ash to the ground where he crushed it beneath his boot. "If Mrs. Mainwearing isn't here by the time the ladies get the food ready, I'll ride over there and check."

"Why wait?" Bran asked.

Larkin nodded. "You're right, let's go. But don't alarm the women, we'll just say we're going to meet them."

"Want us to tag along?" Hank Clay asked.

"No," the marshal said as he mounted his horse. "Don't want to make the women worry. You and Cribbs stay here, in case there's trouble."

Bran borrowed a horse that was already saddled and rode out behind the marshal, giving a quick wave to Macky, whose look of alarm wasn't going to be satisfied without more explanation. But that would have to wait. Besides, it wasn't safe for her to know any more than she already did.

They rode leisurely back toward town until they came to

the fork, then took the other path that ambled up the trail into the mountains. After ten minutes of riding, the marshal spoke. "I've been thinking about where I've seen you before, preacher, but it hasn't come to me yet. I'm sure we've crossed paths before."

"Could be," Bran admitted. "I've ridden all over the West for the last fifteen years. Not many men wear an eye patch."

"More than you think out here. Too many Indians. Oh, well, it'll come to me. I never forget a face."

At that moment shots rang out up ahead. Bran instantly pulled his gun.

Larkin glanced at Bran's gun and frowned for a second. "Most preachers don't carry firearms."

"I do," was all Bran said as they spurred their horses into a gallop. They reached the crest of a hill and caught sight of a buggy being driven hard toward them. The bushwhackers were hidden in the rocks above.

"It's Sylvia," the marshal called out and began returning fire. "I'll go for the crooks. You see to her."

Bran rode hard toward the buggy, circled around and came alongside. The judge was slumped against Sylvia. He'd dropped the reins and the horses were running wild.

"Hold on," he yelled and drew even with the frightened animals, sliding from his mount onto the back of the lead horse. Moments later he had them under control. Behind him the gunfire had stopped. Then the marshal was galloping to catch up to them.

"Are you all right, Mrs. Mainwearing?" Bran asked, worry making his voice sound almost angry.

"I'm fine," she snapped. "But the judge got his hair parted by a bullet. Did you get them, Marshal?"

"No, by the time I got up there whoever was shooting at you was gone. All I saw was a man riding away on a horse with a silver-trimmed saddlehorn."

"Silver trim?" Bran asked.

Sylvia looked curiously at him. "That mean something to you?"

"No, it's just that most bandits aren't so well equipped," Bran responded. The marshal had gotten close enough to see the silver-trimmed saddle, but he couldn't catch the rider. Of course he was concerned about Mrs. Mainwearing, but Bran would have thought he'd at least have tried to follow whoever had been shooting at the buggy.

"The judge?" Larkin asked.

"I'm fine, just took a chunk out of my scalp," he replied, trying to right himself. "Caught me by surprise or I wouldn't have dropped the reins. Didn't even get a chance to draw my gun."

"You carry a gun too, Judge?" The marshal looked from the judge to the preacher and back again.

"Certainly. The West is a wild place," he said, then groaned and glanced at his blood-splattered shirt and vest. "Don't suppose there's a doctor at your party, is there, Adams?"

"No doctor in Heaven, Judge," Larkin replied. "But I imagine Lorraine can fix you up."

"Lorraine?" Sylvia repeated, a frown marring her face.

When the buggy reached the parsonage, the members of the congregation were waiting. "What happened?" Preston asked.

"The preacher's horse came hightailing it back. We knew there was trouble," another commented.

"Some bandit riding a horse with a silver-trimmed saddle decided to take potshots at me," Sylvia said, climbing down from the buggy. "He got the judge instead. Help him down and get . . . Lorraine Lake to look at him."

The judge, blood streaming down his face, was carried inside. The women stood back to let Lorraine treat the wound.

Macky, who'd forgotten her injured ankle, walked away from the doorway, stunned by Sylvia's revelation. Pratt.

Inside the cabin, Sylvia pulled a small bottle of whiskey from her purse and handed it to Lorraine. "This ought to purify the wound."

"That'd do me a sight more good if it was in my stomach instead of on my head," the judge growled.

"I suppose we could manage that," Lorraine agreed, "if there's any left."

He'd lost some blood but the bullet hadn't done any real damage, other than leave him with a giant headache. After settling him down and cleaning away the blood, Lorraine poured whiskey on the wound, then handed the bottle to the judge and turned away.

Sylvia was watching. "You did a good job, Miss Lake," she said. "Moose always thought a lot of you."

"I thought a lot of him, too. He was a good man."

Sylvia let out a laugh. "No he wasn't. He was an ornery old coot, lied for the hell of it and drank like a fish, but he did know how to appreciate a good woman."

Lorraine, startled for a moment, recognized a hint of friendship in Sylvia's eyes, and nodded. "You're right. He said that once he found you, he knew he'd met his match."

Sylvia walked over to the judge and studied him. "Think you can amuse yourself here while we feed these men? No point in wasting all this good food."

The judge pulled himself to a sitting position, and leaned against the wall. "By all means," he said, his voice revealing the depth of his pain.

Sylvia brushed the wrinkles from her dress, and stepped out the door, stopping for a moment beside Bran. "I know you don't approve, but I won't have anybody else shot at because of me."

Before he could stop her she walked to the center of the clearing. "I'd like your attention," she said, waiting for everyone to gather around. "I have an announcement. The trouble in Heaven has gone far enough. I don't intend to lose another gold shipment, or have anyone else hurt. In that regard, I've hired a gunfighter to find out who is behind these attacks."

A murmur of conversations spread through the crowd.

"When will he be here?" Clara Gooden asked with worry etched across her face.

"You know what happens when a gunfighter comes to town," Preston Cribbs added. "Every would-be killer in the territory suddenly turns up to prove he's the best."

"Yeah," Hank agreed from where he was standing behind Lorraine. "Who is he?"

"His name is Night Eyes and I received a notice from my solicitor. He'll be here any day."

The collective gasp of the onlookers effectively covered Macky's, but she couldn't stop herself from turning her gaze toward Bran.

He was looking at her. Night Eyes? Eyes That See in Darkness? It had to be. His expression hadn't changed, but she knew that he was giving her the chance to reveal that he wasn't the preacher he claimed to be.

Macky had known from the beginning that Bran was dangerous. But a gunfighter?

She held her breath and the moment of decision passed. He had allowed her to pretend to be his wife when she needed to hide, the least she could do in return was protect his identity. She owed him that much, until she knew the truth. Besides, she knew something that they didn't. The man riding the horse with the silver-trimmed horn was Pratt, the bank robber.

Bran waited. He inclined his head slightly, as if he could read her mind and understood her confusion. She couldn't give him away. No matter what Sylvia said, she wasn't afraid. She went to stand beside Bran, laying her hand on his arm, ready for whatever came next.

Larkin, waiting under a tree by the tables, felt the pieces fall into place. He didn't know why he hadn't seen it before. The man with the eye patch wasn't a preacher; he was Night Eyes, the gunslinger. Larkin didn't much like competition, either in his job or his personal life. He was in charge here and he didn't intend to let anybody else mess up his plans. Too bad Bran wasn't a wanted man. It would make Larkin's life easier if the preacher could be arrested and carried off to jail. But this gunfighter was too careful for that. He never killed a man who wasn't trying to kill him first.

But his job as marshal was to find the man behind the trouble in Heaven. How better to find the criminal he was looking for than to use Night Eyes to do it? He bit back a smile.

"Mrs. Mainwearing, I wish you hadn't done that," the marshal finally said. "The judge sent me here to look into the matter. I assure you that I've done everything possible. By bringing in a man with that kind of reputation, you'll only make matters worse."

"Maybe, and maybe whoever is after me will understand that I mean business," Sylvia snapped, then turned toward Bran. "I understood I was invited to supper and all this has given me an appetite."

"Of course," the mayor spoke up, recognizing the undercurrent of unease rippling through the crowd. "Preacher Adams, will you say grace?"

Bran's arm stiffened beneath Macky's touch. There was only silence. She caught his hand. "Maybe you'll allow me?"

There was a moment of surprise, then the mayor nodded and bowed his head.

But it was Bran's strong voice that spoke. "Let brotherly love continue. Be not forgetful to entertain strangers; for thereby some have entertained angels unawares. May the angels remain among us."

"Amen," Hank said, and was rewarded with a puzzled look from Lorraine.

"I'll say amen, too," the marshal agreed, taking Sylvia's hand. "May I escort you, Mrs. Mainwearing?" he asked and, on her nod of acceptance, led her to the tables piled high with food.

Bran leaned down to whisper in Macky's ear. "I don't know why you protected my identity, but thank you."

"You did the same for me."

"As you said, maybe we can look after each other." He

didn't have to say that this kind of thinking was new to him. "As for you, Mrs. Adams. I think you'd better limp back to your stool and let me serve you if you plan to continue the ruse that you have a sprained ankle."

She flushed. "You knew? How?"

"I don't tell everything I know, either."

Sylvia insisted on taking a plate to the judge and remained inside while she tried to get him to eat. However, he refused, choosing instead to empty the bottle. By the time the musicians began to tune up their fiddles, Judge Hardcastle was singing boisterously and threatening to get out of bed to dance.

One of the women brought a low bench from the back of her wagon and sat beside Macky. She held one child on her knee while discreetly nursing a newborn beneath a faded shawl.

Macky smiled at the little girl who ducked her head against her mother's arm. "What's your name? I'll bet it's Sunshine."

The child shook her head.

"Then it must be Gingerbelle. I once had a friend named Gingerbelle who looked like you, except she had only one arm and I'm sure you have two, don't you? Of course Gingerbelle did very well with only one, except when she had to draw water from the well. Then do you know what she did?"

The little girl, caught up in Macky's story, forgot to hug her mother's body. "What did she do?"

"She whistled," Macky exclaimed. "That worked every time. Can you whistle?"

"No."

Macky knew that the little girl wasn't buying her story, but she was intrigued. Macky slid closer. "It's a secret, but I'll share it with you if you'll sit on my knee. Of course, you can't tell the baby. Babies don't understand about big girl's secrets.

Solemnly the child slid from her mother's knee and let

Macky lift her into her lap. "Secret?" Her eyes were as large as saucers.

Macky lowered her voice. "What she did was whistle and her mule named Solomon came running. He took the end of the rope and lifted the bucket of water from the well. Once it was up high enough for Gingerbelle to reach it, she'd pull it to the ground and let Solomon have a drink."

"She did?"

"Of course the secret was that her mama never knew that Solomon drank out of the family water bucket. And you must promise not to tell anybody what I did."

"You're really Gingerbelle? But you have two arms."

"Well, yes, but you have to keep my secret. I wasn't strong and Solomon got awfully thirsty. Would you like to meet him?"

"Solomon is here?"

"Solomon is here," Bran answered. "But Trouble has a sprained ankle so she can't introduce you. But if your mother will let you, I'll take you to the corral to say hello."

The grateful mother nodded and watched as her child confidently held up her arms to the man dressed in black. "You know she doesn't usually have anything to do with anybody. She hardly ever talks, not since her real papa died."

The woman finished feeding the baby and plopped her against her shoulder where the baby let out a satisfied burp. "I'm Rachel Wade—I mean Pendley—and that was Rebekah. The baby is Louis. Mr. Pendley is Louis's daddy. He and I aren't really married yet. There wasn't a preacher. That's what made it so hard, me having another baby and all. Some people were pretty outspoken about it."

"I'm Macky Calhoun, I mean Macky Adams. Don't pay attention to gossip. Nobody can know what's best for someone else. God gave you a child and I'm sure He understands. I'm so glad you came."

Gratitude filled Rachel's face. "My ma always made us youngens go to church. Mr. Pendley wouldn't come, but

maybe he will when I tell him how nice you are. Maybe your
man will say the words?"

Macky nodded, though she didn't know what Bran
would say, or what it meant to have a legal marriage. She'd
find out and help Rachel, if she could.

Soon, members of the congregation, caught up in the
judge's good spirits, began to dance merrily. The marshal
took one turn around the floor with Lorraine, then turned
her over to Hank Clay and set his sights on Sylvia. Bran
didn't dance, but after he returned the child to her mother,
he began to mingle with the guests, laughing and giving
every indication that he was having a good time.

To Lorraine's surprise, she was asked to dance not once
but twice. It wasn't much, but it was a beginning, all because of Macky. She'd thought that the women of Heaven
had tolerated her because she'd made them welcome in her
saloon, but she was no longer sure. She sighed. They
seemed guardedly friendly but she didn't want to get her
hopes up for nothing. She didn't know why she'd come to
the party. She didn't belong.

Lorraine turned toward the creek, feeling more lonely
than she'd ever felt. She never had real friends.

And except for Moose, every man she'd ever known had
used her. She'd thought the marshal was different and she'd
been lonely. But it was obvious that it was Sylvia he had his
eye on and Lorraine wouldn't be second choice.

The music behind her had turned slow and soulful. Just
what she needed when she already felt like throwing herself
into that creek and letting it sweep her away from this
godawful little town in the middle of nowhere.

She stood at the edge of the water, listening as it
splashed against the rocky barriers and moved off into the
night.

"It's hard being different," a male voice said.

Lorraine whirled around. It was Hank Clay leaning
against a tree behind her. Had he followed her, or had he
been there all along?

"Yes," she answered. "Though I don't know how you'd know. You're one of the city fathers."

"No, they just include me so that I'll agree with whatever they say. They don't think I'm very smart. I let them believe they're right."

"You're smart enough to know what they're up to," she said. Odd, she'd never paid much attention to the burly man across the street from her business. He never came in; she'd thought it was because he was too frugal. And he was always dirty, until tonight. Tonight was probably the first time she'd ever seen Hank Clay in clean clothes. And the stains on his fingers were probably burned into his skin.

"What about you, Miss Lake?"

"What do you mean? I'm a saloonkeeper. They know it and I know it. I'm only tolerated tonight because of Macky. You don't think they'd ever invite me on their own, do you?"

"Maybe not. But you're not the only one. How many times do you think I've broken bread with them? This is the first."

"I'm sorry," Lorraine said.

"I'm not. I am what I am and I don't have to prove anything to anybody. Neither do you."

Lorraine listened to Hank in shocked silence. She'd never heard him say more than two or three words before. Yet he clearly understood the truth and he was sharing himself with her. Why?

"What do you want from me, Hank?" she asked. "You know I don't spend private time with my customers."

"I'm not a customer, Lorraine. I'm just a man you're passing the time with at a housewarming." He took a step forward and held out his hand. "Will you do me the honor of going walking with me, Miss Lake?"

Lorraine stifled a gasp. His manners were perfect. Someone had trained him in the way to approach a lady. And she was a lady, even if only she knew it.

She surprised herself by saying, "I'd be delighted, Mr. Clay."

He folded her arm across his and led her away from the sound of the music until they reached an open meadow beneath a starlit sky. Hank removed his coat and laid it on the ground. "Miss Lake," he said, "would you care to sit for a spell and look at the night sky?"

"I think I would, Mr. Clay."

Moments later she was sitting on the damp, cool earth and Hank was lying on his back staring up into the heavens. "Look, there's a shooting star."

"I wonder if it's going some happy place and if it wants to go?"

"Maybe it hasn't any choice. Look, there's the evening star."

"It's so bright, close enough that you could almost reach up and touch it."

"Do you see the Big Dipper?"

Lorraine studied the sky, trying to follow the path of his pointing finger.

"Come down here beside me and you can see it better. There are seven stars, three in the handle and four in the bowl."

Lorraine lay down, arranging her crinoline so that the back side pulled up, exposing her bottom to the ground, the front side lying flat across her. Hank leaned against her so that she could see where he was pointing.

"I read about the Big Dipper, but I've never been able to find it."

"There. It's in the north sky now. By summer it will move to the west with the bowl down and the handle pointing upward. By winter its handle will point down. When I was a boy I always thought that the snow was water being emptied from the dipper."

Lorraine turned her head toward him. "That's pure poetry, Hank. How did you learn all this?"

"My mother was the mistress of a very learned man. He taught me many things—before he died."

Lorraine didn't comment right away, studying him in

the fading light. His face took on new angles, new character in the shadows. "It's hard to know things and have nobody to share it with."

He turned to his side and rested his weight on one elbow. "No. What I know is mine. What I allow people to know is my choice, Lorraine."

"And you're choosing to let me know you?" Her voice was barely above a whisper.

"If you wish."

"I wish."

Then he kissed her. It was sweet and gentle and her response came unexpectedly out of nowhere, filling Lorraine's mouth with the magic of the night. She sighed and opened her lips to him, knowing that the moment was special and that she might never find it again.

When he pulled back she was stunned. "Why did you stop? I mean, other men don't—"

"I'm not other men," he said quietly. "I want you to know that."

"Why should you be different?"

"Because," he said simply. "I'm the man you're going to marry. When I touch your body like this," he lightly ran his fingertips across her breasts, "it will be a thing we both enjoy. When you come to know my body"—he took her hand and pressed it against his arousal—"it will be because I have the right to know yours."

Lorraine stared at him in disbelief. "My goodness, the town blacksmith is a poet."

"And the town saloonkeeper is a teacher."

"No, I only offered."

"And as the new newspaper editor, I'm going to see that it happens, as soon as my equipment arrives from back East. It's time you and I got back to the party," he said, moving to his feet and pulling her up.

"But—"

"Come along, Miss Lake."

"Where did you come from, Mr. Clay?" she finally asked as they made their way back to the cabin.

"Where we came from isn't important, it's where we're going that counts."

"And where is that?" she asked breathlessly as they came to a stop at the edge of the woods by the creek.

He kissed her again, this time more deeply, then answered. "To the stars, Lorraine."

As they entered the clearing where the dancers were whirling around, Hank stepped back and suddenly Lorraine was alone. She still wasn't sure that she hadn't dreamed what had happened. Except for the tingle in her lips and the thudding of her heart.

Imagine that. She'd been kissed by the town blacksmith, a man she'd scarcely noticed before, and she was practically floating on air. And he was offering her a future.

"Lorraine," Aaron Larkin said, interrupting her state of magical intensity. "I'm going to escort Sylvia back to her ranch. Will you drive the judge into town?"

"Yes, of course. Tell him to get into my wagon."

"I think it's more a matter of pouring him into the back. He's had too much to drink."

"Just like Moose," Sylvia said. "Will you check on him, Lorraine? And let me know how he gets along?"

"I'll be glad to, Sylvia. I wonder if you'll ride along with us, Mr. Clay?" she asked. "I mean, in case the shooters are still around."

Moments later Lorraine was in the wagon and Clay was riding alongside. Halfway back, the judge passed out. Lorraine waited for Hank to say something. He didn't, and for the first time in her life, Lorraine Lake didn't know how to talk to a man.

Once the judge had been driven away, Aaron Larkin suggested that, considering what had happened, the members of Preacher Adams's flock all ride back together. "There's safety in numbers," he reminded them.

Subdued now, the women quickly packed up the left-over food, leaving what they thought the preacher and his wife could make use of. They accepted Bran's thanks for their help and promised to be in church the next day as they started back to town. This time, one of the older Cribbs boys took the reins in Rachel Pendley's wagon.

"Reverend Adams was worried about Mrs. Pendley being able to see to her babies," Ethel Cribbs said. The other women quickly agreed, basking in the afterglow of such Christian concern. Rachel gave Macky a timid wave as they drove away.

Aaron assisted Mrs. Mainwearing into her buggy, tied his own horse to the back, and followed the townspeople. "I don't think the outlaw will dare come to her house, but I think I'll stay the night with Mrs. Mainwearing," he said to Bran.

Bran didn't comment. He couldn't help but wonder if the bushwhackers had been after Sylvia or the judge. At least the marshal was with her tonight.

Tomorrow he had to set things straight with his employer. Tonight he had to set things straight with his wife.

Bran stepped inside the cabin. "That was a nice thing you did for Rachel Pendley."

"I like her," Macky said.

"And inviting Lorraine turned out to be a good idea. I think she and Sylvia have more in common than they thought."

"I think, Reverend Adams, that you are very good at flattery. Did you see Sylvia dancing with Otis Gooden? How'd you get her to come?"

Bran pursed his lips and considered how best to proceed. "You know Mrs. Mainwearing was talking about me, don't you? I'm the gunfighter."

Macky was standing in the middle of the cabin looking around at all the things the women in the church had brought to make the place more livable.

She turned. "Yes. I knew. Does she?"

"Yes. I told her after dinner last night. I thought she wasn't going to announce that she'd hired me just yet."

"I think she wanted to send out a warning to whoever shot at her. She doesn't want anybody to get hurt."

"Aren't you going to ask me why a gunfighter is pretending to be the preacher?"

"Not unless you ask me why I'm pretending to be your wife."

"When I allowed the congregation to believe that, I thought it was because you needed a husband. I wanted to protect you. And I always use a disguise."

"I would have thought," Macky mused aloud, "that the marshal would know Night Eyes, or at least about him."

"The world knows Night Eyes as a half-breed gunfighter, but there is no detailed description and no reason to arrest him. Night Eyes has never killed except in self-defense."

"Well, it still seems odd that he didn't say anything. But thank you for being honest."

"I'm glad it's out," Bran said, "I've kept too many secrets for too long. I want you to know them all."

"There's more?"

"Yes. Night Eyes isn't wanted by the law, but John Brandon Lee is. When I was seventeen, I killed a man, a soldier who was beating an Indian boy. I ran away. I'm wanted for murder."

"If you killed him, he must have deserved it. Why didn't you stay and stand trial?"

"I was young and the only witnesses were Indians. I knew I wouldn't have a chance. But I'm not sorry for what I did. The Indian boy was my brother, Blue. I couldn't let anybody get away with killing another member of my family." Bran turned toward the fire.

"Well," she said, searching for something to say to ease his pain. For a moment she was tempted to confess that she was the kid who'd taken part in the bank robbery. But she was guilty and confession would mean that she'd have to go to jail. Yet, to stay would only put Bran's safety in jeopardy. She needed time to think.

Tonight she just wanted to enjoy the odd feeling of companionship they were sharing. Like her father, who always delayed dealing with problems in the hope they'd disappear, she'd confess tomorrow.

"If it's all the same to you, Bran, I'd rather save any more truth until later. There's something else I want to do tonight."

"What?"

"I want you," she said, and held out her arms, "to teach me how to dance."

Her answer was so beautifully Macky that he lost his self-imposed iron will before he'd put it in place.

Chapter

Seventeen

BRAN SUCKED IN A HARSH BREATH. For a few seconds he only looked at her, not trying to conceal the hunger in his eyes.

"Dance?"

"Surely you know how?" she said softly, revealing her uncertainty as she dropped her gaze to his boots. "I mean I thought that you must have had some occasion to learn. I'm sorry." She turned away. "It was a foolish idea."

"Only because it means that I'll have to put my arms around you," he said, catching her shoulder and turning her back toward him. "I don't know how smart that is."

"Why? Am I such a clod?"

"Oh, Macky, you're not a clod. You're a temptation. And I," he said, leading her out the door, "have discovered that when I touch you, I have no control."

"I'm sorry. I suppose dancing could be a temptation for a preacher, but since you're a gunfighter I'm not going to worry any more."

"You should worry. Not because I'm a gunfighter, Macky, but because I'm a man."

She let out an exasperated breath. "And wearing these silly shoes, I'm a clumsy oaf. Just a minute."

Seconds later, she stood in her stocking feet, hesitated, then held out her hand. She was asking for more than dance lessons. He could see it in her eyes and, damn it, he couldn't refuse.

Bran placed her left arm on his shoulder and took her right hand in his. "I'm going to put my foot between yours. I'll show you how to move with my hands. Just relax and move with me."

Macky wanted to laugh. If only he knew the kind of heat that pooled inside her and intensified with every glance. It came not only when they were alone and touching, but when she looked up and caught his gaze.

But she wished there were fewer clothes between them. She wished they were really married. She wished she'd never robbed a bank.

With a sigh Macky allowed him to slide his knee between her legs and use his body to direct her movements. She didn't think that the other dancers had been so close, but perhaps this was necessary until she learned the steps.

"I'm sorry we don't have music," he said, "it makes it easier for you to feel the rhythm."

She didn't need music. The rhythm of her heartbeat was enough. And soon they were whirling around the clearing. Her hair came loose and fell across her shoulders. She let out a laugh of joy. Bran laughed in response, dipped her to the right, then back to the left as he swung her around. Her body was a music box wound tight. Then, as if it were running down, they began to move slower and slower, fitting their bodies together in slow seduction until they were barely moving at all.

Bran watched Macky's look of pleasure. She was like a cat, her eyes closed, purring in satisfaction. What she lacked in womanly skills, she more than made up for in honest emotions.

Every touch was an invitation, every sigh a reminder that they were alone, that this woman was as close to a wife as he'd ever have.

His breath was as rough as a cowboy wrestling a steer to the ground, a lumberjack taking the last cut at a tree ready to fall, a lover nearing the moment of penetration.

Finally, Bran caught his foot on the hem of Macky's dress and toppled her. In an attempt to break her fall, he pulled her even closer. Before he could stop it, his lips were against hers, his hand holding her bottom, and her breasts were crushed against his chest.

The moon slipped behind a cloud. The wind kicked up. With his lips still devouring hers, Bran lifted Macky in his arms and carried her inside, allowing the door to swing closed behind them.

Macky didn't hold back. One hand was already unbuttoning his shirt, the other threading through his hair, pulling him closer. She used her tongue to speak the language she was learning from this man who'd set her body on fire.

Suddenly her dress was gone, along with her petticoats and her chemise. Her skin was bare, her nipples hard and aching and her lower body trembling from a sensation that she couldn't begin to describe.

And Bran. Forcing her eyes open, she saw the fire cast a flickering light across his bare chest. He'd shed his boots and trousers and now his drawers were falling down his legs, revealing . . .

Macky gasped. He was like some wild animal, one of the Greek gods in Papa's books. He was beautiful, his dark hair touching his shoulders, his breath coming hard and fast, his arousal throbbing. Then he stopped and looked at Macky.

"Make me stop, Macky." His voice was so hoarse that she could barely hear him. His fists were clenched. He was a man almost past control.

"I can't," she whispered.

"If you don't, there'll be no going back."

"I don't want to go back."

"I could hurt you."

"Probably. You are very large."

"One last time," he rasped. "Do you want me to stop?"

She didn't answer. Instead she lay back on the bed, parted her legs, and let a shudder ripple through her body. "It hurts so bad, Bran. Help me."

He caught her nipple roughly in his mouth for a moment while he sought the mound between her legs. She was wet and trembling. Just a touch and she moaned and tried to impale herself on his fingertips.

"I want—I want—" she said, eagerly lifting her body against his thigh, urging him with her hands.

"I know," he said, and lifting himself over her, he plunged inside.

She cried out and tried to move away as he penetrated a barrier. Then he felt her begin to move again and he was lost in the tumultuous response that wouldn't be held back.

He couldn't stop. And even as he began to spill himself inside her, he knew that she wasn't there yet. She was still taut with anticipation when he collapsed against her.

Stunned.

Dazed.

Possessed.

For a moment he lay there, unable to comprehend what had happened, what he knew but refused to believe, what he'd built to a point of no turning back, then failed to fulfill.

Macky was whimpering softly, trying to control her body, embarrassed at its frustration, but unable to find a source of relief.

"Bran," she whispered, planting desperate little kisses against his face, squeezing his bare bottom as she tried to recapture what he'd taken away. "What's wrong with me?"

"Nothing's wrong with you, my darling Macky," Bran said, knowing he couldn't leave her like this, knowing that he had to finish what he'd started.

"It's me, not you."

"But I'm on fire. I feel—"

And then Bran felt himself come back to life, filling her even more fully than he had before. This time he was going to give her the same pleasure he'd had.

"Don't hold back, Macky. What you feel is good and natural. Dear God, let me show you."

He kissed her again at the same time he slipped his hand between them, finding the swollen nub of her pleasure and caressing it. Slowly at first, he began to move, afraid that he would hurt her. But she folded her legs around him and arched to meet his thrusts. He pulled his hand back and, forcing her to slow her movements, he built her higher and tighter.

"Ohhhhh. Bran, I feel something. I'm going to explode. I'm . . ."

And she did, taking him with her to a place he'd never been and never wanted to leave.

Much later, when Macky's head lay on his shoulder, her eyes closed in sated sleep, Bran let himself face the truth.

His wife had been a virgin. She was telling the truth.

McKenzie Kathryn Calhoun couldn't be carrying any man's child.

Unless it was his.

"I told you to shoot at her, to scare her, not hit anybody."

"Sorry, how'd I know she'd whip that horse into a frenzy and bounce somebody into a bullet?"

This time Pratt was on horseback. This time he was eye-to-eye with the man who was pulling the strings.

"There's one piece of bad news, Pratt. She's hired a gun-fighter."

"So?" The outlaw spoke in a voice filled with bravado. "I've taken care of my share of gunfighters. Who is he?"

"A man called Night Eyes. Ever met him?"

"Nope, but I've heard of him. They say he's half Indian

and half white, spent fifteen years searching for one man. Nobody knows what he looks like, keeps to himself. The few folks who have seen him won't talk about it. When's he due?"

"I think he's already here."

"Here?"

"Yeah, our Messenger from God, the Reverend Adams."

"The preacher is a gunslinger?" But this time Pratt's voice wavered. He didn't understand men who worked in secret, men who instilled both loyalty and fear. Half of Pratt's success was based on making his presence known.

"Crazy, isn't it, but it's a good cover. Who'd ever expect a preacher?"

In spite of the bad feeling that made him look over his shoulder, Pratt chortled. "A preacher? It'll be a fine day when I can't take a one-eyed preacher."

This time when Pratt listened for his instructions, he knew he'd have to make a few alterations of his own. Somebody had spent some of the gold coins from the bank job right here in Heaven. Pratt intended to find out who it was. There was still the matter of the kid who'd escaped with *his* loot.

He'd already intended to take care of the reverend. The preacher knew about his saddle. He'd seen it when Pratt tried to hold up that stage, then again that night in town. Pratt wasn't sure why the man hadn't said anything. Maybe he was afraid. Maybe he needed to be taught a little lesson about the wrath of God, and Pratt was just the one to do it.

Pratt felt his self-confidence return. If he did it just right, he'd take care of the marshal and the judge at the same time.

There was little activity around Sylvia's ranch the next morning. It was Sunday, a day of rest for all. Bran watched for a long time, until he was satisfied that the marshal had not spent the night.

Sylvia had jumped the gun on announcing that she'd

hired Night Eyes. They had an agreement and it was important that she follow it. Bran slowly rode his horse into the courtyard, dismounted and tied his reins to the fence.

As if she'd been expecting him, Sylvia herself opened the front door and stood back to let him in. "I wondered when you'd get here," she said and closed the door behind him. "We'll have coffee while we talk."

Bran followed her into a dining room large enough to feed the entire town council. There were coffee cups on the table and silver pots filled with cream and sugar.

"Why'd you do it?" he asked as she filled the cups and waited for him to pull out her chair before sitting.

"Too many people have died. The judge getting hit was the last straw. By the way, I like your wife."

"I like her, too. But I'm thinking of sending her to Denver. And I want you to go with her."

"She looks like she's about as likely to follow orders as me. Sit down, Preacher, and tell me who is trying to run me out."

"Hard to say. Whoever it is hides his tracks so well that, in spite of how unlikely it sounds, the best prospects are the judge and the marshal."

"Actually, it could be one of them. Both have tried to buy me out. Now they want to marry me."

"Doesn't surprise me."

"You know, you'd be a lot more appealing choice," she said, with a twinkle in her eye. "But then you already have a wife. Or is she part of your cover?"

Bran slowly nodded his head. "She's my wife."

"Too bad."

"For her," he acknowledged. "Not for me. As for your problem, it seems to me there is one unknown player in the game."

"Who?"

Bran took a sip of the strong, hot liquid. "I can't get a handle on him. I only know he rides a horse with a silver-trimmed saddle. He's tried to hold up the stage and he's been seen in town."

"The man who fired at us?"

"At you, I think. I believe he was warning you."

"Or the judge. You know he stands to become an even wealthier man if some of the claims he's bought prove out."

"I didn't know that."

"So, what happens now? I don't want to lose any more gold and there's no way I'm selling the mine."

"I don't know. I need more time."

Sylvia studied her cup, then answered. "I don't think so, Preacher Adams. I think that time is running out. If you don't know who you're after, you aren't going to catch him. I think the settlement needs to know you're the gunfighter."

The thought chilled Bran. Making himself a target didn't bother him, but announcing his true identity would put Macky in danger. That he couldn't do.

"No, not yet, Mrs. Mainwearing. I'll find out the truth, but I'll do it my own way."

"I'll give you a week, Night Eyes. If you're as good as they say you are, you'll find him. If not, I'll bring in someone else."

Sylvia rose.

Bran followed her toward the door. She stopped before opening it. "You know, you're a very attractive man, Preacher. If I didn't like that young wife of yours so much, I'd offer you a permanent job, something you might not want to turn down. What would you say, I wonder?" She gave a laugh and opened the door. "Relax, Preacher. You're safe."

Bran let out a silent sigh of relief. There might have been a time when he'd consider her offer. But not any more. He was already anxious to get back to the parsonage, to McKenzie Kathryn Calhoun. It was time for her to confess her sins.

Bran took Sylvia's hand and tipped his hat. "I thank you for the offer, ma'am, but I already have a woman and I'd better get back to her."

*   *   *

As Bran rode up to the cabin he could hear Macky singing one of the popular miners' songs about a woman named Clementine. She had a full voice that made a man feel good just listening. She'd make a good wife and mother.

And she'd been a virgin.

Bran hadn't let himself face that yet. Obviously she'd been honest about not being with child. But who was the man following her and why? He hadn't pressed her last night. But now, he needed to know.

He put the horse inside the makeshift fence and went toward the cabin, pausing to watch Macky through the window as she fried bacon and cut slices from a loaf of bread left by the women the night before. She was wearing her man's shirt again, hanging loose over her drawers.

Every now and then Macky stopped and stared off into space. When she woke this morning and found Bran gone she'd been disappointed, then grateful. It gave her a chance to make plans. She didn't know how Bran felt about her now, but she hoped that Lorraine was right when she said that he cared.

For Macky knew the truth. She was in love with her gunfighter husband. Being wanted for murder didn't change her feelings. She'd have killed anyone trying to hurt Todd, if she'd had the chance.

He didn't want the folks in Heaven to know he was the gunfighter. She wasn't sure what that meant, but until she returned the money, she wanted to keep her identity secret as well.

As she worked, she'd gotten an idea. She didn't hold any stock in Bran's belief that she had any influence over the town, but if she could find a way to use her ill-gotten fortune to do good, the church members might understand and forgive her.

Bran could retire and give up his life as a hired killer and they would use her money to build a church. If anybody lost their savings in the robbery back in Promise, they could be repaid from the banker's portion of the money.

Surely Sylvia had enough gold that she'd be willing to go along with the plan until they could pay her back. Maybe she'd just consider it a donation to the Lord.

Macky and Bran could leave their wicked pasts behind and no one would ever have to know. She was creating one of those lovely fantasies, the kind she'd never indulged in before.

But suppose Bran didn't want to marry her? And what about the marshal and the judge?

She'd have to wait, to be sure before she confessed her crime.

Macky heard the horse greeting Solomon. Bran had returned. A moment later, she turned around slowly to face him, forgetting that she was only half dressed. She'd wait until he let her know where they stood before she put forth her plan.

He caught sight of her hair spilling across her shoulders, falling into the space between her breasts, and he smiled.

Macky knew he hadn't intended to smile; none of his smiles came easy. That made them all the more special. Then a grin slashed across his mouth like the sun cutting through a cloud.

She grinned at him, took a running leap and landed with her arms around his neck and her legs around his waist. With all the pent-up anxiety and residual desire fed by the memories of what she'd felt the night before, Macky kissed Bran. And before he could ask the questions he'd intended to, he was lying on the bed with her on top of him, returning her kisses and her caresses.

"Macky. Macky," he said, trying to pull back and regain control. "Don't do this."

But his protest was swallowed up by her mouth and he soon discovered that containing Macky was like trying to stop a prairie fire. It was blazing too hot and moving too fast to escape. And then he was caught up in its heat and giving as much as he got.

Their coupling was over almost before it began and then Macky was urging Bran to hurry and dress.

"We don't have long. Eat your food. We'd better get moving."

"Get moving where?" Bran asked incredulously as he watched her washing herself and pulling on her clothes.

"It's Sunday, Preacher. You have a service to lead, remember?"

"The devil I do," he swore.

"No, you're God's messenger," she said. "Your sermon will be on the Temptation of Man."

"That's a subject I'm well acquainted with," he said.

"I cleaned your clothes. I'll hitch up the wagon while you dress."

Macky left Bran inside, knowing that if she didn't, they'd never get to church. She flew out the door, as if she had angel wings. She pushed her hair beneath a straw bonnet, not noticing the long tag of curls hanging down her back.

"Get away from me, Satan!" Bran growled and began to dress. Macky was no angel. He'd do well to listen to his own words, else he was going to end up on a spit, being roasted by the fires of hell.

Even now he felt breathless, as if he were flying, and nothing he could do would wipe away his joy. This couldn't be happening. He'd never done something so irresponsible. Without a thought about the consequences, he'd burned all his restraint.

Bran swore. He left the meat and bread on the table and followed Macky outside. She'd climbed into the wagon and was humming the song the citizens of Heaven had sung on their arrival.

Bran didn't feel much like he was bringing in the sheaves. He was afraid that he was the fatted calf.

Chapter

Eighteen

"MACKY, WE HAVE TO TALK about what happened," Bran finally said, after they had ridden for awhile.

She didn't want to talk. She just wanted them to be like any other man and his wife going to church on Sunday. "Why? Can't we go on just as we are now? The people in Heaven don't have to know the truth, do they?"

She was serious. For a moment he allowed himself to consider her suggestion. Not telling the truth meant that he'd go on being a preacher and Macky would be his wife. Could he? No. Neither option was reasonable.

"Who are you hiding from? Why did you let the people of Heaven believe that you are my wife?"

"I want to tell you, Bran, but I can't. Especially now. It could put you in danger."

"Telling me what's wrong will put me in danger but keeping me in the dark won't? I don't believe that, Macky. It doesn't make any sense."

Bran didn't make any better sense to Macky. They weren't married, but they'd been as close as two people could be. He'd been ready enough to go along with the pretense in the beginning. And he'd had all kinds of opportunity to correct the mistake. But he hadn't. Why?

Sylvia Mainwearing. The mine. The accidents and thefts. Was he somehow involved in the trouble in Heaven? Even the idea overwhelmed Macky. That would mean that he hadn't cared about her at all. That he was using her.

No. She would never believe that; he'd been too careful to see that she felt what he had. Macky didn't think other men would be so concerned.

When he'd made love to her, it had seemed like he cared about her, wanted her. A lump filled her throat and she felt tears well up behind her eyelids. She couldn't have misunderstood that.

Swallowing hard, she finally forced herself to speak. "I'm sorry, Bran. I have no right to expect anything of you. I'll tell the people at church this morning that I'm going back East to visit my folks. You don't have to worry about protecting me any more."

The wagon hit a rut and bounced Macky against Bran. He moved quickly away. He knew that she was waiting, giving him the chance to say that he cared about her, that they had a future. But he didn't say the words. He had to tell her that no woman could be a part of the kind of life a gunfighter led and survive. Not even Macky.

"I care about you, Macky. You're obviously in trouble of some kind and I have a job to do. We're stuck with each other, whether we like it or not. I don't want you hurt, and to protect you, I need to know the truth."

"The truth?" she said softly. How could she expect honesty from him if she withheld it? She owed him that much. "All right, the truth is that I'm a wanted woman."

Bran scoffed. "I don't believe a word of that. What on earth are you wanted for?"

"Bank robbery. The man I am hiding from is Pratt, the

man with the silver-trimmed saddle. He—we held up the Bank of Promise the day your stage stopped in town."

"I don't believe you. Why would you hold up a bank? You couldn't possibly be a part of Pratt's gang."

Then she told him how it happened. "Now Pratt is here, in town, looking for his money."

"It was his horse you were searching that night outside the saloon? I thought he was the father of your child."

"Oh, my goodness. You thought that I'd have something to do with a man who murders people?"

Bran looked down at the gun sheathed in the holster he was wearing. "You did, didn't you?"

"You're different, Bran," she said softly. "I know you've killed men, but you're not a murderer."

"And I don't believe that you're an outlaw, Macky."

"Believe it, Bran," she said. "You saw the money hidden under the mattress and the gold coins in my handkerchief. They were from Sylvia's mine."

"How can you be sure?"

"You saw them. They were imprinted with an *S*."

They'd reached Hell Street and Bran could see the wagons filled with churchgoers arriving. They'd run out of time.

"So what are we going to do, Bran?" Macky asked.

"First, unless I can figure a way out, it looks like I'm going to preach a sermon, Macky. Then I'm going to find the man behind Sylvia's troubles. And if he happens to be Pratt, all the better."

"And me?" she asked. "I'll go to jail."

"I won't let that happen, though how I'll stop it, I'm not sure."

Heaven's bell, atop the saloon, began to toll. Bran knew that he and Macky could be approaching the hour of their unmasking and, for the first time, he had no idea what he could do to prevent disaster.

As their wagon stopped in front of the saloon, Preston Cribbs came forward. "Welcome, Preacher Adams. We're looking forward to having you share the word. Let me help you down, Mrs. Adams. Can't have you falling, now can we?"

Macky ducked her head. She wished she didn't have to lie. Having a child was something she'd never thought about, but . . . She touched her stomach for a moment, then caught sight of Bran watching her. She lifted her head proudly and strode inside.

She might not have been with a man before, but she had now. And she knew what that could mean. For a moment she remembered Rachel Pendley, nursing her child, fearing the censure of her child's illegitimate birth. Macky made up her mind that she and Rachel would be friends. After all, until Bran decreed otherwise, she was the preacher's wife and charity began at home.

Moments later everyone was inside the saloon. The chairs that held gamblers and drinkers in the evening were arranged to face the bar.

Bran followed Preston Cribbs to the front as the congregation filled the chairs, leaving a scattering of men and older children to find seats on the stairs behind. Macky sat at the end of the row, watching the man in whose arms she'd spent the night and part of the morning. The man who knew her terrible secret.

From her position she could see the entire saloon, including the steps leading up to the room where she'd spent her first nights in Heaven. But Rachel Pendley and her children weren't there.

At the last minute Hank Clay came in, climbed over several men and sat down on the top step. Apparently nobody except Macky seemed to notice when Lorraine slipped down the hall and sat down beside him.

As if by request, Preston Cribbs stood and motioned the worshipers to join him in song. His voice, thready and high, began a hymn which Macky had never heard. Had she been asked, she'd have to confess that she was unfamiliar with hymns in general. But this song, "On Jordon's Stormy Banks

I Stand," seemed very appropriate. Though Bran wasn't looking at her, she couldn't keep her eyes from him.

When they finished the song, the congregation bowed their heads. Bran looked out over the citizens. "We have come here today," he said, "to share our praise and our gratitude for gifts we are given. To promise to hold each other in the wake of the wind, to keep each other warm when the winter is cold, to bring food to the hungry. This we can do. This is our duty to our Father who has given us life. We do so now. Please be seated."

The congregation sat slowly, studying each other with questions in their eyes. They'd never had a minister who spoke in rhythm, in quiet, even tones. And they weren't sure how they were expected to respond.

Bran opened the Bible he carried in his hand. He studied the pages, then asked, " 'Am I my brother's keeper?' The answer is yes. We are our brother's keepers and the keepers of the land and the animals who live among us. But there are those of us who are overcome by weakness. This is the temptation of man, to covet that which does not belong to him and take it if he can. That which tempts man is, and always has been, greed."

A few uneasy "Amens" rippled through the room.

"This morning we come to ask forgiveness, even me," Bran said, "for I am a man like you. I too have coveted that which does not belong to me. I too have taken that which I wanted without regard to breaking the laws of God."

A murmur went through the saloon and Macky felt the eyes of the women planted on her. She looked at Bran, waiting for him to tell the truth, to explain that she wasn't his wife, that she wasn't carrying a child.

But he remained silent.

For a long moment the world seemed to be silent. Then sudden rifle fire shattered the quiet, followed by the sound of horses riding hard. Quickly the men rushed outside as one of the wagons carrying Sylvia's gold came to a ragged stop, the driver slumped over the horses.

"Where's the marshal?" one of the escorts called out.

"I'll get him," someone said.

Bran left his place in front of the bar and hurried to help the wounded man from the wagon. "What happened?"

"The thieves were waiting for us. Took the entire shipment. Never made it to Denver City."

The marshal rode in from the other side of town. "What's wrong?"

"They fired on us," the second man said. "Killed two of the guards and drove the others off. Took the gold and sent us back to town with a warning."

The marshal pulled his gun from his holster and checked the barrel. "What kind of warning?"

"Said that I was to tell you that the Sylvia would never ship another load," the wounded man said. "Swore that not even that gunfighter can stop them."

Larkin pressed his lips together. "Nobody threatens me," he said. "Preacher Adams, I'd appreciate it if you'd explain to Mrs. Mainwearing what happened. I'm forming a posse to go after the bandits. Who'll ride with me?"

Moments later the men with horses mounted up and rode away, leaving the women of the church behind, worried and huddled together. "Let's take care of the wounded," Macky said, springing into action. "May we use your saloon, Lorraine?"

"Of course, let's get them inside." Hank Clay stayed behind long enough to assist the preacher in helping the two wounded men inside. Then, while Bran rode toward the mine, Hank and another man loaded up the wagons and escorted the women and children back home.

Macky, still shocked by the possibility that Bran had been about to confess everything, stood by the window trying to decide what to do. She hadn't known what to expect; church was as foreign to her as the corset and crinoline she was still learning to tolerate. Understanding Bran was even worse.

"Can you help me, Macky?" Lorraine called from the upstairs hall.

"Yes, as soon as I get out of this fish trap I'm wearing," she answered and lifted her skirt to unfasten the steel-spoked contrivance and let it fall to the floor.

Little had changed since Bran's early-morning visit to the widow when she'd offered him a full-time job and issued him a personal invitation to call.

He wasn't surprised when Mrs. Mainwearing opened the door. "Have you changed your mind, gunfighter?"

"No," he said and stepped adroitly around her. "I have bad news, about your gold shipment."

"What about my gold?"

"There was another holdup. They took the gold and either killed or wounded your men."

"Oh, dear God!" Sylvia stumbled toward a love seat inside the parlor. "What am I going to do?"

"There's more, I'm afraid," Bran said. "They sent you a message. No more gold will be allowed to leave. They said nobody can stop them, not even the gunfighter."

"And what do you intend to do about it?" she asked wearily. "I hired you to save gold, not souls."

She had a right to be angry. "I intend to, Mrs. Mainwearing, but you can't identify me just yet."

"Why shouldn't I? I can't see that you're accomplishing much as a preacher. At least if the murderer knows that Night Eyes is here, he'll think twice about taking him on."

"That's what I want to talk about. I'm afraid you may be in physical danger."

She cut her gaze to Bran. "You mean you think he might . . ."

"He's already sent you a warning by shooting the judge. Then he follows up with stealing your gold and making a threat. He's getting desperate."

Sylvia came to her feet and began to pace. Finally she

turned toward Bran. "Somebody killed Moose, Reverend Adams. People thought I didn't care about him, but I did. I don't intend to lose his mine."

"There are times," he said, "when we can't control what happens."

"Maybe, but I'm not going to give up. One way or another, I'm going to find and punish the person behind all this."

Bran finally convinced her to keep his secret a little longer. He had to make arrangements for Macky before he allowed the truth to come out. But as he rode to town, he knew that he couldn't hold Sylvia back for long.

He understood the pain of failure and her need to find and punish Moose's murderer. He also understood the helplessness she felt. He'd lived with that helplessness for most of his adult life. He'd been driven by pain, by his need for revenge, so much so that he'd sacrificed his life to it, even when he was no longer certain that the men responsible for slaughtering his family were still alive.

Being wanted for the murder of the man who'd nearly killed his Indian brother had never slowed Bran down, though the possibility of capture was always there. But the wanted poster of an eighteen-year-old boy bore little resemblance to the thirty-two-year-old gunfighter he'd become. The only thing that tied him to that killing had been his real name, John Brandon Lee.

He was sorry he'd had to shoot the soldier, but he'd had no choice. Even if the Indian being tortured hadn't been Blue, Bran would still have come to his defense. But Blue had almost died and that had filled the last crevice in a heart already turning to stone.

Afterward, Bran never intended to become a gun-for-hire, but once it happened, the work seemed to come easier and more often. He never walked away when the only way to stop suffering was to punish the one causing it. Never once did he punish unfairly, nor was he blamed.

Night Eyes was an avenger who never used his anger

against the innocent. He'd always worked alone and those who knew his real identity either died or kept his secret.

Age, an eye patch, and several name changes left John Brandon Lee in the past. He'd never stopped looking for the river pirate who'd killed his real family.

But what had he gained?

A reputation as a gunfighter and a life of loneliness.

And now there was Macky.

When he reached the place where the judge had been wounded, Bran pulled off the main road and followed the trail of hoofprints leading up in the rocks. Finding the spot where the ambusher had waited was easy.

After learning about Macky's part in the bank holdup, Bran was certain that Pratt was the man after her. Pratt must feel secure in his activities. He hadn't even been careful to cover his tracks.

The scene struck Bran as odd, particularly since the marshal had said he couldn't find the bushwhacker who'd fired on the buggy. If Larkin hadn't found Pratt it was because he hadn't looked or taken the time to track him down.

The sun was directly overhead and warm. The wildflowers blooming among the rocks had been trampled by a horse that had been ridden hard, or was carrying a heavy load. That didn't mesh with what happened to Sylvia and the judge. Unless someone else had ridden through here since.

Bran wiped his forehead and peered upward. It was time he did a little investigating on his own. Flipping the reins against his horse's haunch, he started the animal up the trail that became rougher the higher he went. Then he heard the sound of another horse.

Nestled between two boulders was an old miner's cabin. A lean-to beyond revealed a black horse, dusty and breathing hard as he drank deeply from a water trough. There was no sign of a silver-trimmed saddle, but Bran was fairly certain that this was the same horse he'd seen in town. It could have been ridden by one of the outlaws who'd tried to hold up the stage. And more than that, it had been ridden hard—recently.

From the look of things, Bran figured there was only one man inside. Bran eased off his horse and tied him to a tree behind a boulder. With the wind blowing down the draw, the black horse wouldn't smell the intruder and give Bran away.

Carefully he worked his way around to the cabin. Why was Pratt still in Heaven if he was searching for the money Macky had? Either he had some idea that the *kid* was around, or this was his normal hiding place. At least Macky was safe. Bran's concern for her bothered him. He'd seen too many men lose their edge once they fell in love.

Love? The Devil! Love was something he'd never even considered, never allowed. He'd failed all the people he'd ever loved—his parents, his sister, and his Choctaw brother. All dead.

For so long he'd beaten down the least little spark of feeling, certain that if he let it free, his love would somehow put the recipient in mortal danger.

Find and punish had been the driving factor in his life, suppressing any human need with cold hate. It had worked —too well. He'd stopped feeling at all. Then Macky had gotten on the stage, and like the snowy peaks atop the mountains, the walls of ice around his heart had begun to melt and he couldn't seem to stop it.

He was still stunned that she'd given him her innocence. That he'd taken it so casually. No. Hell, no! It hadn't been casual. It had been intense. It was the kind of temptation that David had felt for Bathsheba.

Damn his weakness! Bran knew what caring could do. But he knew about desperation as well. He couldn't fault Macky for running away. He'd done the same thing. He'd run away because people refused to believe that the men who'd killed his family were river pirates, not Indians.

He'd run away from the charge that he'd murdered a man because he'd known that nobody would believe him then, either. He'd run because his word meant nothing.

Macky also ran away because nobody believed in her and she never thought they would. But that was changing. Her simple honesty was contagious. And he wouldn't allow Macky to be hurt. So long as the townsfolk didn't know that he was Night Eyes, they'd accept Macky as the preacher's wife and she'd be safe. Until he'd dealt with Pratt, he'd have to make certain that the charade continued. But he'd have to find a way to stay away from Macky. He couldn't stop wanting her, and wanting her could cause her more grief than the law.

The sun was moving toward the west. In the higher elevation the temperature was growing cooler. He needed to move quickly, before Macky decided to return to the parsonage alone. He found a spot close to the house where he could see the man inside the cabin and he knew that he'd found Pratt. On the floor was one of the saddlebags containing Sylvia's gold.

Pratt hadn't shaved in a couple of days and the beginnings of a scruffy gray beard smudged his face, covering the wrinkles of age. Bran felt a moment of recognition, an uncertainty that left him almost immediately. This man could hurt Macky.

Confronting him now could be a mistake. Now that Bran knew where Pratt was, he could always find him. What was more important was learning who'd hired him, for Bran didn't think that the outlaw was working alone. This was simply more of the sinister cat-and-mouse game being played with Sylvia. Someone stood to gain much more. And Bran intended to find out who.

Hank Clay drove the judge from Willa's Boardinghouse to the stage Sunday afternoon.

"You sure you ought to be leaving, Judge?" he asked.

"Can't stay. I need to get back to Denver to report that the gunfighter is on the way. I'm not a bit pleased about that," he confided. "Not a bit."

"Mrs. Mainwearing might be safer with him around."

That observation, however casually made by Hank, didn't please the judge. Everybody in Heaven knew that the judge had his eye on Sylvia. It was obvious that he didn't like the thought that she was turning to an outsider for help.

Hank also knew that the marshal spent a lot of time with the widow and hadn't made much progress in finding the bushwhackers. Now, according to the town gossip, Sylvia seemed to have cast a favorable eye on the preacher.

The only thing Hank knew for sure was that there were a lot of people in Heaven with secrets to hide. Including Lorraine. Including himself.

As he drove past the saloon he glanced up and caught sight of the flutter of the window curtain. Someone was watching. He didn't have to see her face. His senses told him it was Lorraine.

"Will you do something for me, Mr. Clay?" the judge asked as Hank stopped the buggy and held his hand out to help the judge climb down. "I'll be glad to pay you."

"If I can."

"Keep an eye on any newcomers. Send me word if anybody suspicious comes into town."

"You mean the gunfighter?"

"I guess I mean anybody who's turned up in Heaven since Moose died. Maybe even before. Whoever arranged that accident could have been here all along. We don't need people in Heaven who aren't good citizens. For all we know, Night Eyes is already here."

Most towns didn't want people who didn't fit in. Hank had learned that well enough through the years. He couldn't believe that a professional gunfighter would be able to keep his identity secret in Heaven. Everybody knew everybody else too well. He didn't much like spying for the judge. He'd spent the last three years of his life trying to be unnoticed.

As the illegitimate son of a wealthy Southern planter, he'd never been left alone. Until his mother died, everybody who knew made his life a living hell.

Once she was gone there was no reason to stay in South Carolina. There was a whole country out there that didn't know who he was. He'd tried a town or two before settling in Heaven. As far as Hank was concerned, anybody here was free to be whatever he or she wanted, even a gunfighter.

Living a simple life as a blacksmith and livery operator had been enough for Hank Clay—for a time. Now he wanted more.

Later that night, Hank waited for the last horse to ride away from the saloon. As the lights began to dim, he crossed the street, made his way into the kitchen and up the back stairs.

Lorraine was standing beside the window as if she were waiting for him.

"Mr. Clay?"

"Hank," he corrected.

"Is that really your name?"

"Is Lorraine yours?"

She dropped her head and turned back to face the window. "My name is Laura Peters. Or at least that's the name my mother gave me. The trapper my father sold me to called me Lottie."

"There's a husband?"

"No. There never was. I ran away. Later, after I learned how to make a living, I called myself Lorraine Lake. I'd run into a piece of bad luck when I met Moose and he brought me here."

"You and Moose?"

"At first—yes. Not in a long time. Does that matter?"

"Not if it doesn't matter to you."

Hank didn't stay the night. Instead, he listened to Lorraine talk. She'd never had anyone do that before, and by the time the moon slid behind the trees, she was asleep in his arms.

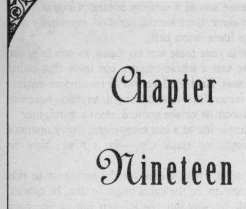

Chapter

Nineteen

Pratt wasn't a man who liked to keep his own company. From the time he'd joined the group of riverboat pirates and lured his first riverboat onto a sandbar, he'd surrounded himself with men who followed blindly.

Through the years, his self-importance had been inflated by his success. He'd made a reputation as a thief and become supremely arrogant. Playing second fiddle now was wearing on his nerves. He'd had no choice if he wanted to avoid prison, but now he was ready to collect his money and move on. San Francisco was the kind of place that offered a man real opportunity.

The bank job in Promise had been a bad idea from the first. It was only now becoming clear that maybe he'd been set up. One of his men had been killed and the other captured. And he didn't even have the money to show for it.

To make matters worse, it left Pratt temporarily broke. That's why he'd gone after the stage, for pocket money. The job should have been easy. It would have, except for that sharp-shooting gunfighter who'd done away with the two newest members of his gang.

Then came the mine disaster. He didn't care that the fool who helped him set off the dynamite had died. But almost being caught himself hadn't been part of the plan. He hadn't picked the two men who helped hold up Sylvia's gold shipment. One of them was killed. The other took most of the gold into Denver and Pratt knew he wouldn't return. Once again Pratt had been lucky.

Or had he?

Nah! Staying up here in the mountains was getting to him. Even getting one of the saddlebags of gold for himself without the other men's knowledge didn't take away the growing sense of foreboding. Pratt was ready to move on. He was becoming a little too well known in the Kansas Territory.

He was all out of whiskey and he needed a drink and a woman. He thought about Lorraine Lake but she'd turned him down once. She had her eye on the marshal. That was one man Pratt didn't want to cross and he'd been told to stay away from town. Until he got his money he'd follow orders.

As far as he could see, he had few choices. There was that bitch Sylvia Mainwearing, but she was surrounded by men. Pratt could always seek out one of the women who serviced the miners, but they were used up and often diseased. That took him back where he started.

He needed to go to town.

Wait a minute. What about that preacher's wife? She was stuck out in the middle of nowhere, just like him. From the look of her, she was a woman with a lot to offer to the right man. Nobody would know if she had a private visitor on the side.

The fact that she belonged to that gunfighter made possessing her all the more appealing. Pratt would have to take the man eventually. Why not have a little fun and begin the eviction proceedings a little early? Besides, he had a score to settle with the man of God. Taking his woman would be a start.

He'd just take a little ride down to the cabin and make a nice Sunday-afternoon call on his nearest neighbor.

Pratt saddled his horse and thought about the possibilities that lay ahead. He slipped his hand inside the saddlebags and pulled out one of Sylvia's gold coins. If Miz Adams were good enough, he'd just make a little contribution to the church.

The Sunday morning services hadn't turned out as Macky had expected. She drove the wagon behind the cabin and unharnessed Solomon. The mule was as docile as he could be, almost as if he realized the trouble he'd caused when he dumped Macky in the road.

Macky led the mule inside the empty, temporary corral, slapped him on the rear and fastened the gate. Bran hadn't returned from Sylvia Mainwearing's mine. Mrs. Mainwearing would likely be upset. Bran would probably have to drive her into town to check personally on her drivers. Maybe Macky should have waited in town for Bran to return, but once the drivers were treated, she'd wandered downstairs to watch for Bran, growing more and more uncomfortable as the miners and drifters began to wander in.

Though it had been Sunday, once Lorraine opened the door to the injured drivers, the rest of the miners made good use of the saloon. One of Lorraine's customers invited Macky to dance. Another had invited her to join their card game.

Finally, she'd picked up a Denver newspaper lying on the bar and walked down to the general store where she took a seat on the bench out front. Opening the paper, she'd read the headline and felt her heart slide down her stomach and draw itself into a knot.

The banker was dead. The man she'd threatened to kill for cheating her father had been shot in the holdup of the bank in Promise. She hadn't known that. Now he'd died. In addition to being a bank robber, she was an accomplice to murder.

"The devil's pitchfork!" She knew then that she was really in trouble. She felt as if she were whirling around in a fast-moving stream, ready to be sucked down with no way to get out.

She couldn't think. Earlier in the day she'd decided to confess her crime, make amends and stay in Heaven. Now she couldn't do that without giving Bran's secret away. Nobody would believe that she was innocent when she'd ended up with the money. She had to do something. But what?

She couldn't stay in town. Too many people were watching her. She studied the situation all the way home, looking for another answer that would get her out of the mess she'd dug herself into. Back at the parsonage she paced back and forth outside the cabin door, searching diligently for solutions that remained illusive.

Papa had told her that one day she'd know what love was. He was right. She'd found it and she was about to lose it. And she couldn't see a way in hell to stop it.

"Lordy, what am I going to do?"

But it wasn't the Lord who answered, it was Pratt. "First off, you and me are going to get acquainted, Miz Adams, is it?"

He was standing right beside her, leaning against the corner of the cabin, flipping a gold coin and catching it in his palm. He'd figured it out and now he'd come for the money. "What are you doing here?" she asked, her heart pounding. Why hadn't she stayed in town as Bran had told her to?

"I've come to call on the new minister," he said.

"I'm sorry but he isn't—I mean, we're busy. If you'll come back later."

She was trying to move past him, get through the door and throw the wooden bolt from the inside.

Pratt smiled. He had to hand it to her. She'd gussied

herself up real good. He liked her red hair and her cool green eyes.

Something about them seemed familiar, a bit troublesome.

"That's all right, ma'am," he said. "We sure don't need the preacher for what I have in mind. Guess I can give you my . . . donation."

He flipped the coin at her. Instinctively, Macky caught it and glanced down at the familiar S on its face.

"You ever see anything like that before, ma'am? It's pure gold. All you have to do is be nice to me and you can keep it. You can be nice, can't you?"

Macky gasped. Her mama had a favorite story she used to tell about going to a fancy ball, and how the lady always had to leave when she was having the most fun. If she stayed too long, the fun would be over and she'd pay the price of misbehaving.

Macky had stayed too long. Now she would have to pay the price.

"No, I don't think so. I've never seen a coin like this before," she lied, her voice trembling. "But our church will certainly make good use of it. You're a very generous man, Mr.—I don't know your name."

She needed him to think she was impressed. Maybe she'd bargain a bit, anything to buy time. If she was right about him, Pratt was the kind of man who liked to see women grovel.

"My name?" He adjusted his gunbelt and rocked back and forth on the balls of his feet. "Reckon you know my moniker, even if you don't know me. Folks call me Pratt."

"The bank robber?" Macky said and gasped as if she were afraid. At the same time she took a step closer to the door.

"One and the same," he bragged. "Everybody's afraid of me. But don't worry, darlin', I won't hurt you. Women like me, you know."

He was leering at her now.

"I wouldn't brag about my identity, Mr. Pratt. Not after that newspaper headline I read back in town."

It was Pratt's turn to be confused. "What headline?"

"Guess you didn't hear," Macky said and walked boldly toward the cabin. "That banker died. Pratt is wanted for murder. Not only that, but Mrs. Mainwearing hired a gunfighter named Night Eyes to protect her gold. The marshal and the sheriff are out looking for you right now."

She almost made it inside when he grabbed her, twisting her arm painfully behind and jerking her close. She could feel the heated, putrid smell of his breath.

"That's a lie," he growled. "I don't know what you're doing here, sweet thing, but you ain't no preacher's wife."

It was time for Macky to confess her sins. The worst was about to happen. "You're the one who's lying, Mr. Pratt. We both know that you're in trouble, don't we?"

She'd had enough of this evil little man. He might not leave, but if he laid a hand on her, he'd regret it. "I think you'd better go now, before my husband returns."

Pratt's desire melted under the intensity of her gaze. Her eyes looked like hoarfrost on winter grass, encasing its green in pure ice. He'd never seen eyes like that except once.

Once. Where?

And then he knew. "You're—you're that kid—McKenzie."

"Kid?" she questioned. "Yes I am, Pratt, and I can prove you're the one who held up the bank and probably the one who shot that banker."

"I found you! I followed you here and didn't even know it. First there was the velvet purse on the trail, the purse with the gold coins. I should have known then, but I didn't put it together. Where's the money?"

Macky couldn't answer. All she could think about was keeping Bran out of it. "You can't prove it," she finally said.

"Oh, yes I can. But wait a minute. Somebody took the cameo and the feather. And the preacher stopped me from going after the thief."

Pratt let go of her arms and stepped back, glancing around as if he'd heard something. "The two of you been working together from the first. And the boss don't have a clue, or does he?"

"Boss?" Macky questioned.

Pratt studied her. "Maybe the boss knows. Maybe he plans on cutting me out."

"What makes you think that?" Bran said as he stepped out of the trees near the stream, leading his horse with one hand. He held his drawn pistol in the other.

The bank robber's eyes grew wide. "What are you going to do with that gun?"

Macky was suddenly afraid. Bran was gone. In his place was the man who'd seen his sister die, who'd killed men and lived to kill again. All the light was gone from his eyes, leaving only cold, dead cold.

"Go inside the cabin, Macky, and bolt the door. And you"—Bran continued to stare at Pratt—"you get on your horse. We're going for a little ride."

"You don't have to worry, Brother Adams, I ain't going to tell nobody. I was just playing a little joke on the kid—I mean your wife."

"I don't like jokes."

"Just give me part of the money from the robbery and I'll leave you and her alone. I ain't got no reason to tell anybody that you ain't a real man of God."

"Oh, but I am, Mr. Pratt. I'm His avenging angel and we're going to have a little talk about your soul."

If he'd moved, Bran would have killed him. For the first time he was ready to shoot a man in cold blood, without mercy. He knew it and Pratt knew it as well.

As Bran mounted his horse, Pratt put his hands over his head and made a dash for his own mount. "I'll come. Honest to God, I'll come. Just don't kill me."

"Don't kill him, Bran," Macky echoed. "He isn't worth it."

"Maybe not," Bran agreed, "but you are."

Bran let Pratt make his own way up the trail until he was satisfied that Macky wasn't following. "Turn off here."

"But there's no trail. There's nothing but rock and snow."

"Don't let it worry you, Pratt. We aren't going far."

Pratt followed orders, riding his horse as far up as he could go. It was growing colder. The sky was turning a leaden gray and the wind was picking up. Pratt began to shiver, his teeth chattering in spite of his best efforts to look tough.

"Far enough," Bran finally said. "Now get off that horse and remove your gunbelt."

Pratt complied, his fingers shaking so badly that he could barely obey. "Forget the money. Just let me go and I'll leave the territory."

"Not yet. I think I'll wait until I get some answers to a few of my questions." Bran rested his revolver on his thigh, his finger resting loosely on the trigger. "I want to know what's happening here in Heaven."

"I—I don't know what you mean."

Before Pratt was even aware that he had moved, Bran fired one shot at Pratt's feet. "You know what I mean. Did you kill Moose?"

"No! It's God's truth, Preacher. I was in prison then. Old Moose was killed before I got here."

"But you know who was behind it, don't you?"

Pratt heard the sound of the hammer being cocked once more.

"You don't know? You ain't in cohoots with 'em?"

"I work alone, Pratt, and I want an answer."

"I'm a dead man if I say."

"You're a dead man if you don't."

"Can't we make a little deal here, Preacher? I don't want to take the fall here. Just let me go and I'll ride west and you'll never see me again."

The last thing Bran wanted was to have Pratt leave. He was the only one who could prove Macky's innocence. But the spineless thief was so scared that he was likely to do something dumb. Maybe there was another way. If Bran could convince Pratt that he was gaining a new partner, one he feared, that might make him stay around. But Pratt had to be convinced that he would be signing his own death warrant if he didn't go along.

"Suppose we make a deal," Bran suggested. "Taking over the Sylvia looks like a pretty good setup. Let's just say I'm considering cutting myself in. I could use a partner, someone who already knows the lay of the land. What about joining up with me, Pratt? I'm not greedy. We'll split the take fifty-fifty."

Pratt looked up at Bran, his eyes filled with puzzlement. "You'd make me a full partner?"

"I'm considering it. But first, tell me everything you know."

Pratt began to smile. This was looking better and better. Suddenly he could see a way out, a way to escape and pin the trouble on a man already known to be a killer. He took a deep breath. Why not? It made sense. Every outlaw from here to the Mississippi would know that Pratt was the king and Night Eyes would take the blame.

As the preacher, Brother Adams would be above suspicion, the perfect partner. And he didn't know that his cover was blown. It was just about perfect. Once he took care of a little problem, Pratt would be in the driver's seat and he couldn't be exposed without the redhead and the preacher going to jail.

"Okay, Rev, I don't suppose it matters none that you know. I work for Aaron Larkin, the federal marshal. He's the man behind all this. He's going to marry Mrs. Mainwearing. I'm supposed to take you out. Then, once he gets your place, he'll have the biggest mining claim in the territory."

"So Marshal Larkin killed Moose?"

"Not with his own lily-white hands, but he had it done.

Pulie, the man killed in the mine, was the one who actually did the deed."

"You got any proof?" Bran asked, his mind racing. It made some weird kind of sense. A federal marshal could go anywhere and do anything. He mingled with the worst of the criminal elements and the town leaders. He could break thieves out of jail and set up bank robberies.

"Just check it out over in Denver. Most of those mining claims have been transferred into Larkin's name, including Moose's."

"Moose's?" That caught Bran by surprise. "You mean Mrs. Mainwearing doesn't own her mine?"

"Oh, she owns the land all right, but the mineral rights belong to Larkin. Moose signed them over one night in a poker game. When he sobered up, he realized what he'd done and tried to buy them back."

"Why'd Larkin have to kill him then, if he already owned the mining rights?"

"Because Moose had already been to San Francisco and married Sylvia. After the poker game, he claimed he'd put everything in her name. Larkin was scared to take the claims to court. He decided that he'd just marry her and then he wouldn't have to worry. But the lady is no fool. She won't make up her mind."

"You mean between Larkin and the judge?"

"Larkin ain't used to being crossed. He's smooth, but he's crazy and he's spent a lot of time getting this thing set up right."

"So he started running off all the prospectors. Then he had Moose killed so that left the way clear for him to marry Sylvia. If she didn't go for that, he'd get rid of her and use his IOU's to claim the mine."

"Yeah, but then he thought Sylvia might pick the judge instead of him."

"Were you trying to kill the judge?"

"No, just scare Sylvia. It didn't matter who I hit. As soon

as she heard the first shot she drove those horses like some wild woman. I never seen nothing like it."

Wild woman. Bran's lips twitched slightly. Sylvia was a lot like Macky. She didn't scare, either.

"Trouble was," Pratt went on, "Larkin didn't know Sylvia was sending for a gunfighter. Now he's running scared. What do you see as our next move, boss?"

Night Eyes had done his job as he usually did, but this time exposing the truth could bring harm to Macky. He wished he could see a way out, but there was no clear answer, not yet.

"All right, Pratt," Bran finally said. "I want you to get back to your cabin and wait for the marshal to contact you. I want to know every move he makes. If we can set him up we'll be secure for life."

"Sure," Pratt agreed eagerly. "I'll let you know everything that happens.

"It would be a mistake for you to run away, Pratt. If you do, I'll chase you down to the ends of the earth."

"I won't run," Pratt promised eagerly. "Why would I walk away from a sweet deal like this?"

"Just to remind you how serious I am," Bran said. He took careful aim and fired, the bullet amputating the tip of the little finger on Pratt's right hand.

Pratt grabbed his hand and screamed. "Son of a—! What'd you do that for?"

"So you won't forget our agreement. I'm a man of God, remember, and I believe in an eye for an eye and a tooth for a tooth. Would you rather I start with your eye?"

As Bran rode back toward the cabin, the sky clouded over. They might have snow, but the temperature seemed too warm.

Everything was coming to a head now. Before he confronted Macky he needed to make sure that his plan could work. She had to be convinced that Pratt was leaving town, and would never tell the truth about the bank robbery in Promise because he'd be implicated by the gold coins Bran had in his possession, the coins that had come from Macky's purse. For the first time, Bran was grateful for his reputation.

He'd have to keep a close watch on Pratt. Even with the little reminder he'd given the outlaw, he couldn't be certain that Pratt wouldn't try to double-cross him. Still, he was counting on what he knew about men like Pratt. They thrived on their own reputations and being a partner with a famous gunfighter would give him the fame he craved. Fame and fear, either one ought to work.

With Pratt under control, the threat of Macky's arrest was lessened. Bran hadn't figured out what he was going to do about the marshal, but she didn't have to know about that. Once the marshal was gone, the sheriff in Promise could be told the truth.

Then Macky could make her own choices about her future. And he'd see that she had every chance to become a farmer if that was what she wanted. As for Night Eyes, he could disappear forever. It was time. He was tired of being on the move. Night Eyes had searched for the killer of his parents for most of his life. That seemed less important now.

Macky was here, and alive and waiting for him.

Bran felt his insides twist at that thought. In the strangest moments, like now, when he should be concentrating on the problem at hand, his mind would catch on some obscure little detail about Macky and he'd lose his train of thought.

Suddenly he was remembering that soot-covered sock on her head. The one she'd accounted for by saying it was a treatment to make her hair more manageable. He laughed lightly. The last thing in life he wanted to be manageable was Macky's hair. He preferred it flying wildly around her face when he was loving her, like some shimmering veil of fire.

Maybe he was getting too involved in his role. He was a

gunfighter, not the preacher he was pretending to be. He was a killer, not the husband he wanted to be. But it didn't matter any more. He knew the minute he saw Pratt at the cabin that he was a liar when he said he didn't love that woman.

"May God smite you dead if you fail, John Brandon Lee," he whispered to the wind.

Chapter Twenty

Wᴜᴛʜ ᴀ ᴍᴜᴛᴛᴇʀᴇᴅ ᴏᴀᴛʜ, Bran pulled his coat tighter and rode his horse back toward the cabin. He'd better be right about Pratt, else Macky's fate was sealed. What happened to him didn't matter, but Macky deserved a future.

He'd known that he had to end their growing intimacy, but every time he'd attempted to do so, Macky had burrowed through his defenses and left him even more vulnerable. And he'd let himself reach out to her. But now, he had to find a way to shut all his feelings for her out of his mind until he could be sure she was safe.

Bran met Macky running to the trail toward him, worry making little wrinkles across her forehead, her glorious hair flying behind her in the wind.

"Oh, Bran, I heard shots and I thought—"

"You thought what?" He swung down from the horse to catch her as she whirled herself into his arms.

"I was afraid you'd been shot. What happened?"

He could feel her heart hammering against his chest. She was holding him so tight he could barely breathe. "Mr. Pratt had a little accident. He decided that he'd make a sacrifice to show repentance for his life of crime."

She leaned her head back and studied him, not sure whether he was serious or teasing. "Is he all right?"

"No, but he's working on doing better. But I don't know how long I can control him. We're going to arrange a little visit to Denver for you. You can stay there until this is settled."

"And what's my reason for leaving my husband?"

"Well, the town still believes that you're carrying a child. Let's let them keep thinking that. You're going to Denver to consult a doctor."

She nodded, then slipped her arms around his waist and laid her cheek against his chest. "Oh, Bran, let's get out of here, go so far away that nobody will ever find us."

"There is no place far enough, Macky. Marshal Larkin isn't going to let us go." A statement more true than Macky could know. "We'd never be able to live without looking over our shoulder. This has to be resolved another way."

"Bran, Pratt knows who I am. Sooner or later, if he doesn't get his money, he's going to tell—whether I'm here or not. I won't let you get involved."

"I already am. The marshal knows I'm the man Sylvia hired. The only thing he doesn't know yet is about your part in the robbery."

That stopped her. "Are you and the marshal working together like Pratt said?"

"Of course not. But I don't trust him and I don't want you anywhere near him."

"Oh, Bran, what if he figures out that you're wanted on that old murder charge?"

"He hasn't yet." *And with a little luck, he'll be so involved in acquiring the mine that he won't. And you'll be long gone by the time he does.*

She'd known that he wouldn't listen. He'd decided to

protect her and he would, at any cost. For now, she'd let him think that she was going. But come morning she'd find the marshal and tell him about her part in the robbery. She'd convince him that Bran knew she was running from an angry husband and agreed to go along. Everybody in Heaven liked Bran. Sylvia would vouch for him. With his reputation they'd believe that he thought he was protecting her.

As they stood, big drops of rain began to fall. Macky grabbed Bran's hand and together they dashed to the cabin, separating as Bran took the horse to the shed and Macky ran into the house. She lit the fire and stood rubbing her hands together over the flame. If Bran had his way, this might be their last time together.

Moments later, she heard the cabin door close. Macky sat down on the bed and began removing her shoes. Bran added another log on the fire and slid out of his wet coat as he tried to gather his wits. Macky unbuttoned her dress. She wasn't preparing supper. She was preparing for bed.

He couldn't stay there without making love to Macky yet he didn't want to leave her alone. " 'Lead us not into temptation,' " Bran whispered. "Pack your clothes, Macky, we're going to town."

"We are not, John Brandon," Macky said, stepping out of her dress. "I may have to leave you, but not tonight. You always pull back as if you're afraid of caring about me. You think that I'll be better off without you." She let the dress fall to the floor.

"You will."

She began unfastening her crinoline. "As far as Heaven is concerned, I'm your wife. As far as I am concerned, I am your wife."

"But you're not. I won't let you do this, Macky."

Ignoring him, she removed her chemise, followed by her drawers. Finally she looked up. "I'm trouble, remember? I told you that in the beginning. Nothing's changed. You can't stop me from loving you one last time."

And he didn't.

He didn't even try.

The pounding that woke Bran the next morning was insistent and loud. It took him a moment to bring himself back to the present, to the now empty bed he'd shared with Macky.

Pulling on his trousers, he made his way to the door and opened it.

He didn't recognize the man standing there, but there was no mistaking his concern.

"Preacher, I need your help. Please. Rachel said you'd come."

"Rachel?"

"My—my missus," he exclaimed, wringing his hands. "I'm Lars Pendley. It's our little girl, Rebekah. She's done wandered off first thing this morning, chasing a stray pup that took up at the house. We can't find her nowhere."

Bran remembered the woman who'd sat beside Macky, the woman with the baby and the blond little girl with blue eyes. Bran reached for his shirt, pulled on his boots, and quickly looked around. Macky was nowhere to be seen. The fireplace was cold, and from what he could tell, the only thing she'd taken was her brother's clothes. A trip to the corral revealed that Solomon too was missing. Bran didn't stop to look, but he'd bet his last dollar that the money from the holdup was gone as well.

With a groan Bran saddled his horse and took off toward town. "We'll mount a search party," he said to the worried man. "You go on back home and tell your wife not to worry. We'll find the little girl."

Bran didn't know where Macky had gone, but he had a bad feeling in his gut. Now this. When he needed to go after Macky he had to help locate a lost child. He gave the horse a nudge. He didn't know how long Macky had been gone. He only hoped she wasn't with Pratt.

. . .

Aaron Larkin had taken over Heaven's empty sheriff's office as his living quarters. Willa's Boardinghouse was too public and an invitation to share Lorraine's bed hadn't materialized as he'd anticipated.

Inside the office there was a desk, a potbellied stove, and one barred cell containing a bunk across the back side. With a mattress and blankets, he'd managed to turn the bunk into a bed. Tobe, the boy who helped out in the saloon occasionally, brought a load of wood. Still, the jail was bare and mean. He'd spent an uncomfortable night and the morning didn't promise much more.

Through the window the sky looked like rain and the wind was cold. He could build a fire to take off some of the chill while he decided what he wanted to do next. He was tired of being cold and living on the pitiful salary the government paid him.

Once he had the mine in his grasp, he'd be in a position to take over the whole town. Then he'd resign from his job as the judge's lackey and he'd never be cold again.

He'd drawn this job out too long. In the past he'd been quick to choose his victim, then he'd move on. That way, nobody ever connected him with the crimes he'd planned.

He'd always avoid his targeted area until after the first crime was committed, then he'd come in to provide protection for the same people he was robbing. Once he'd taken enough, Larkin managed to find the criminal, who would be killed in the arrest. His reputation as a law officer was growing, as was his purse.

But this time he'd delayed his departure. Sylvia was proving to be more resistant to his charms than Larkin had expected. Instead of arresting Pratt for the crimes as he'd intended, Larkin had been forced to continue using him. The fool thought that Larkin didn't know he was helping himself to some of the gold, but Larkin knew. He'd let Pratt go for a while, but the time had come to get rid of him.

Larkin laid some wood in the stove, then looked around, searching for something to start it. The desk. He opened the desk drawer. Inside, he found a stack of wanted posters. Perfect. They'd been here so long that they were practically falling apart. Larkin wadded up the first two and stuck them under his twigs. But the next poster stopped him cold, the truth settling over him like a bear claw around his heart.

The aged drawing was of a kid with one eye. Wanted for murder in Oklahoma fifteen years before, for killing an army officer who'd been attacked by a Choctaw boy.

Larkin had been a soldier himself back then. He hadn't been assigned to reservation duty, but he'd heard about what happened. Every officer in the West kept the troops riled up by retelling every incident that resulted in trouble on the reservation.

Later, interrogation of the tribe had brought forth a name from one of the Indians in exchange for the food they so desperately needed. The killer was a white boy named John Lee. But John Lee was long gone.

The sketch on the wanted poster was as accurate as the artist could make it, but John Lee had never been found. In fact, Larkin suspected that neither the army nor the law officers had ever really searched.

Over the years the kid had been forgotten.

Until now.

The kid had grown up. The kid still had only one eye, but now he covered it with a patch. The kid, wanted for murder, was the preacher. He should have recognized the man right away, but he hadn't.

Larkin smiled. The preacher who was in Heaven to find out who was responsible for Sylvia's trouble was wanted for murder. And Larkin was the marshal in charge of bringing him in. It couldn't have worked out any better. He could hardly keep from chuckling. The end was in sight. Pratt would take care of the preacher. Then Pratt would be shot when the marshal tried to arrest him.

Larkin pushed the poster to the bottom of the stack.

Life was good.

When Macky rode into town, there was no sign of the marshal or his horse in front of the jail, only Hank Clay building up the fire in his blacksmith's shop.

"I saw him riding off a while ago," Hank Clay said when she stopped at the livery stable. "Surprised you didn't cross paths."

"Nope, I didn't see a soul."

"Speaking of souls," Hank said, "where's the preacher this morning? Something I want to talk to him about."

"Ah, he's working on the fence to keep the animals in the corral."

"He let you ride in without him?" Hank eyed her speculatively.

"I can take care of myself."

"And what brings you to town?"

"I just came in to see Lorraine."

Hank smiled slightly. "I doubt you can see Miss Lake yet. She keeps late hours, you know."

"Mrs. Adams." Clara Gooden was heading straight for Macky. She arrived just in time to hear Hank's comment. "See Lorraine?" she said, surprise in her voice. "Whatever for?"

The last thing Macky wanted to do was get caught up in conversation with every resident of Heaven. She needed to find the marshal and confess to her part of the crime so that she could clear the charges against Bran before he caught up with her.

"About using her saloon," Macky said, making up her story as she spoke. "For a—a special prayer meeting on Wednesday night."

Clara snorted. "With all those no-accounts who come in there to drink and carouse?"

"Well . . . that's just the point. We need to reach the

men who don't come on Sunday morning. We'll just pray for their souls."

And mine, too. Macky was, as her mother would have said, digging her hole deeper and deeper. The only thing that was going to save her was the fact that she was leaving. Everything she owned was packed in the saddlebags on Solomon's back.

Clara nodded her head in agreement. "According to Marshal Larkin, the sheriff in Promise is on his way here. Seems to think there's a possibility that the killer of that banker has something to do with holding up Mrs. Mainwearing's gold shipment. They think he might even be here in Heaven."

"The sheriff is coming here?" Macky wanted to groan out loud. "Well, good, we need all the help we can get. Speaking of that," she said, backing away from the door, "I'd better get on down the street."

It wasn't enough that Pratt was on her trail, now the sheriff was coming. Pratt might know that Mrs. Adams was the kid named McKenzie, but she couldn't believe that the sheriff knew. And the last thing she needed was to have him get here before she'd spoken to Marshal Larkin.

Everything was becoming too confused.

Clara Gooden was talking a mile a minute. She was having no part of Macky slipping away. Once they reached the store, she pulled Macky inside to give her some canned peaches that had been left out of her donation to the parsonage.

"Thank you, Clara. I'm sure the reverend will enjoy them. Now, I really have to go."

"Not yet," she insisted, then called out to her husband. "Mr. Gooden, come and listen to what Reverend Adams is going to do. He's holding a revival in the saloon during the week."

"Well, it isn't certain yet," Macky interjected helplessly.

"A revival?" he questioned from the back room, then came into the store. "Don't know as I'da thought of it, but if

Preacher Adams wants to try it, the congregation will back him up. I'll get the word out. Being as how this is Monday, we don't have much time."

"Well, I didn't necessarily mean this week," Macky began. And she certainly didn't mean a revival. The only revivals she'd attended had been held in a tent. The leader had spent the better part of two days yelling and chanting until people confessed their sins and pledged their souls just to get the thing over with.

"How nice of Miss Lake," he said, "to give up a working night for our cause."

"Well, that's what I was trying to say. I haven't asked her yet. It's still in the planning stages."

"Then you better get on down to the saloon," Otis advised.

Macky wanted to talk with Lorraine, but she knew that the hour was too early to disturb her friend. To change the subject she fastened on another idea, a purchase she'd intended to make while in town.

"Before I go, Mr. Gooden, I'd like to buy a pistol." At Clara's horrified look, she explained, "The parsonage is so far out of town and Bran will be away a lot, I just thought I'd feel safer."

"Well, certainly," Otis said, reaching into his case. "But do you know how to shoot?"

"Yes, I do. My—father taught me about weapons when I was just a girl. He operated a trading post, though not as well stocked as your establishment."

Pleased at the compliment, Otis withdrew several models, describing the merits of each. Macky selected a small derringer that would serve her purposes without alarming the townsfolk. She slid both the pistol and bullets into her coat pocket and left the store promising that she'd be very careful with her new weapon.

Macky strode down the sidewalk to the saloon. Though it was approaching mid-morning, it was still far too early to expect to see Lorraine. She walked to the marshal's office. Maybe she'd wait for him to return. If the sheriff came, at least she'd have a chance to be heard privately.

When Todd was alive, she and the sheriff had crossed swords over her brother's behavior several times. Though she'd changed, Macky was afraid that he'd recognize her. Convincing him that she was innocent of the bank holdup might be hard to do. But by returning the money and leading him to Pratt, she'd hopefully absolve Bran of any wrongdoing.

The door wasn't locked and she pushed her way inside. Someone had attempted to tidy up the place. A thick layer of dust had been partially wiped away and the bunk inside the cell had a mattress and blanket. Macky walked over to the potbellied stove. Its door was standing open as if the marshal were about to start a fire. The wood was laid and some crumpled paper peeked out between the dry sticks.

A fire would make her wait more pleasant. The temperature was still chilly, and the street acted like a funnel, whipping the wind straight through the cracks in the wall. All she needed were the matches she carried in her pocket.

Quickly she lit the stove, fanning the small red licks of flame into a full fire before adding more limbs.

Soon there was a warm glow inside the office. Macky glanced at the barred cell at the end of the room with its hard bunk and small boarded-up window and shivered. Spending time in a place like this would be awful. She liked her freedom, the open fields and blue sky. She didn't even want to think what the law did to murderers.

Worried now, she sat down on the barrel behind the desk, pressing her hands to her temples. She'd had little sleep, though the cause had been worth the headache she was brewing. The pain wasn't as bad as it had been after drinking Harriet Smith's sherry-laced tea back at the way station, but it was getting there.

Macky opened the desk, pulled out the posters and began to flip through them. There was Pratt, wanted for robbing a bank in Missouri and another in Texas. He was younger in the sketch, with an untamed bushy beard that looked out of place on a man that young. But the wild-eyed look was there, even then.

As Macky stared at the posters she wondered why the marshal hadn't recognized Pratt in the crowd that first day the stage arrived. Of course the churchgoers were thronging around their new preacher, and Pratt had shaved his beard, but he'd made no attempt to hide himself. Either he was the most brazen outlaw Macky had ever seen, or he knew he had no reason to fear the marshal.

Still, the bank robbery in Promise was too close for Pratt to take that kind of chance. It was more likely that the marshal never saw Pratt. She'd have to think about that.

And then, at the bottom of the stack, she came to the sheet that stopped her cold. It was a sketch of John Lee, wanted for the murder of an army sergeant in Oklahoma. If she hadn't known Bran, she might never have recognized him. The sketch was smeared and poorly drawn.

The young Bran was thin, his hair hung dark and stringy, cut Indian style, and his wounded eye looked like a pucker in his face.

Bran was right to fear the marshal. He was still wanted, and if Macky was any judge at reading people, the marshal had seen this poster, too. Did he know it was Bran? Larkin didn't seem like a slow-thinking man. Sooner or later he'd recognize Bran and arrest him, no matter what Macky did. If he'd known who Bran was all along, what was he waiting for? Whatever it was, she'd better rethink her original plans to confess her crime. For now, she needed to warn Bran.

Macky folded Pratt's wanted posters and slid them into her pocket. She fed Bran's poster into the fire, then headed for the stable to claim Solomon. After she told Bran what she'd discovered, they'd both leave together. There had to be someplace where they'd be safe.

But she never got the chance. As she stepped into the

street, Bran rode up, firing his pistol. Reining the horse to a stop, he dismounted, calling out, "Hank, round up the men in town. Rachel Pendley's little girl is lost in the woods. We need to make up a search party."

He didn't speak to Macky, but she felt his displeasure and took a step back. She knew he'd demand an explanation for her presence but there was no time now. Finding the lost child had to come first.

Moments later, Otis Gooden, Preston Cribbs, and Hank Clay were ready to ride.

"Don't know why they're so worried about that child," one of the townswomen said with a sniff. "Like mother, like daughter. If she don't get lost in the woods, she'll end up at a place like Lorraine's sooner or later."

Macky didn't allow herself to speak. To say that about a child was unforgivable. The glare of anger she focused on the woman was more than enough to dry up any further comment.

"Shame on you, Eva, that child is one of God's children," Clara said. "And I remember a passage where he said that we should look after the least of them."

Somehow that didn't sound exactly right to Macky. But Clara's comment brought a smile from two others who'd been on their way inside the store.

Macky let the men leave before she climbed up on Solomon and rode behind them. She didn't know how she could help, but Macky knew that she had to try. Even if it meant letting the sheriff and the marshal meet up and compare information before Macky found a way out.

Macky gave Solomon a kick in his side and forced him into a reluctant gallop. She saw dark clouds gathering in the sky. More rain, she thought. And the child was out there, alone, unprotected. Macky shivered. She knew how that felt.

"Solomon," she said, as she leaned close to his ear, "we need a miracle. And you and me have to make one." There was a lump in her throat the size of a hailstone.

Resting her head against the mule's large neck, she whispered, "Lord, if it's not too much to ask, give Solomon angel wings so that he can lead us to Gingerbelle."

But there was no trumpet from on high sending an answer.

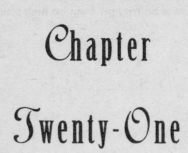

Chapter

Twenty-One

LARKIN CRESTED THE HILL and stopped to check out the cabin. A plume of smoke sketched an *S* in the sky. He let out a deep breath and urged the horse forward. Once the message had arrived last night that Sheriff Dover was on his way to Heaven from Promise, Larkin began to worry.

Dover planned to talk to Mrs. Mainwearing about the recent troubles she'd had in shipping her gold back East. Larkin could handle the sheriff, but there were too many people asking questions. Larkin had to work fast to get rid of anybody who could connect him to the trouble. He still intended to have the mine, but he could wait.

The gunfighter had to be eliminated. Then Pratt would die and be blamed for all of the holdups. Using criminals, then eliminating them had worked well for Larkin in the past. He could see no reason why it wouldn't work again, so long as he didn't wait too long. First there was Pratt to deal with.

"Ahoy, the cabin. Pratt!"

Larkin! Inside the shack, Pratt pulled the rag tighter on his finger and winced. Who'd have thought that losing the tip of a finger could hurt so bad? He made his way out the door. Damn the man, he was still sitting up there on that horse like some kind of lord looking down on his slave. He was tired of all this.

"What happened to you?" Larkin asked.

"Nothing. Just a little accident with my knife. What do you want?"

"The sheriff from Promise is coming in. I want you to get rid of that preacher now and get out of town for a while."

"Funny," Pratt said, studying Larkin shrewdly, "I had the same thing in mind. Maybe I'll just pick up my pay and ride over to Boulder City."

Larkin gave a laugh of disbelief. "Pay? You expect to be paid after you fouled up the bank job in Promise and shot the banker? You'll be lucky if I don't decide to hang you for murder. Or let you have an accident right now. That would take care of everything, wouldn't it?"

"You still need me to do your dirty work, Larkin." Pratt's voice wavered just a bit, though he didn't want Larkin to know he was worried.

Pratt wasn't fooled. He knew that Larkin would kill him. He'd claim that he'd tried to arrest Pratt for the bank holdup and Pratt had resisted. Too bad he'd been killed. His association with the gunfighter was just as risky, but Night Eyes had never murdered a man in cold blood.

"All right. I'll do this one last job, then I'm heading for Alaska. Somebody said that there's gold up there and I have a hankering for snow."

He untied the bandage and it floated to the ground. "Don't suppose you'd help me with this, would you?" he asked and knelt to pick it up, putting the horse's head between him and Larkin, for just a moment. That was all the time he needed. But Pratt missed, causing the horse to shy. The marshal got off one good shot and Pratt fell.

Larkin gave a cynical laugh. Pratt was dead before the marshal dragged him into the rocks beyond the trail. Larkin retrieved the stolen gold and Pratt's silver-trimmed saddle from the cabin.

Pratt was a fool. Larkin hadn't intended to kill him yet, not until after he'd gotten rid of the preacher. Now Larkin would have to do it himself. That was no problem. He'd used gunfighters as fall guys before, but he didn't like it when things went wrong.

Farther up the trail, Sylvia closed the ledger she'd been writing in and leaned back in her chair. She was tired; her eyes were strained from the squinting as she entered the tiny figures into the columns.

Her losses were growing. Even hiring men to work in the mine was becoming a problem. Since the explosion, workers had gradually drifted away, whispering that the Sylvia was jinxed.

She'd hired that gunfighter to stop the trouble and he was making no progress in doing so. Though she'd promised to hold off revealing his true identity, she wasn't certain if that was smart. Nobody knew how dire her situation was. Nobody knew that, in the explosion, she'd lost the main vein.

The truth was, the gold had shifted when the explosion occurred and so far nobody had found it. Even after shoring up the tunnel and clearing away the debris, nothing seemed to be in the same place. It had to be there. A vein of gold didn't just vanish. But this one had.

Sylvia closed her eyes.

"Moose, you old fool, why'd you marry me in the first place? You could have had any of those fancy women back East. Why me?"

But she knew the answer. She knew how to please a man. In spite of her airs, underneath it all, Sylvia Mainwearing was a former saloon girl who'd struck it rich. She bit back a smile as she thought about all the women in Heaven who'd bought her act. Nobody knew that she and Moose were two of a kind. And she'd loved him, even with his loud voice and tendency to drink too much.

And somebody had killed him.

She'd refused to believe it at the time, refused to think that anybody had deliberately pushed him into that ravine and left him there to die. An accident, the marshal had called it, and she'd had no reason not to believe him. Until the other trouble started.

At first it was just little things: timbers that fell and injured miners, mules that spooked, ore spilling down the canyon. Then came the fires and stolen gold shipments, followed by the explosion and murder. And finally someone had taken a shot at her.

Somebody wanted to frighten her and they had. Sylvia was scared to death. She could marry again, and she might. She had to laugh at a former saloon girl being courted by a judge and a U.S. Marshal. The marshal was younger, but Sylvia didn't delude herself about his sincerity. The judge was an old teddy bear and she was comfortable with him, but he was about as much protection as an old shoe.

Still, something was wrong, and Sylvia had learned long ago to take care of herself first.

And she might have found a way. One of the workers had just come from town with two pieces of news. First, a child had gotten lost and everybody had gone looking for her. Sylvia had sent some of her men over to help. It never hurt to keep up a good image with the townspeople.

It was the second announcement that caught her fancy. The preacher was going to hold a revival meeting on Wednesday evening, in the saloon. Sylvia glanced up at the painting of her crest with the S and smiled. That would work very well for her purposes. She'd attend his revival. It was time for Sylvia to confess her sins and let the town know that she was out for blood.

They needed to know that their preacher wasn't a man of God after all.

When the search party for Rebekah Pendley rode out of Heaven, Bran knew that Macky was behind them. One part of him wanted to climb off his horse and turn her over his knee, the other was just glad to know that she wasn't with Pratt.

But why had she gone to town?

The sorry little cabin where Lars Pendley's family lived was barely more than a lean-to, built in the side of a hill. The back walls were dirt and the main house was poorly insulated from the wind and cold.

But he could see Rachel's pitiful attempts to make the place into a home. There were small trees and shrubs planted across the front of the house and a flower box had been nailed beneath a shuttered window.

Rachel, baby on her hip, stood in the doorway, face pinched and anxious as she watched Bran organize the search. Macky rode in, dismounted and stood behind Rachel, listening as the men were directed to ride away from the cabin like the spokes of a wagon. They would go forward and zigzag back and forth until they heard a single gunshot. Then they were to move to their right fifty paces and move back to the cabin. If anyone spotted the child two shots were to be fired as a signal.

Macky glanced at the sky in concern. Heavy gray clouds hung over the mountains, ominously concealing the snow-covered tips. Macky had a bad feeling about this. A child following a mischievous puppy could cover a great deal of territory.

After what seemed like forever, Macky heard a single gunshot. The signal to turn back.

Rachel gasped. "They aren't stopping, are they?" she asked.

"Of course not. They'll just return, reset their directions, and move out again. We'll find her, don't you worry."

But Macky was worried, and she began to pace back and forth. Even Solomon seemed to sense the tension. He moved about in agitation, shaking his shoulders and slinging his head. Finally Macky walked over to the big animal.

"What's wrong, boy? Do you know something we don't?"

For a moment Solomon only looked at her, his big brown eyes piercing and stubborn. He pulled against his reins, stomped his feet and pulled again.

Following a hunch, Macky untied Solomon's reins and climbed on his back. "Let's me and you have a little look," she said, allowing the mule to go his own way.

Macky didn't know how much time passed. Nor did she know exactly where she was, as the mule wandered down the draw, away from the mountains into the thick brush. Branches dug into her bare skin, and slapped her face, leaving red splotches. But the animal seemed to know exactly where he was going and wasted no time in doing so.

"Rebekah! Rebekah!" Macky called from time to time, but there was no answer. In fact the woods were curiously silent, not even a bird calling out to another.

Finally the sound of running water broke the silence. Solomon burst through the brush and stopped at the edge of a swift-running creek. Something about the scene looked familiar. Solomon reached down and took a long drink from the cold stream.

"Solomon, you old fool. Did you bring me all this way just so that you could get a drink of water? How dare you, you selfish, ornery old thing?"

And then she heard a whimper, not of a child, but an animal. "The puppy." Macky slid from Solomon's back and made her way down the bank. "Here, puppy! Here, puppy!"

The whimpering grew louder. And then she saw them. Rebekah and the puppy were caught by a pile of brush midway across the stream. Macky fired her new pistol twice, then stepped into the icy water and waded out to Rebekah and the puppy, grateful that the water only reached her thighs.

The little girl had a gash on her forehead and she was cold as ice, but she was breathing. The puppy seemed fine, but afraid of the current. Moments later, with the squirming puppy under one arm and the child in the other, Macky managed to mount Solomon and head back to the cabin.

"After the trouble you've caused me, you'd better get us there quick, Solomon, or you're going to have to live on snow and creek stones forever!"

The mule must have believed her, for a short time later, they reached the shack where the searchers were waiting anxiously.

"We heard your shot," Otis said. "Where'd you find her?"

Lars Pendley took his stepdaughter inside by the fire. Rachel began to remove her wet clothes and wrapped her in tattered warm blankets.

"She must have fallen into the creek and been washed downstream. She was caught in a pile of brush," Macky answered.

"How'd you know where to look?" Hank Clay asked curiously.

"I didn't. Solomon found her."

The men shook their heads then started back to town.

"Odd," one man said, "the marshal never showed up."

"Wonder where he is?" another asked.

"Maybe he had a lead on Sylvia's trouble at the mine," Hank said.

Bran rode beside Macky. He didn't speak. He didn't even say goodbye to the men he'd organized into a search party. Instead he turned his mount toward their cabin, paused and waited for Macky to do the same. Macky hadn't known what to expect, but being ignored was making her feel very uneasy.

"I'm sorry if I worried you, Bran," she said. "But I had some thinking to do."

"In town?"

"Well, yes. I went in to talk to the marshal."

"And did you?"

"No, he wasn't there. Hank Clay said he left, heading this way just before I got into town. He thought I might have seen him on the trail but I didn't."

Bran was facing straight ahead. His voice cut through the air clean and sharp. "And what business did you have with the marshal?"

"It doesn't matter. I've changed my mind. I'm sorry if I worried you."

"Why should I be worried? I awaken in an empty bed, one, I might add, I'd tried to avoid, and you're gone."

"Wasn't that what you wanted, Bran?"

"Yes, but not like that."

Solomon had fallen behind. Macky planted her heel into his side and brought him even with Bran.

He *was* worried. He really didn't want her to go. Macky wanted to smile. She'd never expected him to let his feelings show, but he didn't have to. He couldn't hide his concern.

"Bran, the marshal knows who you are."

"I know."

"No, I mean he knows you're John Lee. I saw the wanted poster in his desk."

That set Bran back. Being identified as Night Eyes wasn't what he wanted, but it wasn't against the law. Being identified as John Lee could get him arrested. "That does it, Macky. You have to go—now."

"I've changed my mind. I won't leave you willingly, Bran. I love you."

Her words hit him in the gut like buckshot. Even his mother never said the words. He forced himself to say, "You have to, Macky. I know who is responsible for the trouble in Heaven and for the bank robbery in Promise as well."

"So, we'll wait for Sheriff Dover and he'll help us."

"No, Macky. You have to go now."

"Not until after the revival. If I leave before, the marshal might get suspicious."

"About that revival. What on earth made you tell the people in Heaven that I was going to do such a thing?"

"I never meant it to happen. Everybody wanted to know why I was in town and you weren't. I couldn't think of a reason. Then it just popped out. A town meeting might be the answer, Bran. The people of Heaven love you. Why not confess, both of us, and take our chances with the congregation?"

"And what about Marshal Larkin? You think he'll just say go and sin no more? I don't think so, Macky."

Macky felt her elation subside as she slid down from Solomon's back and walked the rest of the way to the cabin. Once in the corral, she gave Solomon an extra measure of the oats.

"You just get rested up, Solomon," she whispered. "We're going to start spring plowing soon. That is, if we're still here."

Macky didn't know exactly what she'd do, or how she'd do it, but instinct told her that come Wednesday night, a way would be provided. It might not be God's will, but it was close enough for Macky.

"Are you going to the revival meeting?" Lorraine asked Hank. They were sitting on the ground, staring up at the sky as they had every night since the evening she'd fallen asleep in his arms.

Forcing herself not to respond to her feelings for the strong, silent man was becoming more and more difficult. Before she'd always put the man off. This was her first experience with a man turning her away.

"I think I'll be there," Hank said. "Though I don't know how smart any of us are to come."

"What do you mean?"

"I don't like crowds. They can turn mean and get braver with numbers," he answered.

Lorraine couldn't see him in the darkness and she held herself back from moving closer. "Is that why you never came to the Sunday services in the saloon before?"

"Partially."

"What makes this different?" she asked, trying to keep her voice casual.

"Well, the sheriff is coming in from Promise. The judge is on his way back from Denver and I haven't seen the marshal in two days. The preacher has been all over town, calling on his future parishioners and sending off letters by the Pony Express riders. I haven't seen Mrs. Adams and there's enough tension in the air to start a riot. Now, we're holding a revival to bring everybody in Heaven together?"

Lorraine knew about tension all right. Surprisingly, she was looking forward to the Wednesday-night service. The more often she came in contact with the city fathers and their wives, the more respectable she became.

Only when Macky had come to Heaven did Lorraine's station begin to change. Macky's generous spirit had touched everyone. She'd become a kind of conscience, forcing Mrs. Cribbs and Mrs. Gooden and the others to live their Christian principles rather than just preach them.

Macky had changed everything for the better. Macky could wear men's clothing. Macky could ride a mule. Macky found that Pendley child and suddenly the child became poor little Rebekah and Mrs. Pendley was invited to church. Macky became Lorraine's friend and now Lorraine was more than just that woman. There was even talk of a school.

Lorraine had told herself that it didn't matter. But now Hank was taking her thoughts of a future in a different direction, which made it all the more important that she be accepted as an equal.

But a revival?

Even Lorraine was having problems with that idea.

"Do you think anybody has seen us together?" she asked.

"Not that I'm aware of."

"Would it matter to you?" she asked. "I mean it might cause gossip."

Hank lifted her over him so that she was gazing straight into his eyes. "Let's get this straight, once and for all. I do what I want and I don't care what anybody thinks. Not now. Not ever. But you and me are different. We're too new to face that kind of hurt."

"Does that mean you don't want anybody to know about us? Are you ashamed of me?"

There was a long silence before Hank answered. "I think you might be more ashamed of me, once you know who I am." And he told her about his father who kept a mistress and had sired him. About the man who already had a proper wife who produced proper children. He told her of the taunts and the fights he'd survived to protect his mother. About how his father had sent him off to school and how, while he was away, his mother died—alone.

"Why send you away, if he didn't care about you?" Lorraine said, tracing his eyebrows with her fingertips as she tried to still the wild urgings of her body's response to his touch.

"Because he couldn't bear to look at me. Because I looked more like him than his own children. Because I was strong and they were weak."

"What happened to your father?"

"He'd always gambled and finally he went too far. He killed himself."

"Oh. I'm so sorry, Hank. That must have hurt you badly."

"No, what hurt was that my mother died before I could take her away from him."

Something in his voice revealed a twinge of uncertainty. "Would she have come with you?"

"I have to think so. But I don't know."

"So, what brought you to Heaven?"

He gave a wry laugh. "I heard that you had to travel through Hell to get to Heaven and I figured that whichever place I landed would be where I'd stay. The people in Hell wouldn't care who I was and the ones in Heaven wouldn't turn me away."

"How awful for you, Hank. But surely you don't keep to yourself because you think the people of Heaven would turn their backs on you now—unless—oh, I see. They might, if they learned about us. You've made yourself a reputation as a city father. Now the shoe's on the other foot and it's pinching you."

"No," Hank protested.

"Yes. You're afraid that you might end up like your father. You don't want to make me your mistress and you're not ready to marry me. You won't let yourself love me because you don't want to give me a child. How noble of you."

Lorraine pulled herself to her feet and looked down at the man lying so still. "Well, never fear, Hank Clay. I'll never embarrass you before the good citizens of Heaven. I make no apologies for what I do. I'm just sorry that I was stupid enough to believe you were different. After all the men who've wanted me, I fall in love with one who is ashamed of who I am."

"Lorraine, no. It isn't like that at all." Hank came slowly to his feet. He didn't know how everything had gotten out of hand. He cared about Lorraine. What she was hadn't mattered to him. She was a lady as far as he was concerned. Keeping what they had a secret was his way of making sure it wasn't destroyed.

"I think it is, Hank. And I think it's over." With that she was gone and Hank was standing there with a hole as big as a mountain in his heart and regret that showered him like the rain that had started to fall.

•   •   •

Macky didn't see Bran for the rest of Monday, or Tuesday. Of course he could have come to the cabin while she plowed her field with Solomon.

She had no seed, nor could she be certain that she'd even be there long enough to harvest what she planted, but there was something about the smell of damp, fresh-plowed earth that made her senses respond.

The Monday-night rains were gone by Tuesday. She rode into town, picked up the other two dresses from Lettie, and bought a plow. Along the way, she decided to face the marshal directly.

He was in his office, pouring coffee from a tin pot on the stove.

"Morning, Marshal Larkin," she said. "Got a minute?"

"Sure. Come in, Mrs. Adams. Something I can do for you?"

"Just wanted to be sure you were coming to the revival tomorrow night. I'm worried."

"Oh? About what?"

"Well, people seem to be a little nervous about the gunfighter coming to town. They think he might be after that bank robber, Pratt."

"Haven't heard anything about it. What makes you think that Pratt is even here?"

"I figure that's why you're still here. Look, Marshal, let's talk straight. I think you know who Night Eyes really is. Suppose he turns Pratt over to you. Do you think the trouble in Heaven would stop?"

Larkin studied her. What in hell was she up to? She was as much as confessing that her husband was the gunfighter. But what connection did they have to Pratt? He'd been a law officer long enough to smell a trap and this had all the markings of one. He'd just play along.

"I don't know. Night Eyes has a reputation as a fair man. 'Course, if he's tied in with Pratt that would change things."

"But Night Eyes has never been wanted for a crime, right?"

"He isn't wanted. Why?"

"You just never know what will come out in a revival. Sometimes criminals are taken by the Holy Spirit and confess to their crimes, even a man like Pratt. Then again, sometimes even honest people are guilty of deception."

Larkin leaned back on his stool. It sounded for all the world like the woman was threatening him. Had he missed something?

One thing was clear, he'd better be at that revival. "I'll be there, Mrs. Adams. I wouldn't miss it for the world."

Macky was almost ready to admit that she'd been wrong to be suspicious of Marshal Larkin. Still, she couldn't bring herself to open up completely. She was almost out the door when she looked back, and caught sight of a saddle with silver trim under the desk. The marshal had Pratt's saddle. Why?

Maybe Pratt had already been found. Or maybe she'd been right all along. The marshal and Pratt were working together. To do what?

Wednesday was warmer with occasional patches of sunshine. For the most part, the sky, still sullen and heavy, draped over Kansas like Mother Earth's gray apron.

Macky prepared the last of the biscuits and meat left by the church women. She didn't know where Bran was eating. She didn't know where he was sleeping either, but from time to time she heard his horse in the corral.

By noon, she went to the creek and bathed, being careful not to go where she couldn't touch bottom. Even as she rinsed the soap from her hair and sat drying it in the disappearing sunlight, she couldn't hold back the memories of the first time Bran had brought her there and the nights that followed.

Macky felt a shiver of concern ripple down her back.

Gathering her clothing, she sprinted to the house to dress for the revival. She might have to go alone, but she'd hoped that her avenging angel would be there. She planned to use the town meeting to confess her own crime in such a way that Bran would never be involved. She hoped he'd understand what she had to do.

Back in town, Larkin reached inside the drawer to retrieve the wanted poster on John Brandon Lee. He didn't know what the revival would bring, but he was prepared to make his move if the opportunity presented itself. He didn't think that Night Eyes would allow himself to be arrested. But if Larkin could force him to draw, he'd be rid of the problem. Aaron Larkin would have Heaven in his pocket. He'd take Heaven's queen, the lovely Sylvia Mainwearing, down a peg. Once she saw Moose's IOU's she'd have to do whatever he wanted.

"Onward Christian soldiers," he said and let out a high, thready laugh. Larkin figured he could consider himself a soldier marching off to war. And he knew before he fired the first shot that he was going to win.

But the poster was gone. Someone had been in his office. Someone knew about the preacher, about John Brandon Lee. But who?

It had to be the redhead. He'd had the feeling when she came to his office that she was fishing. Now he was sure of it. She had the poster and she thought its absence would protect the gunfighter. He smiled. They'd underestimated him. He didn't have to prove anything. The redhead and the preacher were about to be exposed as the biggest sin in Heaven.

Chapter
Twenty-Two

THE SULLEN DARKENING clouds raced across the late afternoon sky as Macky placed the money from the bank holdup in her market basket and covered it with a cloth. If asked, she'd say she was bringing a gift to Lorraine. Bran met her as she stepped out the cabin door. Solomon was already hitched to the wagon and complaining stubbornly.

"Good morning, I mean afternoon," Macky said uncertainly. As Bran had once said, the good part remained to be seen. With a certain amount of delicious wickedness he'd said that he'd much prefer the bad. Today he'd get his wish.

Bran helped her into the wagon, noting without comment that she was wearing a new dress. He'd missed her. Her declaration of love had tormented him and he'd had to struggle to stay away from her.

For the last few days he'd used every favor he had coming to him to build his case against the marshal and the proof was on its way to Heaven with Sheriff Dover.

"Macky, about us—" he began.

"There is no us, is there, Bran? I know I said I love you, but I understand you're not ready for that."

The old Macky was back. She never expected love so she was swallowing her disappointment. He only hoped his plan would bring back the woman he loved. It was the only way he could show her how he felt.

The couple driving into Heaven had come a long way from the two awkward people who'd arrived in town only days before. Bran and Macky had been wild, passionate, full of pride. The Reverend and Mrs. Brandon Adams were polite and genteel. They reached the saloon and greeted their neighbors with stiff-lipped smiles and barely concealed tension.

Gathered outside the makeshift church were the same townspeople who'd met their stage that first day. Lorraine waited in the doorway to the saloon. Across the street, Hank Clay leaned against the post under the roof of the blacksmith shop and watched with a stern frown.

"For a revival, the sinners seem a bit sullen," Judge Hardcastle said under his breath to Mrs. Mainwearing, who was still seated in the smart black buggy down the street. "Do you intend to go inside, or do we just wait out here to be saved?"

"Don't be sacrilegious, Judge," Sylvia snapped. "I told you that you didn't have to come along."

"Which is precisely why I did. You're not going to put me off any more, my dear. I think you ought to know that I made a few inquiries about you and I was surprised to find that you were the rage of San Francisco."

Sylvia gasped and turned her blue eyes on the judge. "You know what I was—before?"

"I do and I'm certainly intrigued by your remarkable success. It's a damned sight more appealing than believing you were some kind of society girl who was down on her luck."

Sylvia couldn't miss the twinkle in his eye. Maybe she'd

misjudged him. Maybe she'd give him just a bit of encouragement, see how things progressed. If the services went as she remembered them from her childhood, there'd be plenty of time for confession and repentance. That was when she'd act.

"Let's get going, Judge. I don't want to miss a thing."

"What do you expect to happen?" he asked, helping Sylvia from the buggy, and ignoring the surprised expressions of the faithful gathering at the doorway.

"I don't know. There are a lot of secrets in Heaven and who knows what the night will bring?"

The churchgoers made their way inside, skirting the eerie pattern of darkness cast by the rays of the sun already setting behind the buildings along the street.

At the last moment a strange wagon rattled into town, carrying a lone woman. Macky looked up and recognized her immediately.

"Harriet!" She ran toward the wagon, clasping the woman in her arms as soon as she stepped down. "How did you manage to get away from the way station?"

"Heard there was going to be a revival. Always did like a little fire and brimstone, especially when it's being served up in such interesting surroundings." She bent her head close to Macky. "Reckon there's any sherry behind that bar?"

Suddenly Macky felt better. Bran might not appreciate what she had in mind, but having Harriet there restored her self-confidence. She looked at the gathering crowd, discreetly searching for and not finding the marshal. Where was the man? Nobody had seen him in at least two days. According to Lorraine he occasionally rode back and forth to Denver, taking care of problems in other parts of the territory. But his disappearing now bothered Macky.

And where was Pratt? He had to be present to make it work. Macky fingered the wanted posters folded securely in her pocket. She hadn't seen him, but she was sure he wouldn't leave Heaven without attempting to get the money from the holdup.

The soft fabric of her new blue dress made a whispering sound as she walked. She looked down at it and sighed. If her plan failed, this could be the worst day of her life. Macky might lose the man she loved who now stood before his congregation with his Bible open. His expression was blank, but Macky could see the pain he tried to hide.

"Dear friends," he began, "we come here this day to confess our wrongdoings and ask for forgiveness."

A commotion broke out as another wagon came in and the passengers disembarked. Rachel Pendley, Lars, and the two children came into the saloon and found places at the back. After the din of whispers died down, Bran began once more.

"All of you have welcomed me—us, making us a part of your lives, sharing your food and your goods to welcome us. I never expected that. I never thought to find friendship here, certainly not love. But a revival is supposed to be a renewing of the spirit, a new beginning."

A few "Amens" were voiced from the audience.

"But a new beginning cannot be built on a lie and that is where I stand. I wish to confess my sins of omission to Judge Hardcastle."

Macky realized in horror that Bran was about to use her event to his own end. He was about to confess her sin and make it his.

"No," Macky called out and stepped to the front of the room. "You don't have to do this for me, Bran. Friends, this isn't his sin he's about to confess, but mine."

"No, Macky—"

"He's protecting me. I'm not his wife. The preacher never saw me before I got on the stage in Promise. I was running away to keep from being arrested for robbing the bank and stealing Sylvia's gold."

"Be quiet, Macky!" Bran shouted, crushing her arm in his grip.

"No, Bran. They have to know. I can prove it. I've

brought the money and the gold coins that I haven't spent." She pulled back the cloth and revealed its contents.

"You're the bank robber?" Sylvia Mainwearing shrieked. "There's no way you could be guilty of holding up my gold shipments and killing my Moose. You weren't even here then."

Sylvia marched up to the bar and stopped in front of Macky. "Don't you go trying to flimflam us by taking the blame for someone else. I think it's time everybody learns our messenger of God is really the gunfighter, Night Eyes. He doesn't rob banks and neither do you!"

This time the entire congregation erupted.

"Night Eyes?"

"But he's that gunfighter, isn't he?"

"I don't believe it. If you're not Reverend Adams and his wife, where are they?"

"I always did think that redhead was odd-looking. Remember how she looked that first day, with that short skirt and that man's shirt?"

"You hush! That's Macky you're talking about and we don't care what she did before she got here."

"I'm telling the truth," Macky insisted quietly, bringing all the conversation to a stop. "Bran may be a gunfighter, but he had nothing to do with the bank robbery. It was me. I'm the one who came away with the money. I was with Pratt, at the bank."

"You were with Pratt?" Lorraine said in disbelief.

In desperation Macky reached into her pocket and pulled the wanted posters from her pocket. "See, this man is Pratt, the head of the gang who held up the bank. The banker from Promise is dead. Pratt or one of his men killed him."

Bran dropped her arm and closed his Bible. "What in hell are you doing, Macky? It's Larkin who is behind all the trouble in Heaven and I can prove it."

He glared at Macky, willing her to be silent. She was going to get herself arrested and it would be to no avail.

He'd resigned himself to going to jail, to having his past exposed. But Macky was to be spared.

In the midst of the overwhelming silence, another familiar voice spoke. "I don't think so, Adams." Marshal Larkin stepped into the saloon. "This man is a gunfighter, not a preacher. He's lied to all of you. He thought he'd take over Heaven and you were about to let him."

Bran looked up at the man standing in the doorway, the light behind him shadowing his face beneath his hat. The sun was setting over the mountains in a flame of red-orange color. It was almost as if the sky were on fire, silhouetting Larkin's outline. Bran's mind began to race. The light—the fire—the shadows. Suddenly it all came rushing back. The last time he'd seen this man he'd thought he was big and tall. He wasn't. He hadn't been old; he'd just been mean.

"You're him," Bran said. "Why didn't I see it before? After fifteen years, I've finally found you."

"What do you mean?" Macky asked.

"I was just a frightened boy. All I could see that night was your beard. The rest of your face was in the shadows. But I heard you laugh. Laugh, Larkin. Let me hear you laugh now," Bran said, his voice deadly cold, "before I kill you."

Just a kid? Larkin felt the blood rush from his face. He'd known Night Eyes was deadly, but this was more than he'd imagined.

"I don't know what you're talking about, Adams, but you're under arrest. I'm taking you in for the murder of an army officer on a reservation in Oklahoma."

"You aren't taking me anywhere. I'm going to kill you, Larkin, right here. Just like you killed my mother, my father, and my sister. But I want you to remember them, Larkin. I want you to know why you're dying."

"You're crazy!" Larkin protested and began to sweat. A picture was forming in his mind of a mean little shack along the Mississippi and a boy who'd stood up to him without fear. Now he knew where he'd seen Adams before. Now he knew what happened to the gunfighter's eye. He started to back up, then stopped and steadied his voice.

"I don't think you want to do this, Adams. Pratt is dead. But before he died, he implicated Mrs. Adams in the bank holdup. You may kill me, but by her own confession, she'll still go to jail."

"Macky's innocent," Bran said quietly.

"Cribbs," Larkin directed, biting back a laugh, "take the holdup money. Gooden, make sure she doesn't try to run."

"Horsefeathers!" Sylvia snapped. "Nobody's running anywhere and nobody's laying a hand on Macky or they'll answer to me."

"You don't understand," Larkin argued confidently. "There is a reward for the arrest of John Brandon Lee. As a U.S. Marshal I'm commanding you to help."

"Can't do it," Preston said. "We're civilians."

"But your Night Eyes intends to take over your mine, Sylvia. Pratt was his man. That's the way he works; he stirs up trouble, then lets himself be hired to settle it."

Now it was Bran's turn to laugh. "You should know about that, Larkin. You've used that method often enough. But this time you had to kill your man before you were ready. I found Pratt's body. And I found out a few other things as well. You scared off all the little miners and took over their claims. But you were too quick to transfer them into your name."

Larkin looked as if he were cornered. He'd expected the town to back him, expected Bran to cower in fear from being publicly identified as a killer. He'd underestimated him.

Bran slowly laid the Bible on a chair and pushed his jacket back, tying the straps of his holster around his upper leg. With a cold smile he started toward Larkin, who was standing in the doorway.

Larkin began to back up, but Bran walked past the members of his congregation and into the street.

"No, Bran, stop this," Macky said, catching his arm.

"Larkin isn't worth it, not now. I won't let you." She reached inside her pocket and found the derringer. She didn't know what she would do, but Larkin couldn't be allowed to hurt Bran.

"I have to do this, Macky. 'Vengeance is mine saith the Lord' and tonight, after all these years, I'm administering God's justice."

"But Bran, what about us? Larkin is right. If you go to jail, what happens to me?"

"There is no us. We've known that all along. As for you, Trouble, this time you aren't responsible. You'll do fine."

They might have been alone, in a world of silence. The townspeople had hushed their chatter and were following them outside, hanging back in confusion.

"Do you remember yet, Larkin? A little shack on the Mississippi. A mother and father you killed and a girl you raped."

"Won't work, gunfighter. I don't have the poster any more, but the warrant for your arrest still exists. Your name is John Lee and you're wanted for murder. I can't see any point in forcing the army to try you when we both know you're guilty." He laughed.

Bran stopped his slow advance and cocked his head slightly. "You find this funny, Larkin?"

"Sure. Don't you?" Larkin replied with inflated bravado, then laughed again. "I think it's real funny. Here we are, you, a minister of God, ready to kill to protect your past, and me, an officer of the law trying to protect the future of Heaven."

Bran felt revulsion sweep over him. He couldn't believe how blind he'd been. He was ready to kill Larkin on the spot, but he had to find a way to force him to confirm Macky's innocence.

"As for his redheaded wife," Larkin went on. "That's another interesting story. You folks have picked yourself a real fine pair to lead your flock." He smiled.

Bran's resolve faltered for a moment. He'd spent the last

three days trying to separate himself from Macky, determined that she should be free to find a new life for herself. He couldn't let her go to jail. He'd failed everyone else in his life, but not this time.

He might die, but Macky couldn't be held responsible for something she had been innocently involved in. Not now that he knew how much he loved her. Even now he fought the need to hold her one last time. He'd let her fill the empty space inside him, dissolving the protective walls he'd built around his heart. But there could never be a wife and a home for John Brandon Lee. What they'd shared in Heaven was all he'd ever have.

A man like him didn't get that kind of lucky. He had to stop Larkin and clear Macky's name. That was the last thing he could do for her. He'd already arranged to leave her all his money in the bank in San Francisco and he'd sent a note to Sheriff Dover. All he had to do was get rid of this man.

"Larkin," Bran said, his voice deadly calm. "You're right. I once killed a man in cold blood. He was about to harm someone I loved. If I have to, I'll do it again."

Bran's legs were spread apart, rocking slowly back and forth, his eyes locked intently on the man whose death he'd made his life's mission. Even knowing that this sad specimen of a man wasn't worthy of the time Bran had spent on him couldn't change what would happen.

"Judge," Macky said, pleading with the man. "This isn't right. You have to stop this. Please!"

The judge looked at Bran with caution. "Reverend Adams," he said quietly, "why not let me handle this?"

"I told you, he's not a preacher," Larkin said, "he's a murderer and the girl isn't his wife."

"And we don't care," Hank Clay's steady voice answered. "If you shoot him, Larkin, you're dead."

"You asking to die, too?" Larkin taunted. "The judge has enough room in his jail for all of you."

"Maybe," Hank said, "but every man in town has a gun on you and the jail isn't big enough for them all."

"Leave it be, Hank," Bran said. "This is between Larkin and me. I'm going to kill him and there's no point in any of you getting hurt."

"Please, Bran," Macky whispered. "Don't do this. I love you. I don't want to lose you."

"No, Macky. It was never meant to be. It's time these folks learn the truth. I am a killer. Now stand back."

"I don't believe that," Clara Gooden spoke up. "If you shot somebody, they needed shooting."

Bran positioned his jacket so that he could get to his gun. "Don't defend me, Mrs. Gooden. Larkin is right."

"No!" Macky cried out, trying to get away from the judge to Bran's side. "It's me the law is looking for, not Bran."

Larkin felt a cold dread catch him at the back of his neck and freeze him in place. He looked around uneasily. When he'd stepped into the saloon it had seemed so simple. Call out the gunfighter and kill him. Blame the bank holdup on Night Eyes. The banker was dead. The preacher would be blamed for Pratt's crimes and Larkin would get the reward. Then he'd get rid of Sylvia and take over the mine. But the boy he'd shot with the arrow had survived.

The boy was Night Eyes and he was daring Larkin to make his move, with the entire town watching.

"There's more," Larkin said, taking another step back.

Bran waited. "Fine, tell us the rest. But let's start with Pratt. Why'd you kill him?"

"I didn't and you can't prove it."

"I can," Macky said. "You have his saddle. I saw it under your desk. He'd never give up that saddle willingly."

Two riders came to the outer edge of the circle of on-lookers. One of the riders was Harvil Smith from the way station, the other Bran didn't recognize.

The stranger spoke first. "Good question. Why'd you kill him, Larkin? Were you afraid that he'd tell how you broke him out of jail to do your killing, how he murdered an innocent boy in a crooked poker game in Promise, how he shot the banker in Promise so he wouldn't reveal your dirty scheme?"

"Innocent boy?" Macky whispered, unaware she'd spoken. "In Promise?"

"Pratt was your man, Marshal," the sheriff charged. "You planned it all."

"You're responsible for Todd's death?" Macky's voice rose in cold anger. "And now you want to kill Bran?"

"Wait just a minute," Larkin growled. "You aren't pinning that on me."

"Todd's death wasn't enough for you," Macky said, striding across the clearing toward Larkin. "Then you tried to blame the murder of the banker on Bran?" She got a good grip on her pistol and started toward Larkin.

"Stay back, Macky!" Bran said, reaching out to pull her away.

But Bran could tell she wasn't listening. She was too close to Larkin. She'd put herself in danger. He might have backed down from Bran, but not a woman.

He tried to draw attention away from Macky. "Larkin, someone asked me where the snake was in the Garden of Eden. We've found him, you liver-livered son of evil. I'm going to kill you."

Bran shoved Macky away just as Larkin drew his pistol. But he wasn't fast enough. A single gunshot rang out before he could fire. Then four others followed and the pistol in Larkin's hand dropped to the ground in a cloud of dust.

A look of surprise opened Larkin's eyes wide as he fell, mortally wounded.

At that moment a ribbon of lightning scissored the sky and the wind swirled rain round the onlookers. The two horses in the street whinnied nervously and danced around. Bran turned toward the redhead who'd stormed into his life and grabbed him by the heart.

A smear of red turned her chest into a bull's-eye. She glanced down at the bright color in calm surprise. Her mouth was open, but no words came. Only the sound of rattled breath and tears that dribbled down her cheeks. As the sheriff pushed his way through the crowd, she held up the gun she'd bought from Otis Gooden.

"You shot him," Bran said.

"Yes," Macky said. "He was about to hurt you."

This time when she collapsed in Bran's arms, it wasn't pretend. This time when he carried her inside the saloon, it wasn't part of a charade.

"Oh, Macky," Bran whispered. " 'A fugitive and a vagabond shalt thou be in the earth . . . My punishment is greater than I can bear.' "

"It's all right," she whispered, "I didn't belong in Heaven anyway."

Outside the saloon the sheriff from Promise was overseeing the removal of Larkin's body from the street. The judge directed the parishioners to go home and pray for their souls and Macky's recovery.

Lorraine and Bran put Macky to bed and treated her wounds.

"Looks like I need to open a hospital instead of a school," she said as she finally pulled up the covers and stepped away from the bed.

"Well, so far your patients are doing well," Bran said, then felt his voice crack. "Lorraine, I love her. I don't want her to die."

"I know," she said, and laid her hand on his shoulder. "I know what it means to find the person you want to hold on to for all your life."

"What am I going to do?" he asked, turning away.

"Pray," was her only answer.

Chapter

Twenty-Three

FOR THREE DAYS Bran prayed beside Macky's bed but nothing helped. Macky was growing weaker. She was dying.

Finally, desperate for answers, Bran loaded the necessary supplies across Solomon, mounted his horse, and rode into the mountains. The snow, gone in the valley below, was still thick between the rocks and on the ground beneath the trees.

For two days he rode, stopping only to feed and water the animals, until he reached a precipice hanging over a deep valley below.

First he dug a pit in the earth, filled it with dry wood and brush, then covered it with rocks. He lit the fire heating the rocks.

Next to the pit he constructed a beehive-shaped sweat lodge out of willow sticks covered with the animal skins he'd bought from Otis Gooden. By the time the lodge was finished, the rocks were ready. Using forked limbs, he moved some of the rocks into the lodge. Then he removed his clothes, tied on a loincloth, and entered the lodge.

As the fire heated the remainder of the rocks, the air inside grew warmer and warmer. Bran poured snow on the rocks to make the steam that would force him to sweat out the impurities of his body and eventually ready his mind for whatever message the Great Spirit world would send.

Replacing the cooling rocks with hot ones when necessary, Bran lost all track of time. He didn't know whether hours or days passed. But finally, when he was almost ready to collapse, he staggered out into the night and fell across the rock extending over the deep river below.

Overhead, the sky had cleared. Stars peppered the black night like a thousand eyes, watching him. The wind whipped across the mountaintop, slashing him with cold. Still he didn't move, waiting for a sign.

But no sign came.

Back in Heaven, Hank took Lorraine away from Macky's bedside. "Come outside with me. I want to talk to you."

"But I can't leave her."

"You can't do any more. Either she will live, or she'll die. It's out of our hands."

Lorraine stood wearily, looking at Macky's pale face, her chest barely moving, her eyes closed as if in death. Lorraine felt Hank throw a shawl over her shoulders and turn her toward the door. She'd never been in a situation where she felt so lost. "She is my friend, Hank."

"She's everybody's friend," he said, taking her hand and leading her away from the buildings and into the open prairie at the edge of town. This time he didn't try to find a secluded spot, rather he slid his arms around her and pulled her back against his chest, holding her openly for all to see.

"Bran has become everyone's friend, too."

"I know," Hank said. "When I first saw them I never expected it, but they've given so much of themselves."

Lorraine shivered and moved closer. "Bran could have gotten away before the sheriff came, but he stayed. Even after Sheriff Dover told him he would have to arrest him for the soldier's murder, he stayed at Macky's side."

"But then he left. Where is he now?" Hank asked.

"I don't know. He said he'd return and the judge believes him. Surely they aren't really going to send him to jail for killing someone who was beating his brother. And nobody believes he was in partnership with Pratt."

"I don't think Larkin's charges will stick. Too many people will say that he was never a member of Pratt's gang. And the murder warrant against Bran is fifteen years old. There's talk about asking for a pardon. Macky is the one in trouble. She did take part in the holdup."

Lorraine turned toward Hank. "I don't believe that for one minute. She may have ended up with the money, but according to Bran she never got off her horse. She didn't even know that banker had been shot. Oh, Hank, it's all so unfair."

"Look at the sky, Lorraine. The Big Dipper has moved."

"So soon? I thought it waited until fall."

Lorraine turned her eyes upward and clasped her arms around the neck of the man she loved.

"Nothing waits," Hank said. "I was wrong about so many things, Lorraine. Life just moves on." His arms went around her, his lips nuzzling her ear. "We have to grab it and hang on to what we can. Will you forgive me for not wanting the town to know what we feel?"

"I suppose I'll have to," she answered with a smile. "After all, everybody in Heaven can see us standing here in the open. You're a ruined man."

"I'm a man who has been restored, Lorraine. Will you marry me?"

"When Bran returns. I won't go through a ceremony without him."

"So? We'll live in sin."

"Oh, Hank, where is he?"

Hank leaned back, fighting the urge to kiss her. He rubbed her upper arms, spreading a gentle warmth with his touch. "He'll be back. Wherever he's gone, it was for a reason. I have the feeling that we'll know soon."

"I hope so. Macky is so very weak."

Suddenly he looked up. "Look, Lorraine, a falling star."

The streak of silver plunged to the earth and disappeared. There was something ominous about that. In the distance a coyote howled and Lorraine was glad she was in Hank's arms.

Bran heard the wind, felt it stroke his body. He watched as the mist from the river below formed a black fog that spread across the valley, enveloping him.

Total blackness surrounded him, smothering him, tendrils of cottony fog filling his nostrils as he tried to breathe. Then the wind died and Bran felt as if he were suspended in the air, buffeted by a gentle motion, almost as if he were inside a living—no, a dying thing.

"Why are you here?" A voice spoke.

Bran didn't answer. He could neither see nor sense another presence.

"I speak to you, Eyes That See in Darkness. Answer."

"Who calls me by my Indian name?"

"I am all those who've gone before, and are yet to come. I answer your plea. You are prepared to offer yourself as a sacrifice to save her life, but it cannot be."

Bran let out a low moan that carried with it the pain of all those he'd failed. His voice grew louder, its anguish filling the heavens above, its agony churning the river below.

"Nooooo! You cannot take her. She must not die. Take me, but let her live."

His cry fell across the emptiness, dying into a profound silence.

Then there was another voice, soft, lost, and afraid. "Bran? Where are you, Bran?" A voice he knew too well.

"Macky? Is that you, Macky?"

"Oh, yes. Bran, I need you. Please . . ."

The darkness didn't change, but Bran focused on her need, on Macky who was calling out for him. Then the darkness was pierced by a sharp slant of sunlight.

"Use your power," the first voice said. "If you wish to, you will see her. It was foretold in your naming vision. The power is yours to use, but only once."

And then he saw her, lying so cold and still, barely breathing. Around her shimmered a haze of silver, almost as if the essence of life were being contained within a net stretched around her.

"Macky," he whispered. "No. You can't leave yet. I haven't told you that I love you."

Even in his state of half consciousness, he saw her eyelids quiver and open.

"Bran?"

"Yes, Macky. It's me."

"But I can't see you."

"No, it's my spirit speaking to you. Feel its strength, Macky. Know that I am with you, loving you, keeping you from harm."

"How is that possible?" she whispered.

"I do not know. Only that you are the vision I did not see as a boy. I see you now. I am the comfort you sought. Be strong, Macky. I give you my strength, my life; and my heart."

And the dark roiled in, surrounding Bran, and he knew no more.

"You're awake!" Lorraine let out a cry of joy and rushed to Macky's bed. "I don't believe it."

Macky looked around, her mind still fogged by the dream. Or was it? She could remember the coldness. Then a voice, Bran's voice. It spoke to her as if he were with her. She looked around again.

"Bran?"

"He isn't here. He disappeared over a week ago. The sheriff from Promise is out looking for him."

"He'll be back soon," Macky said confidently.

Lorraine looked at Hank and then back at Macky. "How do you know?" she asked.

"I just do. He loves me, Lorraine. He told me. Bran told me that he loves me."

"That can't be. Bran hasn't been here, Macky," Hank said. "We don't know where he is."

"Neither do I, but he'll be back and I have to get well. I know what I have to do. Get me something to eat and some clothes."

"Macky, you may be filled by the Holy Spirit, or by the spirit of love, but you're not moving from that bed. You hold her down, Hank, while I get some broth."

But Macky didn't attempt to move. She merely lay there, a secret smile on her lips.

"What really happened, Macky?" Hank asked.

"I don't know but I heard Bran's voice. He said that he loves me. That he's coming back."

"He ought not to," Hank said. "The judge will have him arrested. There's something you don't know."

"There are probably a lot of things I don't know. What I do know is the most important thing."

"The marshal is dead."

"I know. I killed him."

"And they found Pratt's silver-trimmed saddle in his office, along with a bag of gold from the Sylvia."

Lorraine returned with the broth and sat down on the bed. Macky opened her mouth to protest, and found it filled with soup.

"You can probably preach a sermon and mine for gold. But this is my saloon. You're in my bed. And if I'm going to give it up, I run the show."

"What day is this?" Macky asked.

"It's Sunday. You've been delirious for ten days."

Macky swallowed the thick, meaty liquid and tried to concentrate. "Is the judge still here?"

"No, he's gone back to Denver," Hank said. "Do you want me to get him?"

"I certainly do."

"And suppose he decides that you're well enough to take off to jail, Mrs. Kate Adams?" Lorraine said, filling the spoon once more.

"Oh, that's all right, as long as Bran isn't arrested. And the only way I can be sure of that is to talk to the judge before Bran gets back. In the meantime, I'll just lie here and drink soup."

Two days later Macky was going crazy with boredom. Finally, after promising that she was only going to walk down to the general store, Lorraine allowed her to leave the saloon.

The short walk from the saloon to the store took what seemed like forever because of the number of times Macky had to stop and assure the townspeople that she was going to live. Finally, almost light-headed from her ordeal, Macky reached the store and sank down on the seat outside.

"Mrs. Adams, I'm so glad you're all right." The woman standing beside her was Mrs. Pendley. The shy little girl who'd claimed Macky's heart climbed up on the bench beside her, while the mother shared her news.

"We heard about what happened, and my Lars and me, we decided that maybe you was being punished for helping us out. Lars, he decided that if you got well, we'd do the right thing."

Macky swallowed back the ever-present lump in her throat and stared at the woman. "Right thing?"

"Yep. We're going to get your man to marry us proper. We're going to have another baby and we want to join your church."

"I'm sure that my husband—I mean the preacher will be pleased to say the words over you, when he gets back."

Mrs. Pendley glanced around. "Oh. He ain't here?"

"No, he's away on business. Say, I don't suppose you'd be willing to give me a ride home in your wagon, would you?"

"Yes, ma'am, we'd be pleased to help you."

On the way, the little girl told Macky about her ordeal in the woods. "It was like you said, I knew that the angel would help me, just like he helped Gingerbelle draw the water from the well. I just waited. But the puppy felled in the water and I had to help him out."

"Angel?"

"You said Solomon helped Gingerbelle. 'Member? Well, I knew what you was talking about 'cause mules they don't know how to draw water from the well. It was my story from the Bible. My mama read it to me. That's where she got my name, Rebekah."

Macky searched her memory. "Rebekah?"

"Rebekah drew water from the well and give it to a strange man. The man was really an angel and God sent him to love her. I just waited for the angel to come and find me."

Macky gave the child a smile and hugged her. She'd reread the story of Rebekah at the well someday. In the meantime she hugged the little girl. Calling Solomon an angel was stretching things. But even her father had said that God worked in mysterious ways.

If he'd just find Bran and send him back, she'd never ask for anything else again.

"I'm really sorry I have to do this, Miss Calhoun, or should I say Mrs. Adams, but until we get to the bottom of this, I have to follow the law." Sheriff Dover's regret was as genuine as his curiosity.

"Just call me Macky. And don't worry, I understand I have to be arrested. I was at the bank and I did keep the money. But I always intended to take what my father was cheated out of and send the rest back."

"I'm sure it's only a matter of getting the prisoner from

Promise to confirm your story and the judge will let you go. Once he learns that Larkin and Pratt are dead, he'll sing like a bird to protect himself. I have to bring him here, then we'll leave for Denver for the trial."

"Why Denver?"

"Because I don't want to be lynched and that's what will happen if I try your case here. I need the judge's protection."

"Just put me behind bars, Sheriff. It doesn't matter where."

"Well, technically you are under arrest, but I can't put you in a jail cell," the kindly man standing in her doorway said. "I already have a male prisoner there. I've arranged to house you at Lorraine's until we leave."

The sheriff took a long look at Macky before adding, "You know you didn't have to stay away from Promise. Nobody blamed you for your brother's troubles. I might have been able to help."

"Thanks, Sheriff Dover, but I didn't know how to ask. After Todd moved into town, it was better if I stayed away."

"So you grew up out there on that pitiful piece of land all by yourself. I don't think I would have recognized you if I'd seen you that day in town."

"I wasn't by myself. My father was there."

"Still, I feel bad about what happened. I'll try to make this as easy as possible for you now."

"Fine." Listlessly Macky climbed the ladder to the loft where she exchanged her dress for her brother's clothes. Without Bran, none of this mattered anyway. She had no future and she'd burned her past. This was as good a place as any for a woman like her.

She allowed her fingertips to caress the green gingham dress one last time, then placed the garment in her portmanteau. Next she added her mother's cameo and Bran's silver feather. She'd joined Pratt's gang as a boy and she'd go to jail as a boy. The redhead who was the preacher's wife would be left behind with the fancy clothes and crinoline petticoat.

She heard Sheriff Dover leave the cabin, while she laced

her boots and braided her hair, giving her a moment of grateful solitude. The tiny cabin had been her home—their home—for only a few days, yet she didn't want to leave. She'd never experienced such joy anywhere else. Now there was only pain.

She couldn't complain; she'd been lucky. Many women never knew the happiness Bran had given her. And she didn't regret one moment of what they'd shared. But as the days passed, she'd given up hope that Bran would return. Without him she was only half a person.

With a deep sigh, she looked around again. Time to go, she decided and stepped out the cabin door where the sheriff waited with an extra saddled horse.

"Mrs. Mainwearing was glad to get her coins back, Mrs. Adams. You know the explosion in her mine repositioned the vein and she's lost it."

"I'd think that she'd be well off if she never found another ounce of gold."

"No. It seems that she'd followed Moose's instructions and grubstaked most of the prospectors in these mountains. That and the charitable contributions she made to some home for wayward women in San Francisco took a lot of her money. She can live comfortably, but she's determined not to let Moose down."

"What about the gold the marshal stole?"

"Except for one bag that Pratt managed to steal, there's been no sign of it or the deeds and IOU's. Until we go through all the banking records in the territory, we won't know where he deposited any of it."

"Does that mean that the prospectors' claims are also missing?"

"Looks that way. Judge Hardcastle seems like a man with a good head on his shoulders," the sheriff observed. "He'll probably rule in absentia for the people who were cheated."

"And Mrs. Mainwearing?"

"Looks like the judge may take care of her future as well. Good man, the judge. I predict that he'll have a lasting influence on the legal system in this country. A hundred years from now, we'll still be hearing about a judge named Hardcastle."

They were almost back to town when Macky remembered what the judge said about putting her under house arrest at Lorraine's. "Who do you have in jail now, Sheriff Dover?"

"A man who is determined to be punished in spite of the possible consequences."

That didn't make any sense. "What consequences?"

"Well, for one thing, my popularity is already at an all-time low. Now the good folks of Heaven will probably make up a necktie party with the judge leading the mob."

There was something about the tone in his voice that told Macky he was hiding something. He almost sounded as if he were teasing her. "Who? Who have you arrested?"

"He says his real name is John Brandon Lee. But the folks in Heaven call him Night Eyes."

"You have Bran in jail? You bully! He isn't guilty of anything except doing your job for you. Where did you find him? When?"

"Now, wait a minute. I didn't find him. He found me. And he's been there since early this morning."

"But why? You don't have any reason to hold him. Pratt held up the bank. I was there. I saw him. I confessed."

"Do you really think that a judge could accept the word of a man's wife? Maybe under normal circumstances, but to believe that this man's wife just happened to ride into town with the gang because she was going to miss her stage?"

"But I'm not his wife, Sheriff. Honest, you have to believe me. My name is McKenzie Kathryn Calhoun. You've known me for ten years. You know I'm not married. And you know I don't lie."

"True enough. And maybe you could testify. Still, it isn't that simple, Macky. The preacher isn't being held for murdering the banker. It's for the killing of that army officer back on the reservation. And Bran has confessed. He did it and he swears he'd do it again."

"But that was fifteen years ago, and the man was going to hurt a woman. He was beating the Indian boy, who was only trying to protect his mother. You have to believe Bran."

"I do, but if there is still an outstanding warrant for him, he'll never be able to live without looking over his shoulder. He wouldn't even let me tell you he was here."

"Why not? Did he think I would try to break him out of jail?"

Now that she thought about it, that wasn't a bad idea. With the trial delayed, she'd have time to get to the bottom of that murder, if she could just get her strength back. Somewhere there had to be records to Bran's claim of brutality by the officer, maybe a witness. She'd send Hank Clay to the fort to ask some questions. She'd send back East for a fancy lawyer.

Catfish and toad frogs! The sheriff had all her money. How on earth could she pay anybody to do anything? Solomon! If he was back she could sell him. But who'd want a mule that thought he was an angel? Then it came to her. The cameo. She still had that. Macky groaned. She was right back where she started, trying to raise money to get out of town.

She had a strange feeling that Sheriff Dover hadn't believed a word she'd said the day of the revival. But if he thought she'd let Bran take all the blame for what had happened, he had another thought coming.

Suddenly, Macky felt a sense of confidence fill her. Bran might not want her help, but he was going to get it. And once he was free, she had the perfect means of repayment. Ah, yes. Revenge would be sweet.

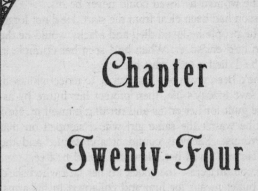

Chapter

Twenty-Four

Bran lay on the bare bunk in the cell and dozed. He felt a sense of peace settle over him, something he'd missed for most of his life. Always seeking, finding, enacting punishment on those who deserved it, then moving on. Never stopping, never giving himself the time to reflect on what he'd done or where he was going. For the first time he had time to reflect on what he'd accomplished.

He hadn't been the one to kill Larkin, but the man was dead. Bran had watched in shock as Macky's gun had fired first, followed a fraction of a second later by four others. The sheriff and the judge had been at a loss to decide who to charge with the shooting. In the end they'd simply said it was death by gunshot misadventure.

There was a time when Bran thought that his life would be complete if he found his family's killer. But it wasn't. There was a hole in it a mile wide and a heart-smile deep.

He couldn't hide behind the truth any longer. He'd fallen in love and the woman he loved could never be his.

The lesson had been clear from the start. He'd not forget it again. The people he loved died and Macky would be the last person he'd endanger. When he'd seen her crumple in his arms, he'd died a little with her.

Then he'd been given one last chance to redeem himself. He could save Macky's life, then protect her future by assuming the guilt for her crime and turning himself in. He'd done so. She wasn't the same girl who'd stepped on that stage in Promise. She was confident and secure and the people in Heaven loved her. Now she would be free.

But he couldn't erase the shock on her face when she'd taken the bullet meant for him and collapsed in his arms. Nor could he forget her words. "I love you, Bran."

Later, on the mountain, when he'd seen her in his vision, he'd told her that he loved her, too. That was the only time he'd ever allow himself to say the words. He'd taken them straight from his heart and left it forever damaged. But he'd learn to live with that.

Macky was safe and that was all John Brandon Lee wanted now.

"What will happen to Bran?" Macky asked the sheriff as they rode into town.

"He'll have to stand trial for the officer's murder. Bran admits he killed the soldier. That doesn't give you people much room to maneuver."

"You people?"

They reached Hell Street and rode slowly toward the saloon. As they passed the businesses, the owners stepped outside and fell in behind the horses as if Macky and the sheriff were the Pied Piper and they were mice following behind.

"It seems everybody in town thinks both of you ought to be set free."

Macky looked around in amazement. Back in Promise, the townsfolk were happy to see anybody in her family leave. Now the people of Heaven were closing in around the sheriff so that they couldn't move.

"All right, women!" the familiar voice of Clara Gooden called out. "Let's go."

Before Macky could dismount, Ethel Cribbs, Clara Gooden, Lorraine Lake, Rachel Pendley, and Letty Marsh followed Sylvia Mainwearing through the swinging doors of the saloon carrying crudely drawn posters and signs. Free Our Macky and Our Preacher, one sign said. Don't Mess with the Folks in Heaven or You'll Find Your Way to Hell, another read. Macky was stunned.

In the jail, Bran stood and looked out the window to see what was causing the commotion. Then he caught sight of a red-haired woman surrounded by people. *Macky. What are you up to now?*

As he watched, Preston Cribbs and a line of men marched out of the livery stable singing at the top of their lungs. " 'Onward Christian soldiers, marching as to war . . .' "

Judge Hardcastle could be seen looking out a window on the second floor of Lorraine's saloon.

"Now just a minute," Sheriff Dover protested. "What's this all about?"

Sylvia drew even with the sheriff and motioned for the protesters to be silent. "It's like this, Sheriff. We've decided not to let you take your prisoners to Denver, not unless you want to arrest every man and woman in Heaven. The judge is here. The jury is here, and if you must conduct a trial, do it here. We've impounded a panel of twelve honest men and appointed someone to speak for the prisoners."

Sheriff Dover bit back a smile. He didn't intend to tell them that this was exactly what he'd had in mind. Let them think they'd pulled it off. That would make the future of his prisoners even more secure.

"Fine," he agreed. "Only problem is that Mr. Lee's trial

will be a military trial and we don't have that kind of authority here."

"Not Mr. Lee," someone called out.

"No, it's Brother Adams," Clara Gooden corrected.

"Quiet down!" Sylvia instructed. "Let me get on with our plans. Sheriff Dover, Preston Cribbs has already drawn up a petition to drop the charges that Bran murdered that army officer. We're going to have Hank Clay and Judge Hardcastle take it straight to the governor. We don't believe that anybody will convict a man of God who was only ministering to one of His children. What do you think about that?"

"Fine move. What about Macky here?"

It was Mr. Cribbs who answered. "Kate—Macky," he quickly amended, "will, of course, have to face the charges, but since your own prisoner knows that she was an innocent bystander, we think that an exception could be made. All we have to do is have the Bank of Promise drop the charges and"—he took a deep breath—"since there is some question about whether or not the banker in Promise was in cahoots with Marshal Larkin, we've decided to reopen the bank in Heaven. We'll honor all the Promise depositors. If the money, less the value of Macky's farm of course, is deposited in our bank, we think everyone will be happy. Macky could be released into the custody of—"

"Me—" one citizen volunteered.

"No, us—"

"But I thought of the idea—"

Macky couldn't believe what she was hearing. At that moment, her gaze slid across the tops of the heads that were bobbing in agitation. Through the barred window in the jail she saw him.

"Bran," she whispered, and slid from her horse, pushing through the throng to reach the wooden sidewalk.

Her smile lit up as bright as a lover's moon flooding the water with light. Wordlessly, the crowd opened a path through which Macky dashed.

"Bran! Bran, you're here."

It didn't matter that he was in a cell. It didn't matter that the entire town crowded into the jail behind her. They were together again.

"Macky, you're really all right?"

"Of course I am, you silly thing. You told me to take your strength and I did. Why did you go away and leave me?"

"I was never there," he said. "Only my spirit came to you."

"But you were so real. You touched me. You kissed me. You—" Her face tilted downward. "You said that you loved me. Don't deny it. I heard you."

"I was miles away, up in the mountains, on a ridge overlooking the canyon below, Macky. I was seeking guidance. I found a way through the night, a vision."

"And it brought you to me. Don't you see, Bran? This was meant to be. Your night eyes don't see in the dark, they see through the blackness of man's pain. They see inside a person's soul and find love."

She clasped the bars and pressed her forehead against them, trying to get as close as possible to the man beyond.

"Don't do this, Macky. I'll probably be hanged for killing a man. I don't want you to think about me. Think about your farm and the life you want to live."

"Tadpoles and catfish! I'm going to have my farm and grow things. What I want is a husband and friends. I have so much love to give. I want to learn to sew and cook and have babies. I want a husband. It's either going to be you, or somebody else. You choose."

Bran's face had crinkled into a frown.

"Well, there's Hank."

"Too late. Hank and Lorraine are getting married."

"Well, then, there's— What about the judge?"

"The judge is old enough to be my papa and besides, he's already spoken for. Mrs. Mainwearing is setting her cap for him."

"What about Sheriff Dover?" Bran asked.

Macky shook her head. "I don't think that's a good idea. I'm not saying that I don't need a lawman to keep me in line, but you know that I'm pure trouble. He would never have time to go after the bad guys."

Bran could only stare at her, at the flush in her cheeks, at the teasing twinkle in her moss-green eyes. Even now, in the middle of all this, he was having a hard time keeping himself from moving his arms between those bars and pulling her close.

"But you and me?" His voice was tight and strained. "What kind of example would we set?"

"The kind of example we need in Heaven," Sylvia Mainwearing said, pushing through the crowd. "It's been decided, Bran, we've got to get you out of jail to keep half the town from living in sin."

"What do you mean?"

"At last count, there are four weddings waiting to be blessed."

With Macky's searching plea pinning him where he stood, Bran couldn't fight them any longer. "But you know I'm not a real preacher, Sylvia. Even if I do get out of this, I'm not legally empowered to perform a marriage ceremony."

"Legal doesn't bother us, but if it's a problem for you, the judge is empowered. And he's on his way to marry you and Macky. And not a moment too soon. After all, she's carrying your child."

"But she isn't," he protested. "That was just a misunderstanding. I wish it were true, but it wouldn't be fair to her."

"Don't I have a say in all this?" Macky asked.

Bran turned to face her. "Since when has anyone ever been able to keep you from having your say? Speak."

"You'd really marry someone like me?" she asked.

"You'd really want me to?" was his response.

"He does. We do! And she will," the crowd echoed. "Don't you want to marry Macky and stay with us?"

Bran felt a lump in his throat. "There is nothing I want

more in my life than to be Macky's husband, and I would like to stay but I don't think the Lord would approve of my spreading His word."

Macky couldn't speak, her heart was so full. She wanted Bran to be her husband because he wanted to be, not because he felt obligated to stay.

Hank Clay spoke up. "The first thing you need to learn is that you've convinced us. The Bible says, 'Ask and ye shall receive.' "

Ethel Cribbs's chins wiggled in agreement. "We asked, Brandon Adams, and He sent you to us. Until another man of God comes along, you'll do just fine."

"And if that don't take up all your time, along with Macky and all those babies she has planned," the sheriff suggested casually, "you could take on the job as an officer of the law in Heaven. I expect the governor would look favorably on that."

"Indeed he would," the judge's voice agreed as he came to stand beside Macky. "Seriously, Bran. I think the governor will be amenable to pardoning you on that old murder charge. He's trying hard to restore the appearance of justice to the Indians and this will make him look good."

"Besides," Sylvia said with a confident smile, "the governor is an old friend of mine, from way back. I think he can be persuaded to go along."

Macky could only hope that the wheels of justice would not move too slowly. "Thank you, Sylvia. Judge. But I'm not at all sure I can handle being the wife of a truly good man. I much prefer the black-sheep variety."

"But what about the trial?" Bran asked, unconvinced.

Judge Hardcastle pursed his lips and studied the floor for a long moment. "I have the solution. I'll have you held in custody until we get back from Denver with an answer."

"Whose custody?" Sheriff Dover asked. "I have to get back to Promise and pick up the prisoner."

The judge glanced around the room. "What about his

wife's? She could see that he stays right here in Heaven and I'd deputize all the rest of you to help her."

Macky's face first brightened, then fell. "You mean he has to stay locked up until then?"

Bran finally took a step forward, pushing against the door, which swung open with a creak. "It isn't locked, Trouble. It never was. I was just afraid to open the door."

Macky flew inside the cell, slammed the door and locked it. "It is now. And just you try to get away from me."

"I promise. I won't move outside this cell until I'm free."

"Maybe it's a good thing I haven't started my newspaper yet," Hank observed.

"Why?" Lorraine asked, standing arm in arm with the big blacksmith.

"How would it sound if the first official ceremony conducted in the city of Heaven was the marriage of two outlaws in the city jail?"

"It would sound as if it were divine intervention," the judge proclaimed.

"Either that, or the work of the devil," Bran agreed just before he kissed Macky.

The morning Bran was officially released from the city jail, he rode a borrowed horse out to the parsonage on Pigeon Creek. He liked the idea of coming home to Macky, like any husband who had been away. As he rode into the clearing he could hear her calling out.

Quickly, he rode through the trees along the creek and beyond until he reached the meadow. Macky, with Solomon strapped to a plow, was cutting a path through the earth. He watched her for a while, content to enjoy the picture of this woman who seemed so right with the world.

After a time, he made out the words she was singing. " 'Bringing in the sheaves'—Gee! 'Bringing in the sheaves.' Haw! 'We shall come rejoicing'—Gee! 'Bringing in the sheaves.' Haw!"

The mule lifted his feet in cadence while Macky and the plow followed along. Bran, his heart filled to bursting, slid from his horse and started toward them, his step scaring up a bird hidden in the brush. The bird flew across Solomon's face.

Solomon brayed, took a right turn and picked up speed, dragging Macky along.

"Let go," Bran called out in horror. "He's heading for that bank."

But it was too late. Solomon turned and skimmed the bank, throwing the plow straight into the earth, pulling Macky with him until she finally let go. Then, as if he realized Macky had fallen, Solomon slowed his gait, his reins dragging behind.

"Macky! Macky, are you hurt?" Bran dropped to the ground beside her, his heart pounding.

She looked up at him, dazed for a moment, then her face broke into a wide smile. "You're home. Isn't it perfect?" she said.

"What?"

She flung herself against him, pushing him back against the freshly turned dirt. "The day. The field. I'm planting beans and corn, and wheat. I'll be a farmer and work God's good earth while you look after the folks in Heaven."

Macky leaned over him, drawing a line from his mouth to his heart, and kissed him soundly. "Oh, Bran," she whispered, moving away for a moment, "we are so lucky."

"Darlin', Macky. What did I do to deserve you?" His hand slid up around her neck, holding her so that he could deepen the kiss.

Even in her joy she knew that the aching, the deep longing that he held so fiercely was still there. When he made love to her, he still held back, as if he were afraid that by opening up he would lose what they shared. She'd never known a man so strong, with such capacity to love with such fear deep inside. She hurt for him, for what he'd missed and what she'd missed.

She'd make it up to him. Tears gathered behind her eyelids and a surge of great tenderness swelled up, colliding with the ever-present knot in her throat.

She felt him tighten his grip on her, lifting her over him, shuddering as his body announced its profound need. In the night, alone in their tiny cabin, she'd cried silently for the boy who'd watched his family die. For the young man who'd tried to protect his Indian brother and failed. For the adult who'd plotted a course of revenge and reparation through his life.

Always alone, conditioned to that course, determined never to be helpless again. Except this once. He'd let himself care and now she knew that he was afraid to lose her.

Somehow, lying in the open field, holding each other in the sun, was different from before. There was no restraint on their loving. There was no darkness, no black nothingness to get through. Together in the sunshine was a kind of timeless commitment, even if Bran didn't realize.

Macky knew and she draped herself over him, settling herself against that part of him she'd come to know so intimately during the night hours. She pulled back and opened her shirt to reveal her breasts.

"You're not wearing anything underneath," he said.

"I may never wear any of those torture racks again, except, of course in church. Will you mind?"

His hands moved across her body in a fierce kind of tenderness, catching one nipple and lifting it up so that he could take it in his mouth. Slowly and deeply he tugged, then pulled his mouth from one to reach for the other. When he turned loose, for a moment she felt a terrible pain of loss.

"Besides," she said, "Rachel Pendley says that my nipples have to get tough, so it won't hurt when our baby nurses."

"Our baby? You aren't making up more stories, are you, Macky Lee? The preacher's wife can't go round telling tales. We have to set an example."

"Well," she said shyly, "He did tell us to go forth and

multiply. Give me a baby, Bran." She put her arms around his neck and rolled over, taking him with her.

He didn't have to hold back any more. He didn't have to fight his desire, and with a cry of joy he gave in, taking her lips with wild abandon. This time when he closed his eyes, it wasn't to hide the passion raging there, but to submerse himself in their mutual need.

And Macky opened herself up to him as if to convince him they belonged together. She tilted her head back, giving him full access to her mouth as her tongue joined his, exploring, demanding, giving.

He knew now what love was, passion, need, freely given. This was Macky, what she'd been from the first, what he'd almost lost. This woman was his wife and he loved her with all the yearning he'd closed off for all the years he'd been alone.

Finally, as if the claiming spent his fierce need, his kisses grew gentler, more promising, until finally he lifted his head. His movement sent a shower of dirt across her, sprinkling her breasts with flecks of silver.

"I love you so much, my gunfighter," she whispered. "My cup runneth over."

He looked down at her and smiled. "Look, Macky." He touched her nipples, brushing away the shiny grains. "You've been crowned with jewels from the earth."

"Diamonds and silver," she said, "do I give to you."

"Diamonds—" Bran raised up, studying the flecks of color. Then he turned his head, finding the place where he'd been lying, the slash of earth Macky had cut into.

"God in heaven!" he said, and rolled away. "Do you realize what you've done, Macky?"

"I've behaved improperly for a minister's wife?"

"No, you've found silver! This is silver. Look at the ore. Your plow cut straight through the vein."

Macky sat up and studied the odd-looking black soil with the grainy silver rock showing through. "That's silver? It looks like plain old gray rock to me."

"It isn't. At least I don't think so. Heaven is rich, Macky, we're rich. The congregation of the First Methodist Church in Heaven is rich!"

Macky already knew that and it had nothing to do with her plow. But this belonged to everyone. She joined Bran in his excitement, shouting and throwing a handful of dirt into the air. "Silver! We've struck silver in God's good earth." She stood up and began dancing across the meadow. After a whirl around the clearing, she caught Bran by the hand and made him dance with her.

When they both tired of dancing, they fell to the ground and there, in the sight of God and one old mule named Solomon, Macky spoke her own vows.

"I, McKenzie Kathryn Calhoun, take thee, John—Eyes That See in Darkness—Brandon—Lee—Adams, to be my husband, my love for now and always. It's your turn."

"But the judge has already said the words, Macky."

"That isn't the same. You must make your pledge. I want to hear the words."

She felt him tremble as he looked into her eyes and made himself speak, slowly, gently, softly. "Because you have filled the dark places in my heart with light, I, John Brandon Lee, take thee, McKenzie Kathryn Calhoun, to be my wife. I will love and protect you through all our life."

"Are you sure, Bran? I still don't know how to cook and I'll never be a proper lady. I'm not very good at womanly things."

His mouth curled into a wicked smile. "Macky, I wouldn't have you any other way. Propriety, goodness, and mercy would be very boring. I love you, Macky. I don't want you ever to change."

Macky nodded seriously, then gave him an impish smile. "Then you, sir, may make love to your wife."

Bran couldn't refuse. He knew that their life wouldn't always be like this, carefree and happy.

But this afternoon, in the sun, in the joy of their love, he accepted what he was being given and he knew that he must give in return.

Shyly, almost reverently, he kissed her. Until this moment he'd consciously tried to remove all gentleness from his life. But this afternoon he reached back in time, into the darkness he'd never tried to penetrate, to find a way to say with his body what he'd never allowed his mind to believe.

Macky's clothes were discarded with each new exploration of Bran's lips and hands. She lay back, smiling at him, allowing him this rare moment of discovery, and each new touch became a commitment.

Finally, when she could hold back no longer she forced him to his back beside her and, following his lead, began to remove his clothes, one kiss at a time.

"You're so beautiful," she whispered as she planted her mouth on his body, marking him with invisible heat that proclaimed her total possession.

"No, I'm scarred," he argued. "Both inside and out."

"Scars only make the beauty more perfect, because they say that you are real."

Her eyes glistened with moisture in the sunlight. He couldn't hold back from touching her, if only to remind himself that this was real.

Then her fingertips, followed by her lips, moved lightly up his neck, across his cheek, to his eye. She removed his patch and kissed him in the place where the pain had begun.

"Now," she whispered, "I'm taking away the hurt. Part of you will forever be mine for part of your pain is inside of me."

And suddenly, the last sliver of ice melted and turned into a torrent of heat that radiated throughout his being.

"Oh, Trouble," he said, "you've done it now." He groaned, then shuddered as he felt the heat intensify.

"Is it bad?" she whispered hesitantly, moving back uncertainly.

"Oh, yes. It's very bad." The stern set of his lips curved in to a smile. "It's very bad, just what I like."

And he kissed her, allowing every newly released feeling to wash over her, cleansing them both of the last shard of doubt.

For just a moment he felt knifed by the thought that he might not make her happy, that something he might do would bring back the darkness and the pain.

"I love you, Bran," she whispered and touched his eye again. "I can't promise you that nothing will ever hurt you again, but I will try to love the pain away when it comes. I've found the place where I belong."

And then he knew that it was there, for them both, for the asking. "I know," he said and caught her shoulders, turning her on her back. "This afternoon I give you all my heart," he whispered and moved to cover her.

She smiled shyly. "I know. But I'm a demanding wench. I want a lot more. I think the part I need right now is a little lower down."

Later, Macky lay in his arms, staring up at the sky. "Isn't this place beautiful, Bran?"

" 'Beauty is in the eye of the beholder,' " he responded, looking at her, not the landscape, "and I don't think I've ever seen a more beautiful sight."

"We've found it, Bran, our Garden of Eden. And we've cast out the snakes. There's only one thing I have to do. Put a marker on Papa's grave. Then everything will be perfect."

She was right. All the demons were gone. Together, they'd found their future and one day they'd have a child, a rebirth to take away the pain of the past.

The sooner the better. And he'd make it a point to tell Ethel Cribbs not to serve any pickled pig's feet at the dinner-on-the-grounds being held on Sunday to celebrate the dismissal of charges against Macky and Bran's pardon by the governor.

"McKenzie Kathryn Calhoun Lee, any place with you

would be heaven, and if this isn't the Garden of Eden, it's close enough. We'll mine the silver and build a city befitting of Heaven's name."

"But Bran, I like Heaven just as it is, and if the streets aren't paved with gold, silver will be just fine."

ABOUT THE AUTHOR

SANDRA CHASTAIN is the bestselling, award-winning author of 32 romances. She lives in Smyrna, Georgia.

DON'T MISS THESE FABULOUS
BANTAM WOMEN'S FICTION TITLES

On Sale in October

BRAZEN

by bestselling author SUSAN JOHNSON

"No one [but Susan Johnson] can write such
rousing love stories." —*Rendezvous*

Susan Johnson "is one of the best!" declares *Romantic Times*. And in
this sizzling new novel, the award-winning, bestselling author of *Pure
Sin* and *Outlaw* entices us once more into a world of sensual fantasy.

_____ 57213-X $5.99/$7.99

THE REDHEAD AND THE PREACHER

by award-winning author SANDRA CHASTAIN

"This delightful author has a tremendous talent that
places her on a pinnacle reserved for special
romance writers." —*Affaire de Coeur*

A lighthearted, fast-paced western romance from bestselling Sandra
Chastain, who is making this kind of romance her own.

_____ 56863-9 $5.50/$6.99

THE QUEST

by dazzling new talent JULIANA GARNETT

"An opulent and sensuous tale of unbridled passions. I couldn't
stop reading." —*Bertrice Small, author of The Love Slave*

A spellbinding tale of treachery, chivalry, and dangerous temptation in
the medieval tradition of Bertrice Small, Virginia Henley, and Arnette
Lamb.   _____ 56861-2 $5.50/$6.99